Ken
Lussey

THE
EYE ⊕F
H⊕RUS

Other books by Ken Lussey

Thrillers featuring Bob Sutherland and Monique Dubois
and set in Scotland and beyond during World War Two:
Eyes Turned Skywards
The Danger of Life
Bloody Orkney
The Stockholm Run
Hide and Seek

Contemporary thrillers featuring Callum Anderson:
A High Road
A Tangled Web

For younger readers:
The House With 46 Chimneys

First published in Great Britain in 2024 by
Arachnid Press Ltd
91 Columbia Avenue
Livingston EH54 6PT
Scotland

www.arachnid.scot
www.kenlussey.com

ISBN: 978-1-0686257-0-1

Cover photograph by Maureen Lussey
Cover design by Carolyn Henry Photography
Printed and bound in Great Britain by Inky Little Fingers Ltd.
Unit 3, Churcham Business Park, Churcham, Gloucester, GL2 8AX.

For Maureen, who shared my Maltese adventure.

PROLOGUE

It was a beautiful morning. The sky was a cloudless blue and the air was still. For the first time in his life, Joseph Camilleri would have preferred it to have been foggy. As he used the tiller to steer *Doriette* out of the mouth of Marsaxlokk's harbour and into the broader bay beyond, he looked around anxiously.

It was still early, even by the standards of the village fishermen, though there were already three other fishing boats leaving the quayside behind them. Another was ahead, visible beyond the Royal Navy vessel guarding the way through the anti-shipping boom across the mouth of the bay. Off to the right were two moored Sunderland flying boats and the more delicate shape of a Catalina, ample evidence of the seaplane base at RAF Kalafrana.

Joseph thought his heart was going to stop beating when a Royal Air Force air sea rescue launch powered into view from behind one of the moored aircraft and rode up onto its wake as it gathered speed. For a moment it seemed to be coming straight towards *Doriette* but then he saw it was merely completing its turn towards the gap in the boom, which it slowed down to approach. Joseph realised he'd been holding his breath and exhaled, a sense of deep relief flooding through him.

As *Doriette* approached the boom defence vessel he found himself holding his breath again. He knew he had to keep calm. There was no reason for anyone to take any interest in what was just another luzzu going about its business. They were only doing what they did most mornings, though perhaps a little earlier.

Like the other fishing boats he could see, and the much larger number still waiting to be brought to life back in the harbour, *Doriette* was cheerfully painted, mainly in bright light blue, with stripes in brown and yellow and much narrower lines of red and white along the hull. At the front was a yellow section, shaped like a moustache, from which a pair of painted wooden eyes with prominent black eyebrows protruded, one on each side of the prow.

The Eye of Horus was a relic of an ancient Phoenician belief that it protected anyone who sailed in a boat that carried it. Joseph hoped the tradition would hold strong today.

A cheery wave to the bored crew of the naval vessel was all it took to get them through the gap in the anti-shipping boom.

Joseph had thought that after they'd cleared the mouth of Marsaxlokk Bay, there'd be enough wind to make it worth raising the sails. In the event, it was as windless out in the open water as it had been in the harbour and the bay. He realised he'd have to rely on the engine throughout the trip and cursed. Now the siege was lifted, it was easier to get hold of diesel for essential purposes, and fishing was deemed an essential purpose. But the price was exorbitant. Once they'd done what they had come to do, they would see if the fishing gods were with them, though it wasn't a prospect that he relished today.

'Where do you think we should go?'

Joseph realised his brother Lawrenz had shouted to him over the noise of the engine. Lawrenz had, until now, been sitting hunched at the front of the luzzu, looking ahead.

'We need to get far enough away from the island, and anyone else, to be sure no one can work out what we're doing. I've said it before and I'll say it again, you're a fool for getting us involved in this.'

'I'm sorry, Joseph. If there had been any choice you know I'd have taken it. But they told me it's the only way to clear my debts.'

Joseph cursed again. Having a younger brother ought to be a blessing. Having a younger brother with a gambling problem was anything but. He and Lawrenz had argued fiercely about this. If gambling debts made Lawrenz open to exploitation by whoever he owed money to - Joseph didn't know who that was and didn't want to - then what they were doing now would enmesh them both even more inextricably in the web.

It was a little later when Joseph decided they were as far away as practicable from prying eyes, and he reduced power. They were well to the east of Delimara Point and the only other vessels in sight were a good way to their south-west. He knew that the guns of Fort Delimara, and the eyes of the men manning them, would be turned towards the approaches to Marsaxlokk Bay, on the far side of the point. There were patrols on its east side, of course, as well as pillboxes and lookouts. Joseph hoped no one on this side of the point was taking any notice of what would seem like just another fishing boat.

He'd been trying to avoid looking at the untidy pile of fishing nets on the floor of the luzzu, in front of the engine compartment. Joseph prided himself on how he kept his nets and this had offended him when he'd boarded the *Doriette* that morning. Though not nearly as much as what he knew was hidden beneath the nets.

'Come on Lawrenz, let's get this over with. Move the nets.'

Joseph watched as Lawrenz moved the nets to one side. Underneath was a canvas package bound in ropes, the size and shape of a large corpse.

He felt his heart sink at seeing such a stark confirmation of what they were here to do. 'Surely that's going to float and could as easily end up back at the island as anywhere else?'

Lawrenz met his eyes for the first time since they'd left Marsaxlokk. Joseph was shocked to see he'd been crying.

'I said that when they told me what they were going to do,' said Lawrenz. 'They said there would be rocks in the canvas packaging with the body. They said it would sink and stay sunk. I'm sorry, Joseph, but I think that means it will be heavy and I'm going to need your help to move it.'

Joseph cut the engine and allowed *Doriette* to drift, then moved forwards to join his brother. 'Let's assume we're being watched through binoculars by an infantryman in a pillbox and push it over the side away from the land. We can make it look like we're doing something with the nets.'

There was only a very slight swell, even this far out from the island, and the canvas package splashed loudly when it entered the water.

Joseph was relieved to see it sink immediately. 'Now we need to head to where the others are and get some actual fishing done.'

'I'm not sure I feel up to it after this,' said Lawrenz.

'Neither do I, but we need to cover the cost of the diesel and show a legitimate reason for being out today.'

Joseph set a course for the other fishing boats that were visible in the distance. 'Please check the nets didn't get tangled when your friends brought the body aboard last night. How did they manage to carry a body around during the curfew anyway?'

'I didn't ask. I don't want to know if I'm honest.' Lawrenz crouched down over the nets and busied himself with them.

They were within two hundred metres of two other brightly

painted fishing boats from Marsaxlokk when the explosion ripped *Doriette* apart.

Although other vessels were on the scene very quickly, no trace could be found of Joseph or Lawrenz amid the scatter of wooden fragments that was all that remained of their luzzu.

It was subsequently concluded by the authorities that *Doriette* must have struck a floating contact mine, one of the large number laid off Malta over the preceding three years by the Germans and Italians. The only nearby witness, a fisherman on one of the other luzzijiet who happened to be looking directly at *Doriette* when she blew up, questioned that. He said that the blast seemed to originate from further back in the vessel, where the engine and fuel tank would have been, rather than from the front as you'd expect if it had hit a mine. But no one important took any notice of him.

*

A second witness to the explosion that destroyed *Doriette* and killed Joseph and Lawrenz was further away but had a much better idea of what had happened. A man wearing a linen suit and a broad-brimmed straw hat was standing astride the crossbar of a stationary bicycle on a track on a hillside well above the barbed-wire lined shore.

He looked around, wondering if any of the British soldiers manning pillboxes and gun emplacements guarding the end of Delimara Point had seen the explosion out to sea. If any of them challenged him he'd simply tell them the truth - part of it anyway - and say that he worked for a fish trading company in Marsaxlokk, keeping track of who was fishing where and watching for boats returning to the harbour. Even though he managed the company, he did sometimes spot for returning boats and the job justified his possession of a pair of binoculars, something the military could get quite sensitive about, even now the siege had ended and the threat of invasion had ceased.

He was surprised to find no one in sight. He wrapped the binoculars in a cloth and turned to put them in the saddlebag. If he had been spotting for returning boats, he'd have called news in from the red telephone box at the Delimara lighthouse, on the side of the point overlooking the bay.

But not today. Instead, he looked down to check the bottoms of his trouser legs were still held in the grip of his cycle clips, then he pulled the bicycle around and began pedalling back along the track towards Marsaxlokk.

CHAPTER ONE

The journey south from Portree was notable for the frequent glimpses ahead of the jagged ridge of the Cuillin Hills, the mountain range that dominated the central part of the Isle of Skye. They were entrancing on this beautiful June day, with a few fluffy white clouds adding interest to an otherwise blue sky.

Bob and Monique were sitting on the left-hand side of the bus. It had, thought Bob, seen better days. The sign on the side proudly proclaimed that it was operated by *The Skye Transport Company*. It wasn't the same vehicle that had taken them from Kyleakin to Portree in time for a nice lunch in a hotel they stumbled across. But it was the same type and smelled the same, of cigarettes and oil. It sounded the same too, that odd combination of engine and transmission noise that only coaches and buses seemed to make.

Bob was sitting beside the window and Monique was leaning against him, apparently dozing.

After lunch, they'd had time to look around the village and explore the harbour before catching the 3 p.m. bus back to Kyleakin.

At 14 shillings for the two return tickets, the fare had surprised Bob when they'd boarded the Portree bus in Kyleakin. Not that money was an issue, but he wondered how local people managed. On the other hand, it was now impossible to get fuel for private motor vehicles, legally anyway, so anyone needing to travel had little option.

The bus to Portree had been about half full, perhaps seven or eight passengers in total. The return journey south was quieter.

Beside Monique and himself, a woman and a young boy were sitting behind the driver and a young girl, who was obviously with them, was sitting one row further back.

The Cuillin Hills were especially striking as they approached what the driver announced was the Sligachan Hotel, about twenty-five minutes after leaving Portree. Beyond that, the road stuck more closely to the shore of the island and the views on Bob's side, of lochs and islands, were magnificent. He followed their journey on an Ordnance Survey one-inch map that showed most of the southern and eastern parts of the island.

'Hello. Are you a pilot?'

Bob looked up, startled, and realised that the young girl had moved over to the seat in front and was kneeling so she could rest her arms on the back of it and speak to him. He wasn't used to estimating the ages of children, but he thought the girl might be about ten. She had long red hair and was looking at him with an intensity he found unsettling.

'Hello. I used to be, but I work in an office now.'

She pointed at the ribbons on his uniform jacket. 'Did you get those medals for shooting down Germans?'

Bob had no idea how to respond. Telling her the simple truth, that officially he had shot down 22 enemy aircraft but that by his count it was 24, didn't seem an option. Admitting to the girl that as a fighter pilot he had killed many young men just like himself, except for the language they spoke and the country they happened to have been born in, seemed very wrong.

He felt Monique stir and was relieved when she spoke. 'Hello. What's your name?'

'I'm Maisie. That's my mother sitting over there, with my younger brother Stuart. We live in Plockton. We should be at school today but my Aunt Emily, who lives in Portree, has just had a baby and Mummy wanted to take us to visit them. I saw you on the bus to Portree earlier, didn't I?'

As if realising that she was being talked about, Maisie's mother turned round in her seat and looked back. 'Maisie! What have I said to you about pestering people? Come back to your seat.'

'It's all right,' said Monique. 'I think Maisie just wants to talk.'

'Maisie always wants to talk to everyone she meets,' said the boy.

'Shush, Stuart. Well, if you're sure she's no bother.' The woman turned back to face the front of the bus.

'Yes, you did see us on the bus going to Portree earlier. My name's Monique, by the way. This is Group Captain Sutherland.'

'Are you married to each other? You were asleep with your head on his shoulder.'

Bob smiled and felt Monique smother a laugh.

'As it happens, we are,' she said. 'We got married in a nice little church near Edinburgh on Saturday. We travelled by train to Kyle of Lochalsh on Monday and have been staying in the Station Hotel there since then. This is our honeymoon.'

'That's lovely!' said Maisie. 'Why did you decide to come here?'

'I visited not long ago for my work and liked it. We agreed it would be a nice place for the two of us to come and stay. We visited Plockton yesterday, on our first full day here. Even in wartime, it's a lovely village. You must enjoy living there.'

Bob had guessed what Maisie's next question was going to be before she asked it.

'What work do you do?'

It was Bob's turn to smother a laugh. Monique had helped him out over the matter of shooting down enemy aircraft and it seemed only fair to return the favour.

'We work together,' he said. 'We're in military intelligence, which means…'

'Do you catch spies together? That really is exciting!'

'Not exactly,' said Monique, laughing. 'Not all the time, anyway.'

'I've not heard an accent like yours before,' said Maisie. 'You're not Scottish, are you? Or English?'

'No, it's all very complicated. I've spent time in lots of different countries since I was born. I live in Scotland now, though.'

The bus pulled to a halt in what Bob thought must be Broadford. He looked at his watch. They'd left Portee an hour and a quarter before and were due in Kyleakin in twenty-five minutes. From his memory of the bus timetable, that confirmed this was Broadford.

Bob saw Maisie's mother turn in her seat again. 'Maisie! People want to get on. Come back and sit behind us again.'

Bob could see reluctance on Maisie's face.

'You ought to do what your mother says,' said Monique, quietly. 'Perhaps we'll have a chance to talk again on the ferry.'

Maisie smiled and returned to sit behind her mother.

The bus was almost full when it left Broadford. An old lady wearing a headscarf sat beside Maisie and placed a wicker basket on her lap. This attracted the girl's attention and Bob saw her strike up a conversation with the woman. He got the impression the basket might have something alive in it, like a chicken or a cat.

*

A few of the other passengers were making obvious preparations to get off the bus as it slowed down in Kyleakin. It pulled to a halt outside the largest building in the village with a squeal of brakes. On Bob's side of the bus, a grassy area sloped gently down to the shore. There was a pier a little further along in the direction the bus had been going. He was surprised when Monique stood up and pulled at his arm.

'Come on, Bob!'

A man in a worn tweed jacket and cap who was getting off had stopped in the aisle to allow Monique to leave her seat. With no time for discussion, Bob followed her to the front of the bus, then down the steps and out of the door.

Once clear of the others who had disembarked, Monique turned and embraced him, then kissed him. Meanwhile, the bus pulled away.

'I think the bus carries on as far as the ferry slipway,' he said after she had released him. 'That's where we caught it this morning. We didn't need to get off here.' He looked around. 'The signs say this is the King's Arms Hotel. I suppose this is the bus stop for the village itself rather than for the harbour or the ferry.'

Monique smiled at him. 'I know we could have stayed on the bus, Bob. But we didn't get a chance to see much of the village earlier. We got straight off the ferry and onto the bus. It's a nice afternoon for a walk. I'm sure Maisie will have no problem finding someone else to talk to on the ferry.' She smacked the side of her neck with her hand. 'Ah, I'd forgotten about the midges. Never mind. The receptionist in the Station Hotel said they don't like direct sunlight or much wind, and we've certainly got the first of those at the moment, plus a reasonable breeze. We should be all right. They weren't a problem in Portree.'

'We could find out if there's a cup of tea available in the hotel,' said Bob.

'Let's just walk. You can see it's not far to the inner end of the harbour. If we stay to the left of it, along the road the bus is taking, we should come to the ferry slipway.'

Monique took Bob's arm and led him off along the edge of the road towards the harbour, not quite into the path of a postman on a bicycle who pinged his bell before offering a cheery greeting.

Bob smiled back at Monique. She'd made sure she was on his right, the side of his good eye. As usual, she was dressed smartly but rather plainly, today in a thin white summery blouse and fawn skirt, with a matching jacket over her right arm and her black leather handbag slung over the other shoulder. This hung and moved awkwardly, as if it carried more weight than it was intended for. The designer probably hadn't expected it to have to accommodate an automatic pistol.

Monique seemed to spend her life trying to blend into the background but usually failed. As always when Bob looked at her, he was struck by her remarkable presence. She'd have stood out in a crowd whatever she was wearing and from the looks she got, she tended to be noticed by both men and women.

Monique's dark hair framed a face that was classically beautiful, but oddly flawed in a way that to his mind made her even more attractive. There were times, too many times, when he had seen her eyes take on a dark, haunted look, as if they'd witnessed things their owner wished they hadn't. She was 30, some seven months younger than him. She'd packed a lot of living into that time and by no means all of it had been pleasant. She had told him her dark and complex story while they'd been locked up together in the cellar of a shooting lodge in Caithness the previous September and Bob knew she carried with her more than her fair share of ghosts.

But as he looked at her now, Bob could only see a beautiful woman without, apparently, a care in the world.

'Why are you staring at me, Bob? You need to watch where you're walking.'

'I was just reminding myself how lucky I am to be married to you, Monique.'

She looked concerned. 'Do you need to be reminded?' Then she laughed. 'Come on Bob, sometimes you are very easy to tease.'

'Perhaps I should tease you later, in bed?'

'That would be very nice!'

They both laughed.

The road they were walking along curved to the left and passed a line of cottages and houses as it reached the near end of Kyleakin's busy harbour, then ran along its northern side. A barrier across the road where it met the near end of the harbour was manned by two naval ratings with rifles, who saluted Bob and then asked to see their security passes.

With an active naval base on the other side of the half-mile-wide Kyle Akin at Kyle of Lochalsh, Bob wasn't surprised to see small naval craft mingling with the fishing boats in the harbour. Two of them were pulled out of the water on concrete slipways at the near end, apparently for repair. Others were moored or coming and going.

A Royal Navy lorry trundled past along the road, causing

Bob and Monique to step onto the verge. There were a few people around who appeared to be local residents, mainly quite old or women with young children. There were also quite a few naval personnel busy around the harbour. Bob found himself having to return salutes repeatedly as they walked alongside it. He noted with amusement that although the naval personnel he and Monique passed saluted him, without exception they looked at her.

'There are times when I wish I wasn't wearing this uniform,' he said.

'We've had this conversation before,' said Monique. 'You're on leave away from your base and have every right to wear civilian clothes if you prefer. But when you tried it in the hotel dining room on Monday night, I could tell how uncomfortable you were. You dined in uniform last night.'

'That's true,' said Bob. 'A senior RAF officer might stand out like a sore thumb in an area overrun by naval personnel but at least it's obvious who and what I am. Wandering round in a civilian suit, especially as so much of the western side of the Highlands is a "Protected Area" under the 1939 Defence Regulations, could give rise to questions and misunderstandings.'

'I'm sure you're right,' said Monique. 'Perhaps it's better for Maisie to have asked if you were a pilot rather than asking why you weren't in uniform as I assume her father is. You don't look like a spiv or an enemy agent, but it's easy to imagine people wondering.'

Bob realised that Monique had no such problem. Despite her elusive accent, which she usually passed off as French if the question arose, she tended to be accepted in almost any setting. She was someone people wanted to be liked by and someone who inspired both trust and desire in others.

'Do you see the ruined castle over beyond the harbour?' asked Monique.

'Yes, I noticed it this morning and again just now when we got off the bus. It would be nice to take a closer look, but we're not dressed to go exploring,' said Bob.

'That's true,' said Monique. 'But that wasn't why I asked. When I was in Kyle of Lochalsh back in April, the captain of the RAF launch I borrowed told me about a legend associated with the castle. He said there had been an earlier fortress on the same site. That was used by a Viking princess who hung a chain between it and the mainland to enforce a toll she charged on any boats passing along Kyle Akin. I don't remember the name of the castle, I'm sure we could find it on your map. But I do remember the name the princess is remembered by, "Saucy Mary". It is said that when a toll was paid, the princess would express her thanks by showing her bare breasts to the passing ship's crew. Hence her name.'

Bob smiled. 'Perhaps we ought to press on to the end of the harbour and catch the ferry back to Kyle of Lochalsh? It's only a short walk from the far side to the Station Hotel and then I can renew my acquaintance with the most beautiful pair of breasts in the entire world.'

'I'll take that as a promise,' said Monique, laughing.

CHAPTER TWO

The ferry that had taken them 'over the sea to Skye' that morning had been quite crowded, with two naval vehicles aboard, a van and a staff car, as well as a dozen or more foot passengers, both civilian and naval - and one Royal Air Force group captain - squeezed in between the vehicles and the wooden railings surrounding them.

Monique had noticed the ferry on her first visit to Kyle of Lochalsh in April. It was only today that she'd realised two different vessels were operating the service, shuttling backwards and forwards. The one she and Bob caught for the return to the mainland from Kyleakin had the name *Cuillin* painted on its bow and seemed to have a steel hull, whereas she thought that the one they'd caught that morning had been made of wood. She was able to confirm that impression when the two passed one another not long after *Cuillin* left Kyleakin.

What the vessels had in common was that during the crossing they appeared to be carrying an area of wooden roadway on their decks, large enough for two cars parked one behind the other with a little space around them, surrounded by either wooden or metal railings, depending on the vessel. At either end of the crossing, they came alongside the sloping stone slipways and the roadway section was swung around a central pivot. Then ramps were lowered to allow vehicles and passengers to disembark and others to board.

Monique stood arm in arm with Bob in comfortable silence near the front of the roadway, where they could watch Kyle of Lochalsh growing slowly in size. They were the only foot passengers on the ferry and there was only one vehicle aboard, a coal merchant's lorry. The driver and his mate sat in the cab and smoked.

Monique glanced up at Bob. She was standing on his left side, so knew he'd not see her movement. She was aware that the blindness in his left eye still sometimes got him down, but felt he'd done a wonderful job coming to terms with what he called his 'acquired monocular vision'. When you looked into his lovely brown eyes it was easy to forget that he was only seeing through one of them. If you knew where to look you could see the scar on his left temple, where he'd been wounded when he'd been shot down in late 1940. He'd recovered from his other injuries but the damage to the optic nerve on that side was permanent.

Bob coped very well with his loss of depth perception, of three-dimensional vision, and of peripheral vision on his left side, though he still avoided driving at night when he could and he never flew an aircraft in the dark.

Monique quite often wondered what Bob saw in her. She knew that a lot of men, and some women, found her extremely attractive and there had been times in her life when she'd used that to her advantage, even very recently. But Bob was not a stupid or a shallow man. She'd once described herself to him as a recovered cocaine addict who had slept her way around Europe by the time she was eighteen and could speak the languages of all the security services that actively wanted her dead. Despite it being an accurate description, he'd continued to pursue her. Eventually, and despite misgivings on her part, she'd ended up as Mrs Monique Sutherland, though she still used Monique Dubois professionally, amongst other names.

It was more obvious to Monique what she saw in Bob. He was a very attractive man who appeared totally unaware of that fact. He was a comfortable amount taller than her, and his brown eyes were paired with dark brown hair, not far removed in shade from her own. What had really drawn her to him was that he was about as far from the type of bastard who had usually tried to get her into their bed as it was possible to be. He was a decent man. Not too decent, though. They'd met briefly in 1941, but it was only a year later that their paths crossed again in the unlikely setting of a castle in Caithness. On that first night, he'd allowed himself to be seduced by the daughter of the household, much to Monique's amusement. As far as it was possible to be amused with German commandos knocking on their bedroom doors in the middle of the night.

More recently, after she'd agreed to marry him, it was the deep gulf between his decency and her ruthlessness that led her to doubt whether they could ever have a viable future together.

A visit to Stockholm earlier in the year had brought back ghosts from the past for them both. In Bob's case, it was meeting the German pilot who had shot him down in 1940. In hers, it was meeting, and ending up being abducted by and in bed with, an old lover who was now a senior German intelligence agent. She had resolved that problem in a particularly gruesome and, for him, terminal way.

That encounter had left her convinced that Bob could and should do better than her. And for her part, she was increasingly concerned by the very decency that also attracted her to him. Despite Bob's very considerable success as a fighter pilot, he had no discernible killer instinct when on the ground. When faced by a man with a gun in Orkney, he had lowered his pistol so he could try to talk sense into his opponent. His life had only been saved by someone else taking the shot he should have taken, and from very much further away.

Monique was reconciled to spending the rest of her professional and personal life looking over her shoulder to protect herself. She had no wish to have to look over Bob's too because he lacked the instinct necessary to do it for himself.

That all changed on a second visit to Stockholm when Bob pulled off a feat that Monique doubted she'd have been able to manage herself, in the process saving her life and probably his own too. She'd realised that she'd agreed to marry a decent man who loved and cared for her; who looked good; who was much better in bed than he realised; who had excellent career prospects; and who when the need really arose could kill every bit as ruthlessly as she could. It wasn't exactly what you'd call a match made in heaven - more in hell - but Bob was as near her perfect partner as she was ever likely to find.

As if reading her thoughts, some of them at least, Bob turned to look at her with his good eye and smiled. 'Coming here for our honeymoon was a great idea. I may gripe about the uniform and the salutes, but it's allowed us to get away from our normal world in a way that would never have been possible if we'd simply stayed on at the North British Hotel and enjoyed a week of sex and champagne.'

'I accept that the champagne wasn't quite as good at the Station Hotel, even before we consumed their final bottle last night,' said Monique. 'But I'm enjoying the sex every bit as much as I would have done in Edinburgh.'

Bob put his left arm around her shoulder and pulled her to him. Monique put her right arm around his waist. She realised how much she liked being close to him and how nice he smelled.

They lapsed into silence again as Kyle of Lochalsh grew closer. The village's Station Hotel stood, rather oddly she thought, next to the slipway for the ferry to Kyleakin and some distance from the railway station, which projected out into Kyle Akin on a broad pier a little to the east.

From the ferry, the hotel could be seen to comprise a three-storey central block with a flat-roofed two-storey extension on the left-hand side. The ground floor of the extension and part of the main block projected slightly forward of the building and had large windows, behind which she knew was the dining room. The absence of the usual criss-cross sticky tape from the glass suggested no one thought it likely this place would be bombed despite the presence, not far beyond the railway station, of an important naval base. The building was finished in a weathered grey harling and the whole width of the central block had been adorned with large white capital letters between the first and second-storey windows that proclaimed the hotel's identity to the world. Perhaps, she thought, this was intended to overcome its rather unexpected location.

Though she couldn't see it from this angle, she knew that the words 'The Station Hotel' were also painted on the slates of the single-storey extension at the end of the hotel facing the village and railway station.

When their ferry arrived at the slipway on the Kyle of Lochalsh side the turntable was pivoted and the ramps lowered by the ferry crew and the man who managed the queue on this side of the crossing. The driver of the coal lorry peeped his horn and waved them off the ferry ahead of him. Monique realised he had no choice as he wouldn't have been able to get past them.

Once on the stones of the slipway, Bob and Monique moved to the far side to let the lorry pass. They then walked arm in arm up the slope. As soon as the lorry was clear, a post van set off down the slipway towards them, with people on foot following it who presumably intended to board the ferry for its return journey to Kyleakin.

Monique wasn't paying attention to their surroundings and was surprised when Bob suddenly stopped walking. She'd taken a step beyond him and was turned by their interlocking arms to face him.

'I think the honeymoon may be over,' he said, looking past her with a grim expression on his face.

Monique let go of his arm and turned. At first, she couldn't see what he meant. Then she saw a naval officer walking down the slipway towards them in the wake of the people heading for the ferry. It took her a moment to realise that it was Commodore Maurice Cunningham, the head of Military Intelligence, Section 11, and Bob's boss. He was a very long way from where he ought to have been, in his office near Westminster Abbey. The look on his face was nearly as grim as the one Bob was wearing.

'He had to cancel his plans to attend the wedding,' said Monique. 'Perhaps he thought he should come and deliver his wedding present in person?'

She was rewarded with a brief smile from Bob. 'Come on, my love,' he said. 'We'd better find out what's caused him to make what must have been a very long journey. Perhaps I was tempting fate by talking about leaving our normal world behind us. I don't think this is a social call.'

Bob stopped a couple of paces short of the commodore, who had continued to walk slowly down the stone slipway. The two men exchanged salutes.

'Hello, Bob. Hello, Monique. I'm sorry I couldn't come to your wedding on Saturday and I'm even more sorry to turn up in the middle of your honeymoon.'

The commodore was a man in his late forties with black hair and a black beard that was just starting to go grey at the sides. Monique thought he looked exhausted. Even his usually impeccably pressed naval uniform was looking creased. She reminded herself that this was hardly surprising given how long he must have been travelling to get to Kyle of Lochalsh from London.

'Come with me and we can talk.' The commodore turned and Bob and Monique walked either side of him back up the slipway. Monique could hear the post van driving onto the ferry behind them.

It was Bob who spoke first. 'Monique was wondering if you were here to deliver your wedding present in person, sir, as you'd not been able to make it to the wedding.'

Even side-on, Monique could see Commodore Cunningham look momentarily puzzled before he smiled.

'In a manner of speaking, you were right, Monique. I'll tell you more in a moment.'

Beyond the top of the slipway, the road broadened out. Monique remembered that this had been where she'd turned the car around on her first visit to Kyle of Lochalsh, in April. She'd then pulled over and parked. A very similar military staff car was pulled off the road just beyond the gateway leading to the Station Hotel, almost exactly where she'd parked.

'We can talk at greater length over dinner this evening. I will be buying as it's the least I can do in the circumstances. Ruth and I have both booked rooms in the hotel tonight.'

'Ruth?' asked Monique. 'Ah, I see,' she said, as Leading Wren Ruth Woodburn got out of the driver's side of the car and turned to face them, looking extremely unhappy.

Monique had met Ruth in Kyle of Lochalsh on her first visit to the village. Ruth had been employed by the Royal Navy as a mechanic and driver, but Monique had quickly come to realise the young woman had the background, education and ability to do far more. She'd persuaded Bob to take Ruth on in his Edinburgh outpost of Military Intelligence, Section 11, to fill a vacancy for a driver. Since then, Ruth had blossomed. She was an excellent driver but had also become a part-time assistant to Monique in her liaison work with the Security Service, or MI5, who were technically Monique's employers while she was on secondment to MI11.

'I've asked Ruth to go for a walk while the three of us have a private chat,' said Commodore Cunningham. 'We shouldn't take very long.'

'Not to worry, sir,' said Ruth. 'I will enjoy reminding myself of all the reasons why I was so pleased to meet Monique and get posted away from this place!'

Bob and the commodore had gone round to the far side of the car. Ruth turned to walk towards the village. She caught Monique's eye. 'I'm sure this isn't what you wanted on your honeymoon, Monique. I'm so sorry.'

Monique smiled. 'Don't worry about it, Ruth.' Then she got into the rear of the car. Bob was sitting on the far side. Commodore Cunningham was in the front passenger seat and had turned round so he could face them.

'First, as I said a moment ago, I am truly sorry to be troubling you with this. I'm here to ask a very large personal favour of the two of you, as friends. I should begin by giving you the cover story that I will use if anyone asks me what you are doing, and which the two of you should use if anyone asks you about it, including your colleagues and Leading Wren

Woodburn.'

Neither Bob nor Monique said anything. The commodore continued. 'I am hoping that Major General Sir Peter Maitland, the Director of Military Intelligence and as you know my direct boss, never gets to hear about this. But if he does, I will tell him that I have asked the two of you to travel to Malta to explore the options for establishing a small branch of Military Intelligence, Section 11, there.'

'Why us, sir?' asked Bob.

'That's a good question, and one I hope I never get asked by Sir Peter because I don't have an even halfway convincing answer. If that was what I wanted to do, there are several officers working for me in Sanctuary Buildings who would be perfectly capable of doing the job. And that's before we consider how utterly inappropriate it is that I should break into your honeymoon like this, or travel to Scotland myself. The best light I can shine on this is that I am offering to extend your honeymoon and relocate it from Kyle of Lochalsh to somewhere I would imagine is rather warmer and usually sunnier, if perhaps not as pleasant in other ways. I will of course make all the arrangements and MI11 will cover all the costs.'

'Only we're not going to Malta to set up a branch of MI11 or to add variety to our honeymoon, are we, sir?' asked Monique.

'No, you're not, Monique. Assuming you agree to go, of course, and I should say I won't hold it against either of you if you decline.'

Monique saw Bob look at her and raise an eyebrow. She smiled and nodded slightly.

'We're enjoying being here, sir,' he said. 'But you wouldn't have made the journey unless this was important. We're happy to help, whatever it is.'

The commodore turned to look out of the windscreen and then back to face them again. 'Let me tell you what it is, first. What I'm asking you to do is irregular, unofficial and quite possibly dangerous.

'I have a younger sister, Amanda. Her husband was a major in the Royal Engineers and he was killed in May 1941 during the German invasion of Crete. Amanda has one son, James Ewing, who's a lieutenant in the Royal Navy serving in a planning post with the 10th Submarine Flotilla in Malta. He was a member of a submarine crew until a very near miss by a depth charge last year badly damaged the hearing in his right ear. He could have returned home if he'd wanted to but he insisted on staying to do his bit, even if he could no longer serve afloat. The submarine he had served on as the first officer disappeared later last year with the presumed loss of its entire crew. That must have hit him hard but, the last time I saw her, his mother said that his letters home suggested he had coped well with that tragedy and with his hearing problems.

'Nine days ago, on Monday the 31st of May, Lieutenant Ewing failed to turn up for duty at the flotilla's headquarters and nothing has been seen or heard of him since. It seems he spent a weekend's leave with a British woman he has formed a relationship with and after parting company, very happily, apparently, with her on the Sunday he didn't return to his quarters.

'It helps to have lots of contacts. I became aware of what had happened because the man he reports to, Commander Lawrence Dowson, is an old naval colleague who knows of my family connection with James. He was unable to get the civil or military police in Malta to take James's disappearance seriously on Monday or Tuesday despite it being, in military terms, absence without leave or even desertion. They took the view that he would turn up hungover in a brothel somewhere and action could be taken against him then. Lawrence wrote a letter to me last Tuesday night which he entrusted to a friend returning to London the next day and I was handed it on Thursday morning without it going near censors or any other prying eyes.'

'You want us to look for your nephew?' asked Monique, looking up from her notebook.

'Not just my nephew,' replied the commodore. 'I need to be honest with you. You are not my first choice for this. The geography makes my involving you very awkward. And that's before we begin to consider the fact that you were getting married on Saturday. My closest friend at school, Edward Price, is with the Secret Intelligence Service, SIS, or MI6 if you prefer, in Cairo. I was able to get a short message to him using a silly old personal code embedded within the normal ciphers, despite the risk that would raise unwanted interest from others in Cairo. Apparently, it didn't. I simply told him I needed his help in Malta and to talk to Lawrence Dowson when he arrived. I know that Edward flew from Cairo to Malta last Friday the 4th of June. It's worth mentioning that Edward wasn't on the best of terms with the man in charge of SIS's office in Malta, which meant that when he arrived he could only call on limited local assistance, essentially from Lawrence Dowson.

'In passing, that was my reason for failing to attend your wedding on Saturday, for which I really should apologise again. I was waiting for a signal from Edward Price, which I hoped would say that he'd found my nephew alive and well. All I got was a very short cryptic signal from Lawrence Dowson on

Monday, the day before yesterday. Edward Price has not been seen since Sunday morning and has also disappeared.

'I spent part of yesterday hoping they'd both turn up and part of it looking into the possibility of a fallback plan. I flew from Northolt to Edinburgh this morning and was met by Leading Wren Woodburn at RAF Turnhouse. She then drove me directly here. Your colleague Lieutenant Commander Dixon is aware that I have come to see you but no one in London, other than my secretary, knows where I am. To be honest, my first instinct was to travel to Malta myself to try to find James and Edward. But there is no chance I could have done that without other parts of the military intelligence organisation, and Sir Peter Maitland in particular, finding out.

'To summarise, in a personal and unofficial pursuit of a missing family member, I have caused a member of the Secret Intelligence Service to undertake an investigation that is off his home ground, and he has also gone missing. Now I am asking the two of you to go to Malta using a cover story so threadbare it might as well not exist. What I'm doing is so irregular that it could easily cost me my career, but I owe it to my sister to try. It's not fair to ask the two of you to join me in this venture but, and please don't take this the wrong way, I am rather desperate.'

Monique saw Bob look at her again and knew what he was thinking. She smiled at the commodore. 'According to the receptionist in the hotel this morning, a local fisherman had told her that the weather here is due to turn tomorrow, with rain for the next couple of days. I don't know much about Malta, but I suspect you are right about it being warmer and sunnier. Of course, we'll go.'

'Hang on, sir,' said Bob. 'You said that you are staying in the

Station Hotel tonight. Given the obvious urgency involved and the time that's already passed, shouldn't we leave immediately?'

'For reasons I'll go into over dinner, there's nothing to be gained by leaving before tomorrow morning, though we will need an early start. And besides, I do want to buy you dinner, both as an apology for not being at your wedding on Saturday and as thanks to you for offering to help. Can we remember, please, that when we get out of this car there should be no further mention of my nephew or Edward Price? Only the two of you, Commander Dowson, and I will know why you are really in Malta. People may think it bizarre that I am sending you there to set up a small branch of MI11, and still more bizarre that you have agreed to go. But if the three of us simply stick to that story it does give us a fig leaf that partly covers our modesty.'

'You talked about this being a possibly dangerous trip,' said Bob. 'Do you have any reason beyond the two men's disappearances to say that?'

'No. But while you will be travelling under your MI11 identities of Group Captain Robert Sutherland and Madame Monique Dubois, I would also like you to take the various documents we prepared before you went to Sweden that would allow you to operate as Mr Robert and Mrs Monique Cadman if the need arises. I assume you still have them?'

'Of course, sir,' said Bob. 'They're in the safe in the office at Craigiehall.'

'Monique Cadman was blonde,' said Monique. 'That's reflected in her passport photograph. I look quite different, which was what we intended at the time.'

'Very true,' said the commodore. 'I'm aware that your

blonde wig was singed in that car fire in Stockholm. My secretary has by now hopefully sourced a replacement. She's also arranging some warm weather clothing for you, Monique. Meanwhile, Bob, we've got the tailor who made your uniforms and your suits for Stockholm working on two RAF tropical service uniforms and a couple of lightweight suits.'

'You seem to have thought of everything, sir,' said Monique.

'I'm so badly in the dark about what's going on in Malta that I feel utterly helpless. Making sure the two of you are properly kitted out for the trip has been my way of trying to exercise some control, however limited. And I know it might seem presumptuous to have organised your wardrobes before asking whether you would go, but I felt I had to have that conversation with you face to face, so had no choice. Thank you for not disappointing me.'

CHAPTER THREE

The Station Hotel's dining room walls were covered in embossed wallpaper featuring botanical motifs that must have been fresh and attractive once, probably before the war began. Monique had noticed on the first night that the management seemed to be fighting a battle to prevent the wallpaper from peeling away in a couple of the corners of the room, while scars were visible where the edges of tables or the backs of chairs had been pushed too vigorously against the walls.

Meanwhile, the ceiling, which was also lined with decorative embossed paper, had probably been white originally, before being exposed to too many years of cigarette smoke.

Everything Monique had seen since they'd arrived at the Station Hotel late on Monday evening suggested that it was run well by people who cared for it. But it was equally obvious that wartime shortages had meant that they'd had problems sourcing everything from carpets to champagne.

She had shared a bottle of the latter with Bob after they'd arrived on Monday evening and another over dinner on Tuesday. When they'd asked for a second after dinner, they'd been told that there were none left, probably for the duration of the war. The French white wine they'd been offered instead was pleasant and they'd decided that drinking a hotel dry of champagne on their honeymoon would make an amusing anecdote to tell their grandchildren one day.

When Monique and Bob entered the already quite smoky dining room, Commodore Cunningham was seated at a table set a little aside from others, in front of the far end of the large windows that ran along one side of the room.

There were perhaps fifteen square tables in the room, each covered by a clean white tablecloth. Monique noted that five of the others were occupied, three by naval officers and the other two by civilians. She'd seen the elderly couple sitting at a table near the door before, the previous night at dinner, while two men who looked like farmers sat at a table in front of the near end of the run of windows.

Two pairs and a trio of naval officers completed the ensemble. Most were smoking. Monique thought that Commodore Cunningham was probably the most senior naval officer in Kyle of Lochalsh or for a considerable distance in any direction from it. She was amused to note that a pair of officers who had entered the dining room just ahead of her and Bob chose to sit as far from the commodore as possible within the confines of the room.

Bob's presence as a senior RAF officer and, she recognised, hers as an attractive woman, had caused ill-concealed interest amongst a similar gathering of naval officers the previous night and the fact that she and Bob now walked over to join Maurice Cunningham, who stood to greet them, would probably be the subject of speculation in the officers' wardroom at HMS *Trelawney,* the naval base at the eastern end of Kyle of Lochalsh, later that evening. She noticed a brown envelope lying on the table beside the commodore's place setting.

'Did you see Leading Wren Woodburn?' the commodore asked.

'Yes,' said Monique. 'She was grateful for your invitation to dinner but thought the idea of her being seen dining with us, possibly by officers who knew her when she was stationed here, might be more excitement than Kyle of Lochalsh could stand. Besides, she met a friend on her walk earlier, a Wren she worked alongside, and they've agreed to catch up this evening. I did remind her she needed to be careful about what she said, but she's no fool and I'm confident she won't compromise security. I also reminded her that we needed to make an early start in the morning.'

As on previous evenings, Monique admired the view out of the dining room window across the water to Kyleakin and the Isle of Skye, with everything lit up by the summer evening sunshine. She'd be sorry to leave prematurely but pleased they'd at least had a chance to explore the island a little while they were here.

'I'm afraid we drank them out of champagne on our first two nights, so we'll have to have something a little less celebratory,' said Bob.

Monique saw that the commodore wasn't sure whether Bob was joking and laughed. 'It's true, sir,' she said. 'Their entire stock was down to just two bottles.'

'It's perhaps as well Leading Wren Woodburn isn't here,' said the commodore. He looked around the room as if deciding how much privacy they had given their distance from other tables and the background level of conversation. 'I talked earlier about your cover story. I've been wondering since then whether it would be best if we don't even mention Malta to any of your people. That seems least likely to raise awkward questions if they innocently mention it to anyone else.'

'I can see that, sir,' said Bob. 'There's no need, just as there was no need for them to know where we were going when we went to Stockholm for the first time.'

'Good.'

There was a pause while their orders were taken and then another while the wine was brought to the table.

'It's also helpful that Leading Wren Woodburn isn't here because I wanted to ask you about her,' said the commodore. 'I was impressed by her skills as a driver on the way up here from Edinburgh, but I was more impressed by Ruth herself. I don't wish to appear a snob, but I got the sense she was a lot more than the uniform and rank had led me to expect.'

Monique laughed. 'I met Ruth when Anthony Darlington and I were here in April. You could say that I've taken her on as a personal project. Her parents are wealthy and sent her to Roedean School in Sussex. She rebelled against their expectations that she'd then marry an earl's oldest son and instead, and to their horror, took up motorcycle racing with her uncle, her father's younger brother.

'When war broke out, she joined the Women's Royal Naval Service. Her parents insisted she should apply for a commission, but she preferred the idea of becoming a motor mechanic and driver, using her pre-war skills. She enjoyed her time in the navy until she was posted to HMS *Trelawney* here in Kyle of Lochalsh at the beginning of last winter. She found the place boring and the choice of men uninspiring. When I first met her, she told me it had become so bad she was even thinking of applying for a commission.

'We were short of a driver in MI11 and Bob agreed to offer her a post. She's worked partly as a driver and partly as my assistant on the MI5 side of things. She's done very well and I think probably will apply for a commission, though I'll be sorry to lose her.'

'On paper, you've still got a vacancy for a leader for your naval team, haven't you, Bob?' asked the commodore.

Bob nodded.

Commodore Cunningham put his wine glass down. 'Perhaps

you wouldn't need to lose her, Monique. You might want to organise things differently, Bob, because I know Michael Dixon heads up your naval team as well as acting as your deputy. But if Leading Wren Woodburn were able to gain a commission, it might be possible for you to retain her if that's what she wanted.'

'That is an interesting thought,' said Bob. 'How do junior ranks go about applying for a commission in the Wrens?'

'I may be able to help. Perhaps you could sound her out in the car in the morning, Monique. If she's interested, I can talk to a couple of people. She sounds exactly what the Wrens need as a junior officer. Ah, here's the soup.'

Monique had found the food at the Station Hotel to be reasonably good, if rather basic and limited in choice. She'd not expected anything else in wartime.

A little later, Bob sat back after finishing his venison main course. 'I'm sad we'll be leaving here sooner than planned. But part of me is quite pleased that we're not going to be spending another eleven and a half hours on trains going back to Edinburgh.'

'Does it really take that long?' asked the commodore.

'Yes, we left Waverley Station in Edinburgh at 10.05 a.m. on Monday, and after changing trains in Perth, Inverness and Dingwall, we arrived in Kyle at 9.30 p.m. Even with wonderful company, first class comfort and magnificent scenery, it was a long journey.'

'You might change your tune after you've been driven back to Edinburgh by Ruth,' said Monique. 'She's an outstanding driver but many of the roads are very demanding, with long lengths of single track carriageway. We'll certainly get back a lot quicker than by train, but it probably won't be a very comfortable journey.'

'I can attest to that,' said the commodore, smiling.

With the dishes that had been used for the dessert of apple crumble and custard cleared away, the commodore ordered a second bottle of wine.

Monique had seen some coming and going amongst the other diners but noted that the clear area around the commodore and his party had been maintained.

'Are you going to tell us why we can leave in the morning rather than earlier this afternoon?' asked Bob. 'Given how late it gets dark, we could have easily returned to Edinburgh tonight without needing to drive in the blackout.'

'Yes,' said the commodore. 'I do need to tell you about the arrangements for the next couple of days. We'll leave at 6 a.m. tomorrow and Ruth will drive us to Edinburgh. She refuelled the car at HMS *Trelawney* when we arrived in Kyle of Lochalsh earlier. I have asked the hotel to arrange some sandwiches and flasks of tea for the four of us as we will be too early for breakfast. You should know that I have also settled your hotel bill for your entire stay here, both the time you have been here and the time you were intending to stay.'

'You didn't need to do that, sir,' said Bob.

'On the contrary, I think it's the least I can do. As I might as well be hung for a sheep as for a lamb, I paid with cash drawn from an MI11 account. When we get to Edinburgh you will need to gather your passports and other documentation, and some clothing. From what you said about your Cadman passports, I assume that will involve a visit to your office as well as your home.

'The three of us will then fly in an Avro Anson that should still be waiting at RAF Turnhouse to RAF Lyneham in

Wiltshire. There we will meet my secretary and make sure your wardrobes are appropriate for a trip to the Mediterranean in June.'

'I assume that we're flying out from Lyneham?' asked Bob.

'Yes. I need to be honest with you about that. Your flight out may very well be the riskiest part of what I'm proposing. I think that in the past, RAF flights to Gibraltar, which is the destination of the first leg of the journey, have tended to take place in daylight. You may have been too busy to read the newspapers last week, but last Tuesday, the 1st of June…'

'Leslie Howard!' said Monique. She saw Bob look puzzled. 'I've always thought he was a wonderful actor. I saw a newspaper article last week saying he'd been lost, presumed killed when his plane disappeared on the way to Britain from… was that Gibraltar?'

'Not quite,' said the commodore. 'He was on board a British Overseas Airways Corporation flight from Lisbon to Whitchurch near Bristol. It took off a few minutes late at 7.35 a.m. and never arrived at Whitchurch. The loss was announced the following day, last Wednesday.'

'Do we know what happened?' asked Bob.

'Probably,' said the commodore. 'BOAC were in touch with the aircraft and at a little before 11.00 a.m., while it was over the Bay of Biscay, they received a message to say that it was being followed by enemy aircraft and then that it was being fired upon. A search was mounted for the missing aircraft. The following day, last Wednesday, a Short Sunderland flying boat searching in the area where the BOAC aircraft had been lost was itself attacked by eight Junkers Ju 88 heavy fighters. In what sounds like a truly remarkable encounter the Sunderland shot down three of the enemy aircraft and claimed three more as probable kills. The Sunderland was itself badly damaged but made it back for a crash landing at Penzance.

'The working hypothesis is that the Ju 88s that attacked the Sunderland also attacked the BOAC aircraft the day before. Despite the Luftwaffe being given a bloody nose, all flights to and from Lisbon by BOAC have since been rerouted to fly further out into the Atlantic and retimed to take advantage of the hours of darkness. The same has been true of the RAF flights from Lyneham to Gibraltar. As I understand it, you will have a pause in Gibraltar to allow the crew of your aircraft to get some rest. Then you will complete your journey to Malta.

'It rather brings it home that the day the Sunderland encountered the Ju 88s was also the day that Lawrence Dowson's friend was flying back via Gibraltar with his letter to me.

'If there's any consolation in all of this, it's that the flight from Gibraltar to Malta will be very much safer than it would have been until quite recently. Since the middle of 1940, Malta has been under siege from the air by the Italian and German air forces, with over 3,000 air raids before the siege was lifted at the end of last year, and more since. You may know that the entire island was awarded the George Cross by King George last year. From what I've heard, at times the population was close to starvation.

'There was always a strong interaction between the role of Allied forces based on Malta in disrupting German and Italian supply lines across the Mediterranean and the ability of the enemy to maintain their stranglehold on the island. Anyway, as you know the Axis forces in North Africa finally surrendered last month and since then access to Malta from Gibraltar has been very much safer than it was before.'

'You are making it sound like a truly delightful place for a honeymoon, sir,' said Monique.

She saw the commodore look at her, perhaps to check if she was joking, before replying. 'I hope it's no longer as bad as it has been. The tide has very definitely turned.'

Bob looked around to see if anyone was within hearing. 'Is there anything else you want to tell us about our reason for going, sir? The real reason?'

'I'm sorry. I would tell you more if I knew more. I appreciate that sending you in virtually blind doesn't improve your chances of success. But it's the best I can do. More generally, I think you might find it useful to read this.'

The commodore picked up the envelope Monique had noticed at the start of the meal and passed it to Bob. 'It's publicly available information about Malta, so only sensitive as far as demonstrating your interest in the island to your colleagues is concerned. Open it if you want.'

The envelope wasn't sealed, and Monique watched as Bob opened it and slid out a hardback book in a dustjacket that had its title and a map on a blue background.

'*The Epic of Malta*,' he said. 'The author isn't specified but it's got a foreword written by the prime minister.' He riffled through the book. 'It's mainly photographs of parts of the island, of bomb damage and air raids.'

'It's a few months out of date,' said the commodore. 'But it should give you a good idea of where you're going and what the island has been through. Look upon it as background reading for your long flights.'

Monique looked at her watch.

Maurice Cunningham smiled. 'You're right, Monique. I've had a long journey today and you are starting an even longer one tomorrow. Perhaps we should call it a day?'

*

After Bob completed his ablutions in the bathroom on the opposite side of the upper-floor corridor, he returned to their bedroom. He was surprised to find Monique standing naked in front of the window, with the curtains open.

She looked around as he entered, smiling broadly at him.

'Is that your impression of "Saucy Mary"?' Bob asked. 'Remember that in the Viking age, passing ships' captains wouldn't have had the benefit of telescopes or binoculars. Anyone sailing past right now is going to get a much better view of you.'

'You're not going to turn into one of those possessive husbands, are you, Bob?' She smiled at him again. 'Besides, the window isn't very large, the sun is low and will be nearly in the eyes of anyone looking this way, and no boats are sailing past at this time of night anyway. And quite apart from all that, to quote Clark Gable's character in "Gone with the Wind": frankly, my dear, I don't give a damn.'

Bob shrugged off his dressing gown and hung it on the back of the bedroom door, then went to stand behind Monique and wrapped his arms around her, looking over her left shoulder at the view across to Kyleakin and the Isle of Skye.

'Your body hair is tickling my back,' she said.

'I'll move if you want.'

'No, it's quite nice when the surprise has worn off. Anyway, it's our last chance to enjoy the view. Let's make the most of it.'

'I do like these light nights,' said Bob. 'It's even better here than in Edinburgh, being further north. I don't think the sun's due to set until after 11 p.m. and it will still be light until after midnight and again not long after 4 a.m.'

'Let's leave the curtains open tonight,' said Monique. She leaned back against Bob. 'How do you really feel about cutting short our honeymoon and going to Malta to look for Maurice Cunningham's missing nephew and friend?'

'Truthfully? I'm extremely sad. Being here with you has been wonderful, even though we've only really had two days. I was getting the sense that we were far enough away from the cares of our normal world to begin to relax properly for the first time in what feels like ages. That all changed as soon as I saw the commodore waiting on the ferry slipway.

'On the other hand, I know he wouldn't have asked unless he was, as he acknowledged, desperate. I also know that his coming here personally, at the cost of considerable time and effort, shows how much this matters to him. And although he is my boss, I also regard Maurice as a friend. I feel we have no option but to help as much as we can. What about you?'

'Pretty much the same,' said Monique. She took his hands and moved them up, so they were over her breasts. He accepted the invitation and began to gently fondle them, at the same time softly rubbing her nipples with his thumbs.

Bob heard Monique's breath catch in her throat before she continued. 'But as I see it, we're still on honeymoon until we get into the car tomorrow morning. And you know what married couples are meant to do on honeymoon.'

Bob felt her push back and wriggle her bottom against him.

She laughed. 'An important part of you agrees with me.' She turned in his arms and kissed him. It was a long kiss. Then she leaned back a little and looked up into his eyes. 'With Ruth and the commodore staying in the hotel tonight, I'm especially pleased that the bed doesn't bang or squeak. Let's go and give it another try, just to get the commodore's money's worth before we need to leave.'

CHAPTER FOUR

The noise of what she recognised as the aircraft's flaps coming down caused Monique to wake up with a start. She'd flown often enough with Bob to identify the thuds that followed a short time later as the undercarriage being lowered. She'd been dreaming, very vividly. Someone had been chasing her along a tunnel. She thought she'd seen who it was earlier in the dream, but the memory dissipated faster than she could pin it down, leaving just a sense of unease that stayed with her as she gathered herself and looked around.

The inside of the aircraft was as she'd seen it when they boarded late the previous night at RAF Lyneham, though now there was sunlight streaming in through the row of windows on the right-hand side of the aircraft. There were nine seats placed one behind another along her side of the passenger cabin, the left-hand side. A similar number had been installed beyond a narrow central aisle on the other side, with, behind them and opposite the door, two more with their backs placed against the side of the aircraft. Further back was a compartment that she knew concealed the toilet.

She realised that Bob, who was sitting across the aisle, was smiling at her and she smiled back and lifted a hand in greeting. He didn't look as if he'd had much sleep. She always thought it ironic that such an accomplished pilot should be such a frail flyer as a passenger.

After their plane had taken off, Monique had covered herself with a blanket she'd been offered by a member of the crew and tried to make herself as comfortable as possible. She'd been aware that Bob's seat had been empty not long into the flight and assumed that he'd gone to talk to the flight crew. She'd managed to sleep through much of the journey, except for a short period when they ran into turbulence in the middle of the night.

As well as herself and Bob, there were a dozen other passengers on the aircraft. She and Bob were sitting in the second row back, with the row in front of them empty, apparently reserved for the occasional use of the aircraft crew. The other passengers were scattered seemingly at random amongst the remaining seats. Most were military officers, two of them French. The inward-facing seats at the rear of the aircraft, the only two that were side-by-side, were occupied by a blonde woman in her thirties and a girl, presumably her daughter, who seemed to be in her early teens. Monique wondered why they were travelling to Gibraltar, and perhaps Malta, but the opportunity hadn't arisen to talk to them.

Monique felt the aircraft bank to the left and looked out of the window beside her seat. She was rewarded with a beautiful view of the east side of the Rock of Gibraltar caught fully illuminated by the light of a summer sunrise under a clear blue sky. The end nearest her was quite peaky and the rock then tailed off a little as the promontory on which it stood pushed further out into the sea, though she recognised that might be an illusion caused by the height of the aircraft. Bob had acquired a map at RAF Lyneham and Monique had had a chance to look at the quite complex physical and political geography of the area. The dark blue of the sea to the south of the rock was replaced, after a shorter distance than she expected and beyond a white line of low mist, by the darker shapes of the Moroccan coast and inland mountains.

They were landing from the east and the angle of the

aircraft's turn was enough to allow Monique a clear view of a runway that looked remarkably short, with a part of it built out beyond a neck of low-lying land that lay to the north of the Rock of Gibraltar. The far end of the runway, the part projecting into the sea, looked like it was still being built, or perhaps extended. She didn't find that a very reassuring thought. She couldn't see what was to the north, her right, of the runway, but knew that the border with Spain was close at hand on that side. The land she could see ahead of them, on the far side of a broad bay beyond Gibraltar's runway, was also Spanish.

Her glimpse of the runway ensured the landing was a very tense experience for Monique. Bob again smiled at her and she was pleased he couldn't have seen the runway from his side of the aircraft. In the event, there were no dramas and it was only a few minutes after the jar of the landing that the engines were shut down, leaving her realising just how loud they'd been. Monique looked at her watch. It was 7.30 a.m.

The cabin door was opened from the outside and a member of the crew helped passengers retrieve baggage from the compartment at the rear of the aircraft, beyond the toilet. Monique and Bob were the last to disembark, carrying their suitcases down the short set of steps to the concrete area the aircraft had parked on. There were other aircraft standing nearby. Monique was sure Bob would have been able to tell her what they were but, despite his enthusiasm, aircraft recognition was a subject she'd never found very interesting.

The weather at Kyle of Lochalsh the previous morning had been grey, windy and quite cold and it had been raining in Edinburgh and at RAF Lyneham. Gibraltar, by contrast, was pleasantly warm, even this early in the morning, and the blue sky she'd seen from the aircraft window extended from horizon to horizon.

The passengers ahead of them formed a straggling line that was making its way towards an open door in a single-storey building perhaps 50 yards away. The windows in the building were covered by the criss-cross pattern of sticky tape intended to reduce flying glass in the event of an attack by enemy bombers. Above the door was a large sign with dark blue writing on a light blue background, flanked by RAF roundels, that read: 'Welcome to RAF North Front'.

A dark-haired man in brown trousers and a khaki shirt was standing about halfway between the aircraft and the door. He had presumably directed the first passengers to where they needed to go and was now largely redundant.

As Bob and Monique approached, the man waved his arm in the general direction of the passengers ahead of them and smiled. 'Buenos días. I hope you had a pleasant journey.'

'Buenos días, gracias,' replied Monique, smiling back. Her eyes briefly met his and she felt a chill run down her spine, though she wasn't sure why. It was as elusive as the dream she'd woken from on the plane. She couldn't pin down why the man seemed familiar but something about him set off warning bells in her head. She managed to keep her smile in place until she was inside the building.

Passengers' papers were being checked at a desk on the far side of the room.

Monique saw Bob turn towards her and a look of concern crossed his face. 'What is it?' he asked. 'You look like you've seen a ghost.'

'I feel like I have. That man outside who spoke to us just now.'

'I'd imagine he's employed locally to make sure chocks are in place under aircraft wheels and to move access steps around. I didn't know Spanish was one of your languages.'

'I'm not fluent, but I know a little. That's not the point, though. What did you make of him?'

'I didn't really notice him, to be honest,' said Bob. 'Do you know him from somewhere?'

'That's what's worrying me. I feel as if I should, but I can't pin him down.'

Bob walked back to the open door out onto the airfield. 'He's not there now. Look, I suggest that once we've had our papers checked, we go and find some breakfast. I don't know about you, but I'm feeling decidedly second-hand after that flight and some food might help. Our plane isn't due to leave for Malta until 1 p.m. so we need to find a way to pass the time until then.'

Monique smiled. 'I like the idea of breakfast. I wonder if they've got a café here?'

'It's an RAF station, which means they'll have an officers' mess.' He held up his right arm with its four rings of braid around the cuff. 'Sometimes this uniform can have its advantages.'

*

The officers' mess at RAF North Front struck Monique as rather utilitarian, though she had to admit that the fried breakfasts that she and Bob were served were superb. The dining room was busy and quite smoky, but they found an empty table beside a window that looked out over the airfield towards Spain. Again, there was anti-blast tape on the glass.

Monique was pleased to see Bob tuck into his food with as much enthusiasm as she felt. The long flight and overnight turbulence had apparently done nothing to diminish his appetite.

'You said that you know a little Spanish,' said Bob. 'How did you pick that up?'

'I think I told you that in 1924, when I was 11, my parents moved from Denmark to Paris. In Paris, I attended the ballet school set up by the exiled Russian ballet dancer, Vera Trefilova. Setting false modesty aside, I was quite good. When I was 16, I was offered the chance to tour Europe with Madame Trefilova's ballet company. We spent two weeks in Spain and performed in Barcelona, Madrid and Seville. This was long before the civil war of course. I find that languages get easier the more you know. Picking up enough Spanish to get by was the most natural thing in the world, even though I wasn't in the country for long.'

'So, in addition to your fluency in Russian, Danish, French, English and German, and an ability I know about to get by in Norwegian and Swedish, you also speak some Spanish?'

'Yes, and some Polish and Ukrainian from my adoptive mother and some Italian, some Hungarian, and a tiny bit of Dutch from the ballet tour. We performed in Amsterdam and Rotterdam, but the Dutch were always keener to talk in almost any language other than their own. You must have noticed that when you walked across the country in December 1930.'

'Yes, I did,' said Bob. 'But, perhaps unlike you, I found that a cause for relief. The thing I've never worked out is how you learned to speak such perfect English. Did your ballet tour get as far as London?'

'It did, but I started learning much earlier. We had English neighbours in Paris, in the apartment above. A family with two daughters. The eldest was the same age as me. Rebecca and I became close friends until they moved away after a couple of years. She went to a British school in Paris and couldn't speak anything but English, so I learned from her. Then, when Vera Trefilova's tour was in London, I fell in love with a painter I met called Benedict.'

Monique saw the look that passed over Bob's face and smiled. 'Yes, I know, I was only 16. He was in his twenties and not long afterwards he moved to Paris so he could be with me. Benedict turned out to be a bastard who left me for one of the other dancers in the cabaret I was performing in. That was in the summer of 1930 when I was 17, and by then my English was quite good. It was not long afterwards that I met Count Sergei Ignatieff, who as you know I married at the end of that year when I had just turned 18. The best that can be said about him was that he provided an excellent refresher for the Russian I'd learned as a young child in Siberia.'

'I'm pleased you can talk to me so openly,' said Bob.

'We agreed to keep no secrets, remember?' said Monique. 'Besides, I'm only filling in some of the fine details in the story you already know.'

Monique had been looking out of the window while they talked, wondering if she'd catch a glimpse of the man she'd spoken to near the aircraft, and trying to work out why he had evoked such a response in her.

'Bob Sutherland!' Monique looked across the table to see Bob twisting around in his chair. A man wearing a khaki-coloured RAF officer's uniform was standing beside Bob's seat and had his hand on Bob's left shoulder. He wore the four bands of a group captain on his epaulettes, matching those Bob wore on the sleeves of his darker blue-grey uniform. The man was about six feet tall and had blond hair. Monique thought he was probably in his late thirties.

Bob stood up and clasped the man's upper arms with his hands. 'Peter Derbyshire! How are you? It's good to see you alive and well. I heard you'd gone on to better things after you abandoned 605 Squadron to the Luftwaffe at the height of the Battle of Britain.'

Monique could see that both men were smiling and realised that Bob was joking.

'Abandoned like hell! You were so good they decided you could do my job better than I could. With no notice at all I was posted away and, the next thing I heard, you'd stolen my squadron from under me!'

To Monique's surprise, the two men hugged. She could see that others in the dining room were intrigued by what was going on.

Group Captain Derbyshire looked down at Monique. 'May I join you? As you'll have gathered, I'm an old friend of Bob's.'

'Of course,' said Monique.

'Sorry,' said Bob. 'Peter Derbyshire, may I introduce Monique Dubois? She also goes by the name of Monique Sutherland because we were married in Edinburgh last Saturday.'

The group captain shook Monique's hand and sat down. 'Congratulations! Sadly, it's much too early in the day for champagne. Even more sadly, we don't have any anyway. What brings you both to Gibraltar? You're not going to steal my command from under me again, are you, Bob?'

Bob laughed. 'No, we're just passing through. These days I'm the deputy head of Military Intelligence, Section 11, based in Edinburgh. We have a responsibility for military security and work alongside others in the military and in intelligence. Monique is with the Security Service, MI5 if you prefer, and is seconded to my unit. We're on our way to Malta to explore the idea of setting up a small branch of MI11 there. We came in on the Liberator transport aircraft that arrived from Lyneham a little earlier and I thought this would be the best place to get a decent breakfast. We've not been disappointed.'

'I assume you'll be re-joining the Liberator when it flies on to Malta this afternoon? That gives you a few hours to kill. I'm happy to show you the sights, such as they are, while you're here. We can leave your suitcases in my office. It's not far from here.'

'I wouldn't want to drag you away from your duties,' said Bob.

'I think that briefing Military Intelligence, Section 11, about the situation in Gibraltar just leapt to the top of my list of priorities. I've already eaten. If you've finished, we can head off straight away.'

CHAPTER FIVE

The group captain's car made its way through what seemed to be Gibraltar's main built-up area before starting a steep climb along narrow roads that zig-zagged their way up the west side of the rock. The driver had to stop several times at military checkpoints for passes to be shown. Monique had the sense that the group captain's pennant fluttering on the front of the car and the fact that Group Captain Derbyshire seemed to be known by sight by many of the men helped ease their way.

The group captain sat in the front passenger seat of the car and spent much of the journey partly turned around to talk to Bob and Monique in the back. 'Did you notice anything about the people we saw in the town?' he asked.

'They were nearly all in uniform,' said Monique. 'I only saw a couple of civilians, and none of them was old or had children with them.'

'That's right,' said the group captain. 'The importance of Gibraltar as a fortress, the expectation of imminent attack and the need to make space for members of the armed forces was such that pretty much the entire civilian population was evacuated earlier in the war. Only those with essential jobs were allowed to stay.'

'Where did they go?'

'Ah, thereby hangs a tale. At the beginning of June 1940, over 13,000 people were evacuated from Gibraltar to Casablanca in French Morocco. Very soon afterwards, France surrendered to the Germans and all those people suddenly found themselves unwelcome in Morocco and were brought back here to Gibraltar. The population was then evacuated again. Most, around 10,000, went to the London area, just in time to be on the receiving end of the Blitz. Smaller groups, of perhaps 2,000 each, were evacuated to Jamaica and Madeira.'

'That's very much like jumping from the frying pan into the fire,' said Bob. 'They ended up swapping the risk of attack here for the reality of attack in London.'

'That's very true,' said Peter Derbyshire. 'We'll pull over just along here. That's right.'

The driver pulled up behind an army lorry parked in a broadening of the road.

'Up ahead of us is the Rock Gun Battery. It's effectively at the top of the North Face of the Rock of Gibraltar. This isn't quite the highest point of the rock, but it gives the best view of the north end of Gibraltar and our situation relative to Spain.'

Monique climbed out of the car and walked round the back to join Bob. A few yards away Group Captain Derbyshire was exchanging salutes with two army sentries who had approached the car.

After he'd spoken to the sentries, he turned to face her and Bob. 'We're fortunate that there's very little wind this morning. We're at 1,350 feet above sea level and it can get quite blustery up here, even on a warm day. The battery was originally built in 1779 during the Great Siege of Gibraltar to house a 24-pounder naval gun they'd somehow managed to haul up here. It's been rebuilt much more recently to house anti-aircraft guns. We don't have far to walk.'

Ahead of them, the rocky ground rose towards a peak. Monique and Bob followed Peter Derbyshire until he came to a halt on a concrete platform partly surrounded by railings. Monique could see gun emplacements on both sides of the platform.

An army lieutenant emerged from the doorway of a concrete bunker at the rear of the platform and walked over to Group Captain Derbyshire, then saluted. 'Good morning, sir, can I help you?'

'No, thank you, lieutenant. My guests have never been to Gibraltar before, and I want them to benefit from what I believe is the best viewpoint on the rock.'

'You'll not find many here who disagree with you, sir. We've got a kettle on in the bunker. If you fancy a cup of tea before you head back down, just let someone know.'

'Thank you, that's very kind.'

The lieutenant turned back towards the doorway, smiling at Monique as he did so. She smiled back.

'If you come over to the railings, you can see what I mean about the view,' said the group captain.

'Wow!' said Bob. Monique could see from the whites of his knuckles that he was gripping the top of the railings very tightly as she came to stand beside him.

'That really is impressive,' she said.

'You'll recognise RAF North Front and the airfield almost immediately below us. The north end of the town is down there to our left, with the harbour round on the west side of the rock.'

'And everything else we can see is Spain,' said Monique.

'That's right. The border, whose course is the subject of some dispute, is taken by the British to cross the neck of land not far to the north of the airfield. Beyond the border is the town of La Línea, more properly known as La Línea de la Concepción. From there, the Spanish coast curves around to the west and then the south as it forms what we call the Bay of Gibraltar and the Spanish call the Bahía de Algeciras. Off to our left, on the far side of the bay, you can see the city of Algeciras, which is a very significant port. It's about six miles from us as the crow flies.'

Bob took a step back from the railings. 'I was puzzled when we arrived to see references to RAF North Front. Wouldn't "RAF Gibraltar" be more obvious?'

'It would, but RAF North Front is only part of my empire. I also command the not-very imaginatively named RAF New Camp. That was established last year in part of the harbour and serves as a base for flying boats and motor launches. As a result, "RAF Gibraltar" would be ambiguous.'

'I noticed from the window of the plane while we were landing that you are extending the runway,' said Monique. 'The view from here is much better and it looks like the builders have started up for the day. Presumably, that will give you more flexibility. I must admit that, to my non-expert eyes, the runway looked quite short when we were landing.'

'You're right, Monique,' said Peter Derbyshire. 'The runway was extended out into the sea earlier in the war but it's still only 1,530 yards long, which can be a bit tight for some of the aircraft we handle. It wasn't primarily due to runway length, but there was a nasty incident last October. An aircraft like the one that brought you here landed too far along the runway in a storm and went into the sea with the loss of 17 lives. Many of those killed were fighter pilots on their way home after serving in the defence of Malta.'

'That's dreadful,' said Monique.

'It was. The main cause of that accident was crew fatigue. The Liberator aircraft involved had flown from here to Malta, then to Cairo, then back to Malta and then back to here, all without any significant time for the crew to rest. That's why you've got to wait until this afternoon to fly on to Malta. We take fatigue more seriously now. But while that crash wasn't caused by runway length, a longer runway might have improved their chances. What you've noticed is land being reclaimed from the sea for an additional 270 yards of runway, making 1,800 yards in all. I hope we can bring it into use within the next two months.'

'Where do you get the material from for the reclamation?' asked Monique. 'I can't imagine the Spanish being happy to supply it from their side. Do you have quarries in Gibraltar itself?'

'We do, but perhaps not in the way you might expect. Digging tunnels into the rock for military defence dates back to the end of the 18th century but we've turned it into something of an industry during the current conflict. You only need to look at the lie of the land to see that in some ways Gibraltar would be highly vulnerable to a determined attack from Spain, whether by Spanish or German troops. It's giving away no secrets to say that tunnelling has been taking place on a huge scale over the last few years. As a result, we've turned Gibraltar into a fortress capable of accommodating tens of thousands of men, with all the services they would need to withstand a siege. All that tunnelling produces a lot of spoil, and the runway extension is the perfect place to make use of it.'

'Given how strategically important Gibraltar is, I find it surprising that no serious attempt has been made to capture it,' said Bob.

'You're in good company,' said Peter Derbyshire. 'That's surprised a lot of us. Back in July 1940, Franco announced that Spain had two million men ready to retake Gibraltar and expand Spanish interests in North Africa. In October of that year, Franco met Hitler to discuss a joint operation to capture

Gibraltar. We may never know for sure, but it's said the two men didn't get on. Apparently, Franco demanded too high a price from Hitler to declare war on the Allies. Perhaps he played his hand badly, or perhaps he wanted to ensure Spain stayed out of the war. For their part, the Germans seem to have thought the Spanish might simply occupy Gibraltar and then sit back and do nothing more.

'I'm told there was a real belief here that a purely German attack was imminent in early 1941, but that threat effectively ended when Hitler invaded the Soviet Union in June of that year and found himself with other calls on his resources. More recently, of course, even someone as barmy as Franco must have realised that Germany is going to lose the war and that pitching in on the Axis side would not be a wise move. Yet when you look down below us and see Franco's border no more than a few yards beyond my airfield, it's obvious that the threat of large-scale invasion still needs to be defended against.'

'Yes, I do see that,' said Bob.

'We have been subject to plenty of lesser attacks over the past few years,' said Peter Derbyshire. 'The Vichy French mounted air raids on Gibraltar from Morocco in 1940 and last year the Italians attacked us several times from air bases in Sardinia.

'There has also been a series of attacks mounted by Italian frogmen using small underwater craft launched, apparently, from bases in Spain. Some of these have been very destructive. Three allied merchant ships were sunk in the harbour in an attack early last month. Meanwhile, the German Abwehr has organised sporadic sabotage attacks, mainly carried out by Spanish and Gibraltarian agents. MI5 appears to be getting on top of that threat but, as an example, in January last year, rather before I arrived here, two aircraft parked down on the airfield were destroyed by explosive charges.'

'I imagine that must keep everyone on their toes,' said Bob.

'It does, I can assure you. If you've both seen enough, perhaps we should head back down,' said Peter Derbyshire. 'It was kind of the lieutenant to offer us tea, but I can run to a decent cup of coffee in my office if you're happy to wait.'

The three of them walked back down towards where they'd left the car and driver. Monique walked a few yards behind the two men, trying to make sense of something she felt should be obvious to her, but which remained just beyond her grasp.

'I was sorry to hear that you'd been shot down, Bob.'

'Thank you, Peter. He saw me before I saw him. It was a common enough story at the time.'

'You recovered, though?'

'Up to a point.' Bob touched the left side of his head with his hand. 'My optic nerve on this side was cut so I'm blind in my left eye. I've learned to fly again, though never at night.'

'I'm sorry.'

'I was too, for quite a while. But without that happening, I'd never have ended up doing what I do now or met and married Monique. Every cloud has a silver lining.'

Bob looked round at Monique and they exchanged smiles.

Bob and Monique again sat in the back of the car. The driver had turned it round in their absence and after setting off they started the steep descent of the west side of the rock.

With a start, Monique suddenly realised what it was that had been tugging at the back of her mind.

'It was kind of you to offer us coffee, Peter,' said Monique. 'Would you be offended if Bob and I did something else instead?'

'What have you got in mind?'

'You talked about MI5 having a role in Gibraltar. Would it be possible to drop in on whoever looks after their operations here and for you to introduce us? I need to discuss something with them rather urgently. Come to think of it, you might find it useful to sit in on the discussion too.'

CHAPTER SIX

Group Captain Derbyshire directed the driver through a series of narrow streets below the west side of the base of the rock. 'MI5 operates from the Defence Security Office, which has premises near the southern end of Main Street, not far from the Convent, the governor's official residence.'

Monique took more notice this time and realised that the displacement of civilians on the streets by men, and a few women, in uniform was obvious when you were aware of the background.

The driver pulled up outside an anonymous beige-coloured four-storey building that Monique thought could have passed without much effort for a slightly seedy hotel in Madrid or Rome. There were brown shutters on all the windows. As she looked up, she saw that those on the top floor, which was in sunlight, were closed.

Group Captain Derbyshire led the way into the building. The hallway beyond had a light-coloured marble effect floor and wood-panelled walls that had probably once been painted white. A staircase led up from the rear of the hall and there was a lift door in the side wall near its foot. A reception desk was occupied by a man wearing the uniform of an army corporal.

'Can I help you, sir?'

'I'd like to talk to Matthew Moore if he's in the office, please.'

'Is he expecting you, sir?'

'No, but I'd be grateful if you could tell him we need to talk to him urgently.'

'Could I see some identification, please, sir?'

The group captain showed the man a pass and Monique and Bob followed suit.

'I know who you are, of course, sir. But I don't think I've come across Military Intelligence, Section 11, before.'

Monique was beginning to find the man tiresome. She pushed another pass across the desk towards him. 'Is this one any more familiar?'

The man looked at the new pass and then looked up at Monique. 'You're Vera Duval of the Security Service in London?'

'That's right. And I'd very much like to talk to Matthew Moore, preferably sooner rather than later.'

'Of course, ma'am. The two doors on the far side of the hall lead to interview rooms. Would the three of you mind waiting in the one on the right while I let Mr Moore know you're here?'

The interview room was as bare and uninspiring as it was possible to imagine. The once-white walls of the hall were replicated, though with a more careworn theme, as if over years, maps or papers had frequently been stuck to the walls and then peeled off again. There were no windows. The light came from two bulbs hanging from the ceiling beneath broad glass shades that were visibly covered in dust and dead flies.

A badly marked wooden meeting table occupied a fair part of the available floor area and around it were six ill-matched wooden chairs. The room smelled of sweat and cigarettes.

'I like to think that even without its civilian population, Gibraltar is usually a little more welcoming than this,' said Peter Derbyshire as Bob closed the door of the room. 'Can I offer anyone a cigarette?'

'No thanks,' said Bob.

Monique smiled and shook her head.

The group captain returned the packet to his breast pocket. 'No, I'd forgotten, you don't smoke, do you Bob?'

The door opened and a man in his late twenties entered. He was of medium height and build and had brown hair. He wore a tweed suit that would fade into the background in most places, though Monique wondered if it might be a little on the warm side for the Mediterranean.

'Hello, thank you for waiting.' He looked at Group Captain Derbyshire. 'I think we've met before, sir.' Then at Bob. 'That means you must be Group Captain Sutherland from MI11.' Finally, he looked at Monique and smiled. 'And you must be Madame Monique Dubois of MI11 or Madame Vera Duval of MI5.'

Monique returned the smile. 'Or just possibly both, of course.'

'I'm Matthew Moore. I'm the representative in Gibraltar of MI5, or the Security Service if you prefer, and although we've not met, your reputation precedes you. I recall hearing an improbable story about you working as a double agent within the Abwehr for the Secret Intelligence Service. If I remember correctly, this came to an end when you landed with two other Abwehr agents on the coast of northern Scotland in late 1940. They were subsequently hanged as spies and you moved from SIS to the Security Service. And more recently to MI11, apparently. Am I thinking about the right person?'

'You are,' said Monique, smiling at him. 'And I'm grateful to you for making it much easier to explain the background to what I'm about to tell you.' Out of the corner of her eye, she could see the look of surprise on Group Captain Derbyshire's face. She was relieved to see that Bob seemed amused by his old friend's reaction.

Monique continued. 'We trained for our part in "Operation Hummer Nord" in Norway. It was a little chaotic, not helped by the Abwehr agent running the operation getting himself killed in a car crash the day before we were due to depart. The training took place in a hotel that the Abwehr had commandeered in Stavanger. They used it for various purposes and people were always coming and going.

'The most popular part of the hotel was the bar. It was said that they tried to get trainees drunk there to see how reliable they were. One night I was in the bar on my own and a man I'd not seen before tried to pick me up. It seems he'd been told that I'd been widowed earlier in the year, and because of that he fancied his chances. I didn't find his approach especially appealing and, although we parted on amicable terms, he went to bed that night a disappointed and lonely man.'

Matthew Moore leaned forwards in his seat. 'Forgive me for asking, but what has this got to do with me or with Gibraltar?'

Monique could tell that Group Captain Derbyshire was wondering much the same thing. She was pleased to see from his face that Bob had already worked out where her story was going.

'Bob and I arrived in Gibraltar early this morning on the flight that left RAF Lyneham late last night. We were sitting near the front, so got off last. There was a man, a civilian dressed in brown trousers and a khaki shirt, directing passengers from the aircraft to the building where the papers are checked. He gave us a friendly greeting in Spanish and English, and I replied in Spanish.

'Something about him rang a bell but, try as I might, I couldn't place him. It nagged at me over breakfast and when the group captain took Bob and me up to the top of the rock.

But then you talked about Abwehr saboteurs, Peter, and in the car coming back down the rock I suddenly realised where I'd seen this man before. He'd tried to pick me up in the hotel the Abwehr was using in Stavanger in September 1940.'

'Are you sure?' asked Matthew Moore.

'Certain,' said Monique. 'The man I spoke to earlier this morning was playing the part of a Spaniard, but when I met him originally, he was German. I think his first name might have been Kurt or Karl or Klaus or something like that. I don't think he told me his second name.'

'If the Abwehr have successfully placed an agent we don't know about on the airfield, that's a real cause for concern,' said Moore. 'We've been doing quite well to limit their activities by capturing their agents and turning them to work for us. But this is one we know nothing about.'

'Do you think he recognised you, Monique?' asked Bob.

'He gave no sign of it, but then I tried to suppress the reaction I had when I saw him, so I don't know.'

'The first priority is to find our man and take him into custody,' said Moore.

'There can't be that many candidates working on the airfield and we have records with photographs for all civilian employees,' said Peter Derbyshire. 'Will you take a look at them, Monique?'

Monique nodded. 'Yes, of course.'

'If he's still playing his role, I'll get my RAF Police detachment to arrest him. On the other hand, if he did recognise you, Monique, I imagine he'll have made himself scarce. At least we'll have his photograph and know the cover name he's been using. It will be a start.'

'I'll round up a couple of people here,' said Matthew Moore.

'It shouldn't take me more than a few minutes. Can I suggest we reconvene in your office to decide on our next steps, Group Captain Derbyshire?'

*

The group captain's office in RAF North Front's headquarters building was more comfortable and much better appointed than the Defence Security Office meeting room. There was a large map of the Gibraltar area on one wall and several framed photographs of military aircraft on others. Monique thought that the coffee was very good.

There were six people in the office. Monique, Bob, Matthew Moore and the group captain sat around the meeting table. Two men who had arrived with Moore stood near the door. Both had politely declined the offer of coffee but otherwise had said nothing. Monique knew the type. They had compact well-toned bodies and hard eyes. Even when standing still, they had a poise and a presence that made her think of professional dancers. Their lightweight suits fitted well, but she had the sense they would have been more comfortable wearing uniforms. These weren't men she would have wanted to get into an argument with. As soon as she saw them, Monique realised what Matthew Moore intended to do.

The group captain brought them up to date. 'Thanks to Monique, we know that our man is using the cover name of Xavier Allende and we have an address for him in La Línea. He has worked for us for four months. I understand that he told his supervisor that he was feeling ill not long after the Liberator arrived this morning and was last seen riding his bicycle along the road that crosses the runway on its way to the Spanish border.'

'That strongly suggests he did recognise you, Monique,' said Bob.

Matthew Moore put his coffee cup back down on its saucer. 'It does. That gives us two things to consider. The first is how he would have responded once he realised his cover was probably blown. The second is what we should do about him, knowing that he has a couple of hours' lead on us.'

'The first of those is my primary concern,' said Peter Derbyshire. 'I have ordered a thorough search of all the parked aircraft on the airfield and all buildings this man had access to. It's unlikely he had explosives to hand at work, just on the off chance he needed to use them, but I will feel much happier once we've had a good look for bombs he might have planted or any other form of sabotage. I've asked my people to make a start on the Liberator as that's the most obvious target, though even if that's clear there's a lot more to look at before I'm going to feel comfortable about the situation.'

'Thank you, group captain,' said Moore. 'Meanwhile, as we have an address for Señor Allende, or whatever his real name is, I propose to try to track him down in La Línea with my two colleagues and detain him. Would you be prepared to join us, Monique? You've met him and will be able to confirm his identity beyond question. I'd prefer not to have to live with the consequences of kidnapping an innocent Spanish citizen from his nominally neutral but rather hostile homeland. I suspect the diplomatic fallout of that would do little to further my career in the Security Service.'

'Hang on,' said Bob. 'All you have is the address he chose to give when signing up for employment here. Isn't that as likely to be as fake as his cover name?'

Monique could see that was only part of the reason for Bob's concern. He was clearly worried about her going over the border with Matthew Moore. She was herself if she was honest. If Allende had recognised her, he could have warned those he reported to in the Abwehr by now. Going into Spain could be highly risky for her.

It was Peter Derbyshire who replied to Bob's question. 'We do have cause to write to employees, including those living in Spain, from time to time. I can't guarantee that Señor Allende lives at the address we have, but mail sent there must get forwarded to him if he doesn't.'

'My money is on him being arrogant enough to assume we'd never dare cross the border into Franco's Spain,' said Moore. 'But there's only one way to find out.' He looked at Monique.

Monique saw that Bob was also looking at her. She knew he didn't want her to go, but also that he didn't feel able to say anything more.

'I'll go,' she said. 'But only if Bob comes too.'

'Hang on,' said Moore. 'Don't you think that an RAF group captain might stand out like a sore thumb when we cross the border?'

Monique pointed at the suitcases in the corner of Group Captain Derbyshire's office. 'We have alternative identities in there, complete with passports and civilian clothes. Mr Robert and Mrs Monique Cadman will accompany the three of you into Spain. Bob will need a few minutes to change out of his uniform and I need to become a blonde.'

'Very well. Can you let me have the Cadman passports? It will take perhaps twenty minutes for me to get suitable visas inserted for the crossing and then we'll go.'

Monique still thought that crossing the border was tempting

fate but the look of gratitude on Bob's face almost made it worthwhile.

CHAPTER SEVEN

The address they were looking for turned out to be just to the north of La Línea's bullring. As they drove through the town, Monique was struck by the contrast with Gibraltar. Young and old thronged the streets with barely a uniform in sight beyond a couple of policemen on patrol.

They left the car in front of a row of single-storey shops and bars facing across the road to the bullring. The street they wanted was called Calle Calderón de la Barca and led north from there.

Monique and Bob held hands as they walked along the narrow pavement. Matthew Moore and his two men walked a little ahead, split between the two sides of the road. Monique thought that it was they who, to quote Moore, stuck out like sore thumbs.

The three men took a right turn.

When she and Bob reached the corner, Monique saw the side street was lined on both sides by four-storey apartment buildings. She looked back the way they had come. 'You can see the north end of the Rock of Gibraltar towering over the bullring from here.'

Bob looked back and smiled. 'It still feels very alien. Thanks again for insisting I should come along.'

'I knew you'd never agree to my coming alone. Anyway, after your performance in Stockholm, I feel much safer with you than I would with just Matthew Moore and his two companions.'

'Not very talkative chaps, are they? They've gone into this building on the right.'

Monique pushed through a door and found herself in the lower hall and stairwell of one of the apartment buildings.

The three men had waited for them.

'Remember, no shooting unless you're fired at first,' said Matthew Moore. 'The sound of gunfire will have the place crawling with Spanish police in no time and we need to avoid that. The address we have is on the second floor. We'll lead and you follow. I have to say that this is rather grand for a casual labourer employed at RAF North Front.'

Moore's two men led the way up the stairs. Monique and Bob again brought up the rear.

As Monique arrived on the second-floor landing, one of Moore's men was fiddling with the lock of the door on one side. She doubted if a property being used by an Abwehr agent would be so feebly secured, but it seemed she was wrong.

The other man removed what appeared to be a length of pipe from a jacket pocket and led the way into the apartment. As Monique entered, she heard an exclamation from somewhere inside and then a thud. She could see Matthew Moore through an open door, standing in the room at the end of a short corridor. She went through into what was obviously the living room. Bob followed her. Moore's two companions were standing on either side of a man dressed in an off-white vest and brown trousers sitting in a chair and dabbing a cloth at his bloody nose.

He looked up. 'Ah, Vera Eriksen. How lovely to meet you again after all this time. When I saw you this morning I wondered if you might bring trouble my way.'

Monique wondered why he was speaking to her in English, then realised he was playing to the audience.

He continued. 'I obviously didn't make the impression I

69

wanted to in Stavanger and I hoped you hadn't recognised me when you got off your aircraft.'

Monique wondered if anger might loosen his tongue further. 'You were a pathetic and extremely boring little man hoping to score an easy conquest by giving out feigned sympathy to a young widow. I barely listened to you. I can't even remember what you said your name was, except that it's certainly not Xavier Allende. Was it Kurt? Or Karl? Or perhaps Klaus?'

'Nice try, Vera. You'll see the radio and Morse key on the table over in the corner. I've been busy telling your old Abwehr colleagues about you turning up in Gibraltar this morning. I'm sure they're going to be very interested.'

Monique looked at the table, careful to avoid any of the concern she felt showing on her face.

Without warning, the man threw his chair backwards and half rolled across the floor. He seemed to be trying to reach a coffee table next to a sofa under a window. Monique could see a box with a switch on top of it. The thought struck her that it might be a bomb.

There was a sound no louder than fingers being clicked and Allende's head exploded, spattering blood and brains all over the far side of the room. His body came to rest on the floor with an outstretched arm just short of one of the legs of the coffee table.

'What the hell was that?' asked Bob.

One of Moore's men operated what Monique realised was a bolt on the rear of a gun, not as she'd thought earlier a length of pipe.

'It's a Welrod pistol,' said Matthew Moore. 'It's not pretty or elegant, but it is the quietest gun you'll find anywhere. I think Brian here has just saved all our lives. You can thank him later.

Who's Vera Eriksen, by the way?'

'That was the name I was using when the Abwehr thought I was one of theirs. And I've remembered that this man's name was Kurt. I never knew his surname.'

'I suggest that you and the group captain sit in the armchairs on the side of the room not covered in bits of Kurt's head,' said Matthew Moore. 'We need to search the apartment for anything that might tell us more about who he was working with and what his intentions were. A diary or a code book would be nice to have. A list of names and addresses of Abwehr agents would be even better, if rather unlikely. We're only going to get one chance at this, so we need to be thorough.'

The three men worked their way around the apartment with a quiet efficiency that Monique found impressive. At one point Moore asked Monique and Bob to accompany him to the smaller of the two bedrooms. There were three tables in the room covered in what appeared to be the parts of perhaps half a dozen bombs under construction.

As the search continued, Monique saw Bob look at his watch.

'I don't think we're going to catch our flight to Malta,' she said.

'I feel like I'm letting Maurice down.'

'It's not as if we have a choice and I'm sure he'll agree that what we've found here is important.'

Shortly afterwards Monique heard movement in the hall and the sound of someone leaving. Then Matthew Moore came into the room with one of his men.

'That's us. I think we can go now.'

'What do we do about our friend Kurt here and the bomb factory we've found?' asked Bob.

'If we assume that he contacted his Abwehr handlers as he claimed, then when he goes quiet on them, they are going to want to know why and come and see for themselves. If you two leave with my colleague, you should find the car immediately outside. I will finalise the arrangements we've made for a little surprise for our Abwehr friends that will kill several birds with one stone.'

'You're going to booby trap the explosives we found in the second bedroom?' asked Monique.

'Yes. That way we inflict damage on the Abwehr both directly and indirectly. With any luck, we'll kill a few of them. We'll also get them blamed by the Spanish authorities for the explosion, which might help damage a relationship that's sometimes much too close for our comfort.'

Monique could barely believe what she was hearing but could see from his eyes that Matthew Moore was serious.

'No, you're not going to do that,' said Bob.

'I beg your pardon, group captain?'

'People are living in the apartments in this building and the buildings on either side of it. There's enough explosive in that bedroom to bring the whole thing down and kill dozens of innocent Spanish civilians.'

'There's a war on, group captain, in case you haven't heard.'

Bob's punch caught Moore on the side of his face and the man went down immediately. Moore's remaining companion took two steps forwards. Monique half pulled her gun out of her shoulder holster, which stopped him in his tracks and caused him to take a step back.

By this time Moore was regaining his feet, his left hand over the side of his face.

Bob stood very close to him. 'Listen to me, you bastard. If

you cause the death of a single innocent person, I will see you hanged for murder. As deputy head of MI11, I outrank you. I am giving you a direct order, with my colleague and yours as witnesses, to make safe whatever it is you have set up, and the bomb over on the coffee table. Then, as soon as you are back in Gibraltar, you will alert the Spanish authorities to the presence of explosives here. That can be through an anonymous phone call if you wish, though I'm betting that there's a deputy chief of police or something similar who you've been cultivating as a contact for just this sort of eventuality. Do you understand me?'

Moore was looking down at his feet. 'Yes, sir.'

'We're leaving,' said Bob. 'I'll get your other man to drive Monique and me back to RAF North Front. He can then come back for you.'

*

Group Captain Derbyshire was apologetic about allowing the Liberator to leave for Malta without them but, as he pointed out, he had no way of knowing when they were likely to be back. In the event, they'd only just missed it. They'd been held up at the barrier across the main road where it crossed the runway, just on the Gibraltar side of the border with Spain. The barrier had been down because the Liberator was taking off and they were able to watch it go.

Peter Derbyshire did try to make it up to them by taking them for lunch in the officer's mess and arranging alternative onward transport.

He also agreed to send a secure cable from Bob to Commodore Cunningham. Bob wanted to say more to keep the commodore in the picture but felt the risks of attracting unwanted attention from others in London were too high. He settled on the briefest and blandest possible message.

'We have missed our onward flight to Malta. We will instead complete the journey in a Catalina flying boat that is due to leave Gibraltar shortly. Please advise your contact that we expect to arrive at the seaplane base at RAF Kalafrana tonight, timing uncertain.'

*

Monique thought that Bob had been very preoccupied since they'd boarded the Catalina from a motor launch in the harbour at RAF New Camp. They'd shared the launch with three of the members of the crew of the aircraft and a considerable number of mail sacks, some of which appeared to contain boxes of bottles that clinked when being moved rather than letters or parcels.

The crew were wary of her and particularly of Bob. If there was some private enterprise going on in the form of trading or smuggling of alcohol - and Monique was sure there was - then the news that at short notice they had been assigned two passengers, including an RAF group captain serving with military intelligence, would hardly be welcome.

The Liberator they'd flown in on the way to Gibraltar had been a converted bomber, but it had at least been converted with the specific intention of providing reasonably comfortable accommodation for its passengers.

The Catalina offered fewer creature comforts. The aircraft had two engines on a high wing. As they approached in the launch, a very striking feature was a pair of clear bubble-like structures, one on either side of the rear fuselage, with guns sticking out of them.

They were greeted on boarding by the aircraft captain, who introduced himself as Flight Lieutenant Stone. One of the other members of the crew then showed them to a compartment just in front of the bubbles with a rudimentary bunk on either side of the fuselage. The compartment was also home to the mail sacks, but it proved possible for Monique and Bob to use blankets to create reasonably comfortable nests, one on either bunk.

Noise levels were high. They'd discovered as soon as the aircraft started to move, even within the harbour, that they weren't going to be able to make themselves understood by one another across the width of the fuselage.

Monique had expected Bob to go forwards to the cockpit for the takeoff, or perhaps after it, but he remained on his bunk and fell asleep once they were airborne. Monique dozed fitfully. She awoke to find Bob using folded blankets to make himself comfortable at the other end of her bunk.

She smiled and then leaned towards him in the hope he'd be able to hear her. 'The crew use this as the main route between the two ends of the aircraft. I love you deeply, Bob, but I'm not about to embark on an airborne consummation of our marriage if that's what you've got in mind. I'm no prude but this is much too public. Besides, you have a reputation to maintain.'

Bob smiled in response before a look of concern crossed his face. He leaned towards her, so their heads were close together. 'It's my reputation I'm worried about. Hitting Matthew Moore was inexcusable. I deeply regret losing my temper with him.'

'I'm pleased you did, Bob. If you hadn't hit him, I might have done something worse. He intended to murder innocent Spanish civilians and as far as he was concerned it was legitimate if he could get it blamed on the Abwehr.'

'But we're meant to be keeping a low profile. If Moore makes a complaint, and remember that one of his men witnessed what I did, then it could raise questions about why we were in Gibraltar in the first place and cause Maurice Cunningham serious problems.'

Monique smiled. 'You can rest assured that Matthew Moore isn't going to report what happened. What he intended to do raises real concerns about his character and fitness to hold his position, and the strength of your response should have made even someone like him wonder whether he was going too far. His main concern is going to be whether you report what happened.'

'I should, of course,' said Bob. 'But with Maurice's private venture ahead of us, I don't feel I can right now.'

'You did tell Peter Derbyshire what happened. At least someone on the ground in Gibraltar knows that Moore has homicidal tendencies. Once we're finished in Malta, I think that you and I should both submit reports about Matthew Moore, you via MI11 and me directly to MI5. If that's at all possible without compromising Commodore Cunningham's position, of course. In the meantime, the fact that Moore lost a fight with a group captain will grow in the telling and do little for his credibility. Remember that one of his colleagues saw what happened and however quiet he seemed will inevitably gossip about it. I suspect Matthew Moore is going to have to explain away a black eye, too.'

'Thank you for stopping that same colleague from joining in,' said Bob. 'I'd have been no match for him.'

'I'm not sure he was all that keen to help his boss,' said Monique. 'He was happy to back off when I gave him an excuse by showing him my pistol. I doubt if we'd have been able to handle him between us if he'd been determined to get involved.'

'I'm grateful anyway.'

'While you've been worrying about Moore reporting what happened, I've been worrying about the report we are fairly sure that Xavier Allende, to use the only full name we have for him, made to the Abwehr. Two things concern me about that. The first is that their knowing I've been in Gibraltar is unsettling, especially if they also work out I'm going to Malta.'

'For all they know you could be staying in Gibraltar or heading for Morocco or Libya or Egypt. There's nothing to tie you to Malta.'

'Are you certain? Surely the first thing Xavier Allende would have done after recognising me was find out why I was on that flight and where I was going. I wouldn't have thought it particularly difficult for him to confirm I was due to fly to Malta on the same aircraft.'

'Yes, that's true. You said two things were worrying you about the Abwehr getting involved,' said Bob. 'What's the second?'

Xavier or Kurt was communicating over a wireless, presumably using a simple code. What if news of my arrival then gets transmitted on to Berlin using a more sophisticated coding device?'

'You're concerned that the Abwehr discussing you in signals that might be decoded could alert the wrong people in military intelligence in London to your whereabouts? We do have a cover story for being in Malta, remember.'

'We do,' said Monique. 'But it's feeble and won't stand up to much scrutiny. Anyway, let's put that to one side. I'm also concerned about our chances of doing anything useful once we arrive in Malta. It's Friday the 11th of June today and we're going to be in Malta some time tonight. Maurice's nephew, James Ewing, was reported missing eleven days ago, or a week last Monday, and perhaps went missing late on the Sunday, or twelve days ago. Even Maurice's SIS friend, Edward Price, went missing last Sunday, or five days ago. I have a growing feeling that if either of those men were going to turn up alive then it would already have happened.'

'Great minds think alike,' said Bob. 'Even when Maurice was talking to us in the car at Kyle of Lochalsh, it was going through my mind that we were at best going to be looking for bodies and accounts of what had happened to the men. I suspect that Maurice thinks so too. But we must make the effort. You never know, they might still be alive.'

'Let's hope so,' said Monique.

CHAPTER EIGHT

The Catalina had a much slower cruising speed than the Liberator they'd missed in Gibraltar, and they'd set off some time after it. It had been dark for nearly two hours when they landed in the bay at RAF Kalafrana a little before 10.45 p.m. A night landing in a flying boat struck Bob as a highly risky venture though the crew seemed to think it was quite routine. He thought back to the Sunderland flying boats he'd seen in Oban the previous September and realised that if they only flew in daylight then they'd not be flying very much at all in the dark Scottish winters.

Bob and Monique were put aboard a small launch that came alongside the aircraft as soon as its engines had stopped. Bob found it difficult to get any sense of where they were in what at first seemed to be pitch darkness when looking away from the aircraft itself. Then his good eye started to adjust and he began to see the outline of a pier with land and buildings behind it in the light of the half moon.

'I'm guessing they have a blackout here too,' said Monique.

'We do, ma'am,' said one of the two crew of the launch, a man at the rear of the vessel who was no more than a dark shape against the lights of the aircraft. 'And it's a lot more needed here than it is at home, though the bombing is far less bad than it used to be.'

Lights on the launch were switched on when they reached the concrete pier and the crew helped Monique and then Bob onto stone steps leading up to the top of the pier. One of the crew then carried their suitcases up for them.

In the launch's lights, Bob could see a man in a white naval uniform striding over towards them.

'Group Captain Sutherland? I'm Commander Lawrence Dowson. I'm pleased to meet you, sir.'

Bob returned the commander's salute and then shook his hand. 'I'm sorry if we've kept you waiting, Commander Dowson. Something came up and we missed the Liberator we were planning to catch from Gibraltar. This is Madame Monique Dubois, who works with me in my northern outpost of MI11.'

'I'm pleased to meet you, Madame Dubois. I heard from Commodore Cunningham that you'd caught the slow boat and the people here were able to give me a fair idea of your likely arrival time. Now, I imagine you could both do with something to eat and some sleep?'

'Both would be good,' said Monique.

*

The officers' mess at RAF Kalafrana was still serving food despite the late hour, though the dining room was empty of diners when they entered. Bob assumed it was kept open for officers working on night shifts on the base or who were members of the crews of aircraft leaving or arriving overnight.

The drive from the pier had been short and Bob had gained little impression of their surroundings in the moonlight. They'd left their cases with the navy driver in the car.

Commander Dowson pointed out the obvious servery before going to sit at a wooden table for four in a corner of the empty dining room. In the glare of the dining room lights, Bob could see he was of around average height and slight build. He seemed to be in his early forties and when he took off his peaked cap and placed it on the table, Bob could see that the commander had blond hair that was thinning on top. This was in marked contrast to his well-developed ginger beard and moustache.

Bob realised that the choice of food on offer was either some sort of stew with mashed potatoes or a spaghetti dish. He smiled at the woman looking at him expectantly from the other side of the servery and asked for the stew. Monique opted for the spaghetti.

'Have you seen this Bob?' asked Monique, pointing at a dark wooden frame attached to the wall next to the servery.

Bob looked. It was a menu for Christmas lunch from the previous year. 'There's a tradition for officers to serve lunch on Christmas Day,' he said. 'I think that explains the seasonal wishes from the commanding officer, officers and senior NCOs at the top. It looks like they ate well.'

'The dessert course looks interesting,' said Monique. 'Mince pies, biscuits and cheese, beer and cigarettes!'

'That, too, is something of a tradition. Anyway, let's go and enjoy our non-seasonal fare.'

As they arrived at the table, Commander Dowson poured water from a jug into three glasses. 'There is no ice, I'm afraid.'

Bob's theory about why the dining room remained open was confirmed when three of the crew of the Catalina they'd arrived on then came into the room and made their way to the servery. The rest of the crew would be doing the same in the sergeants' mess, he thought.

'For obvious reasons, Commodore Cunningham's not been able to tell me much about what the two of you know or don't know, sir,' said the Commander. 'Perhaps the best thing might be for me to simply tell you about the disappearances of James

Ewing and Edward Price while you eat?'

'That's a good idea,' said Bob. 'Though as this is all rather unofficial, perhaps we should overlook the formalities? I'm Bob and this is Monique.'

'Fair enough, Bob. I should say that once you've eaten I will drive you to a hotel we've booked for the two of you in Valletta. There's far less bombing by the Germans and Italians than used to be the case and Valletta is as safe as anywhere at the moment. And before I forget, I have some cash for the two of you. You'll find that your UK pounds won't be accepted in Malta, not officially at least. Instead, we use currency issued in the name of the Government of Malta. This is printed in the UK, on one side of the notes only for cost reasons, then shipped out here before being stamped with the signature of the government's treasurer, at which point the notes become legal tender. They come in various denominations from a shilling up to a pound. In his latest signal, Commodore Cunningham asked that I provide each of you with enough to cover all your food and other expenses in various denominations. Your hotel bill will be paid by the commodore.'

'Is a Maltese pound worth the same as a UK pound?' asked Monique.

'Nominally, yes. Earlier in the war, Italian propaganda made much of their claim that Britain was stealing Malta's stock of real currency and replacing it with worthless paper. Another view was that the change was made to ensure that if Malta was invaded by the Italians and Germans then large quantities of UK currency wouldn't fall into enemy hands.

'Whatever the real reason, most people on the islands, whether Maltese or British, have become used to our usually rather tatty currency. Having said that, there is some grumbling at the moment because of rising prices which people believe are due to the arrival of increasing numbers of American servicemen in Malta.'

Dowson took two envelopes out of an inside pocket and passed them over. 'I'm afraid I need to ask you each to sign for the cash, here in my pocketbook.' He opened a leather-covered notebook and passed it to Bob with a pen.

Bob signed above his name and below a short handwritten receipt and passed the pocketbook and pen to Monique.

Dowson took a drink of his water and then placed the glass back on the table. 'You'll understand that other than in my initial letter to the Commodore, we've had to be very circumspect in our communications with one another. One thing he said in a signal did puzzle me. He asked me to arrange accommodation suitable for a honeymoon couple in the names of Group Captain and Mrs Sutherland. I wondered if that was a joke or if something got scrambled in the decoding?'

Monique smiled. 'No. Bob and I got married last Saturday in Edinburgh and until Wednesday afternoon we were enjoying our honeymoon in Kyle of Lochalsh. We'd just got off a ferry from the Isle of Skye when Maurice Cunningham turned up and suggested we might like to try a warmer location instead.'

'Good grief!' said Dowson. 'He does have a knack for inspiring loyalty amongst his friends. I'm pleased I took that part of what he said literally, though it might have been embarrassing if you'd just been colleagues. Anyway, at this rate you'll have finished your meals before I've even begun to bring you up to date on the reason you are here. And this isn't a conversation we can have with a navy driver present in the car to Valletta.'

Monique took a notebook out of her handbag. 'I've finished

eating. Perhaps I should summarise what Maurice Cunningham told us in Kyle and you can fill in any gaps?'

Bob saw the commander nod and Monique went on to give an excellent summary of what they'd been told by the commodore. When she finished she looked up at Lawrence Dowson.

'That's pretty much it,' he said. 'As a result, we have two men unaccounted for. You won't need me to tell you how to go about this, but I thought you might want to make a start in the morning at the headquarters of the 10th Submarine Flotilla on Manoel Island. I'll have a car pick you up at your hotel and can give you a little more detail then. I will also show you Lieutenant Ewing's accommodation and belongings, and the room of Edward Price, who is staying - perhaps I should say was staying - with us for his convenience and ours. You can if you wish also talk to the lieutenant's colleagues.

'The other obvious starting point is Anne Milner, James's girlfriend. She's been in Malta throughout the war, initially as a dancer in a cabaret and then as a member of a concert party entertaining the troops. More recently she's worked in the RAF headquarters in Valletta as a clerk helping manage supplies of fuel to the airfields in Malta. The first thing I did when Lieutenant Ewing failed to report for duty was talk to her. She had no idea why he might have disappeared and seemed very worried. I know she was also spoken to by Edward Price. I'll tell you how to find her in the morning.'

The commander looked at this watch. 'One thing you need to know if you don't already is that we have a curfew in Malta, which extends from 11 p.m. to 5 a.m, so is underway already. Your official passes should ensure you can move around between those times if you need to. But my advice would be to adhere to the curfew whenever possible. When you combine it with a blackout that is very strictly observed and streets that are in many places still home to piles of rubble from three years of bombing it's best to stay indoors at night if you can. And with that in mind, let's get you to your hotel and me back to Manoel Island.'

*

'This is rather grand,' said Monique. She watched as Bob walked through a door to an adjoining room. He was back a moment later.

'It's as the receptionist claimed,' he said. 'We have a fine bedroom with a nice large bed and windows on two sides,' he swept his arm around to indicate the space they were standing in. 'We're on the top floor, two storeys above street level and unlikely to be disturbed by any noise from outside short of a Luftwaffe bomb. If the air raid warning does sound, then there's a secure shelter down in the basement and there are gas masks in the bottom drawer of the chest of drawers. The room we came in through is our drawing room. Last but not least, we have our own bathroom through that door, complete with a bath, a sink and a toilet. We've got electric lights in every room and there's even a radio in the drawing room. I'm not sure "rather grand" does it justice. I could grow to like the Osborne Hotel. God knows what this is costing Maurice Cunningham's MI11 budget.'

'I don't know about you, Bob,' said Monique, 'but it feels pretty stuffy to me. I got the sense outside that it's warmer in Malta at night than it is in Kyle of Lochalsh during the day. That might take a little getting used to. It doesn't help that it smells like the last resident was a keen pipe smoker.'

'We could work out how to open one of the windows in here,' said Bob. 'Though we'd need to be sure we didn't compromise the blackout curtains. You heard what Commander Dowson said in the car, about the general belief during the worst of the air raids that someone lighting a cigarette in the open at night could be seen by an enemy aircraft six miles away and at 6,000 feet. That sounds fanciful but it does show how seriously they take their blackout regulations. Those shielded torches he gave us take me right back to visiting London during the Blitz.'

'If we turn the light off in here we can open a window without causing a problem,' said Monique. 'We can use the drawing room as a dressing room. Or an undressing room.' She walked into it. 'There's an electric fan on the side in here. We can move it into the bedroom to give us a bit of a breeze.'

Bob turned off the light in the bedroom and walked over to one of the windows. 'It looks like there are closed outside louvred shutters with a window inside them. Perhaps inevitably the glass is taped to cut down blast damage. We can open the window to get some fresh air. Then there's a net curtain that I imagine is intended to keep out mosquitos when the window is open and finally the thick blackout curtain. I've adjusted it so there's air getting in without, hopefully, any light getting out.'

'Do you like the idea of a bath?' asked Monique. She saw him smile and nod. 'I'll run one. After two days of travelling, I'd love to get properly clean again.'

It turned out that the hotel's hot water system wasn't intended for late-night bathing but given how warm she felt, Monique found that a cool bath was perfect.

Afterwards, she lay in bed next to Bob in the dark, still

warm despite the open window and electric fan, which they'd placed on a chest of drawers on her side of the bed.

'Bob, who is Admiral Prince Louis of Battenberg?'

'I think it's "who was" rather than "who is". If he's the man I'm thinking of he was a German prince who married a granddaughter of Queen Victoria and became First Sea Lord, that's the title given to the senior admiral in the Royal Navy, in the years before the Great War. Why do you ask?'

'There was a framed picture in the reception downstairs showing the hotel with a description saying that he was a notable patron. If he was a German prince then that's an interesting marketing approach for a hotel in a city that's still being bombed by the Germans and their allies.'

'I'm no expert on naval history but I seem to recall it was concern in parts of the press about his German background that led to him ceasing to be First Sea Lord when the last war broke out. It would appear Maurice Cunningham has put us up in a haunt of admirals and minor royalty.'

Monique reached over. She could feel that Bob was uncovered and lying on his back. She ran her hand down his chest, gently brushing it over his body hair.

'You know that if we resume our honeymoon activities at this point, you're going to end up feeling even warmer than you do already,' he said.

Monique could hear the smile in Bob's voice.

'I'll take that chance,' she said, then giggled as Bob rolled towards her, pushing her over onto her back and bumping her nose with his as he tried to kiss her but misjudged where she was in the dark.

CHAPTER NINE

The Royal Navy staff car was waiting on the far side of the very narrow street outside the front of the Osborne Hotel as agreed at 10 a.m. The driver was a naval rating and Bob returned his salute before going around the far side of the car and getting in the back. He smiled as he realised that the driver had opened the other rear door of the car for Monique.

After he got in, the driver half turned to look at Bob. 'I'm told you want to go to the headquarters of the 10th Submarine Flotilla on Manoel Island, sir?'

'Yes, please, we've got a meeting with Commander Dowson.'

Bob sat back as the car pulled away. At the end of the street, the driver turned right and the car began a steep descent.

'My God, look at that!' said Monique.

The descent had opened up views along what Bob knew to be the north-west side of the peninsula Valletta stood on and over a large harbour to the built-up area on its far side. He didn't know what to say in response.

'I spent more time than I would have liked in and around London during the Blitz,' said Monique. 'I've never seen bomb damage on anything like this scale.'

Bob could see what she meant. Wherever he looked there were destroyed buildings, near at hand and in the distance. In places, it seemed that individual buildings had been hit while those around them had survived. Elsewhere it looked like larger areas had been damaged. On the flight to Gibraltar, he'd looked at the photographs of bomb damage in the book about Malta that Maurice Cunningham had given them but that did little to prepare him for the real thing.

'Have you just arrived in Malta, ma'am?' asked the driver.

'Yes, we flew in last night. We've not seen it in daylight until now.'

'Believe it or not, it was a lot worse until the back end of last year. When the siege was lifted and bombing raids became fewer and further between it felt like a miracle. What you're seeing is the result of six months' work to clear some of the rubble and repair some of the damage. I think it's going to take a few more years before anyone's going to want to come here on holiday.'

Bob saw Monique catch his eye and smile. He knew she was wondering how the driver would respond if they told him they were here on their honeymoon.

'At least we've got enough to eat now,' the driver continued. 'It got to the point last year that you could tell who the new arrivals were because their ribs weren't sticking out. And it's going to take a long time for Malta's cat population to return to pre-war levels.'

'People ate cats?' asked Monique.

'Not officially, no. But rabbit dishes have always been popular in Malta and there were stories about the supply being supplemented on the quiet. It can't be a coincidence that you pretty much stopped seeing cats on the streets last year.'

They were now driving alongside the harbour, with the water on their right. 'Is that Manoel Island, over there?' asked Bob.

'Yes, sir. The three moored submarines are a bit of a giveaway. The island sits in the centre of Marsamxett Harbour, which is the harbour between Valletta and Floriana on this side and Sliema and several other towns over on the far side. We'll drive around the inner end of this arm of the harbour. The island is accessed by a bridge at its west end.'

'All of this is rather impressive,' said Monique.

Bob could see what she meant. They were driving past a part of the harbour that was packed with landing craft, first a long row of large vessels moored end-on to the quayside and then a mass of smaller craft moored multiple layers deep. More could be seen moving around further out into the harbour, amidst other craft both large and small.

'It is ma'am. The reason we were so vulnerable to enemy air attacks during the siege is that Malta is only 60 miles from the coast of Sicily. You don't need to be a military genius to think of a reason why they've now filled parts of the harbour with landing craft. What we're seeing here is far from all of them. Meanwhile, areas of the countryside are being turned into tented towns. The word is that large numbers of troops are going to be brought here from North Africa as a staging post for an invasion of Sicily.'

'Let's hope the Luftwaffe doesn't get to see any of this,' said Bob.

'They must have a good idea of what's coming because you can't possibly hide all these ships, sir,' said the driver. 'It may be a strange thing to say but the few German and Italian pilots who still come this way to drop bombs or take photographs have my respect. We seem to have more Spitfires than we know what to do with these days, with more airfield building still going on, which the enemy must also know about. Any German or Italian pilot coming this way is really putting his head into the lion's mouth.'

By now they had left the harbour and were driving through a built-up area that had been badly damaged by bombing. Nothing more was said as they emerged back beside the harbour and drove over a short bridge onto Manoel Island, where they were stopped at a security barrier manned by naval ratings in white shorts and tops who were carrying rifles. After passing a second security checkpoint a few minutes later the driver came to a halt amongst a collection of military vehicles behind a large stone building that looked like it had been badly bombed.

The driver led Bob and Monique past sentries who asked to see their passes and into the building, then up a broad set of steps to a galleried corridor that was open on one side and gave views back across the harbour and over the moored submarines to Valletta. The place was busy with men in naval uniforms and Bob found himself having to return salutes several times. The driver knocked on a door carrying a printed label saying 'Executive Officer'. He then opened the door and ushered Bob and Monique in before closing the door behind them.

'Welcome to my humble home,' said Lawrence Dowson. 'I hope you had a comfortable night.' He was standing behind a desk on the far side of the room. He waved towards a meeting table. 'Let's sit down. If my planning works out, some coffee will arrive shortly.'

'We had a very comfortable night,' said Bob. 'The hotel is superb, thank you for arranging it.'

There was a knock on the door and two naval ratings came in and set out cups and saucers on the meeting table before putting a coffee pot on a cork mat beside a milk jug, a sugar pot and a plate of digestive biscuits.

'It's nice to have an excuse to be civilised for once,' said Dowson. 'I'll be mother.' He poured coffee into the cups. 'Help yourselves to milk, sugar and biscuits. You'll have to excuse me if I don't introduce you to my boss, Commander Richard

Oliver, who commands the 10th Submarine Flotilla. He's away at a meeting in Alexandria.'

'It's quite a place you have here,' said Bob.

'It is, though it's seen more than its share of knocking about by our neighbours in Sicily over the past couple of years. We occupy the buildings along this side of the island, which originally formed the Lazzaretto, a quarantine hospital that dates back as far as an outbreak of the bubonic plague at the end of the 1500s. Most of what you see today was built fifty years later. At the start of the war, the original idea was to build an underground submarine base in Malta, but this is what we ended up with.

'It works quite well most of the time though I'm told it got a bit fraught last year. The upper level of the long frontage is used for office space, meeting rooms, dining areas and some of the accommodation, while the lower level gives direct access to the submarines moored on our front doorstep and has space for workshops and storage. Bomb shelters and additional accommodation have been dug back into the rocky slope behind us.

'I only arrived when the worst was over but I gather it was a damned close-run thing last year. We were attacked repeatedly with considerable damage being caused to the buildings and the submarines moored here. It got to the point where the boats had to submerge in the harbour during daylight hours, which wasn't sustainable. For a while we moved out entirely, relocating to Alexandria to join the rest of the Mediterranean Fleet which had already left Malta because of the bombing. Anyway, that's the history. Let's turn to the matter at hand. I floated a couple of ideas last night. How do you want to proceed?'

'As I see it, we have a bit of a problem,' said Monique, 'and not just the obvious one of two missing men.'

Bob and Monique hadn't discussed their next steps the previous night as sleep had swiftly followed the sex, and this morning had been a rush to get ready and get down for breakfast, so Bob was caught a little unaware. 'In what way?' he asked.

'Our cover story is that we are here to look at the possibility of establishing an office of Military Intelligence, Section 11, in Malta. I can almost hear Maurice Cunningham's voice when he was telling us that only the two of us, and you Lawrence, should know why we are really in Malta. It may be that none of us has properly thought this through. Given that you and Maurice know each other, Lawrence, it is just about plausible that he might have asked you to help us find our feet rather than, say, using the local office of the Secret Intelligence Service or, assuming there is one, of MI5.

'But the moment we start asking questions about Lieutenant James Ewing or Edward Price, it's going to be pretty obvious to anyone with any interest in us that we're not here for the reason we claim.'

'You have a point, Monique,' said Lawrence.

'You do, but I suspect we have no option but to brazen it out,' said Bob.

'What do you mean?' asked Monique.

'As far as anyone else is concerned, you and I have been sent to Malta by Maurice Cunningham to look at the possibility of setting up a small branch of MI11. The logic of that doesn't bear much scrutiny. The island has been on the front line since the beginning of the war. MI11 might have usefully had a presence here during that time, as military security must really have mattered, but why set up an office now, when everything suggests the focus of the war in the Mediterranean is about to move from here to Sicily?'

'That's just a rumour,' said Lawrence Dowson.

'Granted, Lawrence, but as the driver who brought us here this morning said, you don't need to be a military genius to work out why parts of the harbour out there are full of landing craft. As things stand, the idea of setting up a branch of MI11 here looks like a non-starter. Yet here we are and, as you say, Monique, our presence here has been assisted by Lawrence. I think we could just put it down to unlucky timing but if you and I were really here for the reason we claim, it would only take us about five minutes to decide to recommend to Maurice that there is no point establishing an MI11 office in Malta.'

Monique smiled. 'I see where you're going with this, Bob. Meanwhile, Lawrence has told us about the disappearances of his lieutenant and of an SIS officer and, to avoid a wasted trip, we have offered to help look for them while we are in Malta.'

'It's better than nothing, I grant you,' said Lawrence Dowson. 'Which brings me back to the question I asked a short time ago. Where do you want to start?'

'Can I ask,' said Bob. 'Has anyone enquired after Edward Price or have you told anyone other than Maurice Cunningham that he's missing?'

'No, and I find the lack of interest from his office in Cairo rather strange. But other than a brief introductory meeting with him, I had no real idea what he was intending to do. I was worried enough to let Maurice know on Monday that Edward Price didn't return the day before, but it didn't seem my place to raise any wider alarm. Especially given how unhelpful the authorities had been in response to Lieutenant Ewing's disappearance.'

Bob put a piece of digestive biscuit down on his saucer. 'Let's just park that thought for the moment and see if the Secret Intelligence Service, either in Cairo or here in Malta, notice that he's gone quiet on them. We probably need to establish a way of keeping in touch in case anything like that happens. I assume we can reach you by telephone here, Lawrence?'

'Yes, I live here so if I'm not at my desk the duty officer should be able to track me down most of the time. And if you find you need a car at any point, simply call the duty officer here, day or night, and we will provide one as quickly as possible.'

'Thank you,' said Bob. 'Is the best bet for you to leave messages at the hotel if something comes up that you want to speak to us about?'

'I may be able to go one better. I think I mentioned to you last night that James's girlfriend Anne Milner works at the RAF headquarters in Valletta. That would be the best place for you to talk to her, at least initially. What you won't know is that the RAF headquarters is at 3 Scots Street and that its north-east end faces across South Street, the street your hotel is on, to its front door. If you agree I'll telephone and, assuming she's on duty on a Saturday, tell her to expect a visit from the two of you later today. More generally, though, if I were a visiting RAF group captain with a need to keep in touch I'd make myself known at 3 Scots Street. It would certainly be a handy place for you to make telephone calls without their going through a civilian switchboard. You might even be able to get the people there to agree to take messages for you, given you are living just across the road.'

'That sounds worth pursuing,' said Bob. 'Returning to the

here and now, is there anything you can tell us about James Ewing that might help us understand him better?'

The commander sat back in his chair. 'I arrived to take up the position of executive officer here at the beginning of January. James was, and remains, an important member of the team here that plans our patrols, deciding who goes where and when in response to the operational needs of the moment. I soon realised that there was something about him that set him aside from the others. There's a sense of detachment. He can weigh up options and make decisions with a calmness that at times I find remarkable. I think that owes much to the pressures he faced as a first officer aboard a submarine. I've also come to think that although James is a good team player when he needs to be, there's a sense that the team he really feels part of is no longer with us. I'm sure that at heart he still wishes he had a post aboard a submarine. He'd have probably been the captain of his own boat by now.'

'Commodore Cunnigham told us that James was injured in a depth charge attack on his submarine last year,' said Monique.

'Yes,' said Lawrence Dowson. 'It was last August off the coast of Tunisia. HMS *Ursus* had attacked and damaged a tanker and was then attacked in turn by enemy destroyers. At least one depth charge went off very close to the submarine and Lieutenant Ewing's right eardrum was badly damaged. I've known that sort of thing to resolve itself or be treatable in others but, as I understand it, his was a serious injury that went beyond a normal perforation and left him permanently deaf in his right ear.

'Medical advice was for him to return to Britain but, as no one held out any hope for the restoration of his hearing wherever he went, he put in a request to stay with the 10th

Flotilla in a shore position, which was granted.'

'And then his submarine, HMS *Ursus*, and its crew were lost later in the year,' said Monique.

'Yes, in November. It just disappeared without a trace off the north coast of Sicily and was presumed lost. As I said, I only arrived after all this happened, but I've never had the sense that Lieutenant Ewing allows his hearing difficulties or the loss of his boat and its crew to distract him from his duties. I talked about a sense of detachment a moment ago, yes, but he is always completely professional.'

'How old is he?' asked Monique.

'Twenty-four. He joined the submarine service straight from his initial training at the age of twenty-one. He was a highly regarded submariner who has become an equally highly regarded planner. He's been based in Malta since the end of 1941, which is a fair time to be living with the constant fear of attack from the skies, and for part of that time with the pressures of being a submariner in an environment in which the only rule is to kill or be killed. I thought you might want to see a photograph of him. I've got one on my desk.'

The commander got up and walked over to his desk, returning with an envelope from which he took a photograph. 'In terms of a description, I'd say he's an inch or two short of 6 feet in height and slimly built. This is what he looks like.' He slid the photograph over towards Bob and Monique.

Monique picked it up and Bob saw her eyes widen in surprise. She turned it so he could see more clearly. It was a head-and-shoulders photo of a man with a black beard in a naval uniform, complete with a peaked cap.

'It's a young Maurice Cunningham,' said Bob.

'Yes, the likeness is remarkable,' said Lawrence Dowson.

'You can keep that print. It perhaps goes without saying, but I can't offer you a photograph of Edward Price.'

'Can you describe him?' asked Bob.

'He's an extremely tall man, probably not far short of 6 feet 6 inches in height and towering well above me. He's in his late forties and has receding slicked-back blond hair and a blond moustache. When I met him he was dressed in a light-coloured suit and a white shirt. Rather strikingly, he was wearing a red and gold diagonally-striped Marylebone Cricket Club tie. He was also wearing a Panama hat with a red and gold MCC band around the crown.'

Bob saw Monique look quizzically at him and knew what she was thinking.

'You're describing a man who isn't going to blend into a crowd,' said Bob. 'He can't do anything about his height, but if he wanted to stand out as obviously English anywhere in the world then it would be hard to beat an MCC hat and tie.'

'That same thought occurred to me,' said Lawrence Dowson. 'But who was I to tell a man from the Secret Intelligence Service how to go about his business?'

'One thing Commodore Cunningham mentioned in passing,' said Monique, 'was that Edward Price didn't get on with the man running SIS's office in Malta. Did he say anything about that to you?'

'No, it wasn't mentioned. I'm aware SIS has a presence here, as does MI5, to pick up on something you said earlier, Monique. But I've not had much cause to cross paths with either except when SIS occasionally asks for a submarine to drop off or pick up agents close to enemy-held coastlines.'

'Fair enough,' said Monique, 'It was worth asking.'

'Indeed,' said Lawrence Dowson. 'I have, however, been

able to do one thing that I hope might help you in your search for Edward Price. When I met him I offered him the use of Royal Navy staff cars, just as I have offered them to you. During the past few days, I have established which drivers were involved and spoken to them.'

Lawrence Dowson got up from the meeting table and walked over to his desk again. He returned with a piece of paper and sat down.

'As a result, I have been able to reconstruct, to some extent, his movements in Malta. He arrived from Cairo at RAF Luqa late on the morning of the 4th of June. That was the Friday, a week ago yesterday. I had a car and driver meet him and bring him here. That was when I had the introductory chat with him that I referred to a moment ago.

'I had the officer who shares a room with Lieutenant Ewing take Mr Price to his accommodation, and then show him James's room. I had a meeting elsewhere but I know Mr Price then had lunch here. In the afternoon a car took him from here to the RAF headquarters at 3 Scots Street, where I had arranged for him to meet Anne Milner. He asked the car to wait for him. Half an hour later he asked to be taken to Ghajn Tuffieha, which is a beach in the north-west of the island. Having spent a little time there he asked the driver to take him to the beach at Mellieha, which isn't far south of the island's northern tip. According to the driver he spent half an hour wandering up and down a section of the beach and bought cold drinks for himself and the driver. Then he asked to be taken to St Paul's Bay, which is a little further around the coast again, on the north-east side of the island.

'The driver said he tried to make conversation with Mr Price but gave up when he was unresponsive. I've no idea why he wanted to visit three of northern Malta's best beaches but it may be worth mentioning that Ghajn Tuffieha is used as a rest camp by officers and men of the 10th Submarine Flotilla and St Paul's Bay is used in the same way by the RAF on the island.

'It was early in the evening by the time the car brought Edward Price back to Valletta and he asked to be taken to Palace Square, one side of which is home to the Governor's Palace. He had the car pull up on the south-west side of the square, not outside the palace, and told the driver he didn't need him any more.'

'Presumably, he wasn't intending to see the governor,' said Bob.

'I very much doubt it. Palace Square is in the heart of Valletta. He could have gone anywhere in the city from there. The next thing I can tell you about his movements is that later that night, after it was dark but before the curfew, a small boat put him ashore at the foot of some steps leading up to Fort Manoel, which is our immediate north-eastern neighbour and currently home to a battery of heavy anti-aircraft guns. I gather this caused some consternation there, but he convinced them to deliver him back to us.'

'Do you have similar information for last Saturday?' asked Bob.

'I do, but it's equally odd. In the morning he asked to be dropped off in Rabat, which is a town west of here. The driver saw him walk towards the bridge that gives access to the walled city of Mdina, which is immediately adjacent to Rabat. He returned to the car about an hour later and asked to be taken to Marsaxlokk, which is a fishing village in the south-east of Malta. It's at the head of the large bay that is also home to the RAF Kalafrana seaplane base, where you arrived last night. He asked the driver to drop him off on the quayside and then pick him up there three hours later.

'He then asked to be taken to Hagar Qim, which is an archaeological site not far from the coast in the south-west of the island. He asked the driver to park nearby and then walked towards the site. He returned to the car forty minutes later. Edward Price was then dropped off in Valletta late in the afternoon in much the same place as he had been dropped off the previous day. And, as on the previous day, he made his way back to Manoel Island by boat much later.'

'And on the Sunday?' asked Bob.

'He seems to have had a lie-in because a little after 10 a.m. he asked for a car to take him to Mosta, which is a city west of here. He was dropped off close to the church in the centre of the city and asked the driver to meet him an hour later. The driver told me that he was there for the pickup at the right time and then waited for an hour more. When there was still no sign of his passenger he came back here to report what had happened. I asked the driver what Edward Price was wearing on the Sunday and it seems he was dressed exactly as he had been when he met me on the Friday, complete with his MCC Panama hat and tie. I'm told he also dressed in the same way on the Saturday. And that's everything I know. You can have the note I made for reference.' He passed the piece of paper over to Bob.

'Thank you, Lawrence, you've been very helpful,' said Bob.

'I said I'd show you the two men's accommodation. I've put a sub-lieutenant who works and shares a room with James Ewing on standby to show you their quarters and the room we made available for Edward Price, which we've kept locked since he disappeared. I thought that would also be the best way for you to gain some informal impressions of James from a colleague who I suspect knew him as well as anyone except Anne Milner. I'll go and track him down.'

After the commander had left the room Monique looked at Bob. 'I didn't have time in the rush this morning, but I ought to tell you how dashing you look in that tropical uniform.'

Bob smiled back.

'What I don't understand,' Monique continued, 'is why they don't make a peaked cap to match in the same khaki colour. The standard blue-grey cap just doesn't go. I noticed it with Peter Derbyshire in Gibraltar. A matching cap would round off the ensemble nicely.'

Bob could tell she was pulling his leg and laughed.

CHAPTER TEN

Monique quickly realised that Sub-Lieutenant David Short was extremely keen to impress her. Aged no more than twenty and with short blond hair he was, she thought, rather out of his depth, but she was amused by his obvious interest in her and acknowledged that a tiny part of her was a little flattered that someone two-thirds her age should find her attractive.

The sub-lieutenant led them away from the grand, old and bomb-damaged parts of the building and into an underground complex that lay behind it. Monique got the impression that the building had been extended organically into the rock. After a series of twists and turns they entered a short corridor with three wooden doors on either side and what looked through a half-open door to be a bathroom at its far end. He opened one of the doors on the right-hand side and led her into the room beyond.

As Bob followed, she caught his eye and could see that he shared her amusement at the sub-lieutenant's desire to please.

The three of them all but filled the space in the room not occupied by two narrow metal-framed beds, two bedside lockers, a wardrobe, a chest of drawers and a desk. There was a large painting of snow-capped mountains attached to the blank stone wall above one of the beds and a battered religious icon on a wooden panel above the head of the other.

'We don't have room to swing a cat,' said Short, 'but there have been times this year when we were very grateful to be living in what amounts to a bomb shelter. I'm told the bombing was much worse last year and accommodation back here where the troglodytes live was highly prized.'

'Where does Lieutenant Ewing keep his belongings?' asked Bob.

'This is my side and that's his,' said Short, making clear what he meant with gestures of his right arm. 'We share the drawers and wardrobe. His stuff is on the left of the wardrobe and in the two top drawers.'

'So you've got the mountain scenery for company,' said Bob. 'Where is it?'

'I don't know, sir. I found it on top of a pile of rubble in a street after a bombing raid in February. As no one wanted it I thought it would brighten this place up a little. It doesn't exactly compensate for the lack of a window, but it does help.'

'And the icon?' asked Monique.

'The same, really. James told me that he found it in a totally flattened church in Sliema in April last year, during the worst of the bombing. He said it was a miracle it hadn't been destroyed and that he was looking after it until he could find someone to return it to. I think he still intends to find it a proper home.'

Monique caught the eye of Bob, who was standing behind the sub-lieutenant.

'Would you mind telling me a little about James?' she asked. 'Perhaps we can talk outside in the corridor while the group captain takes a look at his things.'

She could see that Short didn't like the idea of leaving Bob on his own in the room but she flashed her brightest smile at the young man and gently took his arm and led him out of the door.

'How long have you known James?'

'I was posted to the 10th Submarine Flotilla in Malta straight from training in January. I was told I would learn most of what I needed to know if I stuck with James and watched how he went about things, so that's what I did. It must be irritating for him at times, having what amounts to a younger brother hanging around when he's working and here in our room. But he's very tolerant and I have learned a lot.'

Monique smiled encouragingly. 'It was before you came to Malta, but does he ever talk about his injury and about the loss of HMS *Ursus*, the submarine he served on?'

'Most of the time, no. I do get the sense that the deafness in his right ear gets him down sometimes. He's young and it's not obvious to look at him that he has a problem. As a result, people tend not to make allowances unless they know him well. There have been occasional instances of other officers taking his failure to respond to things they've said to him as stupidity. Usually, they're put right by those who know what happened to him, but I'm sure he'd prefer it if that wasn't necessary.'

'And what about the loss of the ship he served on?' asked Monique.

'We always call submarines "boats" rather than "ships" ma'am,' said Short, smiling. Then his face took on a more serious expression. 'Again, it was before my time here. I think if you asked most people who know him, they'd say that he accepted the loss of HMS *Ursus* and her crew with a typical British "stiff upper lip" stoicism.

'I thought that for a while, too, though it's been obvious that he's had trouble sleeping the whole time I've known him and I sometimes get the sense he has nightmares when he does manage to sleep.

'I got a better understanding of the real James one afternoon a month or so back. A few of us were getting heavily into the beer in a bar in Sliema when something someone said, I wasn't sure what as the conversation had seemed quite innocuous, caused a complete change of behaviour. James threw a half-full glass of beer against a wall and stormed out.

'I followed him and found him sitting on a pile of rubble in a side street. I thought he was going to burst into tears. It seems someone had mentioned one of the men lost with HMS *Ursus.* Suddenly James was in full flow, in a way I've never seen before or since. What came over was a deep sense of guilt that he'd survived when everyone else on HMS *Ursus* was presumed lost. He felt it was his fault for getting injured in a way that he thought should have been easily curable. The guilt then turned into anger at himself that his shipmates had died because, in his view, he'd not been there to save them. I tried telling him that made no sense and that no one except him thought it was his fault, but there was no consoling him. It took 48 hours for the normal sanguine James to return. By that time I'd begun to realise that the man I thought I knew was only a veneer and that the angry and guilt-ridden James I'd met that day was never far beneath the surface.'

'Did you talk to anyone about him?' asked Monique.

'He wouldn't have thanked me if I'd tried. Besides, there's a war on. Even from my relatively comfortable shore posting here, I've seen how common it is for men to be suffering from dreadful stress, especially those actually doing the fighting.'

'What about Anne Milner?' asked Monique.

'James seems to want to keep his life here and his relationship with Anne quite separate. I know that Anne has a flat in Floriana and I think he's there whenever the two of them can match their time off. That seems to mean a night away from here perhaps once or twice each week and then every couple of weekends. It works well from my point of view as it means I have a twin room to myself when he's away. I'd never tell him, but I sleep better when I'm not listening to James trying to get to sleep or having a nightmare.'

'Do you know Anne? Have you met her much?'

'I've only met her twice, both times by accident. The first time I was with James and two other officers in a bar in Valletta when she came in with some friends. She saw him and came over and asked to be introduced to us. He seemed embarrassed, though I wasn't sure why. She's an absolute stunner and I'd have thought that any man would be proud to be with her. The second time was the weekend he disappeared. On the Saturday I took Nina, a Maltese girl I'd met a few weeks before, to Ghajn Tuffieha on the bus. It's a beach in the north-west of the island that the 10th Submarine Flotilla tends to favour as a rest camp.

Short blushed. 'We were sitting on our towels on the beach and kissing when, over Nina's shoulder, I saw James and Anne walk past wearing bathing costumes and carrying towels. I looked up and said hello and they both replied but kept on walking. I thought at first that they didn't want to intrude or didn't approve of our kissing in public. Then I wondered if they'd been arguing. There was nothing definite, it was just the way they were walking together and the expressions on their faces. I've not seen James since.'

'So he was due to return on the Sunday evening but didn't?'

'That's right.'

'Did you get any sense that James was worried about anything before he disappeared? Did he have money problems that you know about? Did he gamble? Did you get the sense he'd made any enemies?'

'No, sorry, ma'am. If he's ever gambled I don't know about it. And he isn't the sort of man who makes enemies. He never really gets involved enough to get into arguments. As far as worries are concerned, well yes, after the incident in the bar that I talked about, I did realise he was much more highly strung and on edge than I'd thought previously. I don't know whether that was a change in him or simply that I was looking more closely for the signs.'

'And you say that happened a month ago?' asked Monique.

'I can't be exact, ma'am, but it was about then.'

'Thank you.' Monique saw Bob loitering in the room, giving her a chance to finish talking to Short. 'Can you show us the other room Commander Dowson said we could look at? The one the visitor used last weekend?'

'Yes, ma'am. It's in a different part of this maze and I'll take you there.'

*

The room that Edward Price had occupied during his very brief stay on Manoel Island seemed to Monique to be about the same size as the one James Ewing and David Short shared but, with only one of each item of furniture, it felt larger.

Monique stood by the door so that when she asked Sub-Lieutenant Short a question he had to turn his back to Bob and the main body of the room. She talked while Bob went through the SIS man's belongings which, as far as she could see, amounted to nothing more than a suitcase that had been left open on the bed and some clothes hanging in the wardrobe and folded up in one of the drawers.

'I understand you met Edward Price while he was here?' she asked.

'Yes, ma'am. He wanted to know the same sorts of things you've asked me about. He also looked through James's belongings in our room. He had to duck to get through the doors into both rooms. I got the impression he was used to doing that.'

'What did you think of him?'

'Mr Price? It's hard to say. Commander Dowson told me that he was with military intelligence, like the two of you. His height gave him quite a physical presence and I thought it odd that someone working in intelligence would shout about his nationality with an MCC tie.'

'Did you tell him as much as you've told me?' asked Monique.

'He covered pretty much the same ground as you have, ma'am. I told him about how on edge James seemed beneath the surface and about meeting him and Anne at Ghajn Tuffieha the weekend he disappeared.'

'What did you think of Mr Price?' asked Bob, who Monique could see had finished going through the SIS man's belongings.

Short turned to face Bob. 'In what way, sir?'

'You were interviewed by him. How good does he seem at his job?'

'That's probably not for me to say, sir. I don't think he missed anything important in asking his questions. When I was talking to him I found it hard to see past his MCC tie, if I'm honest. It seemed so incongruous that it was distracting.'

'Did he talk at all about what he was proposing to do to find James?' asked Bob.

'No, he said nothing about that.'

'And do you know if he removed anything from James's belongings in his room?'

'No, I'm fairly sure he didn't. He was talking to me while he went through James's things. I'm sure I'd have seen.'

There was a pause and the young man turned back towards Monique. She turned her full-beam smile on him again. 'We're both very grateful. Thank you for all your help, Sub-Lieutenant Short.'

CHAPTER ELEVEN

'All I'm saying, Monique, is that Maurice Cunningham is paying for a perfectly good drawing room for us as part of our suite in the hotel. What's wrong with using it? We could be sitting in comfortable chairs in the shade sipping something nice, cold and refreshing. Instead, you've dragged me back out into the sunshine and the mosquito bites on my arms are beginning to itch.'

They'd returned to the hotel for a light lunch and, afterwards, found they had over an hour before they were due to see Anne Milner in the RAF headquarters building on the other side of South Street from the hotel.

Bob had wanted to return to their suite after lunch but, instead, Monique had led him out onto South Street and they had walked, in the road rather than on either of the very narrow pavements, in the direction they'd driven that morning in the navy staff car. There were a few people about, in uniform and civilians, but it was hardly busy.

Where the car had turned right to begin its steep descent to the harbourside, Monique carried on for fifty yards slightly uphill between buildings that had been badly damaged. Piles of rubble were still in evidence, though they'd been pushed aside to leave a clear roadway in the direction she wanted to go.

Monique said hello to two old men sitting on kitchen chairs and smoking pipes in the sun outside a small damaged building that had been partly reroofed with corrugated iron. The taller ruin behind it seemed to be a gathering place for the area's pigeons, whose collective cooing was quite loud.

A few steps beyond the men the sound of cooing from

behind was displaced by that of shouting and swearing from ahead. A moment later Monique and Bob came out into an open area with a low stone wall on its far side. The shouting was being done by a man wearing just a pair of khaki shorts, boots and a steel helmet standing next to an anti-aircraft gun whose similarly-dressed crew of five sweating men was going through some sort of loading exercise. She led Bob to a section of the wall a little distance away from the gun.

She saw one of the men look over in their direction. 'You're going to have to watch your language, corporal, there's a lady present!'

Monique smiled. Otherwise, the gun crew ignored her and Bob and they reciprocated.

'Wow!' said Bob. 'How did you know there was going to be a view like this from here?'

From where they stood they could see a large part of the north-western side of Valletta to their right and, feeling like it was immediately below them, the whole of the large harbour on this side of the peninsula. It was bustling with boats and ships of all shapes and sizes, either moored or on the move. Prominent in the view was Manoel Island with, she noted, just two moored submarines. She hoped the crew that had gone out on patrol, presumably while she and Bob were enjoying their lunch, returned safely.

'It felt like there had to be something like this here. The thing that I find most surprising about this place, apart from the bomb damage, is how high Valletta seems to be above the harbour.'

'I'm glad you decided to explore, Monique. But you didn't answer the question I asked in the street about your aversion to using our drawing room.'

'I'm sorry, Bob. You're going to have to trust my instincts on this but something just doesn't seem right. When time permits, I'd like to take a closer look at our suite to see whether anyone's put in any hidden microphones. In the meantime, I'd feel more comfortable discussing what we're doing in places where we can be fairly sure no one can hear us.'

'Is that really likely? Who would do that?'

'If we were just looking for Maurice's nephew, then I don't think the thought would cross my mind. But Edward Price's disappearance feels altogether different.'

'Fair enough,' said Bob. 'One thought that does worry me is that if anyone has put a microphone in our bedroom they will have heard what we were doing last night before we went to sleep.'

Monique smiled 'Don't worry about that, Bob. We're here on honeymoon, remember? Newlyweds are meant to do that. Besides, if anyone was listening to us, they might have found it educational. You really are an exceptional lover, you know.'

She saw the blush spread up Bob's neck and across his cheeks and laughed. 'I don't understand how someone so good doing it can be so embarrassed by talking about it. There's only the two of us within hearing.'

They spent the next few minutes in comfortable silence, standing side by side with their arms touching and leaning against the wall, looking at the view beyond it.

'Perhaps it's time to change the subject, Bob. Did you find anything helpful in our missing men's rooms while I was distracting Sub-Lieutenant Short?'

'You first, Monique. I heard the conversation you had with him about Edward Price but did you uncover anything interesting about James Ewing? I missed most of that.'

Monique ran him through what the sub-lieutenant had said.

'There's some food for thought there,' said Bob. 'It will be interesting to see how Anne Milner's impressions of James square with the sub-lieutenant's.'

'Very true. Now it's your turn, Bob. What did you find?'

'Not as much as you. Certainly not amongst James Ewing's belongings. I got the sense he wouldn't have called that room his home. I've probably got more belongings in our hotel than James has on Manoel Island. There was the usual kit: uniforms, washing and shaving equipment, a towel, footwear and so on. But nothing at all personal beyond an Agatha Christie novel that looked as if it had been through many pairs of hands and the icon on the wall above the bed. I specifically looked for a photograph of Anne Milner, which you might expect in the circumstances. But there wasn't one, either beside his bed or anywhere else I could find. There were no other photographs either. Nothing of his mother and father, for example. Most importantly, if he kept a diary – and I accept most people don't – then he didn't keep it in his room. I suppose that was too much to hope for.'

'Perhaps he kept his personal belongings at Anne Milner's flat,' said Monique. 'Until we know more about their relationship I don't think we're going to find out much more about him based on your rummage through his things. We also need to remember that Edward Price had been through James's belongings before you. Sub-Lieutenant Short didn't think Edward Price had taken anything of James's, but what if he did while the young man was fixated on his MCC tie?'

'That's true, if unhelpful,' said Bob. 'Which brings me to Mr Price's room. I wasn't expecting to find anything personal there, and I didn't, and there was nothing of James's there either. But two light-coloured suits were hanging in the wardrobe as well as three white shirts. He also had a spare MCC tie in his case, which I borrowed as it matches the one he was wearing when he disappeared. Last but perhaps not least I found this in the outside breast pocket of one of the suits.'

Bob took a small bright blue object from his tunic pocket and handed it over to Monique.

'It's a matchbook,' she said, looking at it. 'It's from a bar called Captain Bianchi's at an address in Strait Street here in Valletta. Two of the matches have been used. It's a lot better than nothing. The fact that you found it in his suit pocket means he must have visited during his first two days in Malta. That ties in with his being in Valletta on the Friday and Saturday afternoons and evenings. We should call in and see if we can discover what he was doing there.'

'We should,' said Bob. 'I find it worrying that pretty much all we have to show for Edward Price's presence in Malta is a matchbook, a description of him as a tall man wearing an MCC tie, and a rather odd travel itinerary.'

*

It took no more than two minutes to make their way from the Osborne Hotel to the RAF's headquarters at 3 Scots Street. Monique let Bob lead her out of the front door and across South Street, then up Scots Street, which sloped uphill and was a continuation of the street running steeply up the side of their hotel.

A few yards up the street was a doorway on the right with no more than a small brass plaque confirming its identity.

The inside of the building seemed, at first sight, to be

grander than its dowdy exterior. White marble with black inlaid patterns floored a short corridor beyond the doorway leading to a wider hall in which there was a wooden reception desk. A man in a khaki RAF uniform with corporal's stripes on his upper arms and a white covering on the top of his peaked cap stood as Bob entered and saluted.

Bob returned the salute, then identified himself and Monique and showed the corporal his pass. Monique did likewise.

'We're here to see Anne Milner. She's expecting us.'

'Yes, sir, I've got your names on our visitors' list. Could you take the stairs over beyond that door up to the first floor? Miss Milner will meet you there.'

Having climbed the stairs, Bob pushed through the door from the first floor landing and Monique followed.

A woman in her mid-twenties was standing in the corridor beyond, looking nervous. 'Group Captain Sutherland? Hello, I'm Anne Milner, I'm very pleased to meet you.'

Bob shook her hand and introduced Monique.

Sub-Lieutenant Short had described Anne Milner as 'an absolute stunner' and Monique could see why. She was a little taller than Monique and had shoulder-length wavy blonde hair that was showing signs of exposure to the sun but was still alluring. With her large brown eyes, long legs and slender build, Monique could easily imagine Anne being highly sought-after by just about any eligible male in Malta, and probably by a fair proportion of the ineligible ones.

Anne smiled as she shook Monique's hand. Monique had the slightly unsettling impression that she was in turn being appraised.

'I've been told to be back at my desk in twenty minutes. We can talk in this office through here. I'm sorry, but I can't

116

provide tea or coffee.'

'That's really not a problem,' said Bob.

Monique was amused to realise that he was slightly awed by Anne Milner's beauty and decided to reverse the plan she and Bob had discussed and take the lead. She introduced them more fully and then leapt straight in.

'I assume that Commander Dowson told you that Bob and I are looking into James Ewing's disappearance?'

'Yes, he did, though I don't know what you'll be able to discover nearly two weeks after he was last seen.'

'Can we start at the beginning?' asked Monique. How long have you been in Malta?'

'It feels like forever. I arrived late in 1939 to take up a contract as a dancer in a club. During the year before the war, I'd travelled around Europe as a dancer in stage shows and cabarets. It was quite a life. Malta was meant to be just another stop on my world tour but I grew to like the place and the people here, so I decided to stay a while.

'Even so, I had my passage booked on a ship to Southampton in the middle of June 1940. With the war on, it felt like the right time to go home. Then we had our first bombing raid on the 11th of June 1940, a date I remember well. Suddenly my booking evaporated and I was stranded here. I thought at the time that there were worse places to be stranded, but that was over three thousand air raids ago.

'Work as a dancer dried up very quickly and, for a while, I performed as part of a troupe entertaining our boys in khaki or any other colour uniform stationed in naval bases, airfields and army barracks. That, too, ceased to be an option when petrol for non-essential uses dried up and we could no longer get around, so I got what I think my mother would call a "proper job" here.

It makes me feel useful and pays the bills.'

'And when did you meet James Ewing?'

'Christmas 1941. The 10th Submarine Flotilla threw a Christmas dance in their main dining hall on Manoel Island. It was destroyed in the bombing last year. He'd only recently arrived in Malta and we got talking and, well, one thing led to another. We've been something of a fixture ever since then.'

Monique saw Anne look away and realised she'd told a lie.

'That's quite an impressive commitment on the front line and in wartime,' Monique said.

'Well, yes.' Anne paused. 'I'm sorry, but what I just told you wasn't the complete truth. We did become something of a fixture and spent as much time together as possible during the times when James's submarine wasn't out on patrol. Everything went well for some months. But then the bombing became much worse and the 10th Submarine Flotilla moved from Malta to Alexandria. I think James met someone there because he stopped writing quite soon after the move.

'They'd not long returned to Malta when James was wounded in a depth charge attack on his submarine last August. He spent a week in hospital and they decided that the damage to his hearing was going to be permanent and advised him to return to Britain on medical grounds. He asked to stay in Malta in a shore position, I think because he'd met a nurse while he was in hospital. I saw very little of him for the next few months. Then I heard that the nurse had been posted to Egypt and soon afterwards he turned up at the door of my flat one evening, asking for forgiveness. That was late last December, almost exactly a year after we'd first got together.'

'And you took him back?' asked Monique.

'I'd not exactly been living in a convent during our time

apart. The problem was that I'd been falling in love with men who then got themselves killed. First, it was a fighter pilot who was shot down into the Mediterranean and drowned while waiting for a rescue launch. Then it was an army anti-aircraft gunnery officer who ran into a burning building during an air raid one night to rescue some trapped children. The building collapsed and no one got out alive. After them, James suddenly seemed like a very good bet. The damage to his ear meant that he couldn't go to sea on operations any more. That meant he could be relied on to be around on a more regular basis and, most importantly for me at the time, it cut down on the chances of him dying before his time. I was beginning to think I'd become a jinx on the men I loved and I hoped he might redress the balance.'

'We're wondering if the loss of HMS *Ursus* in November affected him,' said Monique.

'Yes, I think it did…'

There was a knock on the door, which then opened. A flight lieutenant came into the room and looked at Bob. 'I'm sorry to interrupt, sir, but something urgent's come up and Anne is needed on the telephone. I'm afraid it can't wait.'

'Yes, of course,' said Bob.

Anne stood up.

'What time do you finish here?' asked Monique, also standing up. 'We really need your help in understanding James better. Can we talk later?'

'I finish at 5 p.m. and I'll do everything I can to help.'

'We're staying at the Osborne Hotel, just across the road,' said Monique. 'Could you meet us there then? We can buy you dinner if you like.'

'Yes, I'll see you then. Goodbye, Monique. Goodbye, Group

Captain.'

After Anne closed the office door Monique sat back down and smiled at Bob. 'You seemed a bit tongue-tied there. Is that the effect a pretty woman always has on you?'

'You should know, Monique. I think I was a little taken aback by the sense that she looked quite like you in your guise as Mrs Cadman, wearing the blonde Ingrid Bergman wig. Anyway, thanks for covering up for me. It was all going well until we were interrupted.'

Monique looked at her watch. We're running out of things to do this afternoon, Bob. Do you fancy a little walk to acquaint ourselves better with Valletta's geography? The hotel receptionist told me of a viewpoint on the other side of the peninsula that's supposed to be even better than the one overlooking Manoel Island and the harbour to the north.'

'We've also got Captain Bianchi's to visit,' said Bob.

'Yes, but I wonder if that might be a job for Mr and Mrs Cadman this evening?'

'You're probably right. In that case, do you want to lead on?'

'The receptionist gave me a map of Valletta and said it was easy to find the place he'd described.'

Monique led the way back down the stairs and into the hall with the reception desk. She turned towards the corridor leading to the outer door but had to stand aside to make way for three men in khaki RAF officers' uniforms emerging from it. The man in front had rank insignia on his epaulettes that comprised a broad band much wider than the four Bob wore, and a narrower band. He also wore pilot's wings like Bob's but sported more medal ribbons than Bob did beneath them. She was aware of Bob, partly behind her and to her right side, saluting and the officer then returning the salute.

The man had his hand on the door leading to the staircase when he stopped suddenly, causing the two men behind to bump into one another. He turned back towards Bob.

'Do I know you, group captain?'

'Yes, sir, you do. The name is Sutherland and I was the commanding officer of 605 Squadron at Croydon in Autumn 1940 when you were commanding 11 Group.'

'Yes, I remember. You had a bad time of it as I recall. I'm glad to see you alive and well.'

'Thank you, sir,'

'You can tell me about it later. I'm hosting a dinner tonight for officers based at RAF Ta Kali in their mess, which is in the Xara Palace at Mdina. I'd like you to join us. Where are you staying?'

'In the Osborne Hotel, just over the road, sir.'

'We'll get a car to pick you up at 5.30 p.m. from your hotel.' The man turned to look at one of the other officers. 'Can you see to that, Briars?'

'Yes, sir.'

'Good. I look forward to catching up with you later, Sutherland.'

With that, the senior officer pulled open the door into the stairwell and disappeared through it, followed by his two colleagues.

'Who was that?' asked Monique.

Bob smiled at her and touched his finger to his lips, then headed for the outside door.

Out on the street he turned to her as she emerged in the sunshine. 'Sorry about that. Which way do we need to go to get to this viewpoint you were told about?'

'Just down to South Street, then we turn right along it. Who was that, Bob?'

'That was Air Vice-Marshal Sir Keith Park, who commands the RAF in Malta. I'm sorry, I'd have introduced you but, as you saw, I didn't really get the chance.'

'From the accent, I'm guessing that he's an Australian?'

'I'm not sure he'd thank you for saying that,' said Bob. 'He's from New Zealand and I don't think they generally like being taken for Australians.'

Monique smiled. 'Wherever he's from, it seems our plans for the evening have changed. What do you want me to do while you are off swapping tall stories with your ex-comrades in arms?'

'I'm hoping that Air Vice-Marshal Park might be a useful ally on the island if things get sticky. That's my MI11 rationale for attending his dinner, though as you saw there's also the small matter of my not really being given the opportunity to decline the invitation. If you are happy with the idea, I see no reason why you can't simply meet Anne Milner as we planned. You seem to have a lot in common with her and I'm wondering if she might be more open with you alone than she would be if the two of us were talking to her.'

'That's probably true,' said Monique. 'The dancing background is the most obvious point of similarity, but it did send a shiver down my spine when she started talking about jinxing the men she loved. That felt much too close to home for comfort.'

'It looks like we're coming to the end of the street ahead,' said Bob. 'There are a lot more people and there's more traffic about. Where do we go when we get there?'

'We're supposed to go straight across Valletta's main street, which the map shows is Kingsway, and past the opera house.

Then we just keep on climbing gently.' Monique stopped walking. 'Ah, the receptionist didn't mention that.'

'It perhaps used to be an opera house,' said Bob. 'Now it looks like a cutaway drawing of one. And the bomb damage is bad in every direction.'

Monique linked arms with Bob and led him across the busy road and the people streaming in both directions along Kingsway's pavements. She found the instructions she'd been given a little harder to follow at the top of the hill, but a policeman was happy to direct them towards iron gates in a grand stone archway.

There were lots of people in the open space beyond the gates. Monique saw that it was a popular place with young couples, with many of the men in uniform. 'Welcome to Upper Barrakka Gardens,' she said. 'I'm told that they were built as pleasure gardens for the knights of the Order of Saint John, centuries back. We need to be over on the far side, beyond this set of roofless arches.'

'Are these the result of more bombing by our friends in Sicily?' asked Bob.

'There's no rubble, so I'm guessing whatever happened here happened before the current conflict. Anyway, this is the view we came for.'

'I'm not going to ask for my money back,' said Bob. 'The anti-aircraft guns on that terrace below us do intrude a little, but you get a fantastic view of the main harbour to the south of Valletta. This is the one called the Grand Harbour, and you can see why. It's difficult to know what to focus on first. It looks so amazing under a clear blue sky and the quality of the light is simply sublime.'

'For me, it's the warships lined up along the harbour below

us that catch the attention first,' said Monique. 'Especially the aircraft carrier.' She watched as what seemed to be hundreds of small boats moved back and forth between the shore and the ships in the harbour. 'Those small boats look from this distance like slightly bulky Venetian gondolas,' she said. 'They are transporting men from the warships to the shore and back.' Then her attention shifted. 'But look at the settlements over on the far side, which form a series of peninsulas divided by inlets that are also full of ships and boats. Seen from here, those areas look as if they have been more badly bombed than Valletta or the settlements beyond the harbour to the north.'

'The naval dockyards are over on the far side of the Grand Harbour,' said Bob. 'I think that they took the brunt of the air attacks, along with the island's airfields.'

Monique took Bob's arm. 'It really brings it home, doesn't it Bob?'

'What?'

'You've got thousands, probably hundreds of thousands of people here who have had their lives turned upside down by bombing over the past few years, and doubtless very many of them have been killed and injured. And yet we've come right across Europe to look for two missing men. What is it that Humphrey Bogart's character says to Ingrid Bergman at the airport at the end of "Casablanca"?' Monique paused and put on an American accent. 'It doesn't take much to see that the problems of three little people don't amount to a hill of beans in this crazy world.' She shifted back to her natural accent. 'In this case that should read two little people. Or four if you count the two of us. Looking at this view puts what we're here to do in context.'

'That's very true, Monique,' said Bob. To her surprise, he

then tried to match her American accent. 'Here's looking at you, kid.'

'Maybe you should let me do the accents, Bob.'

'Unless it's one from New Zealand, perhaps?' He laughed when she smacked his arm, then looked at his watch. 'Do you fancy getting a quick drink somewhere and then heading back to the hotel to get ready for our separate evening activities? This wasn't quite how I imagined we'd be spending our one-week wedding anniversary, but life is full of surprises.'

CHAPTER TWELVE

Anne Milner came in through the front door of the Osborne Hotel a couple of minutes after 5 p.m. and looked around, rather uncertainly.

'Can I help you, miss?' asked the elderly man behind the reception desk.

'She's with me,' said Monique, standing up from a chair in the entrance hall. 'Hello, Anne! I'm pleased to see you again.'

'Isn't your colleague joining us?' asked Anne, smiling.

'No, something came up and Group Captain Sutherland has to go to Mdina this evening. But I need to eat and I'm happy to treat you to dinner. Do you know anywhere good?'

'I'm told your hotel has an excellent dining room, but how would you feel about eating out in Floriana? That's Valletta's south-western neighbour, beyond the city's defensive walls and bastions. I live in a flat there and if you don't mind a short detour we can call in so I can get changed out of my office clothes. It's not much more than a twenty-minute walk from here, less coming the other way if I've overslept and don't want to be late for work.'

'That sounds perfect,' said Monique. She'd wanted to find a way of looking at any of James's belongings in Anne's flat, so the idea that they went there first really was perfect. 'Do you want to show me the way?'

Anne walked beside Monique along South Street to Kingsway. It was busier than earlier so there was little opportunity to talk.

They turned right into Kingsway and Anne linked her arm with Monique's as they walked along the pavement on the right-hand side of the road.

'Bob and I saw the ruins of the opera house earlier,' said Monique. 'We were walking to the gardens that give such a wonderful view over the Grand Harbour. You do get a sense of the scale of the bombing when you see something like this.'

'That may be the worst thing about living through years of constant attacks,' said Anne. 'You start to become impervious to it. There was a time when I knew what these streets looked like with complete buildings and without rubble, a time when I might walk past the undamaged opera house or even enjoy a performance there. But gradually the experience eats away at you and you come to accept as normal what must seem truly shocking to someone new to it. There were times last year, especially in spring when the attacks were at their worst, when there would be new piles of rubble on my walk to work almost every day. And sometimes it wouldn't just be buildings. I tripped over someone's burned and severed arm one morning, just lying in the street. I have no idea where the rest of them was, though I doubt if they were alive.'

'That must have been dreadful,' said Monique.

'It was. Anyway, ahead of us is the City Gate or the Kingsgate. It's not what you'd call pretty, is it?'

Monique looked ahead to see the road and its pavements going between two rising sets of broad stone steps. It then passed through an arch and, in the darkness underneath, Monique could see that the outer face of the gate was formed by two smaller arches for traffic with, on either side of them, further and even smaller arches for pedestrians.

After they emerged from the far side, Monique realised they were crossing a bridge over a very deep, wide ditch and that imposing stone walls protected this side of the city. 'I suppose the people who built all these defences never imagined that one day an enemy would fly right over the top of them and drop bombs from the sky,' she said.

'Very true,' said Anne. 'You can still see where a bomb blew a hole in the bridge. They've repaired it, but I'm not sure I'd like to drive over that part.'

Monique was relieved when they reached the far end of the bridge.

Anne picked up her commentary again. 'Ahead of us, as you may have guessed from all the buses, is Valletta's main bus station. Most people here travel by bus if it's too far to walk or cycle, or they use the steam ferries that cross the harbours to the north and south of Valletta, linking it to Sliema and the Three Cities.

'This open area separates Valletta's defences behind us from the buildings of Floriana ahead of us. There was a time when this was probably a wonderful view but, as you can see, the skyline of Floriana is punctuated by gaps and stumps of buildings. Over there, a little to our right, is what's left of what was intended to be Malta's finest hotel, the Phoenicia. It was taken over by the military at the start of the war before construction was finished and then it was badly bombed in April last year.'

Once beyond the open area, Anne led Monique into a grid pattern of streets largely comprising apartments rising to four or five storeys high. Again, there was obvious bomb damage but, for the first time in Malta, Monique began to think she could see what the area had been like before the war.

'You get a really good sense here of these wooden balconies that protrude from the fronts of the buildings,' said Monique. 'I've seen them in Valletta, of course, including on the first and second floors of our hotel. I get the impression they are particularly prone to blast or fire damage, so a lot of them in Valletta are in poor condition.

'The Maltese call them gallariji,' said Anne. 'Lots of buildings have them, as you've seen. I think they are partly ornamental, in that they make the front of the buildings look more interesting. They also add a little space to the interior. Much less common is the stone version. I live on the top floor of the block over there.' She pointed at a four-storey building on the opposite side of the street. 'As you can see, I've got what looks from the outside like a small stone balcony that then got enclosed.'

Anne took some keys from her handbag and unlocked a door from the street. She then led Monique up communal stairs to a landing at the top of the building, where she unlocked the door on one side.

'I wasn't expecting visitors so you'll have to excuse the state the place is in,' said Anne. 'As you can see, this is the hall, complete with a stone floor. The open door on the left is to the main living room overlooking the street from the stone balcony. On the right are my tiny kitchen and my equally small bathroom, while at the end is my bedroom.'

The glimpses of the rooms that Monique had from the hall suggested that Anne kept the place very well.

'Come on through to the bedroom. It will only take me a couple of moments to change into something that doesn't make me think of work.'

The bedroom was large enough for a metal-framed double bed with a wardrobe and a chest of drawers against one wall. Light was coming in through shutters covering a window. The floor was stone and large, slightly threadbare, oriental carpets had been used as wall hangings to decorate the two walls not occupied by the window or the furniture. The top of the chest of drawers was used to display half a dozen photographs in free-standing frames, though Monique was too far away to see what they depicted.

'Why don't you sit on the end of the bed while I get changed?'

To Monique's surprise, Anne undid the zip on the back of her dress and let it fall to the floor. Then, in just a white bra and slip, she went and stood in front of a mirror on the wall above the chest of drawers.

'One of the worst things about the siege was the way the rations kept getting cut. I was relatively lucky as I could sometimes eat in the canteen at 3 Scots Street. I also registered for a Victory Kitchen near here, a communal kitchen where you could get a basic meal each day for 6d. Yet I was still hungry more often than not. After we got back together, James would complain that he had nothing to get hold of when we were in bed together and even I could see that my ribs stuck out in a way that made me look more like a skeleton than a living woman. For a time I was so underweight that my periods stopped.' She lifted her arms and did a twirl. 'The last few months have been better. I don't look like a skeleton now, do I?'

'No, you don't,' said Monique. 'You look amazing. Does James spend much time here?'

'We get together when we can,' said Anne, as she took a blue floral dress out of the wardrobe and started to put it on.' Sometimes it's hard to coordinate our days off. Perhaps once a month we can have a complete weekend together which we usually spend here. Beyond that, it's an evening and night every week or ten days and then he has to return to Manoel Island early the next morning.'

'One of the things that struck us in his quarters on Manoel Island was that he doesn't seem to keep anything personal there, just his uniforms and essential military kit. Does he keep his other belongings here?'

'Not really,' said Anne. 'Obviously, he keeps a toothbrush and shaving kit here. But beyond that, no.'

Monique had gained the impression that Anne wasn't a very good liar at their first meeting and was sure of it now. For whatever reason, she wasn't telling the truth.

'Are you sure?' asked Monique. 'It could be a real help in working out where he's gone if I was able to take a look at his belongings. There could be something amongst them that wouldn't be obvious to someone who knew him well but which could give me an important clue.'

There was a moment's silence in the bedroom. Monique saw indecision on Anne's face, which was then replaced by determination. Having lied, she was convincing herself that she had no option but to stick to the lie.

'No, sorry.'

'That's a shame,' said Monique, smiling brightly. 'Anyway, where did you want to go for dinner?'

'Give me a minute to sort out my lipstick.' Anne walked over to the mirror and busied herself. 'There, that's better. As you're offering to pay, Monique, I started by thinking through the most expensive places I know of. But that doesn't seem fair and what I'd like to do instead is take you to enjoy some of the best food I've eaten in Malta.'

'That sounds good, though I'd have happily gone the expensive route if you'd preferred.'

'No, it's not far away and you'll be amazed. I only

discovered it a few months ago and it's been an important part of building back my shape after the skeletal months. It's called the King Edward Hotel and it's right here in Floriana.

*

The King Edward Hotel was one of a line of buildings along a side street leading off a main road, many with the projecting balconies she'd asked Anne about earlier. Anne was obviously well-known to the staff and, although the basement dining room was crowded on this Saturday evening, she had no difficulty getting a table for two against a side wall.

Monique ordered a bottle of one of the more expensive red wines on the wine list. Anne might be concerned about appearing too grasping, but Monique saw no reason to go for less than the best quality wine. It was, after all, the man who had interrupted her honeymoon who would be paying for it.

Anne offered Monique a cigarette, which she accepted, and then took one for herself and lit both.

'What do you recommend we eat?' asked Monique.

'The rabbit spaghetti is absolutely superb,' said Anne, 'and comes in generous portions. Ah, I can see from the look on your face that someone has told you about the demise of Malta's feline population.'

'Yes, the navy driver who took us to Manoel Island this morning.'

'I can promise you that the rabbits served here really did once have long ears and bobble tails. It's up to you, of course, as they have other options.'

'I'll go with your recommendation, Anne. Good, here's the wine.'

The wine was excellent. When the rabbit spaghetti arrived it turned out to be as good and as generous as Anne had promised.

'Anne, this afternoon we had to end our meeting when you were about to tell me about James's reaction when HMS *Ursus* was lost in November. What were you going to say?'

'He was different after we got back together. He never had problems sleeping when I first knew him and he does now, and I think he has nightmares too, though he refuses to talk about them when I ask.

'Other changes have been more difficult to pin down. I get the sense that he's sometimes rather distant, as if his thoughts are elsewhere. He can also lose his temper over stupid things that wouldn't have bothered him when we first knew each other.

'Since December we've certainly argued more often than we did before he was wounded. I don't know if that was because of the loss of his submarine or because we'd both been with other lovers while we were apart. Sometimes I've wondered whether I should end things with him and move on. I've not followed that through because there are still times when he's a wonderful man to be with.'

'Thank you, Anne. The officer he shares a room with on Manoel Island talked about a sense that James is hiding feelings of guilt about the loss of HMS *Ursus* under a veneer of normality. Does that ring any bells with you?'

'I suppose it does. I've never quite seen it like that, but it could make sense.'

Monique poured more wine for them.

'Do you want anything else to eat?' asked Anne.

'I'm happy to go for a dessert if you want one, but I don't feel strongly about it myself.'

'I'm full, to be honest,' said Anne. 'Should we just enjoy the wine?'

'Perhaps I'd better order a second bottle,' said Monique, attracting the attention of a waiter.

After she'd ordered the wine she turned back to Anne. 'Can you talk to me about the weekend that James went missing?'

'Yes, he came round on the Friday evening. We had a meal here and then went back to my flat. On Saturday we caught a bus to a particularly nice beach on the other side of the island. I'd been wanting to go there with him for ages, but James had always found reasons not to. I think the problem was that it's very popular with the officers and men of the 10th Submarine Flotilla. Sometimes I get the feeling that James is a little ashamed of me, as if he doesn't want people to know he's with me. I always find that quite hurtful but he never says as much and there are other times when I think it must be my imagination.

'Anyway, we had a wonderful time there, and then we got a bus back late in the afternoon.'

'Did you notice anything odd about him?' asked Monique. 'Were there any tensions or issues between you?'

'No, we had a lovely day. We did see Sub-Lieutenant Short, who James shares a room with, while we were there. He was kissing a girl on the beach as we walked past and we said hello.'

Monique again had the sense that Anne wasn't telling her the whole truth but saw little benefit in pressing the point. 'And what happened on the Sunday?' she asked.

'We had a quiet day in the flat. Well, not so quiet as there's a squeaky spring in my bed. You might have noticed when you sat on it earlier. I made lunch for us, which is something I don't do very often. Late in the afternoon, James set off back to Manoel Island. I heard the next day from Commander Dowson that he hadn't arrived back and hadn't reported for duty. I don't know what to make of it. I'm obviously extremely concerned about him and just hope against hope that he turns up alive and well.'

Anne again seemed far from convincing to Monique. 'Have you discussed this with anyone else?'

'Just the tall man Commander Dowson asked me to talk to, Mr Price. He came to see me at 3 Scots Street during the afternoon on Friday of last week.'

'Did you tell him what you've told me?'

'Yes, the stuff about James. He certainly didn't get to see me in my underwear and I didn't talk about my ribs.' Anne smiled and took a drink of her wine.

'What did you make of Mr Price?'

'He listened to what I had to say and seemed very professional if a little detached. Beyond that, I didn't make much of him. He's old enough to be my father.'

'Did he ask you anything about places James might frequent in Malta? Either on his own or with you?'

'Yes. He asked how we spent our time together and if there were places we liked to go. I mentioned a few places we'd been when we could get entire days off together. I also told him about going to the beach on the Saturday, and James staying at my flat whenever we can manage it. That's about it.'

'Against that background, what I'm about to ask might seem a little odd. Have you and James ever been to a fishing village called Marsaxlokk in the south-east of the island?'

'I've heard of it, but I've never been. And as far as I know, James hasn't either, unless it was on official business. He's never mentioned it to me.'

'And how about an archaeological site called Hagar Qim?' asked Monique.

'Again, I've heard of it, but that's not really my sort of thing. Nor James's.'

'The beach you went to with James on the Saturday was called Ghajn Tuffieha, wasn't it?'

'That's right.'

'What about the beaches at Mellieha and St Paul's Bay?'

'Yes, we've visited both of those a couple of times and I mentioned both to Mr Price.'

'The final places I want to ask you about are Mosta and Mdina.'

'We've been to Mdina together. It's a lovely place where you can forget the outside world for a little while. And I've also been to Mosta with James. We visited a couple of months ago by bus. The church there has a magnificent dome. Last year a bomb dropped by an attacking aircraft passed through the dome during a service and landed amongst the congregation, but it didn't go off. The locals say it's a miracle. James was keen to see the church and I enjoyed our visit too. I think I mentioned both places to Mr Price.'

'Thank you, Anne. I've only got a couple of concluding questions. You must know James better than anyone else. How did he seem immediately before he disappeared? How did he manage financially? Did he have any enemies?'

Anne took another drink of her wine and Monique topped it up from the second bottle. 'He seemed fine. And there were no money problems that I knew about. He didn't make close friends and certainly didn't appear to make enemies. I'm really sorry I can't be more help, Monique.'

'There's nothing to be sorry about, Anne, you've been very helpful. Let's just enjoy this lovely wine.' Monique realised that it was her turn to lie, about how helpful Anne had been if not about the wine.

'Have you ever danced, Monique? You move like a dancer.'

'Yes. My background is rather complicated, with a childhood that started in Siberia and moved on to Denmark. In 1924, when I was 11, my parents moved to Paris. In Paris, I started attending the ballet school set up there by the exiled Russian ballet dancer, Vera Trefilova. If I say so myself, I was pretty good. I had a variety of roles and toured Europe with Vera Trefilova's ballet company when I was 16. A year later I was performing as a cabaret dancer in Paris. By the time I was 20, I was dancing at the Folies Bergère and had worked with the Russian Ballet in Paris.'

'How exciting! It seems we have even more in common than I'd imagined. How long did you dance for?' asked Anne.

'For reasons that would take too long to explain, my career then lurched sideways into the shady world of intelligence and ten years later I find myself working with Military Intelligence, Section 11.'

'And you travel the world in the company of a very handsome group captain. I'd like a job like that. After being trapped in Malta for three-and-a-half years I'd love the opportunity to travel again.'

'You never know what tomorrow might bring,' said Monique, thinking as she said it how trite it sounded.

'You do know that your colleague is very keen on you Monique, don't you?'

'What makes you say that?'

'The way he looks at you when you're talking. He didn't

seem to be able to take his eyes off you this afternoon.'

'As we got married in Edinburgh last Saturday, I'm pleased to hear that,' said Monique.

'Really? That's wonderful! Congratulations!'

'Thank you. Let's divide what's left in the second bottle between us.' Monique topped up their glasses again.

'You aren't wearing a ring,' said Anne.

'I don't when I'm on duty,' said Monique.

Anne smiled and looked at her watch. 'I can walk you back, at least as far as the City Gate.'

Outside, dusk was setting in. Anne linked arms with Monique again. They walked in silence through the still-busy streets of Floriana. As they approached the bus station, Monique prepared to try one last time to get Anne to agree to her looking through James Ewing's belongings, which she was certain were in Anne's flat. It was too late tonight, but she still needed to get her permission.

Then the wail of a nearby air raid siren started up, quickly followed by others further away. Monique felt the hairs rise on her arms and the back of her neck.

'Damn!' said Anne. 'Don't worry, Monique. These days the warnings we get often come to nothing. Either the attackers get intercepted before they get close to the islands and give up or it's a false alarm in the first place. I suggest we press on as planned. You know how to get back from here, don't you? There's still enough light to see your way and there are still quite a few people about despite the sirens. You can see the City Gate beyond the bus station. You just need to go a short distance beyond it and then turn left into South Street, the street your hotel is on. I doubt if you'll be stopped by the police or special constabulary but, if you are, I'm sure your military intelligence pass will justify your being on the streets after the alarm has sounded. I'll have no problem getting home.'

'Thanks for walking me this far, Anne. Look, I know you're worried about James. It really might help find him if you would let me take a look at his belongings. I know you must keep some of them at your flat. It wouldn't need to be done officially. I could just drop by myself as a friend tomorrow morning if you're going to be in. Perhaps we could then go and have lunch somewhere?'

Even in the gathering darkness, Monique could see the indecision return to Anne's face. This time it stayed there for longer and she began to hope that Anne might be having a change of heart. But as had happened earlier, the indecision was then replaced by something harder.

'I'd love to see you again, Monique, but I'm working tomorrow. The war sadly doesn't stop for the weekend and our airfields still need fuel deliveries. And you'd be having a wasted trip anyway. Other than the sort of stuff I talked about earlier, there's nothing of James's at the flat.'

'I'm sure our paths will cross again, Anne' said Monique. 'Take care on the walk back.'

Anne hugged Monique and the two women kissed cheeks. Then she turned and walked back towards Floriana.

Monique watched Anne go for a moment, then walked towards the bus station and the City Gate beyond it.

Suddenly the sound of guns firing started up. To Monique, the noise seemed to be coming from all around her.

She heard running feet behind her and turned as Anne caught hold of her arm. 'Those are anti-aircraft guns. We do need to take shelter after all. It's not just the danger of bombs. Everything fired by those guns has to come back down to Earth somewhere.'

Anne turned to one side, still holding Monique's arm. 'I suppose if you want the authentic Malta experience then I'm about to show it to you. I came to know all the air raid shelters near my route to work during the siege and there's a good one quite close to us. Quickly, follow me!'

CHAPTER THIRTEEN

The RAF staff car followed the route Bob had taken in its naval counterpart that morning, descending steeply to the harbourside and then driving south-west alongside it. At the far end of the harbour, where the Royal Navy driver had turned right to follow the waterfront round towards Manoel Island, the RAF driver instead headed straight on, taking Bob into unknown territory.

'How far is it to Mdina?' he asked.

Bob saw the driver catch his eye in the mirror. 'It will take about half an hour, sir. Are you new to Malta?'

'Yes, I arrived last night, so this is my first day.'

'I'd imagine it's a bit of a shock to the system, sir. I've been here long enough to get used to it, though the talk is that a lot of us are going to be relocating to Sicily sooner rather than later. You'd know more about that than I do, of course.'

'I understand I'm going to somewhere called the Xara Palace in Mdina,' said Bob.

'Yes, sir. It's used as the officers' mess for RAF Ta Kali. You'll like Mdina. It's been bombed, of course, like just about everywhere else in Malta, but it's not been as badly knocked about as Valletta and the built-up areas around the harbours, or the airfields for that matter. You still get the sense of what it is at heart, a compact medieval walled city built on top of a hill. The Maltese call it the "Silent City" though, with the airfield at Ta Kali being only a couple of miles to the north-east, it's not all that silent now. It used to be the capital of Malta. When the Order of Saint John took over in 1530 they moved the capital to Vittoriosa, one of the cities on the south-east side of the Grand

Harbour.'

'I'm looking forward to seeing it,' said Bob.

Bob sat back and watched parts of Malta pass by the windows of the car. The intensity of the bomb damage got less severe as the car drove further from Valletta and its harbours. The most striking thing was the way the people of Malta seemed to be getting on with their normal lives in the midst of what amounted to a modern battlefield.

'That's Mdina you can see on the ridge ahead of us, sir,' said the driver.

'Bob leaned forwards to see through the windscreen. 'It does look rather spectacular,' he said.

The car climbed a hill and entered a built-up area.

'We're driving into Rabat first,' said the driver. 'It's immediately to the south-west of Mdina. To get into Mdina itself we cross this stone bridge, hoping that no one wants to come the other way, and then drive through the ornate gateway you can see at the far end of the bridge.'

Beyond the gateway and a security checkpoint manned by RAF airmen carrying rifles, the car entered what felt to Bob to be a honey-coloured stone maze. The driver turned right, then stopped and reversed to let two RAF staff cars coming the other way get past. After another fifty yards, the car came to a halt in a square that had buildings to the left and right and what appeared to be the outer wall of the city directly ahead.

'The two-storey building to our left is the Xara Palace, sir. The sentries will direct you.'

Bob hadn't noticed the two RAF policemen wearing khaki shorts and shirts, one standing on either side of the door to the palace. He thanked the driver and got out of the car, then walked over to the sentries, who came to attention.

Bob saluted in response and then, when requested, showed his security pass. Inside he was asked for his pass again, this time by an RAF corporal holding a clipboard.

'Thank you, sir. Pre-dinner drinks will be served in the atrium, which is directly ahead and then through the arches you will see on your right.'

Bob looked and could see officers milling around at the far end of a broad corridor, holding glasses and smoking.

'First, though, Air Vice-Marshal Park has asked if you could spare him a few minutes. He's waiting for you in the office through there.' The corporal pointed off to Bob's right.

'Yes, of course, thank you.' Bob wasn't entirely surprised by the request - it wasn't really a request - for a private audience.

The office door was open and Bob could see Sir Keith, wearing his peaked cap and sitting on the far side of a desk, looking down at some papers. Bob knocked on the door and Sir Keith looked up.

'Come in Sutherland and close the door behind you.'

Bob did so, then walked over to the desk, came to a halt and saluted.

Sir Keith stood up and returned the salute, then gestured towards a seat. 'Make yourself comfortable.' After they'd both sat down, Sir Keith leaned back in his chair. 'After we bumped into each other earlier I asked my people to find out why there was an RAF group captain I knew nothing about wandering around Malta. I'm a little bemused that no one could come up with any answers, so I thought I'd ask you myself.'

Bob had been expecting the question. 'I'm semi-detached from the RAF these days, sir. Late last year I accepted a post as the deputy head of Military Intelligence, Section 11, based in Edinburgh. We have a responsibility for military security and

I've been asked to come to Malta to assess the suggestion that we might set up an office here.'

Sir Keith looked at him without saying anything in a way that Bob found unsettling. It was a relief when the air vice-marshal eventually spoke. 'I hear what you say, Sutherland. Have you come across anyone who's believed you when you've told them that's why you're here? It doesn't sound very plausible to me. Never mind. Perhaps it's best if I don't know the real reason. I am very pleased we met, however, and I very much hope you enjoy the evening. You'll doubtless have been to this type of thing before.'

'Yes, sir, though perhaps not to as many as you.'

Sir Keith smiled, 'Probably not. Anyway, now we've had a chance to clear the air I'd like to ask whether you have any plans for tomorrow morning?'

'Nothing I can't change, sir.'

'I know it will be a Sunday, but there's something I would like to show you in Valletta. I'll pick you up in my car at your hotel at 10 a.m. Right, now we've got that out of the way let's go and join the others. I'm sure there's a drink out there with your name on it.'

The atrium of the Xara Palace was a magnificent open-topped space, rising two storeys within the structure of the building like a narrow courtyard. One of the long walls had vines strung out along its length at first-floor level and there were groups of small trees in terracotta pots at ground level. Bob found himself drinking very nice sparkling white wine and casually chatting with some of the many other officers there. Perhaps it was because of his pilot's wings and medal ribbons, but he found himself instantly accepted as a member of the group in a way that felt very comfortable.

Drinks were brought to an end when a handbell was rung and dinner was announced.

Bob followed the throng into a dining room that was as attractive as the atrium. Large windows lined one wall, offering distant views across the island, only interrupted by the criss-cross pattern of anti-blast sticky tape across individual panes of glass.

Other walls housed large paintings, mainly of Malta or of aircraft. Bob was directed to a top table that stretched along one side of the room. Three further tables were placed with one end of each touching the top table, so the pattern when seen from the ceiling would have looked like a capital letter 'E'.

Bob found himself sitting with the wing commander responsible for operations at RAF Ta Kali on his left and a squadron leader who worked as the station medical officer on his right.

The food was excellent, with a fish starter followed by pork and roast potatoes with cauliflower.

'I heard someone say that you were a squadron commander reporting to the air vice-marshal during the Battle of Britain, sir,' said the wing commander.

'That's right,' said Bob. 'I thought he was an inspirational leader. He appreciated the efforts and sacrifices of those of us doing the flying and he had an outstanding grasp of the tactics most likely to achieve success against the enemy we were facing at the time. I suppose that shouldn't have been surprising. He'd been a very successful fighter pilot during the last war and he'd helped Dowding establish the operational defence system that we rely on so heavily in this one. He'd even written manuals on fighter tactics. I know he fell foul of internal RAF politics after he'd won the battle and I always thought he was treated rather shoddily, being shunted off into a training post only a month or so later. I was pleased when I read he'd been posted to take over as Air Officer Commanding in Egypt. I gather he took command of air operations in Malta last July?'

'Yes, he did,' said the wing commander. 'His arrival had a remarkable impact here. His predecessor was a good man, but he didn't have the same background in fighter tactics and control. Air Vice-Marshal Park arrived on a flying boat on the 14th of July last year, during an air raid, ordering the pilot to alight despite instructions to stand off while the raid was in progress and getting into an immediate row with his predecessor.

'What happened then was little short of incredible. Until he took over, the standard practice here had been for fighters to take off and climb to the south to gain height, and then turn and fly north to intercept incoming enemy aircraft, which by that time had often reached their targets. The availability of Spitfires had been steadily improving for a while and on the 25th of July, just eleven days after he arrived, the air vice-marshal put in place what he called his "Forward Interception Plan". He insisted that we were prepared for takeoff at much shorter notice than before and once in the air we climbed as we flew north and formed into wings of three squadrons. This allowed us to attack enemy formations long before they reached Malta. The result was that we shot more bombers down before they reached their targets and, perhaps even more significantly, it caused many attacking formations to break up and scatter, often ditching their bombs into the sea and running for home.

'It was typical of the man that he backed up his plan by beefing up the strength of the RAF Air Sea Rescue service in

Malta. Carrying out interceptions much further north meant that more of us had to swim for it if we were shot down and he made sure he did what he could to preserve the lives of his pilots. As I said, the changes were made on the 25th of July 1942. By the end of that month, only a week later, the Axis powers had all but given up on large-scale daylight bombing raids on the islands. As turning points go, it was a remarkable one. I think everyone in Malta was delighted when they announced his knighthood in November.'

After the dessert course was cleared away the noise level in the dining room increased and the atmosphere became smoky. Bob didn't mind as supplies of the sparkling white wine were apparently inexhaustible and it seemed the waiting staff had been briefed never to let a glass get empty. He wondered how Monique would react when her new husband returned to the hotel more than a little drunk.

Speeches then started. Air Vice-Marshal Park gave what seemed a well-judged vote of thanks to the officers of RAF Ta Kali, talking about their achievements and ending with rousing words about taking the war to the enemy in new and even more effective ways in future. There was enthusiastic applause afterwards. The group captain commanding the base replied with thanks for the air vice-marshal's comments and some humorous barbs aimed at his colleagues, which raised a lot of laughs in the audience.

While still standing, he then turned to look along the table at Bob. 'I'm sorry to drop this on you without warning, group captain, but we have a tradition here that the most senior guest gives a short speech. You can take whatever you like as a subject and, judging from your medal ribbons, I'm sure you've got a good story to tell.'

Bob felt stunned as cheers went up around the room. It was obvious he'd not been the only one drinking wine freely.

He looked at the wing commander he'd been talking to about Sir Keith. 'You might have warned me,' he said, quietly.

'I'm sorry, sir, but those are the rules we play by. You'll be fine.'

Bob stood up and looked around at a sea of expectant faces. 'Very well,' he said, pitching his voice at a volume that he hoped would carry across the room. 'I want to tell you a story that's in two parts. For the first part, I want to take you back to the evening of the 1st of November 1940. It was a little after the last of the light had disappeared from the western sky and I was flying a Hurricane back towards Croydon Airport, some 70 miles to the west. I was tired. It was my second flight of the day. I'd shot down a Messerschmitt Bf 109 fifteen minutes after sunrise that morning, ten hours earlier.'

There was a lone cheer from someone at the far end of the room which was quickly cut off, presumably as someone shushed the cheerer.

Bob continued. 'The 1st of November 1940 was a Friday. I'd shot down another Bf 109 on the Sunday before, and another the day before that. On the previous Sunday, I'd shot down two Bf 109s. And a little under two weeks before that, on Monday the 7th of October 1940, I had shot down five Bf 109s in a single day.' He held up his hands to forestall any response from the audience. 'But this isn't a story intended to glorify my achievements. It's a story about how easy it is to let your guard slip, however good you think you are.

'As I said, I was tired, deeply tired. I'm sure many of you have felt the same way after prolonged periods of action. I worked hard to drum into my pilots on 605 Squadron the old

148

maxim that you should never fly straight and level for more than 30 seconds in a combat area. It was a rule I believed that I applied instinctively myself, especially when flying alone. Incidentally, flying alone was something I repeatedly told my pilots not to do, yet there I was, doing it myself.

'I never saw the aircraft that got me. There was a noise like nothing I'd ever heard before and flashes as machine gun or cannon rounds impacted with parts of the structure of my Hurricane in the dark. Then there was a sharp pain in the side of my head and I could smell hot oil and coolant and my aircraft began to spin vertically downwards towards the ground. Despite the huge gravitational forces created by the spin, I fought to open the canopy. I couldn't see the ground in the dark, but I knew it was getting closer and closer.'

Bob stopped and picked up his glass and took a drink of his wine, finishing the glass. 'Is there any more?' he asked.

'You can't stop there, sir!' shouted someone in the room.

Bob smiled. 'The fact that I'm standing here before you today is proof that I survived, so it's not that much of a cliffhanger. The truth is that I have no idea how I got out of the aircraft, but I came down by parachute at a place near Adisham in Kent. They didn't find me until the next morning. It seems I was in a pretty bad way for a while.

'I largely recovered, though a wound to my left temple,' he instinctively touched the side of his head, 'severed the optic nerve on that side and left me blind in my left eye. It took me a while but I eventually found ways of working around my lack of three-dimensional vision and taught myself to fly again, mainly when I was meant to be running training schools and teaching others to fly. I will never again fly at night, when depth perception is just too difficult for me. I also avoid driving at night when I can.'

Bob thanked the waiter who had topped up his glass and took another drink. 'So that was the first part of my story, a cautionary tale the like of which I'm sure you've all heard many times before. Let me now move the clock forward. Thanks to a very odd chain of circumstances, late last year I was offered a post as the deputy head of Military Intelligence, Section 11, based in Edinburgh. Before the war, I'd been a policeman in Glasgow so, in some ways, you can see it as a return to my roots.

'Anyway, this brings me to the second part of my story. In March this year, a colleague and I were sent to Stockholm.'

'Was that the same beautiful colleague you were seen with at 3 Scots Street today, group captain?' asked someone, presumably one of the officers who had been accompanying Sir Keith Park earlier that day.

Cheers went up around the room.

'As it happens it was. And, as it happens, the two of us were married in Edinburgh last Saturday, so she's spoken for.'

There was more cheering.

Bob held up his hands for quiet. 'One day my colleague was out of the city and I was at a bit of a loose end so I took a taxi out to Bromma Airport, which is quite close to the city centre. I'd hoped to meet with the BOAC Mosquito pilot who'd flown us out to Sweden from Leuchars, who was an old colleague. Instead, I ended up chatting with the manager of the BOAC office there.

'While we were standing on the tarmac close to the passenger terminal, a Junkers Ju 52 landed and the passengers got off. It was a scheduled flight arriving from Berlin. The man I was talking to recognised the pilot and took me over and introduced me to him. His name was Oskar and he was a charming man. When he offered to show me around the Ju 52, I jumped at the chance.

'Afterwards, the three of us enjoyed some excellent coffee - a very scarce commodity in Sweden - in a first-floor café in the airport that offered views out over the aircraft parking area and runway.

'The discussion quickly moved on from how bad the coffee usually was in Stockholm and always was in Berlin to aircraft. It turned out that Oskar and I shared a love for single-seat fighters, though in my case that has been diluted since I started flying a Mosquito regularly. Oskar had a very pronounced limp and when he tapped his right leg it was obvious it was artificial. That's why he had moved from fighters to transport aircraft.

'At least, he told me, the RAF hadn't got him. He'd been flying his Messerschmitt Bf 109 over Kent at night from his base in northern France when he lost touch with his two wingmen. Then he happened upon a Hawker Hurricane on its own whose pilot had been unaware of him until he shot him down. Back at his airfield in France, he overturned his aircraft while landing, perhaps because his wheel hit a molehill in the dark. He lost his leg as a result.'

Bob took another drink and looked around the room. 'I can see that some of the more sober of you have worked out where this little story of mine is going. When I asked, Oskar told me that his accident had happened on the 1st of November 1940. It's almost certain that he was the man who shot me down and here we were, sharing coffee and stories in an airport café in Stockholm.'

'How did you react when you realised, sir?' shouted someone.

'How would you react?' asked Bob. 'He and I were doing the same job. It's just that on that particular night he did his a little better than I did mine. Neither of us had come out of the encounter very well. We agreed to meet after the war, assuming we both survive, so we can have a proper drink together.'

There was a round of applause and Bob raised his glass to the room before sitting down.

The wing commander was still clapping when he leaned in towards Bob. 'I told you that you'd be fine.'

Then Bob heard a sound he'd not heard for some time and would be happy never to hear again, the rising wail of the start of an air raid warning.

The group captain commanding RAF Ta Kali stood up and, to Bob's surprise, suggested that everyone top up their glasses and make their way up to the roof terrace.

Bob looked at the wing commander to his left. 'Did I hear that correctly?'

'You did, sir. It's highly unlikely to be a significant attack and the roof terrace here offers superb views over much of the island. Air raid watching is something of a spectator sport for those of us not on duty actually trying to intercept the attackers.'

Bob still had his doubts but followed everyone else up several flights of stairs to a large outside area on the roof of the palace. The terrace was crowded with officers from the dinner and in the last of the day's light, Bob could see that what he'd been told about the view was correct. The Xara Palace was hardly an imposing building from the outside, but when you added its height to the hill on which Mdina sat, the result was spectacular.

Bob found himself standing next to a flight lieutenant

wearing pilot's wings.

The man looked at him. 'We've already got Spitfires in the air from Ta Kali, sir. If you look in that direction you can see the airfield lights.' He pointed.

As Bob looked, he saw all the lights go out. He assumed they had everyone in the air they wanted in the air and were now ensuring they didn't make the location of the airfield too obvious to the attackers.

The flight lieutenant touched Bob's arm. 'If you look over that way, sir, you can see searchlights around Valletta' He pointed out over the plain below Mdina towards where Bob could see thin fingers of light pointing upwards in the gathering gloom. 'By the way, I very much enjoyed your story. I'd like to think I'd have reacted in the same way if that had happened to me.'

'Thank you for saying so,' said Bob. 'Can you tell me, is that a pair of Lewis guns on an anti-aircraft mount over at the end of the terrace?'

'That's right, sir.'

'Do they ever get used in anger?'

'Not while I've been here, sir, which is six months. But it's said that early last year a wing commander put down his gin and tonic for long enough to use those guns to shoot down a Messerschmitt Bf 109 that was strafing Mdina.'

A moment later Bob saw flashes coming from the direction of Valletta, followed a little later by the distant sound of anti-aircraft guns. He hoped Monique was safe but knew he'd not be able to travel across the island to be with her during an air raid.

Drinks were topped up but Bob had put his glass down and declined the offer of another.

The officers on the roof terrace milled around for a while,

waiting for something to happen. Then the airfield lights at Ta Kali came back on, making the airfield very obvious in a landscape that was now quite dark despite the light of the slightly more than half moon. When the all clear siren sounded a short time later, Bob looked at his watch and realised that though it was still early by most standards, he felt exhausted. He made his way downstairs. His seniority had earlier let him in for a speech. It was only fair that it should now give him the first call on any staff cars heading back to Valletta.

CHAPTER FOURTEEN

It sounded like more guns had begun firing as Monique followed Anne towards a doorway in a stone wall on the south side of the bus station. She'd probably have walked past it without noticing, except for the stream of people filing into it. Beyond the doorway was a set of steps leading downwards under electric lights attached to the arched stone ceiling. She was too busy watching where she was putting her feet to pay much attention to her surroundings but was aware of descending a further set of steps, at right angles to the first, before she emerged into an enormous space. She stopped and someone bumped into her from behind and cursed.

'Sorry,' she said, as she moved to one side.

'Come this way, Monique,' said Anne, turning to take her arm and leading her away from the entrance.

Monique became aware that they were in what felt like a section of the London Underground, only here everything was finished in stone rather than tiles and no adverts were being displayed. There was also a marked absence of rails. A broad, arched stone tunnel headed off in a straight line in both directions, perhaps for a hundred yards or more either way before it came to end walls. Illumination came from dim electric lights hanging at intervals from the shoulders of the arched roof.

There was enough light to see that most of the space was filled with very wide wooden bunk beds. There were three lines of double-height bunks extending along the length of the space, one in the centre and one set a little apart from it on either side. Two further lines of bunks along the walls were stacked three high. A lot of people were in the shelter, and more were coming in through several entrances, but it was far from crowded.

Anne walked to a relatively unoccupied area and sat on the mattress on a lower bunk, slightly hunched so her head didn't hit the one above it. Monique sat beside her.

'What is this place?' she asked.

'It's part of the Floriana railway tunnel,' said Anne. 'I can't give you much detail but, late in the last century, they built a railway from Valletta to Mdina. It closed at the beginning of the 1930s. Valletta station was built underground, beyond the City Gate from here and off to the right. The tracks then crossed the defensive ditch over a bridge that's still there, at a much lower level than the bridge carrying the road to the City Gate. Then the railway passed under parts of Floriana in a tunnel, and this is one section of it.

'Air raid shelters in Malta come in all shapes and sizes. A lot of them are like rabbit warrens and can get really claustrophobic. Many were dug officially, but then people could pay to dig out private areas for extra space and comfort, or just dig their own under their houses. Most rely on oil lamps or candles rather than electric lights as here. These railway tunnels form the biggest of the shelters and, as you can see, they can accommodate a huge number of people.'

'This brings back memories I'd prefer to leave buried, of nights spent on underground railway platforms during the Blitz in London,' said Monique. 'Do you think we are likely to have to be here for long?' She was beginning to wonder how Bob would feel if he returned to the hotel and found she was unaccounted for in an air raid.

'No, I don't. There was a time when I'd have given you a different answer, but the darkest days do seem to be well behind us. To give you an idea of what I mean, I saw some figures in 3 Scots Street quite recently that said that during the worst month, in April last year, over 6,700 tons of bombs were dropped on Malta. The document I saw compared that to around 18,000 tons of bombs dropped on Britain during the whole period of the Blitz from September 1940 to May 1941. Given how small Malta is in comparison, just 17 miles long by 9 miles wide, that gives you an idea of how badly we were hit. The same document said that in the first half of last year, the islands were attacked on 154 successive days and nights, often with many raids every day and every night. To look at that another way, there was only one 24-hour period during the whole of the first half of 1942 when there were no air raids on Malta.'

'Have many people been killed?' asked Monique.

'I sometimes think it would be better not to know, but the same document said that over 1,500 civilians had been killed by bombing in Malta and more than twice that many seriously injured, and that's from a civilian population of only 270,000.

'It didn't say so in the document, but I can tell you from personal experience that there were times when a large part of the population of Malta was effectively living in air raid shelters, day after day and night after night. Life has got a lot easier since then but just imagine what this place would be like with thousands of people down here, with entire families on every tier of every bunk.'

'It doesn't bear thinking about,' said Monique. 'Let's change the subject. Do you mind if I pick your brains about something else, Anne, something totally unconnected? Someone I was talking to mentioned a bar on Strait Street called Captain Bianchi's. Do you know anything about it?'

'Only by reputation, Monique. I've heard the place associated with the black market and prostitution. To put that into context, you could say the same of a good many other bars, music halls, restaurants and lodging houses on Strait Street. The street is the place in Valletta where the crews of visiting ships and other servicemen go for a good time and it's often referred to as "The Gut". It was badly damaged in parts by bombing, but I get the impression that its popularity never really waned and I believe it's seen a resurgence since the end of the siege. My dancing used to be done in rather more salubrious places and I've always made a point of avoiding most of Strait Street.'

'Thank you, that's helpful,' said Monique.

'It's difficult to tell down here, but I think the guns have stopped firing, which is a good sign,' said Anne. 'While we're here, is there anything else your personal guide to Malta can help you with?'

'One thing has been intriguing me. I like to think I'm good at picking up languages and can speak several. But I'm finding it hard to make much sense of it when I hear people speaking Maltese. I get the impression that just about everyone also speaks English here anyway, but I'm fascinated to know more about the Maltese language.'

'Yes, dancing your way around Europe is a good way of acquiring an ear for languages,' said Anne. 'I can't speak Maltese but after being here for so long I find I can pick up the meaning of quite a lot of what I hear around me. Someone told me once that Maltese is made up of a mix of about 30% of an old form of Arabic with 50% standard Italian and Sicilian. The remaining 20% comes from English and other sources. A complication to watch out for is that there are lots of words in English that can have two different Maltese equivalents, one from Arabic and one from Italian or Sicilian.'

'Thank you,' said Monique. 'I'm going to have to listen more carefully when I'm out and about.'

Anne lay back on the bunk and closed her eyes.

'Are you all right?' asked Monique.

'I'm just trying to convince myself that after the wine we drank I don't need to go to the toilet. They're a little less dreadful here than in most air raid shelters I've been in but, to be blunt, pissing into a smelly bucket with just a curtain for privacy isn't my idea of the best way to end a night out.'

Anne closed her eyes again. Monique watched her for a while, letting her thoughts drift over things she and Bob needed to do. She wondered how his evening was going.

'Thank God for that,' said Anne opening her eyes and sitting up. 'That's the all clear.'

It took Monique a moment to tune in to the muted sound of the sirens.

Anne looked around. 'I'll show you the best way out to get to the City Gate.' She picked up Monique's handbag from the mattress and held it out to her. Then she looked at it with a puzzled expression. 'This is very heavy, Monique. What do you keep in it?'

Monique watched Anne's face as realisation dawned.

'Ah, I see. A lipstick, a powder compact and a pistol. Essential companions for every girl on her night out in Malta.' Anne smiled and handed over Monique's handbag without further comment.

*

Bob's look of concern as he entered the drawing room of their suite was very touching. 'Are you all right, Monique?'

'I'm fine, thank you, Bob. I had an excellent dinner with Anne Milner and we drank some very nice red wine at Commodore Cunningham's expense. I then had what Anne called the "authentic Malta experience" when we were caught in an air raid while walking back and we ended up in a railway tunnel beneath Floriana that is used as a shelter.'

'I didn't know Malta has any railways,' said Bob.

'It doesn't, not any more.' said Monique, 'That's why they use the tunnel as a shelter. Anyway, I think we're perhaps getting away from the point.'

'You're right,' he said, walking over and giving Monique a deep hug and then a kiss, which she returned.

'I'm glad to see you, too, Bob.' She looked around the drawing room. 'Do you want to sit down? There's some white wine chilling in the ice bucket over there. I had plenty to drink over dinner but, after my air raid experience, I wouldn't say no to more. We don't need to open it if you don't want any.'

'No, I'll join you. I think I had too much to drink at the Xara Palace but worrying about you in the car on the way back had a sobering effect.' Monique saw Bob look around. 'Do you know if we can talk freely in here?'

'Yes, I think so,' said Monique. 'I've had time to give the suite, including the bedroom, a close look for microphones and am fairly confident that there are none. The corkscrew is over there. You open the bottle.'

Bob poured drinks and they sat on the two armchairs in the room.

'I think you may have more that's relevant than me to tell,' he said. 'Perhaps you should talk me through your evening in more detail?'

160

Monique did.

'So what do you make of her now you've had a chance to think things through a little?' asked Bob.

'I find the way she's obviously lying about James keeping some of his belongings at her flat hard to explain,' said Monique. 'As I told you, I did push quite hard, and more than once. At the end of the night, I thought she was going to relent but something was holding her back. There's some reason why she doesn't want me looking through his stuff.

'I also think she's lying about the weekend he disappeared. According to her, it was all sweetness and light on their Saturday trip to the beach that the 10th Submarine Flotilla frequent. Yet even from what she said there was something in the background about his reluctance to be seen there with her which she admitted to finding hurtful.

'Then we have Sub-Lieutenant Short's impression that Anne and James might have been arguing when he saw them on the beach that Saturday. I asked her about tensions between them and she denied there had been any. I'm also less than convinced by her account of the Sunday. As she tells it, he was with her all day at her flat until he left to return to Manoel Island late in the afternoon. It could be true, but that's the point really, her account means there are no witnesses one way or the other. Unless anyone saw him leave on the Sunday, we've only got her word for everything that happened after they got the bus back to Floriana on the Saturday. She didn't mention whether they ate out that evening and I'm afraid I didn't think to ask her. Now I think about it, it's more than that. We've only got her word for everything that happened over the entire weekend after they walked past Sub-Lieutenant Short on the beach.'

'Is there anything else that came out of your talk with her?'

asked Bob.

'Something has been nagging away at the back of my mind. It's very subtle, but I get the sense that if you take Sub Lieutenant Short's account of the time that James spends away from Manoel Island to be with Anne, it amounts to rather more than if you take Anne's account of the time that James actually spends with her.'

'What do you read into that?' asked Bob.

'I simply don't know,' said Monique. 'It could just be different perceptions or different ways of using language when talking about it. But what if James Ewing was spending some of his time away from Manoel Island somewhere other than with Anne at her flat? That would open up an entirely new set of questions we'd need answers to.'

'I think you've achieved a lot, Monique. Have you had any thoughts about Edward Price in light of Anne's comments about Captain Bianchi's?'

'She was open about only knowing the place by reputation, but what she said convinces me we need to be careful. I also got no sense that she knew of any connection between Captain Bianchi's and James Ewing, and those parts of our conversation were so separated that I'm sure she didn't think I was making any connection myself.'

'I must admit that I find parts of Edward Price's travel itinerary as worked out by Lawrence Dowson to be rather inexplicable,' said Bob.

'I agree,' said Monique. 'He seems to have questioned both the sub-lieutenant and Anne Milner fairly effectively. He then appears to have spent a fair bit of time visiting the places Anne mentioned to him that she had been to with James. I'm not sure I'd view it as a good use of our time if you suggested doing the same thing, Bob, though it might have given him a better idea of them as a couple.

'But he also visited other places that appear totally unconnected with either Anne or James. Why did he go to the fishing village or the archaeological site? And where does Captain Bianchi's fit into the picture? I just don't have any answers to those questions. Our glasses are empty, do you want some more wine?'

Bob nodded and Monique poured them both another drink.

'That's my evening accounted for,' said Monique. 'What about yours?'

'I achieved very little in comparison,' he said. He went on to tell Monique about his visit to Mdina.

Monique found the idea of Bob, after drinking too much wine and without any preparation, being trapped into giving a speech highly amusing. 'It sounds more like a bunch of schoolboys at an illicit midnight feast in their dorm than respectable military officers. Did they really cheer when you said we were married?'

'Call it high spirits or letting off steam. It's something of a tradition. Do you remember when we were at RAF Lossiemouth last November? I told you that the party we saw taking place in the officers' mess was likely to end with the mess piano being taken out through the French windows and set on fire. What happened tonight was similar, though in this case, the idea was to put a senior officer on the spot rather than burn a piano.'

'It sounds like you acquitted yourself well,' said Monique.

'I hope so. They seemed to appreciate it. What I found most bizarre about the evening was the way everyone wanted to watch the air raid from the roof. You were in an air raid shelter with the guns going off overhead while I was watching it from a distance with men who saw the whole thing as entertainment.'

'Have you any idea why Air Vice-Marshal Park wants to see you again in the morning, Bob?'

'No, none, and I am conscious that I can't let him eat into the time we are meant to be using to find our two missing men. As I said, though, he could be a useful ally in Malta. I also begin to think he's someone it would be best not to get on the wrong side of. I'm just sorry it leaves you a bit out on a limb again tomorrow morning.'

'That's not a problem, there are things I can usefully be doing while you are with him.'

'Hang on,' said Bob. 'You're not thinking of going to Captain Bianchi's on your own, are you? That would be a very bad idea.'

'No, I promise, Bob. Besides, I get the feeling it may not be the sort of place that's open on a Sunday morning.'

'As you said yourself, Monique, we need to be careful when we visit. We can give it more thought tomorrow. Adopting the personas of Mr and Mrs Cadman may be the solution, as you suggested earlier.'

'Look, Bob, I know there's still some wine left in the bottle, but it's been a very long day. Do you mind if we go to bed?'

*

'Are you sure you've properly trapped the edges of the mosquito net behind the blackout curtains, Bob?' asked Monique, in the dark of their bedroom. 'I'd prefer it if we don't get any more visitors in through the open window. You talked today about mosquito bites and I also got a few last night.'

'I'm hopeful that I've done a better job tonight.'

Bob kissed her in the dark and Monique put her hand on his shoulder. She could feel that he was lying on his side. She moved her hand down from his shoulder and across his stomach and then carried on down. 'Part of you doesn't seem to want to go to sleep just yet.'

'That's the effect of your hand, as you well know.'

'Whatever the cause, let's not let it go to waste.' She pushed Bob over onto his back and climbed astride him. 'I always sleep well after good sex so I'll probably not notice the mosquitos anyway,' she said.

CHAPTER FIFTEEN

Bob looked at his watch again. He was standing just inside the front door of the Osborne Hotel, waiting for the RAF staff car that had been due three minutes earlier at 10 a.m. When he thought back to what Sir Keith Park had said in the Xara Palace, the implication seemed to be that he would be in the car himself.

Bob again checked his watch. At least he and Monique had enjoyed a slightly more relaxed morning. Unlike the previous day, they'd not overslept. That had allowed time for baths and a leisurely breakfast. And it looked as if he'd done a better job of securing the mosquito net in front of the open window.

Monique had smiled but been a little evasive when he'd asked, as he had the previous night, about her plans for the morning. He knew her well enough to suspect that she intended to do something she thought he'd prefer only to know about afterwards. She'd again promised not to go anywhere near Captain Bianchi's, and he knew she wouldn't break her promise. He couldn't think what else she might have in mind and that left him feeling a little on edge. He just had to trust her judgement. They'd faced enough together for him to know that his trust in her was at least as justified as hers in him.

The sound of a car horn brought Bob back to the present and he went out onto South Street, stopping sharply as he reached the pavement. Outside, on his side of the street and pointing towards the heart of Valletta, was a bright red open-topped MG Roadster. Behind the driving wheel, with a field service side cap perched jauntily on the side of his head, was Air Vice-Marshal Park.

Bob saluted.

Instead of returning his salute, Sir Keith beckoned for Bob to get into the car. 'Come on Sutherland, we haven't got all day!'

Bob complied and Sir Keith pulled away. Bob looked around. The brown leather seats complemented the colour of the car beautifully, though those in the back didn't have a lot of legroom. The polished chrome windscreen surround was folded forward, giving Bob an uninterrupted view ahead.

And, although Sir Keith was only going at a sedate pace along the narrow street, the folded windscreen also caused Bob's peaked cap to shift backwards as the passing air got at it. He took the hat off and tossed it onto the back seat. Sir Keith's side hat behaved as if it had been glued in place.

'I was expecting a staff car, sir,' said Bob. 'This is lovely.'

'Thank you, Sutherland. We don't have access to many luxuries in Malta, so this is my pride and joy.'

From Bob's limited knowledge of the geography of Valletta, they appeared to be making their way towards its south-eastern side, the side adjacent to the Grand Harbour. They took a zig-zag route and it seemed to Bob that while some roads had been cleared of rubble to allow traffic to pass, others remained blocked. It also seemed to him that the original builders of the city had never had the motor car or the lorry in mind when they chose the width of their streets.

No sooner had that thought occurred to him than they turned a corner and slowed to a crawl behind a horse and carriage, which seemed no more suited to the streets than the motorised traffic.

Sir Keith glanced across at him. 'I thought the story you told last night was very good, Sutherland. If you only got married last week, then offering your wife a ride in a traditional horse-drawn Maltese cab, or carrozzi, might be a suitably romantic gesture. God alone knows how any of them are still in business. When I arrived on the islands everyone was so hungry I was surprised that all the horses hadn't been eaten.'

They turned into a side road, Bob assumed to get clear of the horse-drawn cab.

Sir Keith looked over at Bob. 'You haven't asked me where we're going.'

'I thought you'd tell me when you were ready to, sir.'

Sir Keith smiled, 'It's not much further now.'

They were now driving with the Grand Harbour on their left and the scale of devastation and partial subsequent clearance seemed to Bob to be even greater than it had in the heart of Valletta. Bob would have had difficulty retracing the route they then took, but Sir Keith turned right and passed under a raised barrier manned by army troops who waved him past and then, beyond a second checkpoint at which they were again not stopped, he drove through a short length of tunnel. At the far end of this, they emerged into what felt to Bob like the bottom of a canyon, with extremely high stone walls on both sides.

Sir Keith stopped the MG in a space that seemed intended for it, between an RAF staff car and a Bedford lorry.

Bob retrieved his peaked cap from the rear seat.

'Welcome to Lascaris, Sutherland,' said the air vice-marshal. What you see around you are parts of the formidable stone defences built at the south-west end of Valletta by the knights of the Order of Saint John. It's difficult to believe from down here, but on top of the bastion that rises high above us on our right are pleasure gardens offering magnificent views over the Grand Harbour and the Three Cities.'

'My wife and I visited them yesterday afternoon, sir,' said

Bob. 'I'd never have guessed that this was down here.'

'What comes next will be even more of a surprise. What I'm about to show you are the modern equivalents of the stone defences that so liberally adorn these islands. What you have to imagine is an extensive labyrinth of tunnels cut into the rock beneath the bastion. Some of the tunnels and underground rooms have been here for several years and can be thought of as essentially defensive in nature. Others have only very recently been excavated and are still being brought fully into use. They are wholly offensive in intent. Follow me.'

Park led Bob a short distance along the floor of the vast stone ditch, past more parked vehicles, and then turned right into the mouth of a tunnel that had been cut into the sharply apex curve of part of the bastion that rose above them.

Two sentries came to attention and Bob joined Sir Keith in saluting them. The lesson he was taking from the experience was that you didn't need a security pass if you were a well-known and popular air vice-marshal who drove what was probably - in Malta - a unique car.

Sir Keith paused to look at Bob. 'We've just entered a tunnel that, as you can see from the distant light at its far end, cuts right across the base of the bastion and emerges on the other side of it. This is primarily intended to give access to the most recent set of excavations down here, part of which I will show you presently. For the moment, assuming I can remember the twists and turns, we will use it to reach one of the more significant parts of the defensive complex.

'We take a left just along here, then climb these stairs. It's a bit of a pull because we're effectively changing levels within the heart of the bastion. Up at the top here is a sight I suspect you will be familiar with.'

Sir Keith led the way, past another sentry, into a large space that Bob recognised as an RAF sector operations room. There were perhaps half a dozen people in the room, men in RAF uniform and women in civilian clothes, and everything came to a sudden stop when the air vice-marshal entered.

'Carry on, please. This is an unofficial visit and I'm sorry to have come in via the tradesman's entrance.' He turned to Bob. 'This room is actually at the end of an underground complex that includes direction finding, filter and signalling rooms and the anti-aircraft operations room for Malta. It is usual to enter from the far end.'

Bob was looking around. They were standing on the lower floor of a double-height room. Much of the floor area was taken up by a table carrying a large rectangular map showing the whole of the island of Sicily and the tip of the toe of Italy. In the lower centre of the map were the Maltese islands. The map was covered in grid squares and there were racks in one corner carrying flags and markers. There were blackboards around the walls, some with maps and others with information about the RAF Air Sea Rescue service and the Royal Observer Corps. There was a gallery running around two sides of the room and partly along a third. Bob could see seats and telephones up there. Then there was a large board at the upper level of one end of the room showing squadron readiness for up to six squadrons.

'I imagine you've been in places like this before, Sutherland,' said Sir Keith.

'Yes, sir. Believe it or not, the last one I visited was near Kirkwall in Orkney, last November. It wasn't quite a twin of this one, but they are both intended for the same purpose, to protect islands that are vulnerable to air attack by a determined enemy.'

'I imagine that Malta in June is more pleasant than Orkney in November,' said Sir Keith.

'I'm getting used to the heat here, sir, and there isn't much daylight in Orkney in winter.'

'I thought I'd show you this to start your tour with something familiar. Incidentally, I didn't see you after everyone went up to the roof to watch the show last night. Did you hear the final score?'

'No, sir.'

'The alarm went up because we detected two aircraft on radar. They turned out to be Junkers Ju 88s, coming in at very low level from the east. Because of their altitude and because they'd come a long way around, we detected them later than usual. Our best guess is that they wanted to take a look at what we've got in the harbours on either side of Valletta in the last of the daylight because they split up as they approached. One was destroyed by anti-aircraft guns over the Grand Harbour while the second was caught and shot down by a Spitfire from RAF Ta Kali over Gozo as it headed north for home. Anyway, now I want to show you why you're here. We need to reverse our course back down to the tunnel we entered by.'

Sir Keith led Bob back down to the tunnel and then into a suite of underground rooms off to the other side of it. Security appeared, if anything, even tighter here. Again, though, it seemed that Sir Keith could go where he pleased without question.

He stopped outside an unoccupied office that Bob could see through the door had a large map of the Mediterranean on the wall, and then entered. Bob followed.

Sir Keith waved his hand towards the map. 'I've told you

that this new complex has been excavated to carry forward the next stage of the war, Sutherland. If you were in charge of Allied forces in the Mediterranean, what would you do?'

'There's an obvious answer to that question, sir,' said Bob. 'It's so obvious that I'm beginning to wonder whether it's right. We've kicked the Germans and Italians out of North Africa. Our eventual aim has to be to capture Berlin. You're asking about the best next step on the way to achieving that. I know nothing about Axis troop deployments but it seems to me that we have no choice but to take on Sicily next. That's a view that's supported by parts of the harbours around Valletta being packed with landing craft and what a navy driver described to me as tented towns being established in Malta for invasion troops.' Bob pointed at the map. 'If an attack is going to be launched from here, then where could it go other than Sicily?'

'That's all very reasonable, Sutherland. But what would you do if you were Hitler and your intelligence people had come up with subtle but extremely convincing intelligence suggesting that the build-up happening in Malta is all part of an elaborate deception intended to conceal our real intentions, which are to attack both Sardinia and Greece?'

'Thankfully I'm not Hitler, sir.'

'No, indeed. Thanks to some very clever people in your line of work, Hitler is in possession of just that sort of intelligence. His response appears to be to hedge his bets. Sicily is certainly very strongly defended, but they haven't depleted the Axis forces in Sardinia and Greece to bolster Sicily's defences. Now I'd like you to follow me.'

Sir Keith led Bob along a corridor and into another very large room, this time at the upper level, and came to a halt on a balcony. There were more people here than there had been in the sector operations room and Bob realised they were wearing both British and American uniforms. Mostly, though, his attention was taken by an enormous map of Sicily and the sea to its south as far as Malta and beyond, that occupied one entire wall. A young man in khaki shorts and shirt was at the top of a tall ladder set at right angles to the map and apparently intended to run backwards and forwards along the wall on runners set into the floor and on rails beneath the ceiling, giving complete access to the surface of the map. Another young man was on the ground and looking up. From the conversation going on between them, it seemed that one of the runners at the top had jammed.

There was a large desk at the lower level of the room, while opposite the map at the same upper level as the balcony was a suite of rooms with windows looking out over the lower level area to the map. Most of the men Bob could see - and unlike in the sector operations room they were all men - were working in these rooms.

'So much for Sardinia and Greece,' Bob said.

'As you say, Sutherland. But every Axis military unit that stays in Sardinia or Greece and isn't transferred to Sicily is one less unit to oppose our forces when they arrive there. The deception may not be effective for much longer. After a few days of intensive aerial bombing and naval bombardment, we launched Operation Corkscrew on Friday, amphibious landings to capture the heavily fortified Italian island of Pantelleria. That's the blob you can see on the big map south of the western tip of Sicily and east of Tunisia.

'When the first troops landed they found the garrison of up to 15,000 men had already decided to surrender. We are now cementing our grip on the island and that will give us an ideal second launch pad for the invasion of Sicily. It's smaller than Malta but is about the same distance south of Sicily's western tip as we are from its southern tip. Hitler has to realise that Sicily is the real target, but the longer it takes him to react to that realisation, the better it is from our point of view.'

'This is hugely impressive, sir,' said Bob. 'But why are you wasting your Sunday morning showing the sights to a group captain in military intelligence who won't even give you an honest account of why he's in Malta?'

Sir Keith smiled. 'Follow me, Sutherland. The office I've been assigned is just along the corridor.'

It didn't take long to arrive in a room that was empty of furniture. There was, however, a large map of the Maltese islands on one wall.

'As you can see,' said Sir Keith, 'I've not taken up residence yet. However, this map will allow me to answer your question. If you go back to the first air attacks on Malta we had to rely for defence on a tiny number of obsolete biplanes that had been found in packing cases on a dockside. They were borrowed from the Royal Navy and reassembled and did well in the appalling circumstances they faced. The Gloster Gladiators were soon replaced by Hurricanes and eventually by Spitfires, but we never had enough. We suffered losses in the air and our airfields were attacked mercilessly, leading to significant losses of aircraft on the ground too.

'Eventually, we turned the tide. However, I now have another problem. The plans are for over thirty squadrons of aircraft to operate from Malta during the invasion of Sicily, most of them fighter squadrons. In the main, we have until now operated from three airfields, at RAF Luqa in the centre of the island, at RAF Ta Kali to the north of the centre, which you saw in operation last night, and at RAF Hal Far near the south coast.' He indicated each in turn on the map with his right hand. 'We then have two seaplane bases, at RAF Kalafrana in the south, and at St Pauls in the north. We also have a diversion airfield at RAF Krendi in the south-west and a maintenance base at RAF Safi, not far from Luqa.

'You've seen the state of Valletta so it won't surprise you to hear that our airfields emerged from the worst of the bombing with more craters than the Moon. Since January I have been deploying every pair of hands I can find to help bring the runways of this mixed bag of badly bombed and not-really-suitable airfields up to a state that will allow the intensive operation of over 600 fighters during the invasion. I also need to accommodate their air and ground crews and have suitable fuel and weapons dumps, operations rooms, power stations, workshops and so on and so on. On Thursday I was on the island of Gozo looking at a completely new airfield being built by American engineers and Gozitan labourers. They have almost finished the first runway in under three weeks, starting from scratch, and they are now also building a second.'

'The key part of all of that was when I referred to "every pair of hands I can find". I'm told there's a fine tradition in the RAF in Malta of simply co-opting suitable men on their way to Egypt to take part in the defence of the islands. Those days are behind us, but the reason why I'm spending my Sunday morning telling you all this is that I badly need a good senior officer to help me get all this ready. I've been asking London for someone for weeks and getting nowhere. You, however, are here and as far as I can tell have enough of the skills I need to do the job.'

Bob started to speak.

'No, hang on Sutherland. I'm sure you are about to tell me that you have left the Royal Air Force behind you and now see your career in intelligence. If you are certain that is the case, then good luck to you. But are you? You fitted in very well with the officers of RAF Ta Kali last night and I wasn't the only one impressed by the story you told and the way you told it. Are you really ready to turn your back on all that for good? I know from what you said that you will never fly operationally again but what I'm offering you is a way back into the service that will allow you to make a real difference.'

'Thank you, sir…'

'Before you get to the "but" in that sentence, can I just ask you to take 36 hours to think about it? If I don't hear from you by tomorrow evening then I will find some other way of plugging the holes in my staff and I won't think any the worse of you.'

'Very well, sir. Thank you. I'll think about what you've said.'

'No, thank you for hearing me out. I'll get someone to run you back to your hotel.'

CHAPTER SIXTEEN

Monique waited until ten minutes after Bob should have been collected from outside the hotel, then went down the stairs to the entrance hall. The reception desk was empty, so she opened the main door of the hotel and looked out into South Street to make sure Bob had gone.

Then she went back up to their room. It took fifteen minutes for Madame Monique Dubois to transform herself into Mrs Monique Cadman, though without the faux wedding ring that she'd have worn if she and Bob had been working together. It was only the second time she'd put on her new blonde wig, and the first time she'd been in a hurry in Gibraltar so hadn't had much of a chance to look at it. She decided it probably wasn't quite as good - or as expensive - as the one she'd singed in a car fire in Stockholm, but she thought it must still have made quite an impact on Commodore Cunningham's budget. It certainly still made her look a little like Ingrid Bergman.

Monique rummaged through her suitcase and pulled out a red and white floral dress that was about as far from what she'd normally wear as it was possible to imagine. She finished off the look with a pair of sunglasses she'd found in the case. Commodore Cunningham's secretary seemed to have thought of everything when preparing a warm-weather wardrobe for Monique. She'd never normally wear sunglasses, but with bright red lipstick that matched the dress they were a perfect way of completing her change of identity. She considered adding a straw sunhat she found beneath other clothing in the suitcase but it hadn't travelled well. She straightened it out and put it on top of the wardrobe in the bedroom, hoping it would recover from its crushing.

Then Monique went back down the stairs, lighting a cigarette as she reached the entrance hall. The man behind the reception desk was talking to two army officers and although the officers broke off the conversation to look at her as she walked past, the receptionist said nothing to the unknown woman leaving his hotel.

Monique smiled at the two officers and said, in her best English accent, 'Good morning. It looks like it's another lovely day.' She thought the accent sounded all right, even if the content was uninspired, so decided to stick with it. It would get better as she got her ear in if she had to do much talking.

Monique turned left outside the hotel and walked along South Street towards Kingsway. There were lots of people about, many of them men in uniform, but she felt strangely detached from what was going on around her.

She had no problem finding her way back to the street in Floriana where Anne lived. She stood on a street corner a little distance away for ten minutes, looking to see if there was any obvious movement behind any of the windows.

From this distance, it appeared that the street door leading to the hall at the bottom of the communal stairs wasn't properly closed. Monique would have had no problem picking the lock but she wasn't about to look a gift horse in the mouth. Once inside, she quietly closed the door behind her. If someone had left the building without a key, they were going to have a problem getting back in.

She slipped off her shoes and, carrying them in one hand, silently climbed the stone steps in her bare feet. On the top landing, she put on a pair of rubber gloves and paused to hear if there was any noise coming from either of the flats, then put her ear to Anne's front door. Anne had told her that she was going to be at work this morning, but then Anne had lied to her about other things. Why not that too?

Monique couldn't hear anything so put her shoes back on and then picked the lock. Once inside, she first checked there was no one in the flat, opening each of the doors cautiously with her left hand while carrying her pistol in her right. Then she put her pistol back in her handbag and started to take a much closer look.

Anne had described her kitchen as tiny and she'd been right. The only means of cooking appeared to be a small kerosene stove with a single burner placed on a worktop. Monique opened each of the four cupboards and three drawers in turn. There were a couple of pans in one of the cupboards, but they didn't look as if they'd seen much recent use, unlike the kettle standing next to the stove, whose base was covered in soot.

She moved on to the bathroom, which was only large enough for a small bath, a sink and a toilet. All were spotlessly clean. The oddity was the absence of any of James's belongings. Anne had said that although he kept nothing else at the flat, he did keep a toothbrush and shaving kit here. Monique had broken in mainly because she was certain James would have kept other belongings at the flat and she wanted a chance to look at them. She wasn't sure what to make of failing to find even the items Anne had admitted were here.

The bedroom was also spotless, though perhaps no more so than it had been the previous evening. Monique went slowly through the chest of drawers, careful not to leave any sign that she had been there. There were two full-width drawers, with two half-width drawers in a single row above them. The two full-width drawers and one of the half-width drawers were full of Anne's clothing. The other half-width drawer was empty. The wardrobe was three-quarters full of Anne's hanging clothes, but there was a gap at the left-hand end, as if something had been removed. Most of the floor of the wardrobe was covered in women's shoes, piled more than one deep at the right-hand end. But, again, there was a bare area where it looked like a couple of pairs of shoes had been removed from the left-hand end without there having been time for those remaining to migrate across and fill the available space.

On top of the wardrobe was a large leather suitcase. She went through to the flat's main room and picked up one of two dining chairs flanking a folding table. She made a mental note of exactly where it had been standing to ensure she could correctly replace it afterwards. Then she took it into the bedroom, placed it against the wardrobe and stood on it. The room may have been spotless, but the top of the wardrobe was less so. There was a thin layer of dust on the uncovered wood and the large suitcase. Then Monique saw what she was looking for. An area of the large suitcase was less dusty than the rest, suggesting that there had been a small suitcase stacked on top of it. Monique got down and returned the dining chair to its correct location in the main room.

Before ticking the bedroom off her list, Monique went to look at the framed photographs she'd seen on the chest of drawers the previous evening. They were still all there. One showed Anne Milner and James Ewing standing close together and smiling, with what appeared to be a vista of the Grand Harbour behind them. Another two were of Anne in different dancing costumes. The remaining three were of Anne with an older couple, presumably her parents, and of each of her parents individually. Monique looked around. With stone floors, there were no floorboards to hide things under. There was a decorative jewellery box she'd not noticed the previous evening behind the photographs. She opened the lid carefully, ensuring that the little ballerina didn't pop up to make the box play its tune. The contents seemed unexceptional. Anne liked her jewellery, certainly, but there was nothing here that was out of the ordinary.

Monique returned to the main room. It was pleasant, clean and small and gave the impression the resident spent most of her time out of the flat. Two more walls were covered in oriental carpets used as wall hangings and there was a battered old sofa and matching armchair. The only other piece of furniture was a sideboard. One end of this opened to reveal a drinks cabinet with two bottles of whisky and one of rum, all partly full, and a metal tray on which there were four crystal whisky glasses.

The rest of the sideboard was unhelpful, with a few novels on one shelf and some board games on another. A draw at the top held writing paper, envelopes and a pen. Monique looked at the surface of the topmost piece of paper. She couldn't see any indentations but folded it anyway and put it in her handbag. Also in the drawer was a roll of sticky tape. Like most windows she had seen in Malta, those in Anne's flat had criss-cross tape to minimise blast damage.

There was a radio on top of the sideboard. Everyone had radios. What was odd was that it was well forward of the wall. When Monique moved it to one side she found a crystal glass decanter behind it. This had clearly formed part of a set with the four glasses. The problem was that the decanter had been badly damaged. It had been smashed into multiple pieces and someone, presumably Anne, had roughly fitted the main pieces back together with the window tape. This just about held the object in shape, but gaps between the pieces meant it was never going to hold liquid again.

Monique moved everything back to the way she'd found it and went out into the hall to stand by the front door. She knew she was only going to have one chance to do this and something was worrying her. She had a sense she'd half-glimpsed something she'd instantly overlooked, but couldn't think what. Then she remembered.

She went back into the bathroom and pulled out from its semi-concealment under the end of the bath a round wicker laundry basket with a lid. It felt as if it had clothes in it. Monique knew she was going to have to be extremely careful. Nobody remembers how the clothes in their laundry basket have been piled, but what if Anne did?

Monique carried the basket out into the hall and opened the lid, finding it a little more than half full. She took out a handful of what seemed to be the underwear Anne had been wearing the previous evening and placed it in a small pile on the floor.

Beneath that were two dresses, neither of which were Anne's office dress or the blue floral dress she had worn the previous evening. Monique realised she'd seen that hanging in the wardrobe. Then there was more underwear, which she placed in a separate pile on the floor. She wasn't sure what was in the bottom of the basket, but it felt like a heavier lump. Tugging gently, she realised it was a dark blue towel with a light blue decorative band across each end, and then a second identical towel, beneath which was a red bathing costume and then a pair of black bathing trunks.

Monique took a step back and thought about the timings. Anne was clearly quite a fastidious woman and Malta was warm enough to cause anyone to sweat. Most of the contents of the laundry basket probably came from what she'd worn during the last week or less. The towels and bathing wear were so dry they must have been left to air before going into the basket, but why were they still there after a fortnight? It suggested Anne had washed other clothes in the meantime while leaving the towels and swimsuits in the basket. Monique had no way of knowing how Anne did her laundry, but this seemed odd.

Monique picked up the towels and swimwear to replace them at the bottom of the basket, but then noticed a dark stain across the light blue band at one end of the bottom towel. When she looked more closely she realised that the stain was larger than it first appeared and extended across a significant part of the dark blue area of the towel. It looked like blood.

She left everything where it was on the hall floor and went into the kitchen. There had been two small sharp knives in one of the drawers, with a selection of cutlery. She found herself looking quite carefully at them for signs of blood before choosing the one that appeared least blunt and replacing the other in the drawer. She took the knife out into the hall and used it to remove, much more roughly than she would have liked, a small part of the bloodstained end of the towel. She put this in her handbag and hoped that if Anne noticed the damage, she'd conclude the towel had been caught and ripped on a piece of barbed wire on the beach.

Monique checked the knife was unmarked and took it back to the kitchen, then returned everything to the laundry basket. She took a last look around the flat to make sure she'd not missed anything or left anything out of place, and then she left.

No one answered when she knocked on the door of the neighbour on the opposite side of the top floor landing, or on the door of the flat below that one.

Then she had a little more luck. Anne's downstairs neighbour was a charming middle-aged Maltese lady who invited Monique in when she said she was a friend of Anne's who'd found she wasn't at home when she called round to see her.

The lady thought Anne was lovely but didn't see a lot of her. When Monique asked if she had been at home two weekends earlier, the woman said that she would have been out helping in her husband's bakery, which was just around the corner, on the Saturday. On Sundays, she cleaned their home while he cleaned the bakery. She couldn't remember seeing Anne at all over the weekend Monique was interested in, but her hearing wasn't as good as it used to be and with stone floors, the flats were quite well insulated. She usually didn't hear people coming and going on the stairs.

The lady had just closed the door of her flat, leaving Monique standing outside and wondering what to do next, when a dark-haired woman in her early thirties and wearing a pleated yellow dress came up the stairs. She was carrying a shopping bag.

'Hello, can I help you?' the woman asked.

Monique was grateful that she'd had a chance to practice her English accent on the Maltese lady because she realised that this was someone who would see through it in no time if she didn't get it right.

'Hello, I was just asking the lady who lives here if she knew when Anne Milner is likely to be back. I was hoping to talk to Anne but she doesn't appear to be in.'

'Are you a friend of hers?'

'No, it's to do with work.'

There was a pause while the woman looked at her. 'My name's Jane Brookes. I live on the opposite side of the top floor landing to Anne. Would you like a cup of tea?'

Monique smiled. 'That would be very nice. My name's Monique.'

Jane's flat seemed larger than Anne's, though Monique only got a brief impression as she was led into the kitchen. Jane's kerosene stove had two burners and she put one of them to immediate use, heating a kettle of water.

Jane gestured towards one of a pair of wooden chairs flanking a folding table. 'Do sit down. Do you mind my asking why you're looking for Anne?'

'Are you a friend of hers?' asked Monique.

Jane laughed. 'I'll be honest with you. We don't get along very well at all.'

'Why don't you like her?'

'My husband Daniel is a major in an anti-aircraft artillery unit. He's based at St Andrew's Barracks, a little up the coast. We've been in Malta during most of the siege but only moved here at the beginning of this year after the army accommodation we were living in was badly damaged in an air raid. They tried to get me to return to Britain in 1941 but we decided to stick it out together.' She paused. 'A consequence I didn't expect was losing our baby daughter Josephine early last year when she might have survived if supplies of medicine and food had been better.'

'I'm sorry,' said Monique, slightly shocked at Jane's readiness to bare her soul to a stranger.

'So am I,' said Jane. 'It's not really a consolation but we weren't alone. They say that a third of the babies born in Malta last year didn't survive.'

There was a silence for a moment, and then Jane spoke again. 'I was telling you about Anne Milner. To put it bluntly, I'm sick of the way she flirts with my husband whenever she sees him. When he told me about it at first I thought he was exaggerating, but I've seen it myself. It makes me angry and it also makes me feel vulnerable because she's younger than me and so attractive. I've spoken to her about it but it's made no difference.'

'I know that Anne has been close to a naval officer, James Ewing,' said Monique. 'Have you seen much of him?'

'I have met him a few times. He has been a fairly regular visitor since we moved in.

'When did you last meet James?' asked Monique.

'Can you tell me why you're so interested?' asked Jane.

Monique wondered how open she should be. 'Can I have your word that you won't mention my visit to Anne?'

'Yes, of course.'

'I'm with military intelligence and we're trying to work out what's become of James Ewing. He's disappeared.'

'Can you prove who you are?'

Monique showed Jane her MI11 pass.

'That's not you.'

'I wanted to ensure that if any neighbours, like the lady downstairs, talk to Anne about me they'll talk about a blonde woman in a red and white dress. Without this wig, my hair is as it appears in the photograph shown on my pass and I don't usually dress this brightly.'

'When did James disappear?' asked Jane.

Monique thought it odd that the woman looked down at the table when she asked the question.

'A fortnight ago. He spent the weekend with Anne and she

says that after spending the Saturday at a beach on the north-west of the island and a quiet Sunday here he left late that afternoon to return to Manoel Island. Only he didn't arrive back on Manoel Island and failed to report for duty the next morning. No one I've spoken to has seen him since.'

'I may be able to help,' said Jane. 'Daniel and I left the flat at about 5 p.m. on the Saturday you're talking about. Being fairly senior, he'd got a staff car arranged to take us to a dance at St Andrew's Barracks that evening. They tend to hold events quite early in the evening to give time for everyone to get home before the curfew.

'As we were going down the last flight of stairs, Anne and James came in the main door and we passed them in the hall. Then Daniel remembered that he'd left his glasses in the flat and as he was giving a speech he needed them. I suggested that he ensured the car didn't go without us while I returned to the flat.'

'When I came back in, Anne and James were having a huge row at the top of the stairs and the noise came right down to me. She was screaming at him that he couldn't leave her and he was trying to placate her. Then he started shouting too. Then they went into the flat and I came up the stairs to get Daniel's glasses.

'When I left the flat, I heard a smash and a bang, as if something large and heavy had broken. The flats are quite well insulated for sound, so that was a real surprise. I went and knocked on the door, but there was no reply. I was concerned about Daniel waiting with the car out in the street, so I left.'

'Have you seen James since?' asked Monique.

'No, I haven't,' said Jane.

Monique felt her heart sink. Why did everyone lie to her

about James? Jane's account had been believable until that moment, but there was something she'd decided to hold back.

'I did see Anne a couple of days later and I asked if everything was all right,' said Jane. 'She said it was. When I asked about James, she said he was fine. I couldn't ask more without giving the impression I'd been eavesdropping on them.'

'No, I understand completely,' said Monique.

'You won't tell Anne I've talked to you about her, will you, Monique?'

'No, of course not. And I'd again ask that you keep quiet about me being here today.'

'You have my word, Monique,' said Jane.

'Thank you, Jane. If you think of anything else I can be reached at the Osborne Hotel.'

CHAPTER SEVENTEEN

Bob was relieved to hear a key in the door and stood up from the drawing room armchair he'd been sitting in.

He was taken aback when a blonde woman in a red and white floral dress, sunglasses, and garish red lipstick walked into the room. Then he laughed.

Monique took off the sunglasses and smiled back. 'Hello Bob, how was your morning?'

'I didn't know you could do an English accent!'

'I have to admit that I wasn't sure myself. After a little practice, it seemed to go all right. I've been wondering if I should give a Scottish accent a try the next time I'm playing Monique Cadman.'

'Where have you been? I'm trying not to play the part of the anxious husband and say I've been worried about you, but I have been.'

Monique smiled. 'I've not been to Captain Bianchi's if that's what you're wondering. You're going to have to wait to hear where I have been until I get this ghastly lipstick off and the wig, which is a bit warm for comfort in Malta's climate.'

She went through to the bedroom.

'Do you want any help?' asked Bob, standing in the doorway between the rooms.

'The wig is too hot for you to imagine that I'm going to let you go to bed with a blonde. Besides, we've got things we need to discuss.'

'That sounds very serious,' said Bob.

'It is.'

'All right, I'll wait for you in the drawing room.'

It only took ten minutes for Monique Cadman to turn back into Monique Dubois, though from the way she kept touching and moving her hair, it was obvious to Bob that she wasn't happy with the way it felt after a morning under the wig.

Bob was sitting in one of the armchairs. Monique sat down in the other.

'Right,' she said, 'I've got a story to tell you. I fear that, unlike the story you told in Mdina last night, this one may not have a happy ending.'

Monique went on to give Bob a detailed account of everything she'd done that morning.

'Wow,' he said. 'I'm at a bit of a loss to know where to start. You've had longer to think things through. What do you make of it?'

'I should start by thanking you for refraining from immediately pointing out that my breaking into Anne's flat weakens any case that might eventually be brought against her. I simply couldn't see any other way of making progress that wouldn't involve lots of bureaucracy and lots of time.'

'Did you think I'd stop you if you'd told me what you were going to do?'

'I just thought that was a conversation it was better not to have. This way you can say you knew nothing about it in advance if you need to.'

'That won't happen. I agree with what you did, for the reason you just gave.'

'Thank you. Bob. The most urgent thing we need to do is get the piece of towel tested to find out if the stain is blood, and if so whether it's the same type of blood as Lieutenant Ewing's. The navy must have a record of his blood type on his file. I hope Lawrence Dowson can help us there. I also want to get a pencil and rub it over the surface of the writing paper I took, to see if there are any impressions from the sheet above it.

'Then it's a question of working through the rest of what I found. I'm at a complete loss to explain why Anne would have said that James kept some of his toiletries at the flat when they were no longer there. Then there's the fact that he obviously did keep other stuff at her flat, despite her denials. There is no other way to explain the empty drawer I found and the gap at the end of the hanging rail.'

'Perhaps she panicked last night after the two of you had talked and decided to clear all James's stuff out of the flat,' said Bob. 'In her rush, she simply forgot she'd told you that he did keep some things there, and put them into the small suitcase too.'

'I don't think so,' said Monique. 'I may not have dwelled on this just now, but my impression was that although the patch in the dust on the large suitcase suggested that a small suitcase had been removed from the top of it, there was still some dust in the relatively clear area, a lighter layer. Someone has probably done a scientific study into the rate at which dust accumulates in different circumstances, but my guess is that the small suitcase was removed a little while back. Perhaps even as far as two weeks back. But it is only a guess.'

'That implies that you think that James Ewing's belongings all disappeared from the flat at about the same time he did,' said Bob. 'That still doesn't explain Anne's lie to you about his shaving kit and toothbrush. But putting that to one side, the really important question seems to be whether James chose to leave and took his belongings with him, which the neighbour's recollection of the argument on the stairs might support, or whether something happened to James and then Anne removed his belongings in his suitcase. The smashed decanter and the bang the neighbour heard, which may well have been the sound of the decanter smashing, suggest that there was some level of violence involved. And that's without what we think may be a lot of his blood on a towel.'

'If we put the niceties of language to one side, Bob, what we're asking ourselves is whether Anne murdered James on the Saturday evening after they got back to her flat, then disposed of both his body and his belongings.'

'That's right,' said Bob. 'You've had a lot more than I have to do with her. Do you see her as a murderer?'

'I don't know. I've seen the most unexpected people do the most dreadful things. Being very beautiful doesn't necessarily make her a good person. On the other hand, I'm struggling to understand how, if she did kill James in her flat, she could then have disposed of his body. We know he's taller than her. We also know that Anne is still very thin and while she must have muscles to be able to function, they are hardly obvious when you look at her without her clothes on. I simply can't imagine her dragging James's body down all the stairs from her flat to the street. And then what would she do with him? She's got no way of transporting a body.'

'What about a hypothetical new boyfriend with a means of transport and perhaps a pass to be out and about during the curfew?' asked Bob. 'He could be one of the very many men in uniform on the island who I am sure would fall under Anne's spell if she so much as smiled at them. This same person could also have helped her move the body down the stairs later that night. It might even be the major who lives in the flat opposite, whose wife dislikes Anne so much. You did say you thought that she was holding something back from you.'

'I think that whatever happened did so in anger and shortly after they returned to the flat on the Saturday,' said Monique. 'It's a shame I didn't think to take a piece of the crystal decanter to have that tested for blood. In any case, I doubt that would have been possible without causing the rest of it to collapse.'

'Until we get that piece of towel tested, it's all speculation anyway,' said Bob. 'There are some envelopes with the hotel's name and address on the side over there. How would you feel about putting the piece of towel in one of them? I could then take it over to 3 Scots Street and telephone Lawrence Dowson and ask him to get someone to pick it up and then get it tested. Meanwhile, you can do your pencil rubbing of the paper you found and when I get back we can have some lunch and decide what we need to do this afternoon.'

'Remember Anne Milner is working in 3 Scots Street today and knows you by sight, Bob. You might need to be a little discreet.'

Bob smiled. 'I promise to try to refrain from shouting about a bloodstained towel while talking to Lawrence on the receptionist's telephone within hearing of anyone entering or leaving the building.'

'Sorry, Bob, I know you didn't need me to tell you that. Lunch sounds good. Hang on, you didn't say why Air Vice-Marshal Park wanted to see you this morning.'

'I can give you the full story over lunch. He offered me a job.'

'What!'

'Don't worry, Monique, I'm not going to take it. I'll tell you more when I get back.'

CHAPTER EIGHTEEN

How does the lightweight suit feel, Bob?' asked Monique. 'I didn't get a chance to ask in Gibraltar.'

They'd turned left on leaving the hotel and were walking towards Kingsway.

'I wore the other one there, but the fit of both is perfect, even around the shoulder holster. I could get used to having my own tailor who makes bespoke uniforms and suits at short notice and always gets them exactly right. I doubt if we could afford him if Maurice Cunningham wasn't paying.'

'You look even more attractive in that than you did in the tropical service uniform,' said Monique. 'I would again question whether it was a good idea for you to wear Edward Price's spare MCC tie. The idea of your assuming Robert Cadman's identity and wearing his civilian clothes was to avoid drawing attention to yourself. The tie undermines that.'

Bob knew that she was right. 'That's true. I just think that it gives me a connection with the man we're looking for. Asking "Did you see a tall man wearing a tie like mine?" seems a good starting point.'

'Does the Marylebone Cricket Club allow non-members to wear its ties?' asked Monoque, smiling.

'I very much doubt it but, as MI5's man in Gibraltar said, there's a war on. I must admit that I'm disappointed not to be enjoying the sights of Valletta with a blonde this afternoon.'

'You'll have to make do with the brunette you married eight days ago. It was your uniform that might have attracted unwanted notice and attention. I feel I stand out less like this than I do as a blonde. Besides, it's too hot for comfort this afternoon, even without that wig. At least Mrs Cadman's sunhat has recovered enough of its shape to be used for its intended purpose and her sunglasses do help cut down the glare.'

'And after your exploits this morning you don't mind shifting our focus away from James Ewing to Edward Price?' asked Bob.

'We don't have much choice, do we?' asked Monique. 'With the 10th Submarine Flotilla's medical officer on weekend leave, Lawrence can't get the piece of towel tested until tomorrow morning and it seems best not to involve anyone else. And if I was hoping for evidence of a farewell note or something helpful from the top sheet of the writing pad I was disappointed. We can decide what to do about Anne Milner when we know if it is blood on the towel and how likely it is that it belongs to James Ewing.'

Kingsway was busy with people and traffic and, for the first time, when they reached it they turned left to head towards the end of the peninsula on which Valletta stood.

As far as the busy pavement permitted, Bob linked his arm with Monique's while she kept track of their progress on the map she'd been given by the hotel receptionist.

'This is Palace Square we're coming into,' she said. 'It's easily the largest open space we've seen within the city itself.' Bob was surprised when she came to a halt and turned towards him. 'Before we go any further, I want to ask you again if you are absolutely sure that turning down Air Vice-Marshal Park's job offer is really what you want to do. I'm worried you're doing it simply for my sake and it might turn out to be the wrong decision for your career.'

Bob looked around to see if anyone was within earshot. 'I told you over lunch why he's offering me the job, including the highly sensitive part about what's going to happen next in the war in this part of the world. I honestly don't believe that accepting his offer would be in the interests of my career. I've no idea how long the job would last, though possibly not for long. And then what? I'd have burned my bridges with MI11 with no guarantee of anything afterwards. Remember, too, that my promotion to group captain is technically temporary and will only be made substantive after a year in my current post, which won't be until October.

'I also got the sense that Sir Keith would have jumped at almost any stray senior officer who crossed his path, and part of me has genuine doubts about whether I'd be particularly good in the role he has in mind. Administration has never been my greatest strength. Those are both important factors in my decision too.'

'But it may be your last chance to find a significant role back within the RAF,' said Monique. 'Are you really happy to let it pass you by?'

'Yes, I am Monique. I enjoyed my time with the officers of RAF Ta Kali last night but I've moved on from that world and I don't want to go back. I see my future doing what I do now in MI11.' He paused, thinking about how to phrase what he wanted to say next. 'There is another reason for my decision. If I turn my back on MI11 and accept Sir Keith's offer then I also turn my back, to some extent at least, on you. I don't want to do that. It took me a very long time to find the love of my life and I'm incredibly lucky to be able to share every part of what I do with you. I don't want that to stop.'

Bob was surprised when Monique stepped forwards to hug him. When she pulled away she was smiling. 'You forgot to mention that I'm armed and dangerous and might have killed you if you'd taken the job.'

'The thought never crossed my mind,' said Bob, smiling back.

Monique took off her sunglasses to dab at her eyes with a handkerchief. Then she straightened her sunhat and looked around.

'It's all right,' said Bob. 'No one's taking any notice. Perhaps it's as well that I'm out of uniform and you decided not to be a blonde this afternoon or wear bright red lipstick. Even in this very public place with all these people around we can still share a private moment. Anyway, now we've resolved the question of my career, we need to give thought to where Edward Price might have gone after he was dropped here by Royal Navy staff cars on both the Friday and the Saturday.'

'This is the south-west side of Palace Square, on the left as we're looking at it,' said Monique. 'We know Edward Price visited Captain Bianchi's in Strait Street at some point before the Sunday morning, when he left the suit with the matchbook in its pocket in his room on Manoel Island. According to the map, Strait Street is one street back from Palace Square on its north-western side. It's quite a long street but I'm willing to bet you a shilling that we'll find Captain Bianchi's not very far from here.'

Bob smiled. 'That's not a bet I'll take, Monique.'

Monique led the way. Strait Street turned out to be a very narrow alley that was bustling with life, even on a Sunday afternoon. Men in military uniforms from all the services but especially the Royal Navy mingled with civilians, mainly older people and younger women, with almost none of the children that Bob had seen everywhere else in Malta. A recurring theme seemed to be young men in uniform sharing cigarettes with young women wearing tight dresses and high-heeled shoes who were standing in open doorways.

It seemed to Bob that the narrowness of the alley was emphasised by the enclosed balconies projecting from the front of many of the buildings at upper-floor level, giving the impression in places that if neighbours leaned out of their windows they could shake hands across the street. In some cases, people were leaning out of upper-floor windows carrying on conversations with others at street level. This partial enclosing of the street made it feel very dark and gloomy at pavement level, despite the blue sky above and the sun catching the upper-floor level of some of the buildings on one side. This sense of enclosure was only relieved by the irregularly spaced gaps on both sides of the street where buildings had been destroyed by bombing. These gaps tended to be filled by rubble made up mainly of large, quite regularly-sized blocks of stone.

'Welcome to "The Gut", as Anne Milner tells me it's called,' said Monique.

Bob had checked the address on the matchbook and was looking for numbers above or beside doorways, while at the same time trying not to get in the way of people making their way along the narrow street, entering and leaving the many business premises or simply standing and negotiating the price of a sexual encounter. As well as the balconies, there were lots of hanging or projecting signs at first-floor level. Some, like one promoting the Oxford Music Hall, were associated with businesses that were boarded up or derelict or had been bombed. Others sought to attract customers to establishments that were clearly thriving such as The Empire Bar and the neighbouring Cape of Good Hope Lodging House or the Westminster Café and Bar opposite. A little further along was the Ben Nevis Hotel and Restaurant. Bob didn't stop to check but doubted if its menu stretched to venison or haggis. Other signs advertised commodities such as 'cigarettes and tobacco', 'cold beer', 'Simonds Ales and Stouts' and, something of a local favourite, 'Cisk Lager'.

'I think it's not far ahead,' said Bob, pointing in the direction they'd been walking. He was right. There was a vertical sign on the face of a building on the left after a hundred yards proclaiming that they had arrived at Captain Bianchi's. The background to the sign was the same bright blue they used for their matchbooks while the signwriting was in black. A faded red arrow painted on the front wall of the building below the bottom of the sign pointed diagonally down at a doorway with a closed dark brown door. The ground-floor windows were covered with closed wooden shutters, but that was also true of many of the other ground-floor windows in the street.

'It doesn't look open,' he said.

'There's only one way to find out,' said Monique, putting her sunglasses in her handbag and stepping forwards to push at the closed door.

*

Monique fully expected to find that the door was locked and was surprised when it opened easily. She looked at Bob who raised his eyebrows in response and then she stepped inside.

Beyond the door, Monique found herself in a narrow bar lit mainly by a few electric lights hanging on cords from the ceiling. Just inside was a counter on her right with an elderly man wearing a red apron behind it, drying a glass with a cloth that might once have been white. Wooden tables and

199

accompanying chairs were arranged close together along both sides of the room with another partly enclosing the far end, leaving space for access to a rear area at a lower level beyond some steps. It sounded like someone was playing a scratched Glen Miller record out of sight in the rear part of the bar and there was a buzz of male conversation drifting through from it.

The walls on both sides were panelled in dark wood up to about a seated customer's head height and, above that, they were largely covered in mirrors advertising a range of alcoholic or tobacco products. This at least made the most of the limited available light. The floor was tiled in black and white marble tiles set in a check pattern. Monique thought that the paint over the embossed paper on the ceiling might once have been white, but it was nicotine brown now.

There were four customers in the room. Two old men in working clothes were sitting at a table just beyond the bar on the right, smoking pipes and drinking beer. Two much younger men in army uniforms were on the other side, also smoking and drinking. One of them whistled as he turned to look at the new arrivals.

Monique ignored him and stopped by the counter, but then had to move to make room for Bob as the outside door opened behind him. Two couples came in. The girls wore tight bright dresses and lots of makeup and each was holding the hand of a young man in a naval uniform following behind. They pushed past Bob and Monique and then, laughing, opened and went through a door that Monique hadn't noticed at the top of the steps descending to the rear of the establishment. In one of the mirrors on the left-hand wall, Monique caught a glimpse of a set of stairs beyond the door, leading upwards. She thought there must be bedrooms up there available for short-term rental by the girls. No one in the bar showed any sign of having noticed the two couples.

'Hello,' said Bob to the man behind the counter. 'I'm looking for a friend of mine who was here last weekend. I think he was here on Friday or Saturday.'

The man looked back at Bob without saying anything.

Bob continued. 'He's a very tall man,' he held up his hand to demonstrate what he meant. 'He's got blond hair and a moustache and is rather older than me. When he was here I think he wore a tie like the one I'm wearing.' Bob touched it for effect.

The man put down the glass and then the cloth and made a show of looking at his watch. 'You need to come back in an hour. Someone will be able to talk to you then.'

Bob looked at Monique and she felt herself shrug slightly. He looked at his watch and Monique instinctively did likewise. 'Very well, we'll call back in an hour.'

Then he turned and pulled open the door, holding it wide so Monique could precede him out onto Strait Street.

Monique put on her sunglasses and led Bob for fifty yards along the street, then came to a halt and pulled him over to one side where there was a recessed doorway with a closed door. 'We need to talk,' she said.

'We do, but don't you think someone might get the wrong idea if we're standing in a doorway in this part of the city?' he asked.

Monique smiled. 'That's their problem, not ours. I think we can fairly say that we've now stuck our heads above the parapet.' She looked back along the street towards Captain Bianchi's. 'You realise that when we return in an hour, we may not get a friendly welcome?'

201

'I do,' said Bob. 'But there seemed no other way of approaching it.'

'I agree. In the meantime, we've got a chance to get to know the area a little better. Do you fancy a walk, Bob?'

'Yes, of course.'

Monique was pleased that he didn't ask where they were going or why. She took his arm and led him on a route that zig-zagged its way around the streets leading down the hill from Strait Street towards the harbour and those that ran at right angles to them.

She found what she was looking for in the form of the ruins of a large church that had, until its bombing, stood on the north-west side of Old Mint Street, a street that ran parallel to Strait Street but was removed from it by the intervening Old Bakery Street. None of the streets they'd been in were anything like as busy as Strait Street. Old Mint Street, though wider, was quite empty in comparison.

It was possible to enter the ruin through a gap in the standing walls that must originally have been a wide doorway and Monique led Bob in.

'Next time we're here,' said Monique, 'you cut back on the side we approached from and stand in the shadow of the angle of the wall there.' Bob walked to where she'd indicated. 'That's right. That partly conceals you from anyone coming in through the doorway. I'll make my way over to this pile of rubble here.' She looked at her watch. 'Good. Now shall we find a cup of coffee somewhere? We've got time before we're due to be back at Captain Bianchi's.'

'I'd prefer one of those cold beers we've seen advertised,' said Bob.

'Later, Bob. We need clear heads for a while yet.'

*

The two old men were still drinking beer and smoking their pipes in Captain Bianchi's, though now they had been joined by two more and they were all playing a noisy card game that involved lots of banging of hands of cards down onto the table.

On the other side of the room, the two men in army uniform had been replaced by six Royal Navy ratings, drinking beer and eating pasta. A wiry man in his fifties with greying hair in a light-coloured suit was sitting on the table at the far end of the room, near the top of the stairs leading down to the back room. There was a nearly-full glass of beer in front of him and he appeared to be watching the card game.

Bob had led the way in and none of the customers took any notice of him or Monique. After a few moments, the elderly man in the red apron climbed the stairs from the rear of the establishment and came to stand behind the counter by the front door.

'I was here earlier,' Bob said, 'looking for my friend.'

The man looked back at him. 'I'm sorry, sir. I've talked to my colleagues and nobody here remembers seeing anyone like the man you described to me.'

Bob thought that he didn't appear very sorry but recognised they were both posturing and replied as Monique had suggested. 'Thank you for asking. I'm grateful to you for your help.' He followed Monique back out onto Strait Street where she took his arm and led him slowly away.

She then followed a zig-zag course that Bob knew was intended to lead them back towards the bombed church they'd visited earlier.

'How sure are you that we're being followed?' he asked.

'Don't look back, but I've just seen the reflection in a window of someone I think is keeping a little behind us. He's wearing a Panama hat and sunglasses now, but I'm fairly sure it's the man who was sitting at the end of the front room of the bar. He was on his own then so hopefully he still is now.'

After a few more right-angled turns, Monique looked at Bob in a way he knew was intended to allow her a view of the street they'd just walked down. 'He's still behind us and there are very few other people about. I'm fairly sure he's on his own. This is our church, coming up on the left. When we go through the doorway you'll only have a few seconds to get into position. And…'

'Please don't tell me to have my Walther PPK ready, Monique. I thought our relationship moved beyond that after our last visit to Stockholm.'

He saw Monique smile. 'Sorry, Bob. You're using the replacement you were issued with after the Swedes kept the old one as evidence, aren't you? Have you practised with it?'

Bob realised that Monique was nervous. He was too. He smiled, 'I could say it's a bit late to have this conversation but of course I have, on the range at RAF Turnhouse. Right, here's the doorway.'

Bob took a sharp left turn as they passed through the ruined doorway and moved out of sight of anyone following them into the church, then he drew and cocked his pistol. He watched as Monique walked over to the pile of rubble she'd identified earlier and turned to face the entrance. He saw that she'd left her pistol in her handbag and realised that responsibility for their safety now rested squarely on his shoulders. Part of him was pleased that Monique had so much confidence in him.

There was the noise of a car going past in the street and then

Bob saw the man from the bar, preceded by his shadow, enter the ruins of the church. He had a revolver in his right hand and walked slowly towards Monique.

'Where's your friend?' he called out to Monique in a Scottish accent.

'He's behind you,' said Bob. 'And he's pointing his pistol at your back. Stand still. Now lean over to your right side and place your revolver on that block of stone beside your knee. That's right. Now put your hands high in the air.'

'You wouldn't shoot a fellow Scot, would you?'

'Quiet please, while the lady finds out who you are.'

Bob watched as Monique walked over to the man and, without getting into Bob's line of fire, went through his pockets. She then took a few steps to one side while she looked at two items she'd retrieved.

'According to his identity card and ration book, this is Mr Stuart McQueen and his address is given as Captain Bianchi's on Strait Street.'

'I own the place and live on the top floor,' said McQueen.

'Why are you following us?' asked Bob.

'To find out why you are looking for Edward Price.'

'The man we work for is an old friend of Edward's,' said Bob. 'He asked us to investigate his disappearance.'

McQueen half-turned to look at Bob. 'Are you with the Secret Intelligence Service? If so then your complexions suggest that you've come from London and not Cairo.'

Neither Bob nor Monique said anything in reply.

'I'm a friend of Edward's too. That's why he came to see me. Perhaps we should talk? It's hot standing here in the full glare of the sun, especially with light reflecting off the ruined walls and rubble around us. How would you feel about a nice chilled beer back at Captain Bianchi's? On the house, of course. Can I put my hands down?'

Monique reached down to retrieve McQueen's revolver from the stone block he'd placed it on. She opened the cylinder and unloaded the weapon. Then she flicked the revolver, causing its cylinder to snap shut, and held it out to McQueen. 'Now you can put your hands down. You can carry this. I'll hang on to the bullets.'

McQueen smiled. 'I'm impressed. You've done that before.'

'If you patronise me again, Mr McQueen, I'll ask my friend over there to shoot you in the backside and we'll just walk away and leave you here to bleed all over your suit.'

'I'm sorry. I get nervous when someone's pointing a gun at me and was simply hoping to lighten the mood.'

'You lead and we'll follow,' said Monique. 'I'll look after your identity card and ration book for the moment, along with your bullets. The idea of a cold beer is very appealing.'

CHAPTER NINETEEN

The back room at Captain Bianchi's turned out to be larger than the one at the front of the establishment. The steps led down into the first of a series of square areas, each partly divided from its neighbours by arches supported on square columns. The whole area was brightly lit, in marked contrast to the front room, and at the back was a full-width bar.

Monique saw there was another contrast, too. This rear area was much busier with men in uniform sitting on chairs at small round tables or standing and talking. The air was heavy with cigarette smoke. She realised why she'd been able to hear the sound of male conversation from here in the front bar earlier. The record player was on the end of the bar and, though she was no expert, it sounded like the same Glen Miller record was playing again.

The uniforms on view represented the three services and there seemed to be a contingent of Australians in too, judging from the bush hats they were wearing. There were other women in the room besides Monique but they were serving drinks rather than consuming them.

McQueen led Bob and Monique over to an alcove on one side of the room. 'We'll be able to talk here,' he said.

'I much prefer that table we can see over in the corner at the back of the room,' said Monique. 'The one that group of sailors has just left.' She knew it might be an excess of caution, but McQueen had had an hour's warning of their visit and she didn't want any conversation between them being recorded. Dictating which table they should use was a good way of reducing that risk.

'As you wish,' said McQueen. 'I'll organise the drinks. Are you both happy with Cisk Lager Beer? It's our local brew and I can highly recommend it.'

Monique smiled and Bob nodded. McQueen waved to attract the attention of a barmaid as they sat down. Monique noted that while there had also been ashtrays on the tables in the front bar, those on the tables here each had two or three matchbooks, just like the one Bob had found in Edward Price's suit pocket, piled next to them. She picked one up and put it in her handbag. When the drinks arrived she tried hers and decided that a cold beer might be the perfect antidote to a hot afternoon.

'You go first, Mr McQueen,' said Bob. 'You said you were a friend of Edward Price's. Tell us more.'

'As you wish… What do I call you?'

'I'm Bob and this is Monique. First names will do for now.'

'It's nice to be able to put names to the faces,' said McQueen. 'Let me take you back four years to 1939 in London. As you might have guessed from my accent, my background is north of the border, in Glasgow. I'm guessing you're from Edinburgh, Bob?' Bob didn't reply. 'Anyway, in the middle of 1939, an unexpected chain of circumstances left me owning a hotel in Bloomsbury in London. You may be aware that parts of that area have an unsavoury reputation and it was establishments like the hotel I acquired that both fed and benefitted from that reputation.

'As I saw it, we provided services that men wanted and were prepared to pay for. As well, of course, as providing food and drink and accommodation in a city in which the demand for all three was very strong. Many of our regulars were highly respected professionals in law, journalism, medicine and so on. We also had customers who were in the police and the armed services. And we had at least two who were, I later realised, in the Secret Intelligence Service. Edward Price was one of them and the other was called Charles Richmond. They were colleagues and often came in together.

'Some of my customers were not very nice people, and anyone harming any of my girls got banned, usually after being taught a lesson about what pain is really like by some associates of mine. Other customers became good friends. Edward Price was one of them.

'In November 1939 something happened between Edward and Charles. Neither ever talked about it to me, but someone else did. As I understand it, two Secret Intelligence Service agents were captured by the Germans in the Dutch city of Venlo, within a few feet of the German border, and then taken into Germany. It was seen as a disaster by SIS and the consequences were significant. Though based in London, Edward Price and Charles Richmond were both involved and, though never officially blamed for what happened, they did blame each other and things became very bitter between them.

'A year later it was my turn to be looking at a disaster in the making. By Christmas 1940 the London Blitz had been raging for nearly four months and showed no signs of abating. I know others were suffering much more badly, but the bombing was crippling my business. People were staying away from the city when they could, and the way they spent their time and money when they were in London also changed.

'In January 1941, I let it be known that I was interested in selling up and was made an offer by someone else in the business. Wider circumstances were enforcing the sale and the price reflected that. If I'd sold six months earlier I'd probably have realised three times as much, but I was grateful to be able to walk away with what I'd been offered.

'It turned out that was the best business decision I'd ever made because two months later the hotel was bombed and destroyed and the insurance cover for war damage would have been, at best, uncertain.

'Then there was a really weird twist of fate. An uncle of mine, on my mother's side, died here in Malta. His name was Christopher White and he'd been a captain in the merchant navy in the last war and for some years afterwards. No one back in Britain knew what he did out here, but after he died it became clear that he was in the same business as I'd been in. He'd established Captain Bianchi's fifteen years or so earlier and he left it to me in his will. As I was told the story he decided that calling it "Captain White's" wasn't interesting enough and obviously naming it after himself might not be a good idea anyway. So he went for the nearest Italian surname he could find. I knew Malta was being bombed too, but this place didn't cost me anything and I reasoned that as Malta is an island, customers wouldn't be able to stay away as they had in London.

'It wasn't easy for a civilian to find transport to Malta but I managed, at considerable cost. I arrived and took over Captain Bianchi's in March 1941. You probably know that the worst of the bombing was last year, in the first half of 1942, and there were many times when I kicked myself for coming out here rather than simply spending my ill-gotten gains on a nice house in the country somewhere peaceful in Scotland. Business did suffer in the worst of the bombing, though not as badly as it had in London. But the building survived and now that the bombing has largely ceased and the timing of the curfew has been relaxed it's looking like a pretty good gamble.'

'And then Edward Price called in on the evening of the Friday before last,' said Monique.

'That's right,' said McQueen. 'As you're from SIS, you'll probably already have worked out that the Charles Richmond who's in charge of the SIS office here in Malta is the same Charles Richmond who Edward Price fell out with in November 1939. I was therefore very surprised to see Edward on the island. He told me that he'd flown in that morning from Cairo to look for Lieutenant James Ewing, the nephew of an old school friend who had gone missing. He said that he had very few leads and wanted to know if I'd heard anything through my contacts in Malta. Had any unidentified bodies turned up in suspicious circumstances? Could the nephew be unconscious in hospital? Had I heard anything at all that might help? I agreed to telephone a few people and make discreet enquiries while he spent the evening enjoying the run of the establishment.'

'You provided a prostitute for him?' asked Monique.

'I did say he'd been a regular customer in London,' said McQueen. 'Back then I saw him as one of those men who marry their profession and never find time for an actual wife. I don't think anything has changed. Back then, it wasn't young women he was interested in anyway, and that doesn't seem to have changed either.'

'Who was he interested in back then?' asked Monique.

'Young men dressed as young women, mainly,' said McQueen. 'Strait Street has long had a reputation for, amongst other things, cross-dressing. Business is business and who am I to judge? Let's face it, we live in a very mixed-up world. I heard that one of the most senior intelligence officers in the British army in Cairo was arrested in Madrid for wearing women's clothing in public not so very long ago.'

'Did you find out anything that might have helped him?' asked Bob.

'Not really. I was told what seemed little more than a rumour that Edward was interested in, but I doubt if it came to anything.'

'What was that?' asked Bob.

'A contact who you might say is involved in the unofficial import of sought-after goods told me that early the previous Monday morning, which would have been the 31st of May, a fishing boat exploded out at sea after leaving the village of Marsaxlokk, which is in the south-east of the island. The authorities said it had hit a mine but some of the fishermen in the village thought otherwise. The part of the story that interested Edward was the associated rumour that two men had been seen putting a body in the same boat the previous night, during the curfew. I've no idea if this was true and told Edward as much.'

'That would be the night and morning after the missing naval officer was meant to return to his quarters,' said Bob. 'I can understand why Edward might have been interested.'

'He also came here the next night, the Saturday night,' said Monique. 'Did he discuss with you what he'd found? We know he visited Marsaxlokk that Saturday.'

'Sadly not,' said McQueen. 'I came down with a dose of Malta Dog on the Saturday morning and was only really functioning again late on the following Thursday, a few days ago. In case you're wondering, that's the local name for dysentery. Everyone who's here for any length of time gets caught by it sooner or later. I know that Edward was here again on the Saturday night and that he again enjoyed our hospitality, but I didn't have a chance to talk to him after he left here on the Friday night.'

'Did either of you mention the archaeological site at Hagar Qim when you talked?' asked Monique. 'We know he also visited it on the Saturday afternoon, but have no idea why.'

'Sorry, no.'

Bob put his empty glass down on the table. 'When you were telephoning your contacts on the Friday night, did anyone mention anything to do with Mosta? We think Edward Price visited it as one of several places the lieutenant's girlfriend told him they had been to together. But as it's where Edward went missing on the Sunday, anything else that has a connection with the place might be significant.'

'I'd help if I could, but again the answer is no.'

Monique saw Bob glance at her and raise an eyebrow.

'I think that's what we wanted to cover,' she said. 'Thank you for being so open with us, Mr McQueen.'

'I didn't think I had any choice. Please feel free to call in any time you are in the area. First, though, can I offer you an exchange? Another beer for each of you in return for my identity card, ration book and the bullets from my revolver?'

'That seems very fair,' said Monique, smiling.

*

Bob followed Monique out of Captain Bianchi's and onto Strait Street.

'Should we go for another walk, Bob? I know it's hot but I thought we might make our way across Valletta to the gardens with the view over the Grand Harbour. I think there were seats with shade there.'

Bob looked at his watch. 'It's later than I thought but we've still got a while before we can think of dinner. Why not? It might help us clarify what we need to do next. I don't know about you, but I found our chat with Mr McQueen very helpful.'

Monique took his arm and led him to the next corner before turning uphill.

'Is this the best way?' asked Bob. If it had been up to him, he'd have started by going the other way along Strait Street.

'I want to go to Palace Square first. It's just up here.'

'Have you any particular reason for going back to where Edward Price was dropped off by his car?'

'That's not why I want to go there. Let's take a left and walk along the north-west side of the square. We're in no hurry.' Monique led Bob along the long side of the square opposite the Governor's Palace. 'Right, now I want us to cross the square diagonally, heading for the corner where Kingsway emerges.'

'You think we're being followed, don't you Monique?' asked Bob, as they reached the far corner.

'Can't you feel anything?' she asked.

'I'm sorry, no. Why would Stuart McQueen want to follow us again? Surely there would be no point?'

'If anyone is following us, and I admit it might be just my overactive imagination, then they are very good at it. That means it's not Mr McQueen. There are lots of people about, which will make it easier for them, but I've not identified anyone acting oddly and our doubling back across the square ought to have wrong-footed any followers. From the far corner of Palace Square, we make our way diagonally across the much smaller Victoria Square, which I admit I didn't really notice when approaching Palace Square earlier. This is it. Presumably, it's called Victoria Square because of the large statue of Queen Victoria over there on her plinth.'

'She has suffered a bit,' said Bob. 'Parts of the crown and sceptre are damaged and she's missing all the fingers on her outstretched left hand. I suppose I'd be feeling a bit worse for wear if I'd spent the last few years sitting on top of a plinth in the centre of a city that's been bombed as much as this one has.' Bob laughed, then stopped when he saw the serious expression on Monique's face. 'You're worried, aren't you?' he asked.

'Let's just stroll on,' she said. 'It's a zig-zag route from here, like earlier though on the other side of Valletta.'

Bob knew better than to turn around and look, but he was aware of Monique using reflections in the taped glass windows of shops she stopped and looked in to try to spot anyone following them.

In Upper Barrakka Gardens, Monique led Bob to a bench that had an oblique view back towards the entrance and they sat in comfortable silence for a while.

'Have you seen anyone who might be taking an interest in us?' Bob asked. 'I haven't, but I think you are better attuned to this sort of thing than me.'

'No,' said Monique. 'Let's go and enjoy the view over the Grand Harbour. I don't want to spoil a pleasant afternoon by imagining ghosts.'

*

They had decided to dine at the Osborne Hotel. There was plenty of time after returning to their suite for cool baths and a change of clothes. Monique had noticed that the hotel offered a laundry service and given how hot it was made a mental note to talk to Bob about getting some washing done.

Monique wrapped herself in a towel and sat on the edge of the bed. She watched Bob standing, naked and with his hair wet and tousled, in front of the open wardrobe in their bedroom.

'I think I should go down to dinner as Group Captain Sutherland,' he said. 'The suit was comfortable but I think I need to keep Robert Cadman in reserve.'

'I agree,' said Monique. 'But first I think you should come over and join me on the bed. We don't have to be down at dinner at any set time and seeing you like that has given me an idea of something we might do first.'

Bob smiled and walked over towards her.

It was rather later when they did go down for dinner, by which time Monique was feeling hungry.

There was no one in reception so she led Bob into the busy dining room.

'Sir!' Monique felt and heard Bob turn behind her. The elderly man whom she'd seen several times behind the reception desk was just beyond Bob, holding an envelope out towards him.

'A gentleman left this for you earlier, sir.'

'Bob took and looked at the envelope, then turned towards Monique. 'It's addressed to Group Captain and Mrs Sutherland. It's in an Osborne Hotel envelope.'

'Can you tell us anything about the gentleman?' asked Monique.

'Yes, of course. He was here only a few minutes after the two of you returned earlier. I'd had to leave the reception for a moment, but when I came back he was waiting. He asked whether the lady and gentleman who had come in were Group Captain and Mrs Sutherland. He said he was an old friend and had seen you in the street but hadn't been able to catch up. When I confirmed who you were, he said that he needed to be elsewhere but would leave you a note, which he then wrote on the letter paper I provided. If you'd not come down for dinner, I'd have had it brought up to your room.'

'What did he look like?' asked Monique.

'He was about the same height as the group captain and had a light suit on. He had dark hair and a black moustache. He's probably aged in his late forties.'

'You said you were away for a moment when he first came in,' said Monique. 'Where was the hotel register?'

'On the lower level at the back of the reception desk, where I can get to it most easily.'

'Is it possible the gentleman might have been able to look at who is staying as guests before he spoke to you?' asked Monique.

'I don't think so, but it's not impossible. Is something wrong?'

'No, not at all.' Monique smiled at the man. 'Thank you so much for your help.'

Monique led the way back into the dining room and they sat at the table a waiter showed them to.

'What was that all about?' asked Bob.

'It was about someone following us from Captain Bianchi's to the Osborne Hotel,' said Monique. 'They did it very well. When he came in, our follower made the most of a quick look at the hotel register and, despite your civilian clothes, decided we had to be the couple registered as Group Captain and Mrs Sutherland. He confirmed that with the receptionist and then wrote us a note. That note.'

'Should I open it?'

'I can't think of a better way of finding out what it says.'

Bob opened and read the note, then passed it across the table to Monique. She looked at the single piece of paper.

'Dear Group Captain Sutherland,

'I understand we may have a shared interest and think it might be helpful to meet to discuss it. I will be at the ancient site at Hagar Qim at 9 a.m. tomorrow, Monday. If you - and your wife if you wish - can join me it might be to our mutual advantage.

'Yours aye, Charles Richmond.'

Monique didn't take much notice as she and Bob ordered food and wine.

'At least we now know who was following us,' she said when there were no waiters within hearing.

'We do, but his approach seems rather odd, don't you think?' asked Bob. 'With the resources of SIS at his disposal, you'd have thought he'd have had a better way of finding out who he's dealing with than by sneaking a look at a hotel register and then asking a question that could quite easily have produced a misleading answer. From our point of view, we have no way of knowing that the man who followed us and wrote this letter really is Charles Richmond, the head of the SIS office in Malta.'

'I'm not so sure,' said Monique. 'We know Edward Price went to Hagar Qim on the day before he disappeared. To my mind, the note suggests that he was there to meet Charles Richmond. It also suggests that it was Charles Richmond who wrote that note. Would anyone else have thought of suggesting Hagar Qim to you as a meeting place?'

The dinner the hotel served was excellent but Monique had the sense throughout that Bob was as distracted as she felt herself.

When the table had been cleared of everything other than their coffee and the last of the wine, Monique looked at Bob and smiled. 'One of us is going to have to ask the inevitable question.'

'What are our priorities for tomorrow?' he asked, returning her smile.

'That's the one,' said Monique. 'I think we need to contact the 10th Submarine Flotilla's duty officer tonight to line up a staff car for the morning. The first stop will be Hagar Qim at 9 a.m. to see what Charles Richmond, assuming it is him, has to say for himself.'

'I agree,' said Bob. 'I know we're waiting for tests on the stain on the towel tomorrow, but I think that when we're finished at Hagar Qim we need to move on to Marsaxlokk. The awkwardness is that I think I'm going to need to be an anonymous civilian in Marsaxlokk, whereas I definitely need to be Group Captain Sutherland, complete with uniform, at Hagar Qim. We don't want to have to come back here between times.'

'There's no need,' said Monique. 'We can ask the navy driver to park somewhere out of the way and go for a short walk while I help you change from your uniform into your suit in the back of the car. Please tell me you aren't thinking about wearing that MCC tie again.'

'I don't have a better plan for the change of identity,' said Bob. 'And I'll wear something more anonymous and carry the MCC tie in my pocket.' He looked at his watch. 'We've plenty of time before the curfew, do you fancy a short walk to the viewpoint you found so we can take in the sights of the harbour to the north and Manoel Island?'

CHAPTER TWENTY

'This is the second time in not much more than a week that I've brought someone here,' said the navy driver. 'I've been in Malta for over a year and had never heard of Hagar Qim, and now I've been twice.'

'Was it you who drove for Mr Price, the tall civilian, on the Saturday before last?' asked Monique.

'That's right, ma'am. He seemed to be doing a bit of a Cook's tour but it was a pleasant enough day.'

'Where did you drop him off?'

'Just here, ma'am.'

'This will be fine for us too, thank you. I'm not sure how long we'll be but I don't expect to be too long.'

'No problem, ma'am. I've got a newspaper and a bottle of water and there's a nice sea view.'

Monique and Bob got out of the rear of the car and walked over to a gate with a sign on it.

'There's certainly a sea view,' said Monique, 'and that breeze is very welcome. But am I alone in finding this place a little bleak?'

'I agree,' said Bob. 'Once you're out of the built-up areas, the island's landscape does seem to encompass a range of different shades of arid, and the blue skies and stone walls only add to that impression.'

Monique watched as Bob opened the gate, then followed him through.

On the other side, he came to a halt. 'I think that's what we've come to see,' he said. 'It looks like a segment of an ancient city made of huge blocks of stone. It's intricate and imposing and rather remarkable. Should we go and take a closer look? I see no sign of Charles Richmond.'

They carried on walking.

'What is this place?' asked Monique.

'I asked the hotel receptionist last night after dinner. He said it was a group of ancient temples that date back much further than the pyramids in Egypt. There's more than one structure here, as we can now see from this angle.'

Monique saw a movement and realised it was a man in a light-coloured suit making his way towards them around the side of what appeared to be the main temple. 'I think this is why we're really here. We might as well wait here and let him walk. His car wasn't back where our driver dropped us off. Presumably, he's parked somewhere less obvious and walked here.'

As the man drew closer, Monique could see that he had dark hair and a black moustache.

'Good morning,' said Bob.

'Group Captain Sutherland, I presume?' said the man, smiling. 'The uniform does help with the identification. And you must be Mrs Sutherland?'

'You signed your letter as Charles Richmond,' said Monique. 'Do you have an SIS security pass proving that's who you are?'

'I do, but I also need to confirm who I'm dealing with,' said Richmond. 'You told Stuart McQueen that you are with SIS and I know that's not true.'

'No, we didn't,' said Monique. 'He assumed we were with SIS and we didn't correct him.'

Richmond smiled again. 'Yes, I see the distinction. Let me see if I can work it out. You told Stuart that the man you work for is an old friend of Edward Price's and had asked you to look for him. I'm betting that the man you work for is Maurice Cunningham and that makes the two of you from Military Intelligence, Section 11.'

'That's very clever, Mr Richmond,' said Monique. 'Perhaps we should show you our MI11 passes in return for you showing us your SIS documents? Then we're all happy.'

When passes had been exchanged and checked, Richmond turned to Bob. There's a nice stroll around the outside of the site, group captain. Should we walk while we talk?'

'As there are three of us, it might be better if we go and sit on those low blocks over there,' said Bob, pointing at two flat blocks placed on the ground at right angles to each other. 'Is this place always so quiet?'

'I've only been here twice, counting today,' said Richmond. 'But in my limited experience, it is. The last time I was here I was told that this is one of the oldest religious sites on Earth. If so, then word of its importance appears not to have spread widely, which to my mind is a good thing. Those slabs do look like they'd make good benches.'

When they sat down, Monique made sure she sat on the same block as Charles Richmond, but on the other side of him from Bob. That ensured he couldn't look at Bob and at her at the same time, which she thought might make him feel at a disadvantage.

'Was it Edward Price who told you about the history of Hagar Qim?' she asked.

'Yes. He telephoned me late on the day he arrived from Cairo and suggested we meet here the following afternoon. He knows a great deal about archaeology.'

'We were told that the two of you don't get on,' said

Monique.

'We had a chance to talk about our differences when we met.' Richmond looked down at his feet. 'I'll not go into details, but we fell out late in 1939 over something that seemed extremely important at the time. When we had a chance to talk things through during our meeting here it emerged that we'd both been suffering from certain misapprehensions back then and may have embarked on years of totally needless enmity as a result. Don't ask me what our original quarrel was about. Very few people ever knew the reason for our falling out and only two of them, Edward and I, cared. I'd prefer to keep it that way.'

Monique thought Charles Richmond was being very pompous and couldn't resist the chance to deflate him. 'It may not be quite the secret you think. Everyone with any involvement in British military intelligence knows about the Venlo incident, of course. But more people than you appear to believe also know that you and Edward Price blamed each other for it, even though others in SIS didn't.'

'Ah.' There was a long pause before Richmond turned to look at Monique. 'Touché, Mrs Sutherland. I'm sure Maurice Cunningham never knew, so I assume your source must have been Stuart McQueen. If someone told him about it at the time then he's always kept it to himself, until now. The important thing to say is that when Edward and I met here, we agreed to have dinner together the following evening, on the Sunday. I hoped to rekindle a squandered friendship that had once meant a great deal to me. I think he felt the same way. I made some discreet enquiries after he failed to arrive for dinner and that's how I became aware that he was missing. His disappearance has weighed very heavily on my mind, but I've not felt able to do any more than I have.'

'Did Edward talk about why he was in Malta?' asked Monique.

'Only very briefly. He said he'd been asked by Maurice Cunningham to look for his nephew, a naval officer, who was missing. I cheated a little when I told you that I had identified you as from MI11 solely based on your comments to Stuart McQueen because I was already aware of Maurice Cunningham's involvement. I assume the two of you are in Malta to look for both Edward and the nephew?'

'That's right,' said Bob, 'under the rather unconvincing cover of our looking at the possibility of setting up an MI11 office here.'

'If you feel there is anything I can do to help you in your quest, then please let me know. I am limited in what I can do. You will appreciate that the role of SIS here is to look outwards from Malta. That means any help I can offer will have to be on a personal basis or through contacts like Stuart McQueen.'

'Thank you for the offer,' said Bob. 'There is one thing that could help. Are you in a position to send signals to Maurice Cunningham without their content raising questions here or in London? I assume that as head of the SIS office here, you don't need to have your signals approved by anyone else?'

'I can do that. What do you want to tell him?'

'Nothing specific at the moment,' said Bob. 'I'd just feel happier with a secure means of communicating with him. We can keep in touch with Maurice over anything that fits within our cover story via our contact at the 10th Submarine Flotilla, but that's very limiting. Could you send Maurice a short signal saying you and I have met and agreed to cooperate? Tell him that I have nothing significant to report yet, but will be in touch when I have.'

'In his shoes, I'd want something in the message that could only have come from you,' said Richmond. 'That way he'll know he can trust what it says.'

'That's a good point, Mr Richmond,' said Monique. 'Simply add at the end that Monique confirms that Malta is rather warmer than Kyle of Lochalsh.'

'What?'

'That's the point. It's nonsense to anyone else, but it will show Maurice that we had a hand in composing the signal.'

'Very well, I'll do that as soon as I get back to Valletta. I'll leave a message at your hotel that you should "contact Alfred" if I need to get in touch with you.' He wrote on a page in a pocketbook and tore it out, then offered it to Bob. 'Here is my office telephone number. Please memorise it and then destroy that note. If I'm not there, the duty officer will be able to take a message. Apologies if this is unnecessary, but be aware that if you telephone from your hotel you will be routed through a public switchboard, so be discreet.'

'I will,' said Bob. 'One thing that's been puzzling me is why his colleagues in Cairo haven't been showing any interest in Edward's disappearance.'

'I can help you there. Edward took leave, starting on the day he flew to Malta. He told me he had just over a week to find the missing lieutenant, which I imagine means he failed to show up for duty in Cairo this morning. He told his office that he was intending to spend his leave visiting some of the more off-the-beaten-track ancient sites in Egypt. It might take a while for anyone in Cairo to discover that he caught a flight to Malta instead.'

'Thank you,' said Bob. 'Changing the subject, did Mr

McQueen tell you about the rumour that had interested Edward, about a body being put aboard a fishing boat in a village in the south-east of the island the night after Maurice Cunningham's nephew went missing?'

'He did, and I'm guessing that you intend to follow that up.'

'Yes, we plan to go there this morning, though not with me in this uniform. According to his navy driver, Edward Price spent three hours at the village immediately before he came to meet you here. Did he say anything about what he'd found when you talked?'

'I'm sorry, group captain. As I told you, he did mention the missing lieutenant in explaining why he was on the island, but we had other things to talk about that seemed more important at the time. Though now I think about it, he didn't talk about the length of time he had available to find the lieutenant in a way that made it sound like he'd just made a breakthrough in his search for him.'

CHAPTER TWENTY-ONE

The village is bigger than I expected,' said Bob. 'Where do we start?'

Monique leaned forwards to speak to the driver. 'Where did you drop Mr Price when you brought him to Marsaxlokk?' she asked.

'At the head of the harbour, ma'am. The road comes in past a church that's ahead and on the left and the harbour is beyond it. Look, it's there.'

'I don't suppose he told you why he wanted to come here or said anything about what he'd done when you left?'

'Sorry, ma'am. He said nothing more than he needed to.'

'Stop near the church and we'll hop out,' said Monique. 'I've no idea how long we're going to be. Could you check back here in an hour, and then every half hour after that?'

The driver looked at his watch. 'Certainly, ma'am.'

Bob brushed down the front of his suit after they'd got out of the car and it had pulled away. 'Getting changed in the back of a very warm car wasn't the most comfortable of experiences,' he said.

'You had help,' said Monique, laughing. 'And at least the driver managed to keep a straight face when he came back to the car. I get the impression that the story of a lady helping an RAF group captain take his trousers off in the back of a Royal Navy staff car might take on an altogether different complexion when it's been told and re-told a few times.'

Bob realised that she was right and smiled. 'We need to work out how we're going to go about this. I tend to favour the idea of asking people if they saw a very tall man wearing a tie like the one I've got in my pocket and a hat to match on that Saturday. The alternative, of asking random strangers if they know anything about a body being put in a boat that then blew up doesn't seem likely to generate a positive reaction.'

'That's probably what Edward Price had to do,' said Monique. 'He didn't have an alternative line of enquiry.'

'And a day later he disappeared,' said Bob. 'I prefer the "tall MCC member" approach.'

The harbour at Marsaxlokk curved around the north and north-west sides of a bay that faced south-east. There were lines of brightly-coloured boats pulled up on the shore and many more moored in the water and at piers that projected out into it. A road ran around the harbour, behind the lines of boats. On its landward side was a curve of honey-coloured stone buildings, mainly of two storeys in height and with flat roofs. Many had open galleries at first-floor level with arches and stone balustrades. Bob could see there had been bomb damage, but it wasn't anything like as intense or widespread as he'd seen in other places on the island.

Monique led Bob across the road to the harbourside.

The place was bustling, both on land and in the harbour. Men were tending to boats, sorting nets, fishing with rods and lines from the quayside or just standing and talking while they smoked. Women gathered in groups, some with children. A little further to the east was a small market. Bob could see stalls that were selling bread, pasta or vegetables, while others stocked clothing.

'Can I suggest a division of labour?' asked Monique. 'We should start here and work our way around to the far end of the market, where the village appears to peter out a little. Then we can come back to this point and begin the larger job of doing the same thing in the other direction, ending up at the south-west end of the harbour.'

'Who gets to do which end?' asked Bob.

'That's not what I had in mind. Let's remember that we may be investigating at least one death and the last person who came here asking questions then disappeared. This is potentially dangerous for us too. By "division of labour" I had in mind that you talk to any men who will engage with you and I do the same with the women. It's important that we stay within sight of one another and don't get too widely separated.'

'You won't be able to show them the MCC tie,' said Bob.

Monique smiled. 'I'm sure I'll manage without it. Or we could borrow a knife and cut it in half if you wanted?'

Bob could see she was joking.

They did as Monique had suggested. The sun was hot and the bay faced directly towards it, offering almost no shade on the harbourside. Bob quickly came to find it an onerous process. Many men, though not all, were happy to talk to him and a few seemed genuinely keen to help. What he found a little challenging was making himself understood at times. Getting over the idea of 'the Saturday before last' proved particularly elusive in some of the conversations he had.

He was careful to stay fairly close to Monique and had the impression she was finding her conversations more engaging than he was his. Or perhaps she was better than him at feigning enthusiasm. At one point she caught his eye and he got the sense that, despite her smile, she was making no more progress than he was. Which was none at all.

He was surprised by how much time had passed when they reached the far end of the harbour and the availability of people to talk to thinned out.

'You didn't look like you were enjoying that,' said Monique. 'Did you find anything useful?'

Bob shook his head.

'No, neither did I,' said Monique. 'There's a bar not far back, facing out over the road to the harbour. I don't care what time of the day it is, I fancy a glass of cold Cisk Lager Beer.'

Bob smiled. 'Are you sure we don't need clear heads for a while yet?'

'I wondered how long it would be before I regretted saying that. Not long as it turned out. Come on, let's get out of the sun.'

There was a row of tables with umbrellas on the pavement outside but they went into the bar without any discussion. Bob found the cool and relatively dark interior very welcome after the baking heat and glare of the sun on the harbourside. The Cisk beers, when they arrived, were a real relief. He and Monique were the only customers and their beers were served by a man in his fifties wearing dark trousers and a blue checked shirt who had welcomed them like long-lost siblings when they walked through the door.

'Are you enjoying the beer?' the man asked.

'Very much,' said Monique. 'It's a nice place you've got here.'

'Thank you. If you come back after 12 we serve lunch too. We make the best lunches in Marsaxlokk.'

Bob looked at his watch. 'I'm not sure how long we're going to be in the village, but thank you for the suggestion.'

'Do you want another beer? It's obvious that the sun has made you thirsty.'

Bob could see Monique liked the idea. 'Yes please.'

'Are you here on business?' asked the man as he served their second round of beers.

'We're looking for a friend of mine. I know he was here a week last Saturday. He's very tall so you wouldn't have missed him and he was wearing a tie like this one.' Bob took the MCC tie out of the side pocket on his suit and showed it to the barman.

'Yes, I remember him. He had lunch here. He ordered the spaghetti pescatore and said it was very good.'

'Were you able to talk to him at all?' asked Monique.

'A little. I'd heard that someone had been asking questions about the deaths of two fishermen from here in a luzzu that hit a mine. Your friend asked me about it. I couldn't help him with that but I could serve him an excellent lunch!'

'What's a luzzu?' asked Monique.

'It's a type of fishing boat. I'm sure you noticed them out in the harbour and lined up along the shore.'

'The brightly coloured ones?' asked Monique. 'I thought they looked lovely with their multi-coloured stripes.'

'Some of those, the slightly larger ones with the pointed rear ends and the more complex masts at the front, are luzzijiet. The smaller ones with flat sterns are kajjikki. Luzzijiet is simply Maltese for more than one luzzu, just as kajjikki is Maltese for more than one kajjik.'

'I liked the way all the boats I saw, of both types, had eyes on either side at the front,' said Monique. 'They looked like they were made of wood and then attached and painted.'

'They are known as the Eye of Horus,' said the barman, 'or sometimes the Eye of Osiris. Although they come in twos on the boats, they are always referred to as if there was just one. They say it's an ancient tradition that came to Malta with the Phoenicians and it's believed that the Eye of Horus protects anyone sailing in a boat adorned with it.

'Someone told me once that the real origin of the belief goes back even further, to the ancient Egyptians. There was a fight between the god Horus and the god Seth and Horus had his left eye ripped out. Afterwards, the god Thoth replaced Horus's eye and magically restored his sight.'

Bob saw Monique look at him with concern on her face. He smiled back and winked. 'It's fascinating how ancient myths can live on in something as real as the decoration on a fishing boat,' he said. 'Do you know where my friend went after he finished his lunch?'

'I think that the questions your friend had been asking about the lost boat and its crew caused some concern in the village. He had just paid for his lunch and was about to leave when one of our local policemen, Sergeant Spiteri, came in and asked him to accompany him to the police station, which isn't far along this same row of buildings looking out over the harbour. I saw the sergeant a day or so later and he told me that he'd let your friend go after they'd had a chat.'

'I've finished my beer,' said Bob, 'and I'm very grateful to you.' He looked at Monique who caught his eye and nodded slightly. 'I'll pay and then I think we should see if Sergeant Spiteri is on duty today.'

*

It only took two minutes for Bob and Monique to walk from the bar to the police station.

Monique wondered if the story behind the Eye of Horus had upset Bob. It seemed a little close to home, with the significant difference that Horus had regained the sight in his left eye

232

while Bob had not. She'd been reassured by him winking at her, something he very rarely did.

Bob led the way in. Without asking for their names the constable behind the desk said that Sergeant Spiteri was on duty and asked them to wait for him in a small room along a side corridor.

'Why do all police stations feel the same and smell the same?' Monique asked as they sat on chairs on two sides of a square table in the room. The table and chairs were the room's only furniture. The walls were painted a glossy light blue and were bare other than for a cork board that had pinned to it various small notices about air raids, gas attacks and rationing.

Sergeant Spiteri turned out to be a dark-haired man in his thirties wearing a khaki shirt and shorts. He sat down on one of the vacant chairs.

'Hello. I was wondering if I might meet the two of you. You've been around the harbour asking about Edward Price, who I recently spoke to after he in turn had been here asking questions. I know that Mr Price is with the Secret Intelligence Service. Who are you?'

Bob introduced them and he and Monique then showed the sergeant their passes.

'Thank you. I have never heard of Military Intelligence, Section 11, and you don't look very much like a group captain, but I imagine you thought a uniform might make it harder to get answers to your questions. How can I help you?'

'I was hoping you might be able to tell us about your discussion with Mr Price,' said Bob.

'If he's your friend, as you say, then why don't you ask him yourself?'

'I can't. The morning after he visited Marsaxlokk he had a

Royal Navy staff car take him to Mosta. Nothing further has been heard of him. That was last Sunday, a week ago yesterday.'

'Are you saying he's disappeared?' asked the sergeant.

'Without a trace,' said Bob.

'That's very worrying. I'm not sure whether it will help, but I am happy to talk to you about the discussion he and I had in this room. The loss of *Doriette,* the fishing boat he had been asking about, shocked many in the village. Dreadful things have happened in the war, but there's a sense that we are emerging from the worst of it. To lose a boat from the village and the two young brothers who crewed it seemed to take us back to the darkest days of the siege.'

'How old were the crew?' asked Monique.

'Twenty-five and twenty-eight. The older brother, Joseph Camilleri, was an important member of the community and the church. The younger brother, Lawrenz, had been in a little trouble from time to time for black marketeering and curfew breaches. I'd heard it said he didn't keep good company, but I never saw anything myself to support that. I should add that in most professions the brothers would have been conscripted under the Compulsory Service Regulation but as fishermen they were exempt. There have been times when providing Malta with food has been far more important than providing it with two more anti-aircraft gunners.'

'What happened to them?' asked Monique.

'Early on the morning of Monday the 31st of May they sailed their boat out of Marsaxlokk Bay. As far as we can tell, in the absence of very much in the way of either wreckage or bodies, they hit a mine. There are a lot of them out there and Joseph and Lawrenz were just unlucky.'

'I've heard that some people question the theory that the boat was sunk by a mine,' said Bob.

'Yes, they do. A fisherman on a nearby boat said he thought the explosion originated further back in the boat, not at the front as you'd expect if it had hit a mine. But that's just an impression that must have been over, literally, in a flash. In the absence of any evidence, we had to go with the most likely explanation.

'I'm sure your next question will be about the body that rumour suggests was put in the boat the previous night. It is just a rumour. I've not been able to find anyone who can give it any substance and, believe me, I have tried. All you get, if you ask, is that a friend of a friend of a friend heard someone say they knew someone who had seen something. You get the idea.'

'Could the younger brother have been involved in anything more serious?' asked Monique.

'He could, but again there's no evidence. Malta is by no stretch of the imagination a crime-free island. The restrictions that helped us survive the siege made life more difficult for criminals, just as they did for everyone else. But the war has also opened up many new opportunities for organised crime. Organised crime most certainly exists here. I heard a rumour that some of the most influential of Malta's criminals had found their way off the island and were running criminal enterprises in Cardiff. On the other hand, many certainly didn't leave the island.'

'Cardiff in Wales?' asked Monique.

'Unlikely as it seems, yes.'

'And this is the conversation you had with Edward Price?' asked Bob.

'In general terms, yes.'

'Did you say anything to him that might have led to an interest in Mosta, which is where he was last seen?'

'No, nothing at all. I'm sorry, group captain. I think I've told you just about everything I can.'

'If anything else does come up that might be relevant, would you mind letting me know? We're staying at the Osborne Hotel in Valletta.'

*

Bob put his napkin down on the table. 'If those weren't the best lunches in Marsaxlokk they had to be pretty close. I'm pleased you managed to wave down the driver as he was pulling away from his half-hourly check-in. I'd have felt guilty enjoying this and knowing we'd left him hungry. I wasn't sure why he felt it better to eat at an outside table.'

'Come on, Bob, he'd have just felt awkward eating with us or even at a nearby table. I'm sure he was being truthful when he said he'd prefer to eat outside.'

'It does mean we won't need to wait for him when we're finished. I have this unsettling feeling there's still a lot for us to do today.'

'I think we should get him to take us to Manoel Island first,' said Monique. 'We need to know whether that was blood on the towel and perhaps whose blood it might have been.'

'Agreed,' said Bob. 'I'm beginning to think we also need to visit Stuart McQueen again.'

'Why?'

'Listening to what Sergeant Spiteri said about organised crime it occurred to me that Mr McQueen must be involved. The way he talked about dealing with violent customers in

London made it sound like he had local gangsters as customers or friends. The word he used was "associates". And how would you survive in the business he's in, either in London or Valletta, without being able to call in favours from "associates" on both sides of the law?

'I think we need to get Mr McQueen to do some more digging with his associates in Malta. Sergeant Spiteri seems a thoroughly decent man and I believed him when he said he had tried to find what lay behind the rumour of the body being put in the boat and had got nowhere. But what if there is some substance in the rumour and what if Edward Price coming here and asking about it led to someone feeling threatened by him? The bar owner talked about Edward's questions causing "some concern" in the village. What if it went further than that? That's why I think we should talk to Mr McQueen again.'

'You're right,' said Monique. 'If nothing else it might help if we could simply tie down more closely the source of the rumour he heard. McQueen said he heard it from someone involved in the "unofficial import of sought-after goods", by which I assume he meant a smuggler.'

'That's settled then,' said Bob. 'I'll pay for the three meals and the drinks if you warn the driver that we're on the move. I'm afraid we might have to stop on the way so I can change back into my uniform.'

CHAPTER TWENTY-TWO

When he came into Lawrence Dowson's office, it seemed to Bob that Surgeon Lieutenant Commander Ian Webb had thoroughly enjoyed his weekend leave. The man was in his mid-thirties and wearing a white short-sleeved shirt, shorts and long socks. With white shoes and his white-topped peaked cap, the contrast with the black rings under his bloodshot eyes was marked.

'Take a seat, Ian, said Dowson, pointing at the vacant side of his meeting table. He introduced Bob and Monique. 'What have you got for us?'

'I can tell you that it is human blood on the piece of towel you gave me, sir. I was able to determine that it was blood type B. I can also tell you from our records that Lieutenant Ewing has type B blood.'

'That's quite rare, isn't it?' asked Monique.

'It's not the rarest, but yes, you're right, Madame Dubois. Only about one in ten people has that blood type.'

'Which makes it probable that the blood on the towel belongs to Lieutenant Ewing,' said Monique.

'Probable but far from certain. You'd need to know whether anyone else who might have used the towel also has type B blood. I understand that it was found in his girlfriend's flat. It follows from what I've just said that there's only a one in ten chance that she also has that type of blood. But if she does, then you suddenly find yourself with only a 50/50 chance that the blood on the towel belongs to Lieutenant Ewing.'

'Thank you, Surgeon Lieutenant Commander Webb,' said Bob.

'We need to talk to Anne Milner,' said Monique. 'She was on duty over the weekend but I suppose she might be again today. Let's try 3 Scots Street first.'

*

The front door leading from the street into Anne Milner's block of flats was locked.

'I was hoping we'd find her at 3 Scots Street,' said Monique. 'Having said that, it might be easier talking to her here. At least we can count on there being no interruptions.'

'And I was hoping to find Air Vice-Marshal Park there, too,' said Bob. 'I wanted to respond to his job offer face-to-face. At least he'll know that I tried to see him and the note I left for him leaves him in no doubt about my position.'

'Still no regrets?' asked Monique. Bob shook his head. 'You might want to look away for this bit,' she said. she unslung her handbag from her shoulder and moved so her body was between Bob and the door.

'You'll have to teach me how you do that,' said Bob. 'I was there when you did it in Orkney but I've never thought to ask how.'

Monique smiled. 'Are you sure you really want to know, Bob? Anyway, that's it open, let's go in.'

'We could just have rung her doorbell or a neighbour's doorbell.'

'True, but this way we get a better idea of whether Anne is in, even if she's pretending to be out. We need to climb the stairs to the top.'

Monique led the way to the top-floor landing. She looked at Bob and put a finger to her lips, then walked quietly over to the

239

door of Anne's flat and put her ear to the door. She was grateful that Bob had understood what she wanted and was standing still at the top of the stairs. After what she thought must be two or three minutes, Monique took a step back from the door and knocked loudly with her knuckle.

She then stepped forwards and put her ear to the door again before knocking a second time. Monique looked at Bob.

'It appears she's not at home or at work,' he said.

Monique walked across the landing and knocked on the other door. This time she heard movement in the flat and stepped back as Jane Brookes opened the door.

'Hello, can I help you?' Jane looked quizzically at Monique then smiled. 'It's Monique Dubois, isn't it? Only this time you've not got your blonde wig on.'

'Hello, Jane. Can I introduce my colleague, Group Captain Robert Sutherland?'

Bob smiled from his position at the top of the stairs.

'We were hoping to have a word with Anne Milner,' said Monique. 'But she's not in and I know she's not on duty today either.'

'I'm sorry,' said Jane. 'I met her on the bottom flight of stairs not long ago. I'd been out to lunch with a friend and was coming back. Anne was just on her way out. Should I tell her you're looking for her if I hear her come back?'

'No, please don't, Jane. Let's keep it between ourselves.'

'Of course, I entirely understand.'

Monique said her farewells and led Bob down the stairs. She very much doubted that Jane did understand but hoped she would keep quiet about their visit if she saw Anne.

The navy car was waiting for them where they'd left it, on a street running parallel to the one on which Anne Milner lived.

While they were still a little distance away from the car, Bob touched Monique on the arm and she turned towards him.

'We'll need to come back later to talk to Anne Milner,' he said. 'I think that makes the next item on our agenda our return visit to Captain Bianchi's. That in turn gives us a slight logistical problem because there's no way I'm going to get changed in the back of the car a third time, especially not in a built-up area.'

Monique realised what the problem was and smiled. 'And there's equally no way you want to visit Captain Bianchi's dressed like that. It's not really the natural habitat of senior officers in uniform, is it? Though I bet that some have had memorable moments there while out of uniform. Let's go back to our hotel and then release the driver for the rest of the day. We can walk from there to Captain Bianchi's, it's not far. Then we can walk back here, via the hotel if you really think you need to change clothes again.'

*

Monique led the way into the Osborne Hotel from South Street with Bob close behind her.

He didn't realise quickly enough that she'd come to a sudden halt and came very close to walking into the back of her. The brightness in the street meant that Bob's good eye took a moment to adjust to the relative darkness of the hotel's entrance hall and it took his mind a moment more to realise that Monique's abrupt stop was caused by the sight of Anne Milner sitting on a chair on one side of the hall.

Anne stood up. 'Hello, Monique. Hello, Group Captain Sutherland.'

'Hello Anne,' said Monique. 'Do you mind my asking why you're here? I'm very pleased to see you, of course, just a little surprised.'

'I bumped into the lady who lives downstairs from me a little earlier, for the first time in a few days. She said that a blonde woman who said she was a friend of mine had knocked on her door yesterday morning, asking questions about me. I couldn't think of anyone it might have been and then wondered if it was you in disguise. I thought it best to come and ask you myself. I was having doubts about whether that was a good idea by the time I got here so I called in at 3 Scots Street for a cup of tea and to decide what to do. They told me that you and the group captain had been in only a short time earlier, asking if I was on duty today. I came straight over to wait for you.'

'You might have been waiting for ages,' said Monique.

'What I've got to say is quite important, so I was prepared to wait. I've not been entirely truthful with you and I want to set the record straight and clear the air between us.'

Monique looked at Bob. It took him a moment to recognise the very unfamiliar look of uncertainty on her face. He thought he knew what was causing it. The hotel had a guest lounge for those whose accommodation only extended to bedrooms but talking to Anne Milner where they could very easily be disturbed by other guests didn't seem a good idea.

'Let's talk in the drawing room in our suite,' he said.

He saw Monique raise her eyebrows as if she'd not been expecting him to suggest that.

Monique turned back towards Anne and gestured along the hall. 'It's this way, Anne. I'll lead and the group captain can follow.'

Once upstairs in their suite's drawing room, Monique waved

towards one of the armchairs and sat down in the other. Anne sat awkwardly, perched on the front of the armchair and leaning forwards. Bob brought a chair through from the bedroom. He'd noticed how Monique had discomforted Charles Richmond at Hagar Qim by where she chose to sit. The layout of the drawing room didn't quite allow the same approach now, but he positioned the chair so it gave the widest possible angle between Monique and himself when seen from Anne's position. Although nothing had been said, he sensed that Monique wanted to take the lead, which suited him fine. He intended to remain quiet unless Monique indicated otherwise and, as far as possible, to stay out of Anne's line of sight.

'I'm not sure where to begin,' said Anne.

'Can we start with the weekend that James disappeared?' asked Monique. 'After we'd eaten at the King Edward Hotel you gave me an account of that weekend that seemed, even at the time, to be questionable. Can you try again?'

'Yes, of course. What I said to you about the Friday was true. James came to the flat in the evening and we went out for dinner at the King Edward Hotel.

'On the Saturday morning, we got a bus to the beach at Ghajn Tuffieha. I think I told you I'd been trying to get James to take me there for ages and was quite upset that he'd appeared embarrassed by the idea of going somewhere where we'd be seen by the officers and men of the 10th Submarine Flotilla. I also mentioned to you the feeling I sometimes get that James is ashamed of me and how hurtful I find that.

'We'd taken packed lunches and in the afternoon we both slept for a while in the shade of some trees at the end of the beach. Afterwards, James began to behave oddly. We had a stupid argument about sand getting in the last remaining sandwich. We were going to share it but he threw it away instead. It wasn't long afterwards that we walked past the officer he shares a room with and his girlfriend. We said hello but didn't stop or ask to be introduced to her and I'm afraid we must have seemed rather unfriendly. We stuck it out but didn't talk much after that and the rest of the afternoon wasn't much fun. Then we got a bus back to Floriana.'

'What time did you get home?' asked Monique.

'I'm not sure, but it was probably about 5 p.m. It's not far from the bus stop to the flat but James stopped me on the way and said there was something he needed to tell me. He said that he needed a change in his life and I wouldn't be seeing him any more. I think I told you when we talked that I've sometimes thought of leaving him and finding someone else. Now I look more like a woman again and less like a skeleton, I ought to be able to find someone. But when he said he was leaving me it was a huge shock. I didn't want to get into an argument in the street so held in how I felt.

'We walked back to the flat in silence. Once inside we bumped into the appalling woman who lives in the flat opposite me and her windbag of a husband, who were just leaving. I think we got as far as the top landing before something snapped and I started shouting at James, with all the hurt and frustration and anger coming out. He gave as good as he got.'

'What about when you went into the flat?'

'That was rather sad. We carried on shouting at each other and then I saw my crystal glass decanter on the sideboard. The decanter and four matching glasses are my prized possessions, a gift from a very dear friend, the man who owned the theatre I was dancing in when the first bombs fell on Malta. He was killed not long afterwards in an air raid.

'Anyway, in a moment of madness, I picked up the decanter and threw it at James. It missed him and went clean through the living room door before smashing into what seemed like a million pieces against the wall of the hall. I just broke down in tears at the awfulness of what I'd done. James tried to comfort me but I was inconsolable. Then he found the sticky tape I've used to put across the panes of glass in the flat's windows and, after sweeping up all the bits, stuck the largest surviving parts of the decanter back together.

'It's hardly a replacement and looks very odd but it was a nice gesture and it showed how kind and thoughtful James can sometimes be. Then, without any warning, he came down with a bad nosebleed. I don't know if it was because of the argument or perhaps something to do with his injured ear but it took ages to stop.

'We drank quite a lot that evening. James likes whisky and I like rum and I've got bottles of both in the flat that came from a friend, who probably got them on the black market though I'm happy to stay in ignorance about that. Then we made energetic love and I think I passed out afterwards, thanks to the rum.

'When I woke up the next morning, James had gone. He has a small suitcase that he kept on top of the wardrobe in my bedroom. He'd been through and taken everything he kept at the flat. It only amounted to a civilian suit, some clothes and a few other things. Not much really. That was when I knew he'd really gone.'

'Why did you make up what you told me about the Sunday?' asked Monique.

'I suppose I was trying to do something to restore my very bruised self-esteem. That was also why I dug myself into that stupid hole by telling you that James didn't keep anything other than his shaving kit and toothbrush at my flat. That wasn't credible and it risked you seeing that the toiletries were no longer there if you'd gone into the bathroom. It was all very stupid and I am truly sorry, Monique.'

'Why do you dislike your neighbours so much?' asked Monique.

'The husband is an army major who thinks he's single-handedly responsible for preventing Hitler and Mussolini from invading Malta. I exchanged pleasantries with him when they first moved in but I fairly quickly found myself trying to avoid him. The woman is called Jane. She seems to think I'm trying to take her husband away from her. She stopped me on the stairs once and accused me of flirting with him. I laughed in her face. Nothing could be further from the truth.

'Maybe I'm falling into the same trap myself, but I did get the impression once or twice that she had taken quite a liking to James despite the age difference between them and the fact that she's nothing to write home about in the looks department. I usually get on quite well with people but there's a lot about Jane and Daniel Brookes that I simply don't like.'

Monique looked at her watch. 'Thank you for coming to see us, Anne. Is there anything else you want to tell us?'

'No, I think we've covered it,' said Anne. 'I'd just repeat what I've already said about how sorry I am for lying to you.'

'Given what you've said, I think I need to go and talk to your neighbour, Jane Brookes. It might be best if you could find a reason not to go back to your flat for the next hour or so. I'd like to avoid even the possibility of the three of us meeting on the landing you share.'

Anne smiled. 'Would it be inappropriate to suggest that I could stay here with your handsome husband while you go and see Jane? No, don't even reply to that. I'll find somewhere else to be for the next hour.'

'That seems best,' said Monique. 'And anyway, Bob will be walking me to Floriana.'

*

They walked together in silence as far as the bus station.

'That was unexpected,' said Bob. 'Do you believe what she said?'

'I think I do. Most of it, certainly. The reason I want to come and talk to Jane Brookes again is to sort out in my head some of the areas of doubt around the edges. I'm not sure how important they are, but this stuff about Anne Milner and Daniel Brookes still troubles me a little. Was Anne making too much of how strongly she dislikes Daniel when talking to us just now?'

'Do you want a male perspective?' asked Bob.

'Yes, of course.'

'I think Anne simply flirts with the people she meets because it's something that has always served her well in the past. She even flirted with me and teased you just now at the end of that interview. She does it without thinking and often, I suspect, without meaning it or even realising she's doing it. If I'm right then I see no contradiction between her disliking Daniel Brookes and describing him as a windbag on the one hand and her flirting with him on the other.'

'Thanks, Bob, that does make a lot of sense. Something else puzzling me is the idea of Jane Brookes taking a fancy to James Ewing. I've been wondering if Anne threw that into the mix simply to mislead us. But I did believe most of what she said.

The story about James telling her he was leaving and the argument that followed rang true. I also believed what she said about the smashed decanter and his nose bleed and him then packing and leaving while she was asleep. All we now need to do is find out what happened to him after he left so, in that respect, we're actually no further forward.'

Monique didn't need to pick the lock on the outside door this time and again led the way up to the top floor landing.

'What do you want me to do?' asked Bob.

'Just stay outside and watch my back. If her husband's inside you might need to come in and talk to him while I talk to Jane. If he turns up while I'm inside, just tell him who you are and that I'm talking to Jane about Anne Milner.'

If Jane was surprised to see Monique again so quickly, she didn't show it.

'Come on in. I'll make you both a cup of tea.'

'I'll come in on my own if that's all right with you, Jane. That way we can keep it completely informal, just a chat between the two of us.'

'Yes, of course.'

Jane turned back into the flat and Monique followed, careful not to fully close the front door. As before, they went into the kitchen and Monique sat on one of the two wooden chairs flanking the folding table while Jane made the tea.

'I hope you don't mind me asking,' said Monique, 'but does Anne Milner really spend her whole time flirting with your husband Daniel?'

Jane placed a cup and saucer in front of Monique and then sat down with her tea. 'From what he tells me and from what I've seen myself she does seem to flirt with him a lot. That might just be her way, but we both find it uncomfortable.'

'What about you and James Ewing?' asked Monique. 'Was there ever any spark between you when you met on the stairs?'

'That's just silly. He's getting on for ten years younger than me and is very attractive. For someone like him, I'm hardly a catch, even without a husband in tow.'

'Did the thought never cross your mind?'

'I can't believe you're seriously asking me this, Monique.'

Monique could see that Jane was avoiding looking at her. 'Why not? You just said how attractive you find him.'

Jane finally looked up from the table and met Monique's eyes. 'Of course the thought crossed my mind. There was one night when I thought about it very seriously. He and Anne seemed to argue a lot. Late one night he knocked on the door of the flat after they'd had a row. He said he'd been kicked out by her without his security pass or his shoes and she was refusing to open the door. It was after curfew so he couldn't leave the building. We've got a small spare bedroom and I made the bed up for him. I should have said Daniel was on duty that night and I knew he wouldn't be back until late the next morning. I spent the whole night lying awake and wondering what would happen if I went into the spare room and took my dressing gown off. I never found out, of course.

'And what happened on the Saturday night he disappeared? I should tell you that I've spoken to Anne and she has told me about their argument and about smashing a crystal glass decanter that she threw against a wall. She says they then had quite a lot to drink and she slept very heavily. She says that while she was asleep he packed his belongings in a suitcase and left. Do you know what happened after that?'

Anne looked down at the table for a while before replying. 'I was really angry. It wasn't Daniel's fault, but the air raid

249

warnings had gone off as the dance at St Andrew's Barracks was drawing to a close. Even though it was a false alarm, Daniel said he needed to stay at the barracks, just in case something else happened. He got a staff car to drive me home on my own. I'd been hoping for a romantic evening, but it wasn't to be.'

'And then what happened?' asked Monique.

'I was awoken a little after 1 a.m. by a noise that I worked out, when it happened again, was knocking on the door from the landing. Daniel keeps a revolver here which he's taught me how to use on the range at the barracks. I took the gun out of the drawer we keep it in, made sure it was ready to fire, and opened the door.'

'Then what?' asked Monique.

'It was James. He was dressed in a civilian suit and carrying a suitcase. He asked if he could come in. I said yes.'

There was a long pause.

Monique felt like she'd been holding her breath. 'And then?'

'He told me that he'd left Anne. He said he needed a change in his life. He had somewhere to go, but couldn't go there until later that morning. He asked if he could sleep in the spare room again.'

'What did you do with the revolver?' asked Monique.

'What? Oh, I see. Did you think I was about to tell you that I shot James with it? I'm sorry if I misled you. No, I made the revolver safe and put it back in its drawer and made up the spare bed for James.'

'And you had another sleepless night thinking about what might have been?'

Jane's smile answered the question before she uttered a word. 'No. My anger with Daniel overcame my self-doubt and

I found out exactly what would happen if I went into the spare room and took my dressing gown off. I'm sorry I lied to you just now about James and me, but it was only one night and it will never amount to anything more.'

'And the next morning?' asked Monique.

'I went back to my room quite early, while James was still sleeping. Later on, we got up and had breakfast as if nothing had happened. Then he kissed me in a way that made me sure it hadn't been a dream and said he had to go. He asked me to go out onto the landing to see if I could hear whether Anne was moving around in her flat and when I couldn't, he went quickly down the stairs.'

'What time was that?'

'9.40 a.m. I remember looking at my watch as he went down the stairs to make sure there was no chance of him meeting Daniel.'

'And he gave you no clue at all about what he intended to do or where he intended to go?'

'I'm sorry, no,' said Jane.

Monique didn't believe her. 'Are you sure?'

She saw the woman's expression change from something like bliss to anger in an instant.

'Yes, I'm sure. I'd like you to leave now, Monique. And remember that I'm trusting you not to breathe a word of what I've just told you to anyone. I deeply regret being so honest with you, but I suppose it's your job to get people to tell you things they'd prefer to keep secret.'

'If you do think of anything else, Jane…'

'Yes, I know, I can contact you at the Osborne Hotel.'

Bob looked at Monique expectantly as she walked out of the door of the flat.

'Let's talk outside, Bob. No, I've got a better idea. Do we have to go to Captain Bianchi's this evening?'

'No, I'm sure it will keep until the morning, why?'

'In that case, let's give ourselves the rest of the day off. I'll treat you to dinner and a bottle or two of expensive wine at the King Edward Hotel. It's quite near here and the rabbit spaghetti is great. I'll tell you about what I've just learned on the way.'

CHAPTER TWENTY-THREE

The more boisterous parts of Strait Street seemed very quiet and had a slightly hungover feel a little before 10 a.m. the next morning. Monique's map of Valletta showed something she'd not previously noticed, that Strait Street crossed South Street not far from their hotel, making their walk to Captain Bianchi's both more straightforward and rather shorter than if they'd gone via Kingsway and Palace Square.

'Don't you think it's a bit of a coincidence Bob?' asked Monique. 'We were intending to call in on Captain Bianchi's this morning anyway, only to have Charles Richmond telephone the hotel and leave a message asking us to meet him there.'

'I agree,' said Bob. 'As messages go, "Meet Alfred at Stuart's" and a time doesn't tell us much, but it leaves me feeling hopeful something might have turned up. Doubtless, we'll find out when we get there.'

'I can't imagine the place being open at this time of the morning,' said Monique.

Bob smiled at her. 'No, I'm counting on it being closed. That's why I don't have a problem wearing my uniform.'

'The street feels very different, doesn't it?' asked Monique.

'What, without young ladies selling themselves in doorways? I'm impressed by the number of people we've seen sweeping up last night's debris, though we still need to watch where we're putting our feet. I nearly trod on a used condom a moment ago.'

'Charming,' said Monique. 'Here we are. It certainly looks closed, but then it did on Sunday.'

Bob pushed at the door, then stood back and knocked.

Monique heard the sound of the door being unlocked before it was opened by Stuart McQueen. He smiled when he saw them and ushered them into the front bar, then locked the door behind them.

'I've got some coffee made in the back room. Be careful on the steps, most of the lights are out.'

The back room did look very different with fewer lights and without its customers.

Monique saw Charles Richmond sitting at the table in the back corner of the room that she'd selected on their previous visit.

'Thank you for being on time,' said Richmond as they approached. 'I'm told you like this table, Mrs Sutherland, so I suggested we use it this morning. Please take a seat.' Despite the dim lighting, he must have seen her doubt reflected on her face. 'Don't worry. I've got more to lose than the two of you if the wrong people learn about this meeting. You have my assurance there are no hidden microphones.'

Stuart McQueen served coffee and then took the vacant fourth chair at the table.

Richmond leaned forwards in his chair. 'I should start by telling you that I have cleared up Stuart's misunderstanding about your being with SIS, so there's no need for formal introductions.'

'We were intending to call in on Stuart this morning anyway,' said Bob, 'so your message was very timely. Why do you want to talk to us?'

Richmond put his coffee cup down on its saucer. 'Would you first indulge me by telling us why you wanted to see Stuart? I suspect that might overlap with why we want to see you.'

'Very well,' said Bob. 'On the Friday night that Edward Price was here, Stuart telephoned some of his contacts to see if he could find out anything that might help in Edward's search for James Ewing, the missing naval lieutenant. The only thing you heard that was worth passing on, Stuart, was a rumour that a body had been put on board a fishing boat at Marsaxlokk at night, a boat that was subsequently destroyed in an explosion.

'The timing seemed to fit with the disappearance of the lieutenant and Edward Price was interested enough to visit Marsaxlokk the next day. He spent some time asking people around the harbour what they knew about the fishing boat that had been destroyed. He then had lunch in a bar. His questions had caused some concern in the village and the local police sergeant subsequently interviewed Edward, telling him that he - the sergeant - had investigated the rumour about the body and believed that it amounted to nothing. We spoke to the same sergeant and came away with the view that he was a thoroughly professional officer who had been straight with Edward and was being straight with us.

'Edward left Marsaxlokk and was driven to Hagar Qim where he met you, Charles. He didn't talk about Marsaxlokk to you but did tell you that he had just over a week to find the missing lieutenant. You got no sense that he thought he'd just made a breakthrough in his search and my impression from following as closely as I can in his footsteps is that he'd probably discounted the rumour about Marsaxlokk from his thinking.

'What I've been wondering is whether the time Edward Price spent asking questions around the harbour at Marsaxlokk did more than give rise to "some concern" locally. What if someone felt threatened by his investigation? The reason we intended to come to see you this morning, Stuart, was to ask you to try once more to find out what people know, this time with specific reference to the fishing boat at Marsaxlokk. It would help, for example, to know more about the person who told you about the rumour in the first place and whether you can find out who told them, to trace it back to its source if possible.'

Monique saw Charles Richmond and Stuart McQueen both smile, almost as if Bob had told an amusing anecdote.

'What you're saying chimed with thoughts I had after we met yesterday,' said Richmond. 'You learned rather more at Marsaxlokk, but what you told me before you went was enough for me to wonder whether the rumour that Edward had shown an interest in might be connected to his disappearance.

'I came here later in the day and had a pleasant evening while Stuart phoned round and called in favours from some of his contacts, just as you were going to suggest, Bob. He carried on talking to people long after I'd left and returned to my flat.'

'What did you find out, Stuart?' asked Monique. 'You must have unearthed something or Charles wouldn't have contacted us this morning.'

Stuart McQueen sat forwards in his seat. 'I started by very discreetly trying to unravel the rumour I'd been told. Remember that if we're talking about a dead body, two further murders and the disappearance of an SIS agent then the people involved are extremely dangerous. I have many friends in Malta who, between them, offer me protection of various kinds. But there are lots of factions amongst the criminal fraternity on the islands and I try not to anger any of them. Getting a bullet in my head as I step out into Strait Street late one night isn't top of my list of ambitions.

'Nonetheless, after talking to a few people, and giving them time to talk to other people and then get back to me, I did end up talking to a man who told me that even though it was during the curfew and the blackout was in force he'd actually seen the body being moved from one fishing boat to another in the harbour. Even better, because they'd been careless with their torches, he could identify one of the two men who had done it. I was given the name of the man involved, in return for a promise of certain services the next time my informant visits Captain Bianchi's.'

'Wasn't that rather dangerous when your calls would have been routed via a public switchboard?' asked Monique.

'Yes,' said Stuart, 'but they can't listen to everyone and the man who runs the telephone exchange is a customer of mine. That affords me a little privacy.'

'Who was the man identified as moving the body?' asked Monique.

'I'll tell you in a moment, Monique. First, I should highlight an aspect of this that neither Richard nor Bob has mentioned. When the two of you spoke to me here, you asked me if anyone I'd talked to had mentioned Mosta as that was where Edward Price disappeared. When I tied that into what I was told last night, an interesting idea occurred to me.'

'Come on Stuart,' said Charles Richmond. 'Let's cut this "dance of the seven veils" routine. Just tell Bob and Monique what you told me when I got here this morning.'

'As you wish, Richard. Two of Malta's more unpleasant residents are the twins, Simon and Victor Micallef. Simon has a wide range of business interests across much of the island while Victor has his focus in the north and on Gozo.

'Both are involved in what you might loosely describe as

"buying and selling" and that covers a very wide range of commodities which are traded both legitimately and illegitimately. They are involved in the supply of everything from fish, vegetables and kerosene for cooking right through to silk stockings, Scotch whisky and guns. They are also heavily involved in gambling and run protection businesses in parts of the islands. They even, I've heard it said, buy and sell people's bodies and souls.

'You might think that what I do here is little better than selling people's bodies, but everyone who works for me at Captain Bianchi's, in whatever capacity, is free to leave at any time. I don't believe that is always the case with prostitutes and others employed by the Micallef twins. In the background, there is talk of a fairly vicious struggle going on for business between them and elements of the Sicilian Mafia who have long been entrenched in Malta and want to extend their reach further. This has resulted in a number of deaths and disappearances.

'Amongst the businesses that Simon Micallef owns is a fish trading company in Marsaxlokk. Last night I was told that the man who manages that company, Anthony Attard, was one of the men who moved the body into the boat that later exploded. The thought that then occurred to me was about location. Simon Micallef lives at and runs his business interests from a farm with offices and warehouses located to the west of Marsaxlokk. Victor, on the other hand, has his business premises on Gozo and lives in a grand villa in Mosta.'

'That sounds like solid progress,' said Monique. 'You're saying that you've linked the Micallef twins to the bomb in the boat and that one of the Micallef twins lives in Mosta. It's a stretch to suggest that's why Edward Price disappeared in

Mosta, but it's the first link we've had with the city and it's a lot more than we had before.'

'Did you find anything to link the Micallef twins with the missing naval lieutenant?' asked Bob. 'If his was the body put in the boat then there must have been a reason for his death, especially if the explosion wasn't caused by a mine. That would suggest that the two fishermen were also murdered.'

'I'm sorry,' said Stuart. 'No one could tell me anything about the identity of the body and, though I stopped short of using his name in talking to people, there was nothing that sounded like it was linked to the lieutenant.'

'Thank you anyway, Stuart. You've been very helpful.'

'What do you intend to do with what we've told you, Bob?' asked Charles Richmond.

'I'm not sure. Stuart, in your experience, how straight are the police in Malta? If I go and have another chat at the police station in Marsaxlokk, is someone going to report my interest to the Micallef twins as soon as I leave?'

Stuart smiled. 'You'll have worked out that if every policeman in Malta strictly enforced the letter of the law in all circumstances then I would have a very hard time running Captain Bianchi's. Having said that, you have less chance of stumbling over a bent copper here than you would in London. There certainly are some and I may have entertained the occasional one here. But the inspector running the station at Marsaxlokk, a man called Farrugia, has a reputation for doing things by the book. I suspect that reputation means that people in the area sometimes aren't as open with him and his officers as they might be if he were a little more flexible. But I think it also means you could talk to him without fear that word of your interest would leak.'

'Thank you again, Stuart.'

'Bob, can you answer a question for me?' asked Stuart. 'Since you came here on Sunday afternoon I've had this sense that you and I have met before.'

'You said you were from Glasgow and ended up running a hotel in London in 1939,' said Bob. 'I suppose it depends on what you were doing until then. When the war broke out I was a detective sergeant in the City of Glasgow Police.'

'I pride myself on never forgetting a face,' said Stuart. 'It's important in my line of business. I have a feeling you might have arrested me once for pimping.'

'It's possible,' said Bob. 'We've both come a long way since then.'

Monique tried not to smile when she realised that Bob was being deliberately ambiguous.

CHAPTER TWENTY-FOUR

'Thank you for seeing us, Inspector Farrugia,' said Bob. 'I'm glad we've come at a time when both you and Sergeant Spiteri are on duty.'

The inspector's office in Marsaxlokk's police station was well-appointed and had windows that appeared to open out onto a stone gallery overlooking the harbour. A large bookcase stood against one dark green-painted wall and there were maps and paintings of fishing boats hanging on other walls. Inspector Farrugia was a muscular man of above-average height with black hair and glasses. Bob thought he was probably in his mid-thirties.

The inspector sat behind a large wooden desk inlaid with a green leather top and from the absence of clutter seemed to be an orderly man. Bob wished he was able to keep his own desk as tidy.

Bob and Monique sat on wooden armchairs pulled up on the other side of the desk, while Sergeant Spiteri sat to one side with his notebook open.

'I'm pleased to meet you, Group Captain Sutherland, and you Madame Dubois. Sergeant Spiteri told me about his meeting with the two of you yesterday and I was quite intrigued by what he had to say. Are you back because you've found out more?'

'That's right, inspector,' said Monique. 'I'll be brief because I can only tell you what we believe we know and not who our sources are.'

'You'll understand that's not ideal from a policeman's point of view,' said the inspector, smiling. 'Carry on.'

'I'm sure you know about the visit to Marsaxlokk on Saturday the 5th of June by Edward Price, who is with the Secret Intelligence Service. You may not be aware of this but Mr Price was in Malta to look for a naval lieutenant who disappeared on Sunday the 30th of May.'

'And Mr Price wanted to establish whether the rumoured body in the boat might be that of the naval lieutenant?' asked the inspector. 'I have been wondering what lay behind his interest. Thank you.'

Monique continued. 'As you say, he was in Marsaxlokk because he'd been told about the rumour that a body was seen being put in the boat that subsequently blew up. The timing seemed to fit well with the lieutenant's disappearance.'

'But it is only a rumour,' said the inspector. 'Sergeant Spiteri told you that we've been unable to find any substance behind it.'

'He did,' said Monique. 'An informant has now told us more. We've been told that even though it was dark and both the curfew and the blackout were in force, a witness saw two men move the body from another fishing boat onto the one that exploded the next morning. Because they were careless with their torches, this witness identified one of the men as Anthony Attard.'

Bob had half-turned in his seat as Monique approached this point in her account so he could see the faces of both Inspector Farrugia and Sergeant Spiteri with his good right eye. Both looked initially surprised, which Bob took as a good sign. Then something else fleetingly crossed the sergeant's face, a sort of smug 'I told you so' look which the inspector acknowledged with a rueful smile before looking at Bob and realising he was being watched.

'Do you know who Anthony Attard is, Madame Dubois?' asked the inspector.

'I understand he runs a fish trading company here. I'm told that the owner of the company is Simon Micallef, who also owns other businesses across much of Malta, some of which operate on the right side of the law and some of which don't. He runs his businesses from a farm to the west of Marsaxlokk. We were also told that Simon Micallef has a twin brother, Victor, who owns a similarly broad range of businesses in the north of the island and on Gozo. His are run from premises on Gozo but he lives in Mosta.'

The inspector had become more guarded in his facial expressions since he noticed Bob watching him and the names of the Micallef twins had evoked little response from him. The sergeant was looking down at his notebook without writing anything.

The inspector leaned forwards. 'Perhaps I'm being a little slow this morning, Madame Dubois, but would you care to spell out as simply as possible what you think happened?'

'Yes, of course, inspector. The missing naval lieutenant was last seen in Floriana on the Sunday morning. That night someone working for Simon Micallef moved a body from one fishing boat to another here in Marsaxlokk harbour. The next morning that fishing boat exploded, possibly because it hit a mine or possibly because someone wanted to cover up the disposal of the body.

'Move the clock forward to the following Saturday and Edward Price arrived in the village having heard a rumour about a body and asked questions about the loss of the boat that caused concern amongst villagers. He subsequently met Sergeant Spiteri and, as a result, apparently decided that the rumour about the body had no foundation.

'What I have to say next is a little speculative. We know that the day after he came to Marsaxlokk, Edward Price asked to be taken to Mosta because he knew that the naval lieutenant and his girlfriend had visited the city.' Monique looked at Bob. 'What we've been wondering is this. What if the questions Edward Price asked in Marsaxlokk caused someone here to feel threatened by him? They would have no way of knowing that his thinking had moved on. And what if the threat they felt was so great that the following day they abducted him in Mosta?'

'I'm sorry, Madame Dubois,' said the inspector. 'Are you seriously expecting me to believe that the Micallef twins were responsible for murdering the missing naval lieutenant and that to cover that up they killed two fishermen here and then abducted and perhaps killed an agent of the Secret Intelligence Service? Have you established any link between the missing naval lieutenant and the Micallef twins?'

'No, we haven't,' said Monique.

'I would be the last person in Malta to try to defend the character of either of the twins, who are without doubt up to their necks in a range of illegal activities. But the motiveless murder of a British naval officer would be further than I suspect even they would want to go. And, other than by saying that Victor Micallef lives in Mosta, which is correct, how are you suggesting that questions Mr Price asked in Marsaxlokk could have had consequences a day later in Mosta? The two places are separated by ten miles or approaching two-thirds of the length of the island. Sergeant Sptieri has told me that Mr Price is the sort of man who stands out in a crowd, but I think your theory is stretching credibility beyond breaking point.'

Bob felt he had sat on the sidelines for long enough. 'You do understand, don't you, inspector, that if Edward Price comes to harm because you've failed to take seriously what we've told you, the responsibility will be yours?'

'Are you threatening me, group captain?'

'No, I'm simply explaining some facts of life that seem to have passed you by. There is every possibility that Edward Price is already dead and he may have been dead since the day he disappeared. But what if he's alive and being held somewhere by the Micallef twins and you do nothing about it? Consider how that is going to look.'

The inspector held Bob's gaze for a moment, then glanced at Sergeant Spiteri, who had closed his notebook. It appeared to Bob that something passed between them, but he couldn't quite decide what it was.

Then the inspector looked back at Bob. 'While some of your ideas run far ahead of any supporting evidence, it was never my intention to ignore what you and Madame Dubois have said to me. I apologise to both of you if I gave that impression. Your naming of Anthony Attard, even without a source, is particularly helpful. I would ask you to give me 48 hours to look into all this and I promise to report back to you within that period. In the meantime, I would ask that you do nothing further to create waves, either in Marsaxlokk or with the Micallef twins. I don't want to find in a day or two's time that the list of missing people has extended from a naval lieutenant to an SIS agent to two members of Military Intelligence, Section 11.'

*

'That was fun,' said Monique. They were walking beside the

harbour in Marsxlokk on another scorching day. At least she'd come equipped with the sunhat and sunglasses. 'Thanks for your support when he decided that taking a woman seriously was beneath him.'

'Do you think that's what it was?' asked Bob. 'Something was going on below the surface of the inspector's responses and I don't know if it was simply misogyny. I didn't come away feeling that he was untrustworthy but he certainly wasn't being open with us.'

Monique grimaced. 'Do you think that was a threat he made at the end: "Back off or you'll both disappear too"?'

'I don't know, but we do need to be careful.' Bob looked at his watch. 'We might not have appreciated having to wait in Palace Square for a navy car to pick us up and bring us here or waiting twenty minutes to see the inspector, but those delays do mean that the bar you found yesterday is serving lunch and I, for one, wouldn't mind repeating the experience.'

'Should we go and find the driver and offer him lunch again?' said Monique. 'That will ease our conscience afterwards and ensure he's on hand for the trip back to Valletta, assuming that's where we want to go. I don't know about you, Bob, but I'm running out of ideas about how we move forward.'

'I feel the same, Monique. We know what Lieutenant Ewing was doing, and who with, until 9.40 a.m. on the Sunday, when he left the Brookes' flat in Floriana carrying a suitcase and wearing a civilian suit. Then he dropped off the edge of the world. And we know what Edward Price was doing from the time he arrived in Malta until late on the morning of the following Sunday when he, too, dropped off the edge of the world.

'Our only remaining leads for both disappearances all seem to point towards the Micallef twins but you and I agree that our trail of logic is tenuous in places. And we've been warned off trying to find out more about the twins by the police.'

'Are we going to take any notice of them?' asked Monique.

'To my mind, we should give the inspector 24 hours to come up with something, rather than the 48 he's given himself. I suggest that this afternoon we take a leaf from Edward Price's book by following in the footsteps of Anne Milner and James Ewing to Mosta.'

'Won't that seem like we're ignoring the inspector's request to avoid creating waves?'

'It might appear that way, but given the breadth of the Micallef twins' business interests, it seems to me that going anywhere in Malta could be considered to be creating waves. I see no reason why a visit to Mosta should be any more provocative than anything else we might do. It's not as if we're planning to knock on the front door of Victor Micallef's villa and ask if he knows anything about Edward Price's disappearance.'

Monique wasn't sure if he was joking or not. 'Is that what you've got in mind?'

'No, I think that really would fall within the category of "making waves". Besides, we don't have Victor Micallef's address, though I'm sure Stuart McQueen could get hold of it if we asked him to.'

*

The navy driver who had picked them up in Valletta and taken them to Marsaxlokk was the man who'd been assigned to them the previous day. He had again accepted their offer of lunch and again he had chosen to sit outside the bar to eat when Monique and Bob went inside. Monique knew that drivers often felt themselves to be invisible to their passengers and that they were usually right. She was pleased that Bob shared her belief that a word of thanks and a little consideration went a long way. It was one of the many things she loved about him.

The driver broke into her chain of thought. 'Is there somewhere particular you want to go in Mosta, ma'am?'

Monique leaned forwards in the back seat. 'We're still following the trail of Mr Price, the tall man you drove to Hagar Qim and Marsaxlokk. Was it you who drove him to Mosta on the following day?'

'Sorry, ma'am, no. Though his driver that day is a mate of mine and he told me what happened. Mr Price had asked to be picked up opposite the Rotunda of Mosta, that's the usual name for the church in English, an hour after he was dropped off there. But he simply never showed up despite my mate giving him an hour extra.'

'So you've got a good idea of where he was dropped off?'

'Yes, ma'am.'

'Good, we'll go to the same place, please.' Monique turned to look through the back window of the car. 'Have you seen any sign of anyone following us since we left Marsaxlokk?'

'No ma'am. There isn't that much motorised traffic if you discount military vehicles and I think I'd have noticed if the same car or van had been behind us for any length of time. We've not come far and it's not a long journey anyway, of course, which reduces the chances of spotting anyone following.'

Monique saw Bob look at her quizzically.

'It's just an uncomfortable feeling, Bob, like when Charles followed us across Valletta and back to the hotel. It wasn't there when we were going to Marsaxlokk, but it is now.''

The driver turned his head for a moment. 'The story on Manoel Island is that the man who went missing in Mosta is with the Secret Intelligence Service. I know I shouldn't ask, but are you with SIS too?'

Monique smiled. 'I'm sure there's nothing wrong with you asking but, if we were with SIS, it wouldn't be very secret of us to say so, would it?'

She was pleased the driver took it as a joke.

Mosta turned out to be more heavily built-up than Monique had expected. The obvious signs of bomb damage on every street seemed just as bad as those she had seen in Valletta.

'You can see the Rotunda of Mosta beyond the end of this street,' said the driver.

'It's huge,' said Bob.

'Wait until you see the inside, sir. We turn left at the end here and the best place for me to drop you off, and wait for you, is opposite the Rotunda where the road curves around to the right again.'

'This will be fine,' said Monique as the driver stopped.

'Take care, ma'am. I don't want to have to go back and report that we've lost someone else.'

Bob and Monique crossed the road running past the side of the Rotunda and climbed up the steps that led to the open area in front of the very wide portico across the frontage of the building.

'This is a magnificent place, Bob, but I'm still not entirely sure why we're here and what you hope to achieve.'

Bob smiled. 'I'm still coming to terms with our driver being the second person today to express the hope we don't disappear like Edward Price. How sure are you that we were followed on the way here?'

'I can never be sure until something happens to prove me right, like Charles Richmond's letter at the Osborne Hotel. Or, for that matter, Maximilian von Moser's letter after his people had followed us back to our hotel in Stockholm. But I'm right often enough to take heed of the feeling. And if that was an attempt to deflect my question about our purpose here, you can consider it to have failed.'

'We may be wasting our time coming to Mosta, Monique. I suspect we very probably are. But let's at least find out why James Ewing was so keen to see the church.'

Bob took her arm and Monique allowed herself to be led through a doorway beyond which was a crowded entrance area. This then opened out into the interior of the body of the church. There were people here too, but they were less obvious because of the sheer scale of the place.

Bob stopped, his head tilted backwards. Monique thought the space they were now standing in was literally breathtaking. Above their heads was an incredibly ornate dome whose size seemed to defy belief. Below it, a gallery ran around the inside of the dome with windows at regular intervals. The perfection of the pattern covering the interior of the dome was interrupted a little above halfway down from the oculus in its centre to the gallery around its circumference by an area of obvious damage.

Lower still and extending up from the floor were a series of apses or side chapels evenly spaced around the circular body of the church. But it was the dome itself that held Monique's attention.

'Hello, can I help you?'

Monique looked down to see an elderly man with grey hair and wearing a cassock standing in front of them.

'Hello, father,' said Bob. 'We were simply admiring this wonderful place. A friend suggested we visit. I was trying to work out how old it is.'

'Work began in 1833 and it was completed 28 years later. That makes it only a little over 80 years old. To my mind, the most remarkable thing is that they built all this around the church it was intended to replace, which was then demolished in 1860.'

'I think it's the sheer size of the dome that amazes me most,' said Bob.

'That is a common reaction. The design was inspired by the Pantheon in Rome, and what you are looking at is the third-largest free-standing dome in the world. We are lucky it's still here, though.'

'We were told about the miracle,' said Monique.

'Yes. I wasn't here at the time myself. It was on the 9th of April last year and over 300 people were in here waiting for the start of early evening mass. Mosta has always suffered badly in the air raids because we are on the route enemy bombers take when attacking the airfield at Ta Kali, which isn't far away. I suspect the Rotunda must be quite a landmark when seen from the air. Three bombs hit the church. Two were deflected without exploding while the third came through the dome, leaving the damage you can see up there.' The priest pointed. 'It, thankfully, also failed to explode. As you say, people talk of it as a miracle and it is easy to understand why.'

'What happened to the bomb?' asked Bob.

'It was made safe by a Royal Engineers bomb disposal team and dumped in the sea off the island's west coast, like the many others that have had to be dealt with in the same way.'

'Thank you,' said Bob, 'I'm very grateful.' He turned to look at Monique. 'Are you happy if we simply spend some time taking this place in?'

She smiled. 'Of course, Bob.'

When they emerged a little later, Monique found it took a moment for her eyes to get used to the sun again. 'That was wonderful, but perhaps not very useful. Are there any more tourist sights you want to see, Bob, given we've run out of actual leads we can pursue short of knocking on the door of one or other of the Micallef twins?'

Bob looked at his watch. 'If we're going to continue with our theme of following Edward Price as he followed Anne and James, there's one other place I think it would be helpful to see. Not because I think we'll discover anything of real value, but because it might help us get just a little closer to the two missing men.'

Monique smiled. 'You're going to suggest an afternoon trip to the beach, aren't you, Bob?'

'That's right. I'm not sure exactly where Ghajn Tuffieha is, but I've come to understand that nowhere is very far from anywhere else in Malta. We are on our honeymoon after all, and we might find somewhere selling ice cream or gelato. And, as you have just said, we are running out of better or more useful ideas.'

*

Monique was excellent company as they enjoyed dinner that night at the King Edward Hotel in Floriana and spent more of Maurice Cunningham's budget on fine red wine. Yet Bob could tell that beneath the surface she was worried about her feeling that someone was following them. She'd not mentioned it at the time, but when they got back to the Osborne Hotel early that evening she'd told him that the sense of being followed had been with her all afternoon and it had been obvious on the walk to Floriana that she was nervous and on her guard. It might have been his imagination or what she'd been saying, but Bob also began to feel very uneasy as they walked.

He told her about his own disquiet after they'd finished their food.

'What worries me is the memory of what happened in Stockholm,' said Monique. 'We had an amazing night out and then nearly got killed on the way back to our hotel. This is shaping up in very much the same way.'

'Or we could both be imagining things,' said Bob.

'We could, but we're more likely to have grandchildren we can tell about our adventures if we trust our feelings and assume the worst.' To Bob's surprise, Monique then broke into a bright smile and waved. 'Look who just walked in!' she said.

Bob heard a shout of 'Hello, Monique!' from behind him and turned to see Anne Milner smiling and waving as she led an RAF flying officer wearing pilot's wings but no medal ribbons on his uniform to a table on the other side of the dining room. Bob smiled back and raised a hand in greeting. The flying officer looked embarrassed.

Nothing was said while Bob and Monique drank another glass of wine.

'Now he's got over his surprise that his girlfriend is on waving terms with a group captain, the new young man in Anne's life appears to be thoroughly enjoying her company,' said Monique.

'Good luck to both of them,' said Bob. 'She supported James Ewing while he tried to deal with his demons. And it wasn't her who jumped into bed with a neighbour or who walked out and ended the relationship.'

'That's very true, if a little judgemental,' said Monique. 'The thing I can't get out of my mind when I look at them is what she said to us about being a jinx on the men she loved. She went on to say that she hoped that James Ewing might end the trend of men getting themselves killed while in a relationship with her. It now seems that he hasn't. How do you think she's going to feel when she finds out about that? And what are the chances of that nice-looking young man over there surviving his time in Malta, whether or not you believe in jinxes?'

'Come on Monique,' said Bob. 'Just be pleased that they are enjoying their evening and we are enjoying ours. I know what you've said in the past about jinxing the men you love and I know that Anne saying almost the same thing had quite an impact on you. But we put that to rest for good in Stockholm. If anyone is waiting for us on our walk back to the hotel tonight, they can't possibly be a match for the two of us.'

Monique smiled at Bob with tears in her eyes and took his left hand in both of hers. 'Thank you, Bob.'

CHAPTER TWENTY-FIVE

Monique was running along a straight path through a dark, foggy forest and could hear someone pursuing her. When she looked back, whoever it was seemed just out of sight in the gloom. However fast she ran, she was unable to leave her pursuer behind, but they never gained on her either. Then something broke the dream apart, leaving just a momentary memory and a deep sense of unease.

It was dark in the bedroom and Monique wasn't sure what had awakened her. Then she heard a loud knock on the door between the corridor and the drawing room. She felt Bob sit up next to her and closed her eyes as he switched on his bedside light.

'Someone's knocking on the door,' he said.

Monique got out of bed.

'Get your Walther PPK, Bob,' she said quietly. 'Come through to the drawing room and stand to one side of the door. Leave the light off in here. We can see what we're doing by the light from the bedroom. That's right. I'll stand on the other side.'

The knock was repeated.

Monique raised her voice. 'Hello, who is it?'

'Hello Madame Dubois, it's Sergeant Spiteri of the Marsaxlokk police. I'm sorry to wake you but it's urgent. I need you both to come with me.'

'That does sound like him,' said Bob, quietly.

'Give us five minutes, Sergeant Spiteri,' Monique said loudly. Then, in a much quieter tone, 'Let's see how fast we can get dressed Bob, and make sure you keep your gun handy.

What time is it?'

Bob had gone back into the bedroom and she saw him pick up his watch. 'It's just after 4.30 a.m.'

It took them nearer ten minutes, mainly because Bob insisted that if he was wearing his uniform he needed to get a quick shave as well. Then Monique opened the drawing room door cautiously, her pistol held out of sight to one side.

Sergeant Spiteri smiled, though his expression became more serious when he saw her putting her pistol in her handbag.

'What's going on?' Monique asked.

'My superintendent has asked me to invite you both to observe an operation we are mounting this morning. I've got a car outside. I'll explain on the way.'

'On the way to where?' asked Bob.

'I'll explain that, too.'

Monique caught Bob's eye. She could tell that he'd also been wondering if this was a trap. But she'd been impressed by Sergeant Spiteri when they'd met him on his own in Marsaxlokk. They now needed to decide whether they trusted him enough to go with him. Bob smiled and shrugged.

'Lead on, sergeant,' she said.

From the look on his face and the state of his hair, Monique guessed that the hotel receptionist had been asleep before the sergeant arrived and that he intended to go back to sleep as soon as they'd left.

Some of the light from the nearly full moon was finding its way down into South Street and Monique could see that the black police car parked immediately outside the hotel's front door was empty.

'Do you mind if I get in the front with you, sergeant?' asked Monique. 'Group Captain Sutherland can sit in the back.'

Monique knew the journey, wherever its destination, would be in the dark, but she wanted to give herself the best chance of judging whether Sergeant Spiteri was telling the truth when he explained why he had woken them up. Even in darkness, a view of the side of his face was better than one of the back of his head.

'Not at all.' He pulled away and drove slowly along South Street in the dim light of the police car's masked headlights and the moonlight.

'So, where are we going and why?' asked Monique.

'When you talked to Inspector Farrugia and me yesterday you struck more of a chord than you could possibly have realised,' said the sergeant. 'Inspector Farrugia's senior officer, Superintendent Zammit, has had a small unit keeping an eye on the Micallef twins for some weeks. The aim has been to gather intelligence to allow us to raid their properties and businesses to collect the evidence we need to bring charges against them and others who work for them. The plan had been to mount these raids this coming Friday morning, the day after tomorrow.

'After your meeting yesterday morning with the inspector he came to Valletta to see Superintendent Zammit. The inspector told me afterwards that what you had said about Mr Price was a factor in their decision to bring the raids forward 48 hours to this morning. That and their concern that you might do something to cause the Micallef twins to change their routines or halt their activities.'

'Did the police follow us after we left Marsaxlokk yesterday?' asked Monique.

She saw the sergeant glance at her in the near darkness of the car.

'Yes. We wanted to know if you were going to "create

waves" as the inspector put it. I have a constable who's quite good at not being noticed by anyone he's following on his motorcycle. He followed your car to Mosta and then on to Ghajn Tuffieha and back to your hotel, where you were dropped off.

'And did you follow us later, when we went out to dinner?'

'No, there would have been no point.'

'Thank you for being honest with me,' said Monique. 'Returning to this morning, what's due to happen and where do we fit in?'

'The aim is to mount simultaneous raids on five properties. They are Victor Micallef's home in Mosta and his business premises on Gozo, as well as the larger site on which Simon Micallef has his home and business premises west of Marsaxlokk. We will also raid the home of Anthony Attard and the premises of the fish trading company in Marsaxlokk that he runs on behalf of Simon Micallef. These raids are planned to take place a quarter of an hour after sunrise, at 6.00 a.m., assuming we can confirm that both Micallef twins are at locations we are going to raid.'

'How will you do that?' asked Monique.

'That's not something that gets divulged to the infantry like me,' said the sergeant.

'And where do we fit in?' asked Bob.

The first of the pre-dawn light was showing low in the sky to their left and Monique saw the sergeant smile. 'The inspector said they had decided we should cooperate fully with Military Intelligence, Section 11. He and the superintendent had also thought that it would be better to involve you directly rather than run the risk of anything you might do compromising our operation.'

'If we don't see them ourselves, can you pass on our thanks to the inspector and the superintendent?' said Bob. 'Not that I think there was ever any danger of our compromising an operation being mounted at this time of the morning. Where are we going?'

'The inspector thought you would like to observe the largest of our planned raids, on Simon Micallef's home and business premises to the west of Marsaxlokk. Our actual destination is a nearby farm. It's ideal from our point of view because it has an enclosed courtyard large enough to conceal our vehicles and it offers approaches that we can use to the front and rear of the objective without giving away what we are doing. It's an area characterised by narrow lanes bounded by high stone walls and the fields are small and have stone walls dividing and subdividing them too. That means we can cover the quarter of a mile from our starting point to the objective on foot without being seen by anyone there.

'The inspector asked me to emphasise that you are taking part only as observers. I will assign a constable to you and he has been briefed to take you close to the property we are raiding, but not to enter it. We are expecting resistance and the Malta Police Force does not wish to have any MI11 agents killed while taking part in one of its operations.'

It was a little lighter when the sergeant brought the police car to a halt in a courtyard that already had a lorry, two ambulances and two other cars parked in it. The sergeant led them through a door large enough for farm machinery into a stone barn. Light was coming from oil lamps set up around one end of the barn, which had four wooden benches lined up in front of a blackboard and easel. The darker end looked like it was used for storing whatever machinery or equipment the

279

farmer had discarded in recent decades.

Perhaps a dozen policemen were sitting on the benches or standing around, some by a trestle table in the middle of the space on which there was an urn and some white enamel mugs.

'This is Constable Grech, who will be your escort,' said Sergeant Spiteri, gesturing to a policeman standing nearby.

The constable was in his forties and had dark hair and glasses. Monique introduced herself and Bob as the sergeant left the barn.

Constable Grech smiled. 'Can I get you both some tea?'

'Thank you,' said Monique, 'that would be kind.'

'I was hoping we might see Inspector Farrugia here,' said Bob. 'It would be good to get a clearer idea of what's going to happen.'

'It looks as if they've already had their briefing,' said Monique, pointing at a hand-drawn map on the blackboard, with added arrows which appeared to show lines of approach to the intended target. She looked around. 'They do seem reasonably well prepared. All the policemen I've seen have revolvers and there are enough rifles for about one between two.'

After he'd brought over their cups of tea, Constable Grech drifted off to join a group of policemen by the tea urn. Time seemed to pass very slowly to Monique and the wooden bench she and Bob were sitting on was becoming more uncomfortable by the minute.

'It's after six and nothing's happening,' said Bob. 'It would be helpful if there was someone here to tell us what's going on.'

A short time later Sergeant Spiteri returned to the barn. 'Can I have your attention, please?' The chatter between the policemen ceased. 'There's been a delay and I'll let you know when we can move out.'

The sergeant walked over to Bob and Monique.

'What's the problem?' asked Bob.

'We're not sure that Victor Micallef is at his home in Mosta, which is where he's supposed to be this morning. We're trying to get confirmation but until we know, the decision has been made to hold off.'

'If you leave it too long then people are going to be up and about and the opportunity will be gone,' said Bob.

The sergeant smiled. 'You and I both know that, group captain. Let's hope that my superior officers know it too.'

'How are the raids being coordinated?' asked Bob.

'By radio. The superintendent and inspector are in the farmhouse trying to act as puppetmasters for the whole operation.'

'Would you mind if we went and sat in the back of the car you brought us here in?' asked Monique. 'These benches aren't great.'

'No, of course not. Just tell Constable Grech.'

With the windows down to reduce any build-up of heat when the sun rose high enough to find its way into the courtyard, Monique found the back of the car much more comfortable.

She must have dozed because the next thing she heard was the sound of running feet.

'I think they've finally decided to get things moving, Monique,' said Bob.

Monique looked at her watch. It was 7.40 a.m.

Constable Grech opened the door on Monique's side of the car. 'Can you both come with me, please? Try to keep your heads below the top of the field walls.'

The constable followed on the heels of a group of six

policemen making their way out of the corner of the courtyard and along the shadowy side of a tall stone field wall. Three were carrying rifles and two of the others had sledgehammers. Monique had seen another group of policemen, similarly equipped, head off along the line of another wall.

After a couple of changes of direction to follow wall lines, they came to a halt behind a more substantial wall with a gateway but no gate in it. Monique had seen through the gateway as they approached that there was a narrow road beyond the wall.

She realised that the man at the head of the group of policemen they'd been following was Inspector Farrugia. She watched as the inspector looked at his watch and then led the way out through the gate, signalling those with him to follow.

'We should wait on this side of the wall,' said Constable Grech.

'As you say,' said Monique. 'But we're going to be able to observe much better if we move so we can see through the gateway.'

When she got to the opening in the wall she could see the six policemen standing on the other side of the narrow road in front of a substantial wooden gate easily wide enough for vehicles and set into a much better-built stone wall. In response to a hand signal from Inspector Farrugia, two of the men swung sledgehammers at the gate, one side of which came off its hinges and fell backwards. The group then went through the gap they'd created. Monique could see part of a flat-roofed stone house but other than that the wall along the far side of the road completely obscured any view of what lay beyond it.

Monique heard the sound of gunfire, first shots from handguns and then from at least one rifle. Then there was a

282

short burst from an automatic weapon that sounded like a Thompson submachine gun, then more pistol fire. Then there was silence.

Constable Grech had moved to stand on the far side of the opening in the wall and had his revolver out.

Monique looked around at Bob, who was crouching next to her with his Walther PPK in his right hand.

'I saw no policemen with automatic weapons,' she said. 'I wonder if they are being outgunned.'

'We need to stay here, Monique, we'd only confuse things if we tried to get involved.'

Monique looked at her watch. The silence from beyond the wall on the opposite side of the road seemed endless but when she checked again she realised that only a few minutes had passed.

Suddenly, Monique saw the constable turn to look to his left, away from her and Bob. She realised that some rubble was moving near the base of the wall, perhaps fifteen yards beyond the policeman.

Constable Grech swung his revolver around but then jerked backwards and fell to the ground as a shot rang out. Monique saw that someone was trying to climb out of a hole that had appeared in the ground. He was covered in white dust and was now pointing his pistol in her direction. Monique fired instinctively and heard Bob's gun go off at the same moment.

Monique ran over to Constable Grech, who had been hit in the left shoulder and was bleeding profusely. She pressed down on the wound with her hand to try to stem the bleeding. Bob ran past her to the man who had, she assumed, been trying to climb out of an escape tunnel. The white dust he'd been covered with was now red and the ground and wall behind him were also heavily splattered. Monique's best guess was that she and Bob had both shot the man in the head, which would explain why there was very little of him left above his neck. Rather grotesquely, his body was still upright, held in place by the hole he'd been climbing out of.

She heard a squeal of brakes come from the narrow road, suggesting a vehicle had stopped, though her view was obscured by the wall. Then Sergeant Spiteri and a constable came through the gateway.

'Over here! Constable Grech needs help,' called Monique.

The constable ran over with a wad of bandage and used it to press on the wound, allowing Monique to move her hand.

'The ambulances have moved up, which will allow us to get him to hospital,' said Sergeant Spiteri.

Other men arrived and put Grech on a stretcher before carrying him through the gateway to the road. Monique stood up, using a handkerchief to try to clean the blood off her hand and lower arm.

Sergeant Spiteri walked over to where Bob was standing beside the body that was half out of the mouth of the tunnel. Monique joined them.

It was the sergeant who spoke first. 'Given his state, it might take a little while to be sure, but I think this is Simon Micallef. He was last seen entering the private air raid shelter in the cellar of the house across the road and bolting shut the access door behind himself. Who shot him?'

'I think we both did,' said Bob.

'I assume he had already shot Constable Grech?'

'That's right,' said Monique.

'That will do as a statement for now. I'll come and take a fuller account of what happened at your hotel at a time that suits you. It's a bit of a mess here, to be honest, and it's going to take us a while to sort things out. A man with a Tommy gun in one of the warehouses beyond the house decided he'd be a hero and was killed by one of my officers.

'The one thing I should tell you is that we've found Edward Price. He's badly dehydrated and dirty and needs a shave, but he was able to walk with only a little help. He'd been locked up in the cellar of one of the outbuildings over there. We'll get him to hospital to ensure there's nothing more seriously wrong with him. I'll sort out a car to take you back to your hotel. I imagine you might want to catch up on some lost sleep.'

'After a bath,' said Monique.

'Please thank Inspector Farrugia for listening to what we said yesterday,' said Bob. 'I'm very grateful.'

'I think our thanks are due to the two of you,' said Sergeant Spiteri. 'I suspect that without your intervention, Constable Grech might have been shot more than once.'

CHAPTER TWENTY-SIX

Bob had trouble deciding what day it was when he awoke. He looked across to Monique's side of the bed and realised that she wasn't there. He reached out for his watch and checked the time. It was 1.45 p.m. and he sat up with a start.

Monique came to stand in the doorway between the suite's bedroom and its drawing room and smiled at him. 'I heard you moving.'

'Have you been up long?' he asked.

'About an hour, but you seemed to need your sleep so I left you to it. I went down to the reception to see if there was a newspaper I could read. There's a very good locally-based paper, apparently, but I found this discarded in the lounge.' She held up a partly folded newspaper in her right hand.

'What's happening in the world?'

'I can tell you what the Daily Mirror was reporting two days ago, on Monday. That seems to be about as recent as it gets for British newspapers.'

She sat on Bob's side of the bed.

'What are the headlines?' he asked.

'It's all very close to home,' said Monique as she turned the newspaper round so she could see the front page. 'The headline story is that Mussolini has ordered the evacuation of all civilians from Sicily and that Palermo is being stripped of port and industrial equipment.

'Meanwhile, a large convoy of Allied invasion barges and troop transports is sailing to the island of Pantelleria from Tunisia under heavy naval escort. The commander of the Axis forces is said to be Rommel, who has been inspecting the fortifications of Corsica, Sicily and Sardinia before, apparently, taking a break on the French Riviera. There is also talk of the Germans massing planes in Crete and Salonika.

'Goering, always an inviting target for a little ridicule, is said to have ordered the Luftwaffe to transfer its headquarters from Sicily to northern Italy. The article concludes by saying, and I quote: "The Allies now hold the three important island bastions in the Central Mediterranean - Malta, Pantelleria and Lampedusa - from which complete control of the Sicilian 'bomb alley' is assured."'

Monique lowered the newspaper.

'I told you what Air Vice-Marshal Park said to me at Lascaris,' said Bob. 'It would be fascinating to know whether Hitler really is still reinforcing possible invasion targets other than Sicily or if that's just more Allied misdirection. It sounds like Mussolini is pretty sure about what's going to happen next.'

'There's another story on the front page that gives the background to the Allied capture of the island of Lampedusa,' said Monique. 'According to this, it lies 70 miles south-west of Malta. What's a Swordfish, Bob?'

'It's an open-cockpit biplane torpedo bomber. It looks like it belongs in the last war rather than this one and you'd not catch me going anywhere near the enemy in one. They're often used on aircraft carriers though I'd not be surprised if some are operating from Malta. Why?'

'It seems a Sergeant Cohen was flying one during an attack on Lampedusa when he had a problem and was forced to land on a bombed airfield. The Italians took his arrival as the opportunity to surrender the island to him and he's now known to his crew mates as the "King of Lampedusa".'

Bob smiled. 'That could have ended very differently for the sergeant and his crew. I once heard a navy pilot say that the Swordfish is so slow that he'd seen an aircraft carrier pulling ahead of one after it had taken off in a strong headwind. Anyway, how hungry are you?'

'Extremely,' said Monique. 'It's been an odd day.'

'It has,' said Bob. 'I'm sorry I wasn't up to breakfast when we got back to the hotel. Seeing what we'd done to Simon Micallef's head didn't do much for my appetite.'

'But it's back to normal now?' asked Monique.

'Yes, let's see if we can get a late lunch in the hotel. Otherwise, I'm sure we can find something nearby.'

'And how's the rest of you doing?' asked Monique.

'Is that a proposition?'

'It can be if you want, though only after we've eaten. I was really asking how you're feeling about the man we shot.'

'I was there when you told Michael Dixon in a pub in London that killing someone never really gets any easier and that's true,' said Bob. 'Most of the men I've killed were anonymous and distant and I could always tell myself that I was only shooting down aeroplanes, not killing their occupants. It's become more personal in this job, especially on that night in Stockholm. What happened in La Línea was pretty gruesome but until this morning I'd never seen a corpse with its head spread over the surrounding countryside because of something I'd done.'

'I do know how you feel,' said Monique. 'They say married couples are meant to share everything. I'm not sure they had in mind what we shared this morning.'

Bob smiled. 'I'm sure I'll cope and being with you helps, Monique. I see a restored appetite as being an important first step on the road to recovery. I'll get dressed and then we can eat.'

'There's one more thing, Bob.'

'What's that?'

'When I went down for a newspaper there was a message to phone Sergeant Spiteri in Marsaxlokk, which I did from the public phone in the hall. He'd like to come here at 4 p.m. to take our statements about this morning. I said that would be fine. I hope we can find out what the police have discovered as a result of their raids.'

*

The hotel had been happy to provide coffee in their suite's drawing room and Bob placed the bedroom chair next to one of the armchairs, allowing Sergeant Spiteri to sit comfortably on the other and talk to them both at the same time.

'I should start by thanking you again for saving Constable Grech,' said the sergeant. 'He's going to be in hospital for some time and he's been told that regaining full use of his left arm might take longer, but he's happy to be alive and very grateful to the two of you.'

'That's a relief,' said Bob. 'As he was watching over us at the time I feel rather responsible for what happened to him. How is Edward Price?'

'He had some bruising in addition to the dehydration and was treated this morning in hospital. I have spoken to him and we have also interviewed Anthony Attard. Mr Attard has been very cooperative and from what he told us it seems that when Edward Price was asking questions on the harbourside at Marsaxlokk, one of the people he talked to, entirely by chance, was Victor Micallef. I should add that Mr Micallef has been anything but cooperative. When he realises how bad his position is, he may change his mind.'

'I thought Victor Micallef lived and worked in the north of the island,' said Bob.

'It is a small island and the twins get on - I should say got on - very well. Victor happened to be visiting Marsaxlokk that day. According to Anthony Attard, Edward Price's questions worried Victor because he was the other man who had moved the body from one boat to another in the harbour, with Anthony himself.'

'Doesn't he employ people to do his dirty work for him?' asked Monique.

'He does. The problem with the body in the boat was that it belonged to Victor's senior right-hand man, George Azzopardi. Mr Azzopardi was suspected by Victor of selling business secrets to someone connected with the Sicilian Mafia in Malta. The two argued and Victor killed him. Victor wanted to avoid anyone in his organisation from finding out what he'd done. Simon Micallef offered to help and volunteered Anthony Attard, as his own most trusted right-hand man, to help Victor dispose of the body. When they put the body in the boat, Victor insisted they also put a bomb in its engine compartment in the hope it would remove the only witnesses and ensure there was no talk. It seems the bomb was armed by the weight of the body being lifted off a trigger, which started a timer, which a little later detonated the bomb.'

'So the body in the boat was real, but it wasn't Lieutenant James Ewing?' asked Monique.

'That's right,' said the sergeant.

'That's good news for us, of course, because it means the

lieutenant might still be alive. But I do feel very stupid because I'd completely convinced myself that I knew what had happened to him.'

'You and me both, Monique,' said Bob.

'I wish you every success in your search for the lieutenant,' said Sergeant Spiteri. 'As I said, Edward Price spoke to Victor Micallef in Marsaxlokk. The following day, he was seen by Victor in Mosta. You did get that part right, Madame Dubois. Edward Price had already decided that the rumour of the body in the boat wasn't going to help him find the lieutenant. But Victor Micallef didn't know that and when he saw Mr Price in Mosta he jumped to the conclusion that he - Mr Price - was there to investigate him and took action. Victor Micallef and Anthony Attard abducted him and gave him a beating to find out what he knew and why he was there.

'Victor discovered his mistake too late and then found himself with a problem as neither Micallef twin wanted to be involved in the killing of an SIS agent. Their short-term solution was to keep him locked away and out of sight in the hope they could think of a better long-term solution. We hope to learn much more about the Micallef twins and their businesses over the coming days but I think that covers everything we know so far that is likely to be of interest to you.'

'Thank you, Sergeant Spiteri, that's very helpful,' said Bob 'I know you want statements from the two of us now. After that, I think we should go and see Edward Price in hospital.'

'I'm afraid you can't. He discharged himself early this afternoon and we've no idea where he went. He's at liberty to do as he pleases, of course. As you say, the real reason I'm here is to take your statements. I don't think this should take long, and a joint statement by the two of you will be fine as you were together throughout the time you were with us.'

The sergeant was right, it didn't take long. Bob and Monique saw him down to the front door afterwards.

As they turned to walk back along the hall the receptionist raised a hand to attract their attention. 'Group Captain and Mrs Sutherland, I have a message for you.'

Monique walked over and thanked the receptionist then took the proffered slip of paper, read it and looked up at Bob. 'I think we know where Edward Price has gone. The message reads "Meet Alfred and friend at Stuart's for dinner, 8 p.m."'

'That will be interesting,' said Bob. He looked at his watch. 'We can go for a late afternoon stroll and still leave plenty of time to get ready. I need to get changed into something less military.' He rubbed his chin. 'And I need another shave. This morning's rush job really hasn't stood the test of time.'

CHAPTER TWENTY-SEVEN

As it turned out, they didn't have a late afternoon stroll. Bob had been very happy to go along with Monique's suggestion that, as it was their honeymoon, they should get their exercise in bed rather than out of it.

When they left the hotel that evening, Bob was again wearing one of his civilian suits. They turned left out of the hotel and walked past the turn into Strait Street. They'd decided that at this time of the evening, it would be best to avoid some of the less salubrious stretches of the street and walk around via Kingsway and Palace Square.

As on their walk to Floriana the previous evening, it was obvious to Bob that Monique was uneasy. Several times they stopped so she could look into shop windows whose reflections afforded views back the way they had come. It was difficult to be sure in the grid of Valletta's streets, but Bob didn't think the sun was due to set for a little while yet, meaning there was plenty of light to spot anyone who was following them.

Or at least there should have been.

'This is becoming very frustrating,' said Monique. 'Charles Richmond was able to follow us here in Valletta without my identifying him. It appears that someone else in the city is equally skilled.'

They were walking arm in arm slowly along the pavement on the north-west side of Kingsway.

'Are you sure there's someone following us?' asked Bob.

'You're not going to suggest it's my imagination, are you Bob?

'No, not exactly. We knew we were followed back to the

hotel on Sunday by Charles Richmond and we were also followed around the island yesterday by a police motorcyclist. What if the knowledge of that has somehow caused your sixth sense to start crying wolf? And before you say anything, I've also got a sense of being followed but I'm wondering if that's simply me being sensitive to the way you're responding.'

'It's a thought,' said Monique. 'Perhaps we can find out for sure, one way or the other, after dinner.'

'What do you mean?'

'We can talk about it then. In the meantime, I see no point in our trying to evade anyone following us because if they're there then they're too good for me to spot them or shake them off. Let's forget about it for now and go and enjoy our dinner.'

'I wonder if the food in Captain Bianchi's is any good,' said Bob.

'Like him or loathe him, I get the feeling that Stuart McQueen is good at what he does,' said Monique. 'I'll bet he uses only the best ingredients the black market can provide in his kitchen, especially for guests or customers who aren't too drunk to notice how good the food is.'

Strait Street was much busier on a Wednesday evening than it had been on a Sunday afternoon and it had been far from quiet then. Bob was pleased they'd taken a long way round to avoid much of the street because more young men in uniform, many of them obviously drunk, smoking more cigarettes and negotiating more sexual encounters with more young women in open doorways or on the side of the street, gave the place an oppressive, slightly threatening feel.

Monique led the way, pushing through the crowd. At one point Bob saw a young man in a khaki shirt and shorts and wearing a green commando beret on his head move to stand directly in front of her as if to block her progress. Bob missed what happened next but Monique shifted slightly to the left and walked around the young man, now doubled up on his knees on the pavement and holding his groin. His face was a mask of agony and, as Bob passed him, the young man turned the other way and was sick.

Monique pushed open the door of Captain Bianchi's when they reached it and went into the front bar. Bob followed her in.

'Christ, it's like a zoo at feeding time out there,' she said.

'What happened with the commando who stood in front of you?'

'He asked me to show him a good time and tried to grab one of my breasts. He might think twice before he does that again.'

'Are you all right?' asked Bob.

'Come on, Bob, you know me better than that. The day I can't take something like that in my stride is the day I know I need to retire. And that's not going to happen for a while.'

Bob turned to the barman behind the counter by the door. It was the same elderly man who'd been positioned there on Sunday, wearing what looked like the same red apron. The difference this time was that he was smiling.

'Are you here as guests of Mr McQueen for dinner?' he asked.

'If he's with two friends, then yes, I think we are,' said Bob.

'Go down the steps to the back room and then over to the left. You'll find Mr McQueen in the alcove with his other guests.'

'Thank you,' said Bob.

Monique again led the way. The back room was even busier, noisier and smokier than it had been on Sunday afternoon. Stuart McQueen smiled and stood up when he saw them approaching and said something that caused his two companions to turn around in their chairs. Bob found himself surprised that SIS agents would sit with their backs to the room and then smiled at himself. Monique would be proud of him for thinking of that.

'Hello, both of you,' said Stuart. 'I'm so glad you could join us for dinner. You've met Charles Richmond of course. And this is Edward Price.'

When he stood up, Price towered over everyone else and Bob wondered if estimates of his height had been too conservative. Otherwise, he matched the description Lawrence Dowson had given by having receding slicked-back blond hair and a blond moustache.

Bob and Monique both shook hands with Price. 'Hello, I'm Bob Sutherland and this is Monique Dubois, also known as Monique Sutherland as we were married in Edinburgh eleven days ago.'

'Congratulations!' said Edward Price. 'I understand that I have the two of you to thank for getting me out of the cellar the Micallef twins had been keeping me in.'

'Up to a point,' said Bob. 'The hard work was done by the police. How are you doing?'

Edward Price touched the side of his face. 'I think the visible bruises have gone now from the beating they gave me. Otherwise, I'm fine.'

'It looks like you were able to reclaim your belongings from Manoel Island,' said Bob.

'Yes, Charles has kindly agreed to put me up at his flat tonight and I'm flying back to Cairo tomorrow. I went to collect my stuff earlier. Most of it was there, but would you believe that some bastard at the 10th Submarine Flotilla stole my spare

MCC tie while I was locked up? The one I had been wearing is looking very second-hand, so I was relying on the spare. I've had to wear this one that Charles lent me instead. No offence, Charles, but it's a little dull.'

Monique looked at Bob and laughed.

'What's so funny?' asked Price.

'Is this it?' asked Bob, smiling and holding out the furled-up tie that had been in his suit pocket.

'That's it! Where did you get it?'

'It was me who took it,' said Bob. 'I've been wandering around the island wearing it and asking people if they've seen a tall man wearing a tie like mine. It doesn't suit me and I'm not a member anyway, so it seems best to return it to its rightful owner.'

Edward Price laughed and took the tie from Bob, then put it on in place of the one he had been wearing.

Bob and Monique sat side by side on a bench seat at the back of the alcove. Stuart poured them drinks, which emptied a part-full bottle of fine Champagne, and then asked a waiter for another bottle.

The food was outstanding. Bob decided Monique had been right in suggesting Stuart used only the best ingredients the black market could provide.

The conversation flowed around the table and Bob enjoyed the sense of being at a reunion of three very good friends. Only slowly did it dawn on him that two of them were more than just good friends. He was pleased that he and Monique had played their part in returning Edward to Charles and thought how difficult it must have been for them to have been separated for well over three years by mutual misunderstandings and recrimination over an event that neither of them had caused.

Bob had found the first glass of champagne thoroughly enjoyable but noticed that Monique had only sipped hers and had then asked for tonic water. He thought back to what she'd said about resolving the question of whether they were being followed after dinner. He turned down further offers of champagne in favour of tonic water himself.

After the dessert dishes had been cleared away, Bob saw Monique look at her watch.

He put his glass on the table. 'We've had a very long day, as have you, Edward. I think it's perhaps time we were on our way.'

'It's good to meet you both,' said Edward Price, 'and thanks again for getting me out of the mess I'd got myself into. I'm happy to pass to you the baton of looking for Lieutenant Ewing and if you're ever in Cairo, please let me know.'

'Where have you got to with your search for the missing lieutenant?' asked Charles Richmond.

'That's a good question,' said Monique. 'Until this morning we'd convinced ourselves that his was the body put in the boat at Marsaxlokk. We were wrong. Our only alternative lead is my belief that the woman who was with him on the Sunday morning isn't being honest with me about knowing where he was going when he left. We're planning to visit her first thing tomorrow.'

'Is that the girlfriend I interviewed?' asked Edward Price.

'No, another woman. I hope you won't be offended if I don't tell you her name.'

'Not at all. I failed in my search for the lieutenant and am going back to Cairo with my tail between my legs. I'm just pleased to hear that you've uncovered more than I did.'

Outside Captain Bianchi's, Strait Street was even more

manic and sordid than it had been when they'd arrived. It had been dark for some time but no one seemed to be taking the slightest notice of the blackout.

'This way Bob.' Monique pulled at his arm.

'You're taking us to the bombed church where we met Stuart McQueen, aren't you?'

'That's right. Let's get off Strait Street.' She pulled Bob into a street running downhill, towards the harbour. 'That's better. It's much quieter here and I'm sure it will get still quieter the further we go from Strait Street. I've already got that sense of being followed again.'

Monique took his arm and they followed the same zig-zag route as before. The only available light now came from the nearly full moon and when they reached Old Mint Street it was deserted. As she had on their last visit, Monique led Bob into the ruins of the bombed church and then pointed towards where he'd waited before. Bob moved as directed.

With the moonlight shining off the stonework of the church walls and the piles of rubble it began to seem quite bright to Bob. He had drawn his Walther PPK and saw that this time Monique also had her pistol in her hand.

By his watch, they'd been standing like statues in the ruined church for six minutes when he heard footsteps, two sets of footsteps, in the street outside. The footsteps stopped for what seemed like an age and then there was a noise like someone inhaling suddenly, as if they'd been holding their breath underwater. Bob could feel his heart hammering in his chest and he was struggling to force himself to breathe. He knew that two people were only a few yards away, in the street just beyond the wall of the ruined church.

Then the sound of two sets of footsteps resumed, this time at a much quicker pace. Bob raised his pistol and saw Monique do the same.

In the moonlight, he saw a young woman in a dress run into the ruin of the church and then turn to clutch at the young man in naval uniform following closely behind her before pulling him into a deep embrace.

Bob realised that what he'd heard was the sound of the couple kissing in the street. Then he saw the young woman look directly at him over the shoulder of the sailor.

She screamed and took a step backwards. 'There's a man over there with a gun!'

'Don't worry,' said Monique. 'I'm sorry if we frightened you.' She walked past the couple and out through the gap in the wall into Old Mint Street.

Bob followed her lead, trying not to make his Walther PPK too obvious but having no time to put it back into its holster.

Once out in the street, Monique took Bob's arm and led him away from the ruined church. She was shaking and he was worried that something was wrong with her.

She topped a hundred yards along the street in the deep doorway of a smaller bombed-out building.

'Are you all right?' he asked.

Monique burst into a fit of giggles, bending over in the middle with her hands on her knees. Bob could see the funny side of what had just happened and found himself laughing too.

'It might have been less funny if we'd shot them,' said Monique. 'I was so tense I nearly did when they came into the church. I couldn't work out what the noise was and it never crossed my mind it might be the sound of kissing. Anyway, let's head back. I think if we simply follow Old Mint Street this way it will bring us to South Street, not far from the hotel.'

'What did that little excursion teach us about our being followed?' asked Bob.

'Nothing at all. I'm sorry Bob. On the bright side, I no longer have the sense that someone is following us. Perhaps it was just an overreaction as you suggested earlier. And perhaps it was cured by what just happened.'

'From what you said at the end of dinner, I gather that we're going to see Jane Brookes in the morning.'

'Unless you've got any better ideas, Bob?'

CHAPTER TWENTY-EIGHT

'Good morning, Jane. May we come in?'

Monique had again picked the lock on the door from the street and Bob had followed her up to the top floor landing. She thought Jane Brookes looked nervous.

'What do you want?'

'We'd like a chat with you,' said Monique. 'It would probably be best if we could talk in the flat. Is your husband at home?'

'No, he was on duty last night and I think he was intending to sleep at the barracks and then come home later. Do you both want to come in this time?'

'That might be best,' said Monique. 'It would look a little obvious if we leave the group captain on the landing and Anne comes out of her flat.'

Jane again led Monique into the kitchen. She sat on one of the two chairs without going through the ritual of offering tea and looked defiantly at Monique. Monique sat on the other chair, realising that this was the only room in the flat she'd been in. Bob stood in the doorway looking smart in his group captain's uniform and, helpfully from her point of view, just a little intimidating.

'We've come back because we want to ask you again whether James Ewing gave you any clue at all about where he was going when he left you here on the Sunday morning he disappeared.'

'I told you, he didn't tell me anything,' said Jane.

'I don't believe you, Jane,' said Monique. 'I know that he said something to you or gave you some sort of clue. That was obvious when we last met. I'd like you to stop lying to me and tell me what you know.'

'I can't,' said Jane, looking as if she was about to burst into tears.

'From our point of view, there are only two possibilities,' said Monique. 'The first is that James Ewing left in the way you described. The problem we have is that your claim that he said nothing about where he was going simply isn't credible. You aren't very good at telling lies and I can tell you are lying about that.'

Jane looked at the table and said nothing.

'The alternative we have to consider is that your husband came home early, discovered James in bed with you and killed him. What other reason could there be for you to deny us the information we need to know about where James went? That would mean that he didn't go anywhere under his own steam because he was dead.'

There was a long pause, which was broken when Jane Brooks started sobbing loudly.

'I'll tell you what we'll do,' said Monique. 'We'll give you until this time tomorrow morning to tell us the truth.' She made a show of looking at her watch. 'If you don't, we will interview your husband Daniel as a suspect in James Ewing's murder. If we can't find him here at home we will look for him at St Andrew's Barracks, where his arrest will be very public. If we do interview Daniel then we will have to tell him why we think he murdered James.'

Jane banged her fist on the kitchen table. 'That's blackmail!'

'It's very much up to you, Jane. If between now and this time tomorrow morning, you think of anything that James said that might help us find him, then contact me at the Osborne

Hotel.'

Monique stood up, pleased that Bob had recognised his cue and had turned to precede her out of the flat. Jane didn't move. Monique closed the front door to the flat behind herself and then followed Bob down the stairs and out onto the street.

He stopped on the pavement. 'I'm not sure I've ever seen that side of you before, Monique. I hope I never give you a reason to use it on me.' Then he smiled. 'You were very convincing. Do you think it will work?'

'Let's hope so. I'm certain she knows something.'

*

Bob and Monique had gone on foot to Jane Brookes' flat in Floriana. As they walked arm in arm back along South Street towards the hotel, Bob felt Monique grow tense.

'What's wrong?' he asked. 'I've not had the impression this morning that you're getting any sense of being followed. I'm certainly not.'

'No, I've not felt anything. But look at that,' said Monique.

Bob looked ahead and for the first time noticed a dark green civilian car parked facing towards them on the street outside the Osborne Hotel. 'It's going to be picking up one of the other guests,' he said.

'Someone's sitting's the driver's seat,' said Monique. 'Turn towards me in this doorway, as if you're lighting a cigarette for me. Now remove your pistol from its holster, cock it and hold it in your right-hand jacket pocket with the safety catch on. That way it's still safe but ready for almost immediate use. I've no pockets I can put my pistol in so you'll need to react first if things do turn ugly and give me time to get mine out of my handbag.'

Bob and Monique walked slowly towards the car, having to move aside at one point to allow an army lorry coming from behind them to pass. It then had to mount the narrow pavement on the far side of the road to get past the parked car.

As they approached the front of the car the driver, wearing a light-coloured suit and a Panama hat, got out. Bob could feel his right hand grow clammy as it gripped his Walther PPK. The driver must have realised the significance of the way Bob was holding his right arm and raised his hands, smiling.

'Hello. Are you Group Captain Sutherland and Madame Monique Dubois?'

Bob nodded. 'That's right.'

'I've been sent by Charles Richmond. My name's Gordon Wynter and I work with him. Something's come up and he needs to meet the two of you. He said you would be out this morning and asked me to pick you up when you got back to your hotel.'

'What's come up?' asked Monique.

'He'll explain everything when you get there. Charles said you'd be suspicious and asked me to tell you that the weather here is warmer than it is in Kyle of Lochalsh.'

Monique looked at Bob and smiled. He made his pistol safe and replaced it in his shoulder holster. 'Very well,' she said.

'Can you give me a minute to call Charles from the public phone in the hotel to let him know we're on our way?'

Bob nodded and Wynter went into the hotel. When he came out again Bob and Monique got into the back of the car and Wynter started it and pulled away.

'Where are you taking us?' asked Bob.

'HMS *St Angelo*,' said Wynter.

'A ship?' asked Monique.

'No, that's what the navy calls Fort St Angelo, the fortress that stands at the end of Vittoriosa, the peninsula that forms one of the Three Cities on the far side of the Grand Harbour. It's used by the Royal Navy as their headquarters in Malta.'

'That's the fort that's so prominent in views across the harbour from Upper Barrakka Gardens, isn't it?' asked Monique.

'That's right.'

Wynter took them on a route that made its way around the Grand Harbour. Cranes, dock installations and ships appeared and disappeared on their left-hand side as the road at times ran alongside the harbour. At other points, they drove through settlements near the harbour, particularly when they rounded the end of it and began to head along its south-eastern side.

'The bomb damage on this side of the harbour is worse than anything we've seen in Valletta,' said Monique.

'It is,' said Wynter. 'We're passing the landward end of Senglea at the moment. It occupies a peninsula formed by French Creek to its west and Dockyard Creek to its east. They are the two inlets of the Grand Harbour used by the Royal Navy for its dockyards, which have been very popular targets for enemy bombers over the past three years. Senglea, located between the two sets of dockyards, has been all but flattened by the bombing. Vittoriosa, on the next peninsula to the north-east, hasn't fared much better.'

'And that's where the Royal Navy has chosen for its headquarters?' asked Monique.

Bob sat in silence in the back of the car. It had been obvious in views over the Grand Harbour that this area had been badly bombed, but distant views did little to prepare him for the reality of the devastation, which in places left almost nothing standing. As they drove along the Vittoriosa side of Dockyard Creek, views across it were obscured by large numbers of moored boats and ships, but it was still possible to gain an impression of how large parts of Senglea were little more than occasional vertical walls rising from piles of rubble. And this was, he reminded himself, after six months' clearance and repair since the intensity of the bombing eased.

'This is Fort St Angelo, ahead of us at the end of the peninsula,' said Wynter.

Bob leaned forwards to get a better view through the windscreen. 'It looks like the fort had more than its share of the bombing,' he said. 'I suppose it must have been a much easier target to see and to hit from the air than dockyards hiding in inlets between peninsulas.'

The fort looked massive, as it had when seen from the Valletta side of the Grand Harbour. The difference now was that the damage was much more obvious. They were stopped at a Royal Navy checkpoint and when they set off again their car crossed a bridge over what appeared to be a moat separating the fort from the rest of the peninsula.

A short distance further on was a large level area that lay almost in the shadow of the fort's enormous walls. Buildings that were much younger than the fort had been erected on much of this area and some of them also had obvious bomb damage, as had parts of the high stone walls of the fort itself. Naval officers and men were going about their business wherever Bob looked.

Wynter parked the car next to a naval lorry and led Bob and Monique to another checkpoint manned by sailors carrying rifles, this time at the bottom of a slope with stone balustrades that Bob could see climbed parallel to the wall before turning to enter an arched gateway set high in the main body of the fort.

One of the men saluted and then compared Bob and Monique's security passes with a clipboard he was holding. Then he turned to a colleague. 'Able Seaman Carter, take the Group Captain and the lady up to the Magistral Palace.'

Able Seaman Carter handed his rifle to one of the other men and set off towards the ramp beyond the checkpoint. 'If you could follow me please.'

Gordon Wynter turned back towards the car.

'Aren't you coming with us?' asked Bob.

'It's a very select gathering and Charles is the only one attending from SIS.'

'Thanks for the lift.' Bob gave a half wave to Gordon Wynter and then turned to follow Monique and the able seaman up the stone ramp, having to return the salutes of several naval personnel coming the other way. At the top, they walked between defensive points constructed from piled sandbags before passing through the gateway into a large arched space set within the wall of the fort. Even here there were signs of damage.

'It looks like the fort was badly bombed,' said Monique.

'You can say that again, ma'am,' said the able seaman. 'I've heard that so far during the war there have been nearly 70 direct hits on the fort and the immediate surrounding area. The place was built to withstand a siege but I don't think this was the sort of siege the builders had in mind.'

Another sloping walkway led them higher within the walls and then out into an open space. Again it was busy. Through a gateway off to one side, Bob saw a large paved area on which there were two anti-aircraft guns protected by sandbag walls.

Both were being cleaned by their crews.

'What's the Magistral Palace?' asked Monique.

'I don't know its original purpose, ma'am. At the moment it's used as quarters for the commanding officer of HMS *St Angelo*, Captain Wilson. You'll find this place operates very much like that. The higher you go in the fort, the more senior the people who are billeted there. Senior officers tend to have their quarters in the upper part, which includes the palace. More junior officers and senior ratings live in the next layer down and us more junior ratings are at the bottom of the stack.'

'Does that mean you are billeted in the buildings outside the main gate?' asked Monique.

'Ah, no. That's where Maltese officers and ratings are accommodated. They take the same risks as us and have the same bombs dropped on their heads. I've never understood why they're kept separate like that, but I suppose that's the navy way.'

Bob saw Carter glance back at him as if wondering whether Bob could hear and whether he'd said too much to Monique. Either way, the able seaman said little more on the rest of their climb beyond giving directional instructions.

The upper part of Fort St Angelo struck Bob as a remarkable place. Very light honey-coloured stone buildings on slightly different levels were surrounded by what, before the war, had probably been beautiful gardens. There were still plenty of trees, though some of them had suffered blast damage.

There had been another checkpoint manned by two armed sailors at the bottom of a short flight of stone steps up to the upper fort and once at the top, there were far fewer people about than there had been lower down.

Carter led Bob and Monique past a badly damaged building

that he said had been the fort's chapel and then through a gateway into a courtyard. To their immediate left was a two-storey building whose first floor was set back behind an arched gallery with a stone balustrade running along its front. The upper floor was accessed via stone steps that ran up into an arched passage in the nearest wing of the building. The ground floor was also recessed behind arches.

'This is the Magistral Palace,' said Carter. 'The reception rooms are reached via the door under that arch over there.' He pointed.

Monique smiled and Bob thanked the able seaman, who seemed pleased to be able to leave them and return to his duties at the gate.

The door was ajar and Bob pushed it open and led the way in. After the bright glare of the sunlight outside, the inside of the building was very dark.

'Hello, Bob! Hello, Monique!'

Bob recognised Charles Richmond's voice before his eye adjusted sufficiently for him to make the man out visually.

Two men had stood from their chairs at a meeting table in the room, which looked like the office of someone senior, complete with a desk, meeting table and chairs, plus a bookcase and the obligatory maps attached to the walls. In this case, they were large maps of parts of the Mediterranean that left little room for any other decoration.

Bob had half-expected the second man in the room to be wearing the uniform of a naval captain. Instead, he was a blond man of medium height and build in his thirties who was wearing a lightweight suit.

'Thanks for coming,' said Charles Richmond. I'd like to introduce you to Wilfred Masterton, who is my MI5 opposite number here in Malta.'

Bob shook the man's hand.

'Hello Wilfred,' said Monique as she shook his hand. She turned to look at Bob. 'Our offices in MI5 were just along the corridor from one another for a time early last year.'

'Hello Vera,' said Masterton, smiling. 'Though I understand you're Monique Dubois now rather than Vera Duval, and Charles tells me you've more recently become Monique Sutherland. Congratulations to both of you.'

'Thank you,' said Monique.

'Should we sit down?' asked Charles Richmond.

'I'm intrigued to know what this is about, Charles,' said Bob as he sat on one of the chairs.

'Perhaps I should start,' said Masterton. 'You'll understand the context in a moment, but first I need to ask how high your security clearance is.'

'We are both cleared to what I believe is the highest level,' said Bob. He smiled, 'Though, of course, I'd not know if there was a higher one. I very much doubt if there is.'

'Does that mean you are aware of the meaning of "Ultra"?'

'Yes, we are,' said Bob.

'Good. I thought that must be the case for reasons that will become obvious. I suspect that there are very few of us in Malta who are cleared for Ultra. Other than the four of us sitting around this table I know that the governor is and I imagine that the officer commanding each of the armed services must be too. But it's not the sort of club where you get a lapel badge to allow other members to recognise you, so I don't know for sure.' He looked at Charles Richmond. 'Over to you, Charles.'

'We've brought the two of you here this morning because of a signal I received earlier from Commodore Cunningham in

MI11 in London. You will recall, Bob, that you asked me to open up a secure channel of communication with him. He has taken advantage of it.'

'Can you show it to us?' asked Bob.

'It's not the sort of signal I could remove from my office and we are meeting here for reasons we'll explain. Instead, I will tell you what it said from memory.

'It was classified Ultra Secret and addressed to you, Bob, via me. The commodore said that late last Friday there was an intercept of a signal from the head of the Abwehr's office in the German embassy in Madrid to the Abwehr headquarters in Berlin saying that an ex-Abwehr agent called Vera Eriksen had been identified arriving in Gibraltar. She was travelling under the name of Madame Monique Dubois and was with an RAF group captain called Robert Sutherland. The man who had identified her had established that the two of you were due to fly on to Malta. The message from Madrid concluded by reporting that the agent who had made the identification was killed later that day.

'The commodore went on to say that late last night he had become aware of another intercepted signal, this time one sent on Tuesday morning from the headquarters of the 29th U-boat Flotilla based at La Spezia in northern Italy to part of the Sicherheitsdienst in Berlin and decrypted early that afternoon. As you both probably know, the Sicherheitsdienst, or the SD, is the intelligence agency of the SS and the Nazi Party. The intercepted signal simply said that the SD agents had been landed as planned on the island of Malta the previous night, in other words, either late on Monday or early on Tuesday.

'Taking the contents of the two intercepts together, the commodore concluded that there was a realistic chance that the

SD agents were in Malta because of the presence of the two of you.'

Wilfred Masterton sat forwards in his chair. 'You should know that I was alerted to the second of those intercepted messages not long after it was decrypted on Tuesday afternoon. Without making it too obvious that we are looking, in order to avoid compromising Ultra, MI5 personnel based in Malta have been devoting pretty much all our resources to finding the SD agents. It doesn't help that the intercepted signal wasn't specific on numbers, so we don't have any real idea what we are dealing with.'

'I should finish my account of Commodore Cunningham's signal to you, Bob,' said Charles Richmond. 'He said that in the circumstances, he thought you should abort your review of a possible role for MI11 in Malta and either catch a flight back to Britain or, at the very least, take additional measures to ensure your safety. He concluded his signal by saying that he was taking soundings about Ruth's commission. I take it that's to prove it's from him?'

'That's right,' said Bob. 'You say you've been looking for the SD agents since Tuesday afternoon, Wilfred. Have you come up with anything?'

'A little,' said Masterton. 'Most of the prominent Maltese who had Italian sympathies were interned in 1940 and then deported to Uganda in February last year. But there are some left in Malta and we have cultivated contacts amongst them. I've been hopeful that the SD agents would get in touch with someone they know to be an Italian sympathiser and we'd get to hear of it. We're also hoping they'll be careless enough to use a radio transmitter we can triangulate on, but there's been nothing on that front so far.

'Our first progress came last night when one of our contacts reported a rumour of German agents on the island intending to mount an attack on the naval dockyards in advance of what everyone expects will be an invasion of Sicily. That report allowed us to step up our search for the SD agents without fear of compromising Ultra. This morning we've involved the intelligence and security personnel of the three services in Malta and we've moved the hub of the expanded search effort from my office to space that's been made available to us here at Fort St Angelo.'

Wilfred Masterton paused for a moment. 'What I'm puzzled about is why Commodore Cunningham thinks the SD agents might be here because of the presence of the two of you.'

'It's a long story,' said Monique. 'The SD tried to abduct me in Sweden at the end of March, to use my background in the Abwehr in their struggle for control of that organisation. I killed two of them, including a senior officer who was betraying the Abwehr to the SD. Bob then killed four members of an SD team and wounded a fifth. Given the enmity Bob and I have seen between the Abwehr and the SD, I just don't see the two organisations cooperating in the way Commodore Cunningham's theory suggests. Someone in the Abwehr might have leaked the content of the first intercepted signal to the SD but against the background of a huge shift in the way the war is shaping up in the Mediterranean, I find it inconceivable that the SD has the time, the resource or the inclination to mount a personal vendetta against Bob and me. To my mind, their presence here must have something to do with the huge buildup of Allied military power in Malta.'

'The reason why we brought you here,' said Charles Richmond, 'was to offer you the use of this building as somewhere safer to stay than the Osborne Hotel if you decide to remain in Malta rather than return to Britain. There's an excellent suite of rooms upstairs that you could use.'

'Isn't this the captain's accommodation?' asked Monique.

'It is,' said Masterton, 'but the commanding officer of HMS *St Angelo* is happy to make it available to you if it helps us track down the SD agents and protect the naval dockyards from attack.'

'None of this makes any sense,' said Monique. 'If we are in danger and need secure accommodation then the SD agents aren't here to attack the naval dockyards. On the other hand, if the rumour you've heard is correct then Bob and I are in no danger at all. You're hedging your bets, aren't you? You don't believe Commodore Cunningham is right but just in case he is, you want us where you have complete control over who has access to us. If the SD agents are in Malta because of us, you want us to stay on the island as bait.'

'That's a fair summary,' said Masterton. 'I don't want to disregard the possibility that the commodore is right. If you continue to stay at the Osborne Hotel then I simply can't spare anyone to watch your backs for you. If you get killed and the SD agents leave Malta, we lose our chance of capturing them. If you leave Malta and the SD agents are here for you, then we again lose our chance of capturing them. If you stay here at Fort St Angelo we can keep you safe and it means you are still on the island.'

Bob had the sense that the calm expression on Monique's face was a mask for increasing anger and decided it was time to intervene.

'We're grateful for your concern,' he said. 'I think the two of us need a chance to discuss what we should do. If we decide to

315

return to the Osborne Hotel then I understand your resource constraints, Wilfred. In that case, we will watch our own backs while you get on with your search for the SD agents.'

'If that's what you do, I can't take any responsibility for what happens,' said Masterton.

'I understand that and will take full responsibility myself,' said Bob.

'What do you want me to say in reply to Commodore Cunningham's signal?' asked Charles Richmond.

'Thank him for his signal,' said Bob. 'Tell him we are considering our options in discussion with MI5 and MI6 and that we will be staying in Malta for the moment. Finish the signal by saying that it's a shame that they ran out of champagne at the Station Hotel. That will ensure he knows it's from me.'

Bob stood up. 'Thank you both again. Monique and I will go for a walk and decide what to do next. We'll see ourselves out. I think I remember the way back down to the main gateway.'

CHAPTER TWENTY-NINE

Bob led Monique out of the palace and then through the gateway and past the bomb-damaged chapel. There was, perhaps inevitably, an anti-aircraft gun on a plinth at the far end of the open space beyond it, without its crew. Close to it was a square stone building standing next to a tall flagpole, from the top of which a large White Ensign was flying. This part of the fort was eerily quiet.

They came to a halt close to the anti-aircraft gun, where a raised area of paving allowed views over the walls of the fort and across the Grand Harbour to Valletta.

'I'm glad you brought things to a close back there, Bob.'

Bob smiled. 'I got the sense you weren't happy about the idea of our being locked away here in a gilded cage on the off-chance we might become useful as bait.'

'That is what it would have amounted to, isn't it, Bob?'

'Wilfred Masterton was quite open about that being his intention. Did you have much to do with him last year? Is he any good?'

'I didn't have much contact with him directly, but I know he was well thought of in MI5. If he's the head of their office in Malta then I think he must have been promoted since I knew him.'

'Now you've had a little more time to think about it, do you still feel the suggestion that the SD might be coming after the two of us here in Malta is "inconceivable" as you put it in the meeting? I must say that I find it odd that Maurice Cunningham should have seriously considered it as a possibility.'

'Perhaps it looks different from London, Bob. We're here at

the personal request of Maurice and I can imagine that when he had those two intercepted signals sitting on his desk next to each other last night he must have felt he'd sent us into grave danger.

'Having said that, the more I think about it the more ludicrous it seems. Mussolini's evacuating civilians and the Allies are massing troops, aircraft and ships here and on other islands within striking range of Sicily. And in the midst of all this, we are wondering if the intelligence agency of the SS and the Nazi Party is taking time out from the war and borrowing a U-boat just because they're not happy that you and I killed some of their agents in Sweden? It's just not credible.'

'And yet since the SD team came ashore from their submarine, you've felt we were being followed on several occasions that we've not been able to otherwise explain.'

'I know, Bob. That thought has occurred to me too. We just need to be very careful. At least we know that if someone is following us, it's not going to be any of Wilfred Masterton's people as they are fully occupied looking for the SD agents.'

'Let's head back to the hotel,' said Bob. 'I'm sure we'll be able to find someone to drive us there if we ask outside the main gate.'

'I've got a better idea,' said Monique.

*

After they descended the access ramp to the open area beneath the fort's main gate, Monique led the way back along the road, across the bridge over the moat and towards part of the harbour that was bustling with small craft.

The whole area was crowded by men in Royal Navy

uniforms and Bob found himself having to return salutes repeatedly.

The quayside was particularly busy but Monique had no difficulty making her way through the crowd and Bob followed. He realised that many of the men were queueing to get aboard small boats that were themselves queueing to get to the harbourside.

Within seconds, Monique's smile had seen her through to the front of the queue and she was being helped down into his boat by a boatman. Bob followed.

'Where do you want to go?' The boatman had grey hair and looked to be in his sixties, but was muscular for his age.

'Valletta, please,' said Monique.

The boat they were in was one of those that Monique had called 'slightly bulky Venetian gondolas' when they had been looking down on the harbour from Upper Barrakka Gardens. Seen closely, that wasn't a bad description. The boatman propelled the boat using two oars but, unlike any rowing boat Bob had ever been in, he stood and faced in the direction they were travelling.

'What's this type of boat called?' he asked.

'It's a dghajsa, group captain. They're the traditional water taxis of Malta.'

The boat pulled out from the quay and made its way past the bulk of Fort St Angelo. Part of the way across the Grand Harbour it passed behind the stern of a large warship.

'Where in Valletta do you want to be?' asked the boatman.

'We're staying in the Osborne Hotel,' said Monique. 'I suppose that after we land we will need to climb up to the higher parts of Valletta.'

'It's a hot day. If you don't mind me taking you a little

further along the peninsula, I should be able to get you back to your hotel without you having to walk at all.'

Monique smiled. 'Go on then. It's nice just sitting here and watching the harbour go by.'

When they reached the Valletta side of the Grand Harbour, Bob realised what the boatman had in mind as they approached the quayside. 'Where are we?' he asked.

'This is Quarry Wharf. It's a good place to find a carrozzi, a traditional horse-drawn Maltese cab. And, as I hoped, there are two waiting.' The boatman smiled. 'It's a very romantic way to return to your hotel. More importantly, it saves a steep climb on a hot day.'

'How much do we owe you?' asked Bob, as they disembarked.

'Three shillings, group captain.'

Bob gave him two two-shilling notes and told him to keep the change.

Monique expressed doubts about the idea of riding in a horse-drawn cab but then appeared to enjoy the experience. For Bob, it was hard to get away from the idea that he was closer to the smelly end of a horse than felt entirely comfortable. But as the boatman had said, it saved a steep climb on a hot day.

As they entered the Osborne Hotel, the receptionist waved to attract their attention. 'Mrs Sutherland!'

'Yes,' said Monique.

'You're also Monique Dubois, aren't you?'

'That's right.'

'There's a message for you.' The receptionist held up an envelope.

'Can you describe the person who left it?' asked Monique.

'Yes, he was a Dominican friar wearing a white habit and

glasses. He was bald on top and the hair on the sides of his head was grey.'

'Thank you.' Monique turned to look at Bob with a surprised expression on her face. 'I'm not sure what I was expecting, but it wasn't that. Let's go up to the suite and find out what it says.'

Bob saw Monique examine the door to their suite before they went in and then she spent a few moments looking around inside.

'The room's been serviced,' she said. 'Otherwise, we don't appear to have had any visitors.' Monique looked at the envelope she'd been given. 'It's addressed to me as Monique Dubois. There's nothing else written on the envelope.' She slipped a fingertip under the flap on the back and ripped it open, then took out a single sheet of paper which she read before passing it to Bob.

Bob looked down at the letter.

'Dear Monique Dubois

'I understand you are looking for James Ewing.

'I may be able to help. Please meet me at 4 p.m. today in the Chapel of Our Lady of Philermos, which is one of the chapels in St John's Co-Cathedral here in Valletta. You should enter the cathedral by the side door from Kingsway. Please come alone.

'Your hotel receptionist will have told you how to recognise me. I am told you have a red and white floral dress. If you wear that it will allow me to recognise you too.'

'Yours sincerely

'Fr Marco Vella'

Bob looked up at Monique. 'In the current circumstances can we agree that neither of us is going anywhere on our own? We can make it look like you are unaccompanied, but I want to stay within a reasonable distance in case this is some sort of trap.'

'I agree, Bob, though I don't think it's a trap. There was talk of German agents parachuting into England early in the war dressed as nuns, but I find the idea of an SD agent disguising himself as a Dominican friar just a bit too outlandish. Besides, there's only one person I can think of who knows that Monique Dubois has a red and white floral dress, and that's Jane Brookes. I'm fairly sure this is a result of our visit to see her this morning.'

'I think I've noticed the cathedral as we've walked along Kingsway' said Bob. 'It's behind some bombed-out ruins.' He looked at his watch. 'That gives us a free afternoon. What do you want to do?'

'Let's find somewhere for a nice long lunch without any alcohol and then we can come back to the hotel. I'm sure we can think of a way of pleasantly passing a couple of hours.'

Bob smiled. 'That sounds perfect.'

*

Monique let Bob enter the cathedral first, using the side door the friar had indicated in his letter. She gave it a couple of minutes and then followed him in.

The interior of the church was amazing, from the magnificently decorated marble panels covering much of the floor to the gilt coating the arches and the painting of the curved ceiling. And yet it felt very sparse, almost empty in places. There were lines of chairs in the nave, but they were plain wood and looked as if they didn't belong, and there were no candlesticks, icons or other ornate fixtures and fittings on view. Looking around, Monique realised that as a large building right in the centre of Valletta, the cathedral must have been exceptionally vulnerable during three years of air raids. She assumed that anything valuable and portable had been moved to somewhere safer.

Despite the size of the building, it seemed to have been left remarkably unscathed by the bombing. There was obvious damage to one area, just to the right of the door she'd come in by, but the contrast with Fort St Angelo and the battering it had received could hardly be greater.

According to an attendant she'd asked as she came in, the Chapel of Our Lady of Philermos was in the far corner of the cathedral, on the far side of the choir, and only accessible from the chapel next along to its right as Monique looked at it. This was also screened by the choir and was in turn only accessible from the one next to it. That made it a rather awkward meeting place as there would be no chance of staying within Bob's view.

Bob was sitting at the right-hand end of the front row of wooden chairs in the nave. That put him not far from the choir and the altar, which from this distance had a temporary wartime utility look to it. He was about as near to the chapel where she was due to meet the friar as possible without making himself too obvious, which she was grateful for.

Monique checked her watch and as there were just four minutes to go she made her way into the first of the chain of three chapels leading into that corner of the cathedral.

She was relieved to see the figure of a small man in white robes standing in the furthest chapel, the one in which they were supposed to meet.

The friar turned as Monique approached and smiled. With his large glasses, he reminded her strongly of an owl.

'Hello, thank you for coming and for being so punctual. May

323

I call you Monique?'

'Yes, of course. How do I address you?'

'Brother Marco is fine. Have you come alone?'

Monique looked at the friar for a moment before deciding that starting the conversation with a lie was not a good idea. 'My husband is sitting in the nave. For reasons not connected with James Ewing, we are a little concerned about our safety at the moment so felt it best if he accompanied me.'

'Thank you for being honest with me, Monique. I asked to meet you because I know you saw Jane Brookes this morning. Before he left, James Ewing gave her a telephone number and instructions to use it only in severe need. Today she used it and spoke to me. Can I ask why you are looking for James?'

'My husband and I work for British military intelligence,' said Monique. 'However, we are in Malta looking for James Ewing because the man we report to is his uncle, the brother of his mother. The family is concerned about James and hopes he is safe and well.'

'Will it end your search if I give you my personal assurance that he is safe and well?' asked the friar.

'No, I'm sorry, Brother Marco. I need to talk to him myself before I can accept that our job here is done.'

'Very well,' said the friar. 'I hoped my assurance might suffice but I must admit that I feared you would respond as you have. I need to ask you to give me a little more time. Can we meet here again at 10 a.m. tomorrow?'

'Yes. I'll return then.'

'Can I ask you not to pursue Mrs Brookes in the meantime? My telephone number was the piece of information she was withholding from you and you no longer need it. You frightened her this morning.'

Monique felt the need to defend herself. 'She lied to me and I needed the truth.'

'Yes, I can see that matters a lot to you. Do you wish to leave first?'

Monique turned and went back through the chain of chapels and then walked over to sit next to Bob at the front of the nave.

*

Bob sensed Monique approaching before she walked in front of him and sat on the chair to his left. He turned so he could see her with his good eye.

'How did it go?' he asked, quietly.

'Hopefully,' she said. 'I'm meeting him again tomorrow morning and I think he's going to tell me more. Don't turn any further. I think he's leaving now.'

'Should we follow him to see where he goes?'

'I think we have to trust him,' said Monique. 'Besides, if Brother Marco doesn't show up tomorrow he's got a pretty good idea that we'll be visiting Jane Brookes again. It was the friar's telephone number that James Ewing left with her, for emergency use.'

'Why?' asked Bob.

'That's what I hope we'll discover in the morning.' Monique looked at her watch. 'We're going to end up getting very fat on an island of thin people if we're not careful, but do you fancy a walk over to the King Edward Hotel later on? I might try something other than their rabbit spaghetti this time. I do like the red wine that Commodore Cunningham keeps buying for us.'

After their conversation with Wilfred Masterton at Fort St

Angelo, Bob was taken aback by the idea. 'Don't you think that's tempting fate?' he asked. 'Are you really looking for a rerun of what happened in Stockholm? We could dine in our hotel and avoid the risky walks to Floriana and back while still drinking fine wine at the commodore's expense.'

'It seems the best way of finding out if the SD agents are here because of us, Bob. We're going to end up looking over our shoulders the whole time if we don't resolve this one way or the other.'

Bob could see how determined Monique was. When he paused to think about it, he realised that his initial shock at her suggestion had been replaced by a nervous excitement that he'd felt only rarely since the days of autumn 1940, when it had been a near-constant companion while waiting for orders to scramble his Hurricane squadron to intercept enemy aircraft over Sussex, Kent or the English Channel.

He smiled. 'I'm sure it will be a nice evening for a walk.'

CHAPTER THIRTY

Monique had been surprised that Bob had agreed so readily to walk to the King Edward Hotel the previous evening. She'd expected him to build on the objection he made initially, which she knew had been entirely sensible. She'd already decided to give way to him when he suddenly changed his tune and came out in support of what she was suggesting.

In the event, they'd had a thoroughly enjoyable evening. Anne Milner had put in an appearance accompanied by a handsome young army officer and Monique had again exchanged waves with her. It seemed that Anne's confidence in her ability to attract men had been fully restored and Monique felt happy for her.

Even better, from Monique's point of view, was that nothing untoward had happened. She'd had no sense of being followed and they'd certainly not run into any SD agents. It had concerned her a little when they got back to the hotel that Bob had seemed almost disappointed that their evening hadn't ended in a gunfight on the streets of Malta to match the one in which he'd done so brilliantly on the streets of Stockholm. On balance, though, she preferred the post-Stockholm Bob. She'd criticised him in the past for a lack of a killer instinct. That all changed in Stockholm and the new Bob was a man she knew she could rely on utterly if things got difficult.

St John's Co-Cathedral was a little busier this morning than it had been the previous afternoon. She and Bob had entered together from Kingsway before separating and she then made her way to the chapel where she was due to meet Brother Marco, arriving two minutes early. The agreed time came and went. Ten minutes later, she decided Bob would be getting worried, so walked back through to the first of the chain of three chapels, where she could be seen from the nave. Bob was in a chapel on the far side of it, talking to a priest, but he looked up as soon as she came into view.

Monique gave an exaggerated shrug and smiled, then acted as though she was looking around what a small plaque on the wall said was the Chapel of Aragon, Catalonia and Navarre.

Brother Marco arrived just after 10.15 a.m. He looked flustered, as if he'd been hurrying despite what was already becoming a very warm morning. Monique thought that the combination of a red face and white garb probably wasn't the image a Dominican friar usually strove to achieve.

'I am so sorry, Monique,' he said in a hushed tone. 'Thank you for your patience. I had to wait for a telephone call and it lasted longer than I had hoped or expected.'

'I'm pleased to see you again, Brother Marco. Forgive me if I come straight to the point, but will I be able to see James Ewing?'

'I hope so and I think so,' said the friar.

Monique must have let her feelings show on her face.

'I am not being evasive, Monique, though I accept it must appear that way. James is currently staying with friends. I have spoken to him twice on the telephone to ask him to meet with you. Yesterday evening he agreed. This morning he was having quite profound second thoughts. I think I talked him around, to an extent.'

Monique tried to sound more conciliatory than she felt. 'If I could just have a chance to talk to him, even for a moment, I'm sure I could convince him of my goodwill.'

'If I tell you where he is, can I count on you not to tell

anyone else unless James explicitly agrees?' asked Brother Marco.

'With one exception. I will tell my husband, who is the RAF group captain you might have noticed me sitting with after our meeting yesterday and who is now standing over on the far side of the cathedral and acting as if he's taking no notice of us. I promise that James's whereabouts will go no further unless, as you say, James explicitly agrees.'

'As he's a military officer, that could place your husband in an exceptionally difficult position.'

'I am confident he'll be able to cope,' said Monique.

'But I do have your assurance you will approach James on your own?'

'Yes, with my husband hovering protectively somewhere a little off-stage, as he is at the moment.'

'Very well.' Brother Marco produced a small piece of paper which he handed to Monique.

She didn't see if he'd taken it from a pocket in his white habit and when she unfolded it she saw a handwritten address. 'What is this place?'

'That's the street address of a building in Victoria, which is the capital of the island of Gozo. Simply say who you are and that you are there to speak to James.'

'Do I have to be there at any particular time?'

'No, and the timing of a visit to Gozo will necessarily be rather imprecise. I can't guarantee that James will be at the address when you arrive, but it is where he's staying so he will return if he's out.'

'Thank you, Brother Marco.'

'Not at all, Monique. Go with God.' With that, Brother Marco turned and walked towards the exit.

Monique slowly walked over to where Bob was standing.

'How did that go?' he asked.

Monique quietly told Bob about her conversation with Brother Marco.

'If I understand correctly,' said Bob, 'we need to find a way to get to Gozo without telling anyone that's where we're going.'

'That's right,' said Monique. 'And I also wonder if we need to be prepared to stay there for longer than just an hour or two.'

'I'll ring Lawrence Dowson from the hotel and ask if he'd be prepared to lend us a car, without a driver, until the end of tomorrow,' said Bob. 'He could get someone to run over and pick us up, then take us back to Manoel Island where we could drop off the driver. That will give us more than enough time to pack our things in case we need to spend a night away. I think we should keep our suite at the Osborne Hotel, but if all goes well we're not going to need to stay in Malta for much longer anyway.'

'You also need to ring Charles Richmond to let him know not to worry if we drop out of sight for a day or two, and ask him to pass that on to Wilfred Masterton. That's another call you can safely make from the public phone in the hotel.'

'Thanks, Monique, that's very true. In the current circumstances, we don't want them to think that something unpleasant has happened to the two of us. Incidentally, I was talking to a priest a little earlier and commented that the cathedral seems to be amazingly undamaged. It sounds like we're looking at another miracle along the lines of the bomb at the Rotunda of Mosta. Buildings all around the cathedral have been damaged or destroyed in the bombing, including the ruins out there between it and Kingsway. But the damage to the cathedral itself was largely confined to one chapel when a bomb landed outside.

'Most of the chapels are named after the lands where the knights of the Order of Saint John originally came from. This is the Chapel of Italy that we're standing in, for example, and the next one along, on this side of the choir, is the Chapel of France. It's widely seen as ironic that the only part of the cathedral to be badly damaged by the bombing was the Chapel of Germany.'

Monique smiled.

*

'I think that means we've seen almost the whole length of the island, Bob, from Marsaxlokk in the south-east to Marfa in the north-west.' Monique brought the Royal Navy staff car to a halt in a widening of the road that ran along the shore behind the harbour.

There were a few typically Maltese fishing boats moored in the harbour and there were people and a couple of vehicles about, but it was much quieter than Bob had expected.

He looked down at the map of Malta and Gozo that they'd found in the car's glove box. 'According to this, Marfa is definitely where boats crossing to Gozo leave from. I must admit I thought we'd find more of a settlement here. It seems the only village near the tip of the island is the place we passed through a couple of miles back, Mellieha. I'm beginning to think that we should have stopped there for lunch.'

'That army lorry parked a little further along appears to be connected to the group of men we can see down on the shore,' said Monique. 'Perhaps they know something about boats to Gozo.'

'We can ask,' said Bob. 'Pull in behind the lorry and I'll go and talk to them.'

Monique complied and Bob got out of the passenger side of the car and walked across a scrubby margin and down to a stony beach. Half a dozen men in boots, khaki shorts and gloves were dragging a large coil of barbed wire along the waterline. There was plenty of wire on the beach already and Bob wondered if they were renewing lengths that had been laid previously.

One of the men looked up and saw Bob. 'We've got a visitor, sarge.'

Another man stood to attention, presumably the sergeant. 'Can I help you, sir?'

'Please, carry on,' said Bob. 'I'm hoping to get to Gozo and I've been told that boats cross from here. Do you know anything about them?'

'I think you take pot-luck a little, sir. There's a hut at the head of the pier on this side of the harbour. I'm sure they'll be able to tell you about sailings and timings.' He turned round. 'You might be in luck. I think that's the *King of England* coming in now.'

Bob looked past the men. In the distance, there was a steamer with a single funnel making its way towards the harbour.

'Thank you, sergeant, I'm very grateful.' Bob turned and started to walk back up to the car.

'Sir! Hang on a moment.'

Bob turned around. 'What is it?'

'That's a navy staff car you're driving, isn't it? Were you hoping to take that to Gozo too?'

'Ideally, yes, though I'm sure we can find another way to get to Victoria and it doesn't look as if the *King of England* carries vehicles.'

'As you've got a navy car, you might think about getting the navy to take it to Gozo, sir. And you, with it. If you go a mile or so west along the shore you come to a place called Cirkewwa. The navy is running a shuttle service from there to Gozo with a couple of tank landing craft. They're carrying construction equipment and material for the new airfield that's being built over there.'

'Thank you, that's an excellent suggestion.' Bob returned to the car and got back into the passenger side.

'Is that our boat?' asked Monique gesturing in the direction of the approaching steamer.

'I think it could be, though we'd need to find somewhere to leave the car, we'd have to carry our luggage, and we'd have to find transport from the other side of the crossing to Victoria, which the map suggests is a few miles away in the centre of the island.'

'You say that like we've got an alternative.'

'According to the sergeant laying barbed wire on the beach, we might have,' said Bob. 'I'm told we need to follow the shore west to find it.'

Monique started the car and followed the road along the coast. A couple of minutes later she slowed. 'I see what you have in mind.'

Ahead of them, the road came to an end in a large cleared area that was busy with vehicles of all kinds and men. Piles of equipment and stores were lined up along one side of the site, with a Nissen hut in a focal position. Large rocks had been piled out into the water to form a breakwater and next to it was a broad concrete slipway that looked very new.

Grounded on the slipway was a large landing craft with its bow door lowered. As Bob watched, two six-wheeled lorries drove off, followed by two Jeeps.

'Let's see how close we're allowed to get,' said Bob. 'Then we'll ask about a lift.'

Bob and Monique were required to show their security passes at a checkpoint at the end of the approach road. After that, no one seemed to pay them any attention, so Monique drove to the top of the concrete slipway, to one side of the landward end of the landing craft.

'Care to join me?' asked Bob as he got out of the car.

'You're thinking that if your rank doesn't get us a ride, then my smile might, aren't you?'

'Something like that,' said Bob, grinning.

Two young naval officers, a lieutenant and a sub-lieutenant, were standing by the landing craft's ramp, looking at a clipboard that the latter was holding. Both saluted as Bob approached.

'Can we help you sir?'

'I hope so. I need to get to Gozo and I'm wondering if you have space for our car.'

'Your car, sir?' asked the lieutenant, clearly wondering why an RAF officer was in a Royal Navy car.

'Technically it belongs to the 10th Submarine Flotilla, but they lent it to us.'

'The volume of kit here that needs moving is more than we can possibly accommodate, sir,' said the lieutenant. 'But that would be true with or without your car on board. Can you turn it around, then reverse it as far back along the deck as you can manage and as near to one side as possible? If you park it on the port side then you'll be able to get out of the driver's door.'

'I'll do it,' said Monique, smiling brightly.

Bob watched as she completed the manoeuvre, reversing the car much faster than she needed to along the deck. He got the sense that everyone else in this makeshift port had also stopped to watch. Monique obviously thought she had a point to prove, and she proved it better than he could have done.

'We don't really go in for passenger cabins on a tank landing craft, sir,' said the lieutenant. 'Would you and the lady mind going up to the deck at the stern, between the Oerlikon cannons, while we get everything else loaded?'

'Of course not,' said Bob, 'and thank you.'

'It's quite an impressive operation,' said Monique, after Bob had led her to the deck on top of the rear of the landing craft.

'I suppose it takes a lot to build an airfield on an island from scratch.'

'Is all this for one of the airfields the air vice-marshal wanted you to help build?' asked Monique.

'Yes, he said they've almost finished the first runway in under three weeks and are building a second. It hadn't crossed my mind they'd need to build a port to transport everything to Gozo so they could build an airfield there.'

Bob looked around as the rising drone of an air raid warning sounded. 'Bloody hell! This may not be ideal. We're standing on top of by far the best and most obvious target in sight during an air raid.'

Monique grabbed his arm and pointed. 'Look Bob, there's a fighter coming in very low over the sea towards us. And another one behind it and to the right of it.'

'They've caught everyone by surprise. We need to find cover, and quickly.'

'I don't think there's time, Bob!'

None of the landing craft's crew were at the rear of the vessel and Bob realised he was standing next to an Oerlikon 20 mm cannon with a metal shield in front of the firing position. 'Get over there, Monique.' He pointed at the cannon on the side of the vessel furthest from the approaching aircraft. 'The metal shield on that cannon will protect you. Get on the other side of it.'

'What are you going to do?'

It must have been eighteen months earlier that Bob had volunteered for an hour's training on the operation of an Oerlikon 20 mm cannon at an airfield in County Durham. He prayed that the drum magazine mounted on top of this one had ammunition in it. The cannon they'd trained on, intended for airfield defence, had a complicated arrangement of ropes and pulleys to cock it. That was necessary to provide the 400lb pull needed to overcome the recoil spring.

But this was a war zone. Surely a weapon that hard to cock would be left ready to fire in case it was needed? Bob couldn't remember how to tell if the cannon was cocked or not, so added that to his list of prayers.

He put his shoulders in the rests at the rear of the cannon then swung its barrel around to point at the nearest attacking aircraft, which he could now see was a Messerschmitt Bf 109. When he looked through the aiming sight on top of the weapon the aircraft looked frighteningly close. Bob pressed the trigger. The thunder of the cannon firing its stream of shells was quickly replaced by the roar of the Messerschmitt passing very low over his head. Bob instinctively ducked, then stepped back from the weapon and looked around. The Messerschmitt was climbing away and trailing smoke, then it banked sharply to its left and plunged to the ground, exploding on impact some distance inland. He saw no parachute.

Bob became aware of the sound of other weapons firing and saw the second fighter turn away, deterred from pressing home its attack by anti-aircraft guns around the harbour. He felt slightly dazed but a lasting recollection afterwards was the smile on Monique's face before she hugged him.

The naval lieutenant, who Bob assumed was the landing craft's captain, then appeared and shook his hand. 'Congratulations sir! From your medal ribbons, I'm guessing you might have bagged a few in the past, but I bet you've never got one while standing on a tank landing craft!'

'He didn't fire back, did he?' asked Bob.

'A split second more and I'm sure he'd have opened fire, sir. Thank you for saving my vessel. If you'd not reacted so quickly that first aircraft would have strafed us and got clean away. No one else started shooting until it was far too late.'

'Whatever you do,' said Bob, 'please pass on my thanks to whoever left the cannon cocked. I'd have stood no chance if I'd have had to do that too.'

'I will, sir,' said the lieutenant, 'though standing orders are for the cannons to be made safe when the vessel is in port. The weapon you fired shouldn't have been left like that. Look at the one on the other side. It's not cocked.'

The lieutenant moved away and Monique hugged Bob again. 'I don't care if public displays of affection embarrass you. There'll never be a better moment than this. You just saved my life as well as the lieutenant's boat.'

'Did you hear what he said about the cannons not being left cocked?' asked Bob.

'Yes, it was your lucky day; and mine; and the lieutenant's.'

'Perhaps the Eye of Horus was looking down and saw that

this half-blind group captain needed a little help,' said Bob, smiling.

CHAPTER THIRTY-ONE

'I'd thought of Gozo as being sparsely populated and thinly developed,' said Bob. 'The village with the harbour where we came ashore, Mgarr, was larger and busier than I'd expected and I must admit that Victoria is also a much bigger settlement than I'd imagined, even after looking at it on a map.'

'Now we're in Victoria, where should we go?' asked Monique.

'The map of Malta and Gozo the navy kindly left in the car has street plans of key settlements in the corners, including Victoria. The focus of the town appears to be on its north side where there's a square called It-Tokk. North of the square is what the map calls the Cittadella which seems to be what its name implies, a defensive citadel. The address the friar gave you is on the road which heads north from one end of the square and along the side of one of the bastions of the citadel.'

'So if we park in the square or somewhere near it we can walk from there?' asked Monique.

'Yes, I think the road we're on should take us right to it.'

Monique saw Bob looking at the buildings they were passing.

'I'm sure Gozo must have been bombed as it's on the direct route for enemy aircraft based in Sicily on their way to attack targets in Malta,' he said. 'But I've not seen obvious damage of the sort you see pretty much everywhere on the main island. Hang on, I think this is the square we want coming up ahead.'

They emerged in the north-east corner of It-Tokk, which to Monique's mind was more of a rectangle than a square. The south side was lined with three-storey buildings that kept the road on that side in the shade. More shade was provided by lines of trees that separated the central area from the roads to its north and south. The space between the lines of trees formed a market and was busy with people viewing the goods on show or standing and talking. The western end of the square was defined by a round-fronted building in honey-coloured stone that reminded Monique of a tier from a wedding cake.

Monique parked the car on the south side of the square. 'What do we do first, Bob? Should we go and visit James Ewing or should we see if anyone is still serving lunch?'

Bob looked at his watch. 'We're well past lunchtime, perhaps we should find something to tide us over? Remember that we don't know where dinner is coming from.'

'There's a café over on the north side of the square, across the main road.'

The café was serving food and both Monique and Bob enjoyed croque monsieurs with, as it was a hot afternoon, cold Cisk Lager Beers.

After their late lunch, they turned right out of the café before taking the first right turn again. This led them onto a steep cobbled street that climbed between large buildings towards the obvious walls of the Cittadella at its top. A few people were climbing or descending the hill, but no one paid any attention to them.

'Given the number of the house opposite, I think it's the next one along that you want,' said Bob, gesturing towards a substantial two-storey building on the left of the street, on a corner with a side road. Like many other buildings in the town, including the citadel in the background, it was made of honey-coloured stone. There was a stone balustrade around the building at roof level and a short open balcony on the side facing the street. The corner was cut away and at first-floor level this had a gallariji overhanging the pavement. The arched ground-floor windows all had closed external shutters, though the shutters on the first-floor windows were open.

The front door was set a little back from the street, beneath the open balcony. A pair of solid external doors had been opened against the inside of the doorway and the space they left, up a step from the street, was protected by a pair of highly ornate waist-high metal gates.

A small plaque attached to the wall beside the door identified the building as St Dominic's House, a name that hadn't formed part of the address that the friar had given to Monique.

'Do you want to walk up the hill towards the Cittadella?' asked Monique. Bob nodded. She paused to allow him to get a little distance away before pulling on the handle of a brass chain hanging beside the plaque. She heard the sound of a bell ringing somewhere within the building.

One side of the wood and glass door was opened sufficiently for her to see a middle-aged dark-haired man wearing a white habit standing inside.

'Hello, can I help you?'

'Hello, my name is Monique Dubois. I believe James Ewing is expecting me.'

'Ah, yes. We didn't know what time you would arrive and I'm afraid James has gone out for a walk.'

'Do you know when he'll be back?' asked Monique.

'I'm sorry, no. But he does want to talk to you.'

'Thank you,' said Monique. 'Perhaps I'll go and explore the Cittadella and then call in on my way back down the hill.'

The friar smiled. 'Yes, that might be best. Go with God.'

Then he closed the door.

Monique could see Bob waiting further up the hill, below the towering wall of the Cittadella.

He smiled as she approached. 'Not in?'

'No, but he does want to talk to me. I told the friar who answered the door that I'd explore the Cittadella and call in again on my way back. That doesn't seem like a bad idea.'

The road they were walking along doubled back on itself before climbing to a gateway in the wall of the Cittadella. Beyond was a broad open area with, on its far side, a set of equally broad stone steps leading up to the front of an imposing church. Large buildings at a higher level on both sides of the open area looked down onto it. There were a few people in view but it was far from busy.

'This is impressive,' said Bob.

'I was expecting something a little more obviously military,' said Monique, 'perhaps like Fort St Angelo. Other than the airfield we saw being built near the road to Victoria, Gozo seems to have much less of a military presence than Malta, where it's overwhelming.'

They climbed the steps and went into an alley between the corner of the church and other buildings. Then they turned left and walked in silence up an inclined stone path.

'The buildings up here are ruined,' said Bob.

As they followed paths between stone walls it seemed to Monique that except for the church and the buildings around the gateway, most of the interior of the Cittadella was in ruins.

'It looks like these steps lead up to the top of the outer wall,' she said. She climbed up them. 'Wow! Look at that view! You must be able to see a large part of the island from here.'

'I suppose it makes sense that you'd build your citadel on

top of the highest and most easily-defended place you could find,' said Bob. 'I find the ruinous state of the place very odd. None of this looks recent. Whoever knocked down all these buildings, it must have happened a long time before the Germans and Italians started dropping bombs on Malta. Let's follow the wall clockwise around the citadel.'

Further round, nearer the rear of the church whose front dominated the entrance to the Cittadella, the views started to include Victoria itself as well as what Monique thought must be another large part of the island of Gozo.

She looked at her watch. 'It's three-quarters of an hour since I rang their doorbell. Let's see if James is back.'

*

'So what do we do now?' asked Monique.

They'd returned to the car and Monique was sitting in the driver's seat, watching the market in full swing in It-Tokk.

'Let's visit again early this evening,' said Bob. 'If James is in, fine. If he's still being elusive we can think about keeping watch on St Dominic's House, which I think will mean a change of clothes for me. We've got a photograph of him. If we see him arriving or departing you can intercept him in the street. It's not ideal, I accept, but it's the only idea I've got.'

'Do you think he's been inside when I've rung the bell?' asked Monique.

'That would mean the friar you spoke to both times was lying to you, which I would find surprising and disappointing,' said Bob. 'Right now, I think we need to find a hotel. The map suggests the heart of the town is around St George's Square, which ought to be at the other end of the street leading off this square just ahead of us. Let's look there. We can leave our luggage in the car for the moment and pick it up after we've found somewhere.'

Monique took Bob's arm as they walked down the narrow street leading to St George's Square. The south side of the square was formed by the front face of a large church with twin bell towers. The square was busy with people coming and going.

'There you go, Monique,' said Bob, pointing to a building on the right-hand side of the square. 'The Victoria and Albert Hotel looks reasonable and has the distinct benefit of being close to where we need to be.'

It turned out that the Victoria and Albert Hotel offered a friendly welcome and accommodation that was clean, if rather more basic than they'd grown used to in Valletta. As they carried their cases from the navy staff car to the hotel Monique realised that it was as well that she'd packed a dressing gown, because while their room offered great views from the third floor of the hotel over St George's Square, the bathroom and the toilet were both a little distance along the corridor.

*

The third time Monique rang the doorbell of St Dominic's House, she was unsure what to expect. Bob, now wearing one of his civilian suits, had again gone further up the road that ran along the side of the Cittadella before doubling back to its gateway.

This time the door was opened by a man in his twenties who had dark very closely-cropped hair and a moustache and was wearing a light-coloured suit.

'Are you James Ewing?' asked Monique.

'Are you Monique Dubois?'

'Yes, I am.'

'Who's my uncle?'

'Your uncle is Maurice Cunningham and until you shaved off your beard you looked like a younger version of him.'

James smiled. 'Hello. I'm not sure if I'm exactly glad to see you, but thank you for all the time and effort you must have put into finding me.'

'Where should we talk?' asked Monique.

'I find the views from the walls of the Cittadella are good for the soul,' said James.

'That's not where you went earlier,' said Monique.

'No. I spent most of the afternoon in St George's Basilica, trying to get things straight in my head. That's not far away in the centre of the town.'

'Is that the church on the far side of St George's Square?' asked Monique.

'Yes. Let's just walk for the moment. I promise I'll tell you everything when we're there.'

James put on a Panama hat and stepped out into the street, closing the door behind himself, and then turned to walk up the hill. Monique had taken off her straw sunhat when she'd rung the bell and put it back on now, though she left her sunglasses in her handbag. Looking ahead, Monique could see no sign of Bob.

James followed the same route she and Bob had taken earlier that afternoon. The views from the citadel walls were just as remarkable now as they had been then. There was no one else in sight in the Cittadella and Monique began to wonder where Bob was.

James stopped and turned towards Monique and then leaned against the wall running along the outer side of the wall walk.

'Can I ask why it's you that my uncle sent to find me?' asked James.

'It wasn't originally,' said Monique. 'He asked an old school friend who's with the Secret Intelligence Service in Cairo to help. Unfortunately, he got on the wrong side of a Maltese gangster who abducted him. Maurice then turned to my husband and me to try to find both you and the missing school friend. We work in Military Intelligence, Section 11, but consider Maurice to be a friend as well as our boss.'

'Is the SIS officer all right?' asked James.

'Yes, we found him and he's gone back to Cairo.'

'That's good,' said James. 'Brother Marco said your husband is an RAF group captain.'

'He is.'

'I will talk to you Monique but I must ask you to keep what I'm going to tell you entirely to yourself, with one exception I'll mention shortly. That means I don't want you to tell your husband. Do you agree to that?'

Monique's second meeting with Brother Marco had left her with a fairly clear idea that this moment might come and she'd had plenty of time to weigh up the pros and cons. 'Yes, I agree.'

James took a deep breath. 'The simple truth is that I'm a deserter. I've abandoned my post and betrayed my comrades. I believe that in the RAF, aircrew who refuse to fly more missions over enemy territory are said to have a lack of moral fibre. That's me. I've had enough of the war and I've decided to leave it behind me.

'Your husband is a senior military officer, as is Uncle Maurice. If you tell either of them that you've found me they

346

will be duty-bound to do something about it. If they don't, they will be aiding and abetting a deserter. By being here now, you've already put yourself in that position, but it would be worse for them. If the authorities do come after me it will bring my family, including Uncle Maurice, into disgrace and they don't deserve that. It will also publicly dishonour the memory of my father. That's why I'm imploring you not to tell anyone else, including your husband.'

Monique could see the young man was deadly serious. 'I won't. You talked about the simple truth, James. Is there a more complicated truth? You served as the first officer aboard HMS *Ursus* until August last year when a depth charge left you deaf in one ear. You could have returned to Britain but you chose instead to remain in Malta in a shore position with the 10th Submarine Flotilla. Whatever has brought you to where you are now, surely no one can ever question your loyalty or your bravery?'

'That's all true,' said James. 'But it's also beside the point. Let's forget for a moment that I only asked to remain in Malta after being wounded because I was in love with a nurse I'd met in the hospital. The inescapable fact is that I'm a serving officer with the 10th Submarine Flotilla who has decided he no longer wishes to serve. That's desertion.'

'What brought this about?' asked Monique.

There was a long pause. James was looking over the wall of the Cittadella and the thought crossed Monique's mind that he might be thinking about jumping. He was physically larger than her and she wondered whether she could prevent him for long enough to allow Bob to come and assist from wherever he was hiding.

Then James looked at her. 'You probably know that HMS

Ursus disappeared in November and was assumed lost. If it wasn't for this damned ear I would have been with her at the time and might have been able to do something to prevent the loss of the boat. I have repeated nightmares about how my friends on HMS *Ursus* might have died that have kept me awake, often night after night, and I've found it increasingly difficult to cope.

'The other thing behind my decision to change my life was more positive. I found a religious icon in a bombed-out church in Sliema last April, during the worst of the bombing. I had to leave it with some of my belongings when the 10th Submarine Flotilla was ordered to move to Alexandria shortly afterwards, but after we returned to Malta I hung it up on the wall of my quarters on Manoel Island. That wasn't long before I damaged my hearing and seeing it there every time I returned to my room got me thinking. After HMS *Ursus* was lost in November I rather fell to pieces internally and the nightmares started, though I think I managed to keep the facade fairly intact.

'I was desperate to find some way of putting myself back together. The icon inspired me to talk to a priest I met by chance in a church and through him I came across the Dominican Order in Malta. Before long I was spending some of the time when I was away from Manoel Island at a priory of theirs in Rabat. I've never been religious but something about what I've learned of the life leaves me wanting to know more.'

This only served to confirm what Monique had already thought likely from Brother Marco's involvement. 'Where does St Dominic's House fit in?' she asked.

'I suppose you could call it a place of retreat. For me, it's been a place of refuge. The Dominicans are fully aware of my situation and said that I'd be less likely to be recognised on

Gozo than in one of their priories on the main island. So far it has gone well. My only regret is that the manner of my leaving my old life meant I had to abandon the icon and I know there's nothing I can do to retrieve it.'

'Am I right in assuming that your fear of recognition explains the removal of the beard and much of your hair?' asked Monique.

'That's right.'

'You talked about an exception to my keeping quiet about what you've told me. Are you thinking of Anne Milner?'

'Good grief, no!' said James. 'What we had in the early part of last year was wonderful. But we both moved on when the 10th Submarine Flotilla was redeployed to Alexandria. I'm not sure what made me want to see her again in December. My involvement with the Dominicans had barely started and I was at a low ebb. It turned out she was doing pretty badly at the time too. I heard that two of the men she'd been involved with after I'd gone to Alexandria had been killed and she was nothing but skin and bone when we started seeing each other again. Everyone in Malta had stories of extreme hunger last year, but I got the sense that she'd eaten even less than she could have done.

'I'm not sure that reviving our relationship was a good thing for either of us. I did help get Anne back into the habit of eating more and enjoying her food, which was good, but I think that in every other way, I was simply holding her back. Meanwhile, I had a growing involvement with a life that would by definition eventually have to exclude her. But it was you who mentioned her, Monique. I'm sure you've talked to her. Do you think she's missing me?'

Monique felt it best not to answer that question. 'Who do

you want me to tell, then?' she asked, though she suspected she already knew the answer.

'I know it's a lot to ask, but would you be prepared to visit my mother, Amanda Ewing, in Devon? I need someone to tell her in person that I'm alive, and also to give her a letter from me. It has to be delivered by hand, for all the reasons I've talked about.'

'Yes, I'll do that. I'll need the letter of course.'

James took an envelope out of an inside pocket. 'This is it. Her address is written on the front.'

Monique took the envelope and put it in her handbag.

'Thank you,' he said. 'I'm very grateful. I should go now.'

Monique saw he had tears in his eyes. 'Go with God,' she said.

James descended from the wall into the maze of ruins on the near side of the Cittadella. She gave him a couple of minutes lead and then set off herself. She was only halfway back to the first of the standing buildings when Bob stepped out of a doorway.

'You gave me a fright,' she said. 'Which is a good thing. You managed to blend into the scenery very well and I didn't see you at all during my meeting.'

'How did it go?' he asked, slipping his right arm through her left and walking beside her.

'I know we enjoyed our dinner in the hotel,' said Monique, 'but the bar looked a little dreary. Let's go and see if the café where we ate this afternoon is still open. I feel in need of a beer, or perhaps three.'

'Was it as bad as that?'

*

'How did it go?' asked Bob again after they were sat on either side of a table in the café with their beers between them.

Monique had done all her soul-searching on the journey from Valletta to Victoria and didn't need to do any more now. 'It wasn't James Ewing,' she said.

Bob looked shocked. 'Are you sure? He didn't see me but I got a good look at him as he left. Except for the lack of a beard, he looked very like the photograph Lawrence Dowson gave us.'

'It wasn't James Ewing,' Monique repeated.

Bob didn't react badly to what she'd said but Monique could see he was having difficulty coming to terms with it.

Neither of them said anything for a while and it took Bob until they'd each started their second beer to work it out which, in the circumstances, Monique thought was pretty good.

'Maybe it's just as well that it wasn't James Ewing you were talking to,' he said. 'If, hypothetically, a naval officer had deserted during wartime to join a religious community, then anyone who knew what he'd done would be obliged to report it. Especially if they were, hypothetically again, an RAF group captain or a Royal Navy commodore. What about his mother?'

'You're going to fly me to Devon so I can hand-deliver a letter to her.'

'And Anne Milner?'

'Did she appear to be missing James the last two times we've dined at the King Edward Hotel?'

'Fair point,' said Bob.

Monique smiled. 'I suppose that tomorrow we should return to Malta, tell Lawrence Dowson that his lieutenant remains unaccounted for, and find out about flights back to Gibraltar and then home. We will need to ask Lawrence not to tell Maurice anything until we've had a chance to speak to him ourselves.'

'I'm not especially looking forward to that,' said Bob. 'Maurice is going to be very disappointed.'

'I'll talk to him on my own,' said Monique.

'Are you sure? You'll need to be careful you don't put him in an impossible position.'

'I managed it with you, Bob. I'm sure I'll find the right thing to say to him.'

'That would certainly make life easier for me,' said Bob. 'On a brighter note, I've been wondering if we should see the sights here on Gozo tomorrow before heading back to Malta later in the afternoon. The captain of the landing craft said they are working from dawn to dusk seven days a week until the airfield is complete, so we know we'll be able to get transport back.'

'That sounds lovely,' said Monique. 'Though getting back late might make it difficult to arrange a flight home for the following day.'

'Would that be such a disaster? We've done what we came to Malta to do and we are meant to be on honeymoon. If we aim to fly back on Monday it would give us Sunday free to look at parts of Malta we've not yet seen. If we can hang on to the navy car we'll be able to get around without any problem.'

'If you attach the idea of a lie-in and a leisurely breakfast at the start of tomorrow's itinerary, I'd certainly sign up for it,' said Monique.

'Maybe we should stay here for the full three beers you were proposing and then go back to our hotel and see if the bedsprings squeak?' asked Bob.

'That sounds lovely,' said Monique, smiling.

CHAPTER THIRTY-TWO

It was a different landing craft that took them back to Malta from Gozo the next afternoon. Bob was highly embarrassed to find that the captain and crew all seemed to know it was him who had shot down the Messerschmitt Bf 109 the previous day at Cirkewwa and he and Monique were treated like honoured guests.

They'd spent a blissful day on Gozo. The receptionist at the hotel had pointed out places they might like to see on their map and they visited deserted cliff scenery on the south side of the island and its west, a pilgrimage church in the north-west, and a spectacular and equally deserted beach on Gozo's north coast, though here the war did intrude in the form of coils of barbed wire along the sand and signs warning of a minefield. They also spent time at the megalithic temples at Ggantija. Given their late breakfast they'd skipped lunch, intending instead to have an early dinner at the King Edward Hotel.

Once back on the island of Malta, Monique drove them to Manoel Island. The 10th Submarine Flotilla's duty officer told them apologetically that Commander Dowson was on weekend leave at Ghajn Tuffieha and wasn't expected back until Monday morning. Bob turned down the offer the duty officer made to contact the commander, instead saying they'd call in on him then. He did, however, accept the duty officer's offer of the continued loan of the car, which saved him from having to ask.

Bob went back to where they'd parked the car while Monique went in search of Sub-Lieutenant David Short. She was gone for a while and when she returned to the car she was carrying something wrapped in a towel.

'What's that?' asked Bob.

'It's the icon that was hanging on James Ewing's wall.'

'Isn't that a little dangerous?' asked Bob. 'What if someone takes an interest in where it's gone and why?'

'I told David Short that I wanted to let James's mother have the icon, which is the truth. She deserves to have a tangible reminder of him. If I'd left it in his room it would simply have been collected with his other effects when they add the words "presumed dead" to "missing" on his record, which I imagine will be soon after we talk to Lawrence Dowson on Monday. It might have found its way to her eventually or it could simply have been taken by someone else or lost.'

They dropped their cases off at the Osborne Hotel and then, at the suggestion of the receptionist, parked the navy staff car in an area clear of rubble not far from the viewpoint they'd found at the end of the street.

After unpacking their cases, which seemed worthwhile even for just the two nights they had left at the hotel, they walked to Floriana and enjoyed another excellent dinner at the King Edward Hotel and more of the red wine they liked so much.

Afterwards, they walked back to Valletta.

Bob was first to see the car parked outside the Osborne Hotel. 'There goes a lovely evening,' he said. 'What do you think the Corps of Military Police want with us?'

'I hope it's not what I'm thinking it might be,' said Monique. 'If it is, I'm sorry, Bob.'

As they approached the military police car, a corporal wearing a khaki shirt and shorts and a peaked cap with a red cover got out of the driver's side and saluted.

'Are you Group Captain Sutherland, sir?'

'That's right,' said Bob.

'I'm told you know Mr Masterton of MI5, sir. I'm instructed to pick you and Madame Dubois up as soon as you get back to your hotel and take you to see him at Fort St Angelo. It's a matter of urgency.'

'Let's go, then,' said Bob, opening the rear door of the car for Monique.

They exchanged glances as the car pulled away. Monique raised her eyebrows in surprise. He could also see reflected in her face the relief that he was feeling.

*

Wilfred Masterton seemed to be doing whatever he was doing from a much more humble setting in Fort St Angelo than the Magistral Palace. Bob and Monique were shown into a meeting room in one of the blocks of buildings standing in the busy open area below the outer wall of the fort.

There were seven men in the room, looking at a large map on a table. Four were military officers while the other three were civilians. Wilfred Masterton was the only one Monique recognised.

He looked up and smiled. 'Hello to both of you! Your hotel said you were back from your travels but had gone out to dinner. I'm glad you've not missed the show.'

'What show?' asked Bob.

'You'll be pleased to know that we've found out where the SD agents have gone to ground and I'm sure you'll be even more pleased to hear that their arrival on the island appears to have had nothing to do with the two of you.'

Monique walked over to the table. She could feel a nervous energy in the room, an excitement as if something significant was about to happen. She thought it odd that Wilfred Masterton didn't introduce them to anyone. It was as if he was in a rush to be somewhere else.

'Where are the SD agents?' asked Bob.

'Earlier this evening we got quite convincing intelligence that they're using a half-destroyed house near the tip of Senglea, which is the next peninsula along from Vittoriosa, the one we're on.' He looked at his watch. 'Your timing couldn't be better. We've got the whole area sealed off with troops and we will be moving in at 8 p.m., which is twenty minutes before sunset. Do you want to observe? I'm about to drive around there myself to give the go-ahead.'

'Why move in at sunset?' asked Bob. 'Anyone who slips the net will have the cover of darkness not much later. If you left it until dawn you'd have plenty of daylight to round up any stragglers.'

'For reasons I'll explain later, it's imperative we sort this out today. I've got to leave immediately, are you coming?'

Monique saw Bob glance at her and she nodded slightly.

They got into the back of a car parked outside the building and Wilfred Masterton and one of his colleagues got into the front. The others in the room had followed them out and were making their way towards another car.

It only took a few minutes for Wilfred Masterton to drive along the length of the busy Dockyard Creek and then back along a road at a higher level along the other side of it. Monique found herself shocked by the scale of the devastation here. They'd been told that Senglea had been badly bombed, and had seen the area from a distance, but the reality she saw on either side of what appeared to be the main road running along the centre of the peninsula brought home what Malta had been through more than anything else she'd seen.

Bob gave voice to her thoughts. 'Good God!' he said. 'This is appalling.'

'Senglea has been the worst-hit area,' said Wilfred Masterton. 'It's got dockyards on both sides so I suppose that was inevitable. They've cleared some of the rubble from a couple of streets including this one which is called, ironically enough, Victory Street. That's allowed vehicles to pass through but it's still pretty much a wasteland. You only have to look around to see that there's far more destroyed than is still standing.'

'Is it the dockyards that brought the SD agents here?' asked Bob.

'Apparently not. I'll explain afterwards. But it might have been the availability of bombed-out houses that caused them to decide to establish their base here. Ironically, it's the fact that many of the people who used to live here haven't been able to return that caused the SD agents to stand out more than they might have done if they'd set up shop in Valletta or Sliema.

'You can see the road ahead of us dips and then climbs again. The ruin you can see at the top of the rise is all that's left of a church that I'm told used to dominate the end of the peninsula. Our SD friends have gone to ground in what's left of a traditional apartment block in a street just beyond the church. We'll stop up here, where it opens out this side of the church.'

There were half a dozen army lorries parked in the open area, which Monique imagined had once been a square in front of the church. Masterton drew a pistol after getting out of the car. 'Would the two of you mind waiting here for now?' he asked. Then he went over to talk to an army major standing with a lieutenant by the corner of the church.

Masterton's colleague from their car and the five men in the second car went over to join them, and then they all disappeared out of sight around the side of the ruins.

'Let's get out,' said Bob. 'I don't know how you feel, Monique, but this is oddly reminiscent of waiting outside Simon Micallef's farm.'

Monique took her pistol out of her handbag and cocked it, then walked over to the corner Masterton had gone around. 'I agree, Bob. All we need is someone popping up out of an escape tunnel disguised as an air raid shelter and the likeness would be complete.'

Bob came to stand behind her. They waited like that for what seemed an age.

Then she sensed Bob move and turned to see him look at his watch.

'Things ought to kick off any minute now,' he said.

A short time later she heard the sound of whistles being blown and an explosion, then gunfire that went on for a surprising amount of time. Then there was a larger explosion, followed by silence. Behind them, she heard vehicles moving and when she turned she saw three army ambulances drive through the square and out of it in the direction the firing had come from.

'At least this time it doesn't look as if we're going to have to kill anyone,' said Bob. 'I seem to have been doing altogether too much of that recently, counting Simon Micallef and the pilot of the Messerschmitt yesterday.'

Shortly afterwards, Wilfred Masterton and the colleague they'd shared the car with came back around the corner of the church. 'I think we can call that a job well done,' Masterton said. 'I'm sorry, I was a little tense earlier and didn't introduce you to Peter Woodruff, who works with me.'

Bob and Monique exchanged nods with Woodruff.

'What happened?' asked Bob.

'There were four of them in the building,' said Masterton. 'Two were killed but the other two are uninjured. One of the dead agents set off a bomb when our men went in that injured three of them, including one who looked in a bad way. We'll take the two healthy prisoners back to Fort St Angelo and see what they've got to say for themselves. Hop in the car and we can head back there ourselves and get things organised.'

This time Peter Woodruff drove. Monique leaned forwards as they returned through the ruins of Senglea. 'I can help question them,' she said.

'Thanks for the offer,' said Masterton, 'but there's really no need. I thought the two of you would like to observe the operation simply out of courtesy as we'd previously thought you might be their targets.'

'Why are you so sure we aren't?' asked Bob.

'That's the piece of the jigsaw you don't have,' said Masterton. 'It seems that King George has been in North Africa since last Saturday, visiting Allied troops and hosting garden parties and doing the sorts of things that a king is meant to do. At some point last night or early this morning it was agreed that the king should visit Malta. Apparently, he has been very keen to do so all along, but the politicians and military men have been arguing that it's too dangerous for him to come here with the Luftwaffe only 60 miles away.

'This morning I had a meeting with Lord Gort, the governor of Malta, about something else and he told me about the king's planned visit. I, of course, told him in return about the presence of SD agents on the island. It would be fair to say that didn't go down well. The king is due to leave Tripoli for Malta aboard the cruiser HMS *Aurora* at 10 p.m. tonight and the governor gave me until 9.30 p.m. to resolve the problem of the SD agents or he would have to send a signal to cancel the king's visit.'

Masterton looked at his watch. 'I've got a line open from Fort St Angelo to the Governor's Palace and it looks as if I'll be able to reassure Lord Gort that the problem is resolved with over half an hour left before his deadline. That will allow the king's visit to proceed. We had been narrowing down where we thought the SD agents were over the past day or so, but through sheer good fortune for us they made themselves too obvious to the wrong person earlier this evening.'

'But how do you know the king was the intended target of the SD team?' asked Bob. 'From what you say, the decision that he should come to Malta wasn't made until long after the SD agents arrived on the island.'

'It's just too much of a coincidence,' said Masterton. 'I imagine that the king's visit to North Africa must have been kept as secret as possible, but a lot of people would have come to know he was there. As he's been there since last Saturday then it's perfectly possible that the SD could have landed its agents here on Monday night simply to cover the possibility that the king would come here. Hopefully, we'll find that out when we interrogate our prisoners.'

'That makes it all the more important that I help question them,' said Monique. 'I speak fluent German. Do you, Wilfred?'

'No, I'm fluent in Italian. My German is much more basic and, before you ask, I think the same goes for my colleagues. But as I said, there's no need. After a couple of minutes with them, it's clear that both the surviving SD agents speak fluent

English.'

Monique looked at Bob, hoping he'd intervene.

'I'm grateful to both of you for coming along this evening,' said Masterton. 'I'll get someone to run you to your hotel when we get back to Fort St Angelo.'

'I'm sorry, Wilfred, but that's not good enough,' said Bob. 'I accept that this is your show and that it's for you to decide whether Monique takes part in the questioning, though I think you're making a mistake in excluding her. But as the deputy head of Military Intelligence, Section 11, I wish to remain at Fort St Angelo with Monique while your questioning takes place and I would like a verbal report from you as soon as you've completed it.'

Monique could only see the back of Wilfred Masterton's head but still felt she could detect him passing through surprise and anger on his way to acceptance. 'Very well, Bob,' he said. 'You may have let yourself in for a late night, but that's up to you.'

CHAPTER THIRTY-THREE

Monique smiled at Bob across the small lounge where Wilfred Masterton had asked them to wait. They were back inside Fort St Angelo rather than in the building outside it where they'd met Masterton before going to Senglea. Monique wasn't sure of the intended purpose of the room they were in, but it had half a dozen upholstered armchairs around two walls, with a small table against one of the other walls and a bookcase beside the door leading in from the corridor they'd approached by, which was buried within the fabric of an old part of the fort.

'Thanks, Bob,' she said. 'I thought Wilfred was going to succeed in removing us from the picture altogether.'

'He certainly wanted to,' said Bob. 'I have some sympathy for him. He must have been under enormous pressure to wrap things up as quickly as possible. Imagine the weight on his shoulders of knowing that the king's visit would be cancelled if he couldn't track down and catch the SD agents. I could feel the relief radiating off him in the car on the way back. I suspect that may have clouded his judgement in excluding you, as a fluent German speaker, from the questioning. He may not have welcomed the idea of you and I remaining here, but it seems the best way to provide him with the support he may still need.'

Bob walked over to the bookcase and returned with what he showed her was a history of Malta. The armchair she was sitting in was comfortable and after an active day and the wine she'd drunk with dinner, Monique felt herself dozing as they waited.

She awoke with a start and the certainty that quite some time had passed. She realised that it had been the sound of the door opening that had awakened her and that Wilfred Masterton had come into the room.

'I think that's us done for the night,' he said.

'What did you find out?' asked Bob.

Masterton sat wearily in one of the other armchairs and looked down at a notebook. 'The two men we have in custody are the leader of the SD team, Helmut Immendorff, and a more junior agent, Carl Stoltenberg. Stoltenberg played it very much by the book, "name rank and number" type stuff. He reminded me of newsreel films of the Hitler Youth before the war. He might be more forthcoming over time but tonight he gave us virtually nothing that was of any use at all.

'I had questioned Stoltenberg first in the hope he would be the more talkative of the two, so wasn't too optimistic when it came to interviewing Immendorff. I was surprised to find him much more open than his junior colleague. He told me that his team of four SD officers had been based at La Spezia in northern Italy since March because of a belief in the SD that sooner or later Winston Churchill would visit Malta. The idea was to assassinate him here and give the Nazis a huge propaganda coup. Immendorff and one of the two dead men had actually visited the island at the beginning of April, being dropped off by U-boat and then collected three nights later. This allowed them to get an idea of the lie of the land and find the safe house they were using in Senglea.

'When they received intelligence last weekend that King George VI was visiting troops in North Africa the SD decided to cover the possibility of the king visiting Malta and moved Immendorff and his team here, with orders to assassinate him if he did.'

'How was the assassination to be carried out?' asked Bob.

'The SD reasoned that if Winston Churchill - or King George - visited Malta, then the one thing he would be certain to do would be to make an appearance on the balcony above the main door to the Governor's Palace in Palace Square to greet the people of Malta. There are many buildings around the square, some damaged by bombing, and Immendorff said the plan tomorrow was to shoot the king from the roof of one of the other buildings in the square.'

'Thinking about how large Palace Square is, that would be quite a shot,' said Monique. 'Has a sniper rifle been recovered from the building the SD agents were hiding in?'

'No, but the explosion triggered by one of them when we raided the property caused a partial collapse. It could easily be under the ruins.'

'I don't want to question your approach,' said Monique, 'but don't you think that Immendorff might have been just a little too cooperative?'

'That's a fair point, Monique, and one that has been worrying me a little,' said Masterton. 'But I don't think we would have found out any more if you'd been present and we'd questioned them in German.'

'No, I accept that,' said Monique. 'But what if you were told a cover story intended to divert your attention from something else?'

'What?' asked Masterton.

'I don't know, but I think we have to try to find out before it becomes all too obvious tomorrow. What if, for the sake of argument, they've already planted a bomb in the Governor's Palace? If so, then telling you about a planned shooting is simply misdirection in the hope we might let our guard down.'

'If the men we have in custody won't tell us more, how can

you resolve that one way or the other short of thumbscrews or a rack?'

'Where are you keeping them?' asked Monique.

'In cells on the floor below this one,' said Masterton.

'And are you keeping them separately?'

'Of course, why?'

'Describe the cells to me. How are they arranged relative to each other?' asked Monique.

'I was only there briefly after we finished questioning Immendorff but I'll try. There's a corridor like the one outside here on the floor below, further down into the body of the fort. It's only accessible from one end and there's a station for a guard there. There are four two-man cells on each side of the corridor with their doors facing each other and we've put Immendorff and Stoltenberg on their own at opposite ends of the run of four on the same side. That seems the best way to ensure there's no communication between them. I should add that a couple of the other cells are occupied by sailors, presumably after fights or too much drink, but I didn't ask. Why?'

'Are you prepared to let me try something?' asked Monique.

'I've got nothing to lose, go ahead,' said Masterton.

'Can we go down to the cells?'

*

Monique asked Bob and Wilfred Masterton to wait out of sight beyond the guard's station. Then she took off her shoes and very quietly walked along the corridor to the first cell on the left, whose inward-opening door had been left ajar. She was able to enter without moving the door and risking making a noise. It smelled strongly of cigarettes and sweaty bodies. Then she stood behind the door.

Stoltenberg's cell was the first on the right, opposite Monique's. As she'd instructed, the navy guard went to the far end of the run of cells, opened the door to Immendorff's cell and ordered him out. He then brought him back along the corridor, opened the door of Stoltenberg's cell, and told Immendorff to go in. Then he closed and locked the door.

The cell doors had a very worn metal finish and each had a vertically lifting hatch at the bottom that was wider than it was high, Monique assumed for meal deliveries, and a square opening at head height that was made secure by five vertical bars attached to the outside surface of the door.

As the navy guard walked back to the guard's station at the end of the corridor, Monique slipped out of her cell and quietly crossed the corridor, putting her back against part of the door and the wall next to it so her right ear was beside the square opening.

'Are you all right?' asked one of the men in German.

'I am, thank you, Carl,' said the other, who she now knew was Immendorff.

'They told me Friedrich and Sebastian are dead,' said Stoltenberg. 'I already knew about Friedrich because I saw his body as they brought me out of the safe house.'

'So did I,' said Immendorff. 'It didn't turn out to be so safe after all, did it? I warned Dieter that we'd be better somewhere more populated during the reconnaissance in April, but he's never been one to listen to his underlings. It's typical that he should be the one who was out when they came looking for us.'

'Do you think we ought to be talking about… Well, someone might be listening.'

'Don't worry,' said Immendorff. 'Even if someone could hear us, they're so used to dealing with Italians that none of them speak German.'

Monique listened for a while longer but the conversation turned to what they thought might become of them now they'd been captured and she quietly walked back to where she'd asked Bob and Wilfred to wait.

'We're going to need to interview them again,' she said. 'There's a fifth man we've not accounted for and he's the team leader.'

*

It was well after midnight when they were admitted through a side door into the Governor's Palace. After showing their security passes to the guards, a corporal led them up a set of stairs and then directed them to enter an office with a scatter of desks that smelled strongly of pipe smoke.

An army colonel with his jacket undone stood up from a chair at one of the desks and walked over to greet them. He was tall and thin with blond hair and seemed to Bob to be in his late forties.

'Hello, I'm Patrick Miller, I'm Lord Gort's private secretary.'

Bob introduced Monique and himself.

The colonel ushered them towards one end of the room. 'I've dragged a few chairs over here. Please take a seat. Right then, Wilfred. What's come up that's led to you asking for a meeting in the middle of the night? I hope you're not having second thoughts about the security matter you discussed with the governor earlier.'

'I'm afraid that's exactly why we're here,' said Wilfred. 'When I talked to the governor earlier this evening, I believed that we had accounted for all the SD agents, with two dead and two in custody. Thanks to Madame Dubois, we've discovered that there is a fifth man still at large, the leader of the team.'

'Are you suggesting that I wake the governor up and ask him if he wishes to recommend to King George that he cancels his visit when he's already at sea and presumably well on his way here?'

'That has to be a possibility,' said Bob. 'Perhaps we should look at the problem in more detail first? That might allow you to decide on the best course of action. For what it's worth, Monique and I both met King George in rather difficult circumstances last September and my own belief is that he wouldn't wish to cancel his visit based on what we currently know.'

'What exactly do we currently know?'

Bob told him.

Patrick Miller then summarised. 'We have a lone German agent on the island whose team was here to assassinate the king. One of the team claims they intended to shoot the king on the balcony outside this building, but we think that is an attempt at misdirection, like his attempt to convince us that he was the team leader. The remaining SD agent, assuming he hasn't gone to ground completely after the loss of his team, might be planning some other way to kill the king.'

'I assume security surrounding the king's visit would be very tight anyway?' asked Monique.

'Extremely. You can't move for RAF fighters on the island at the moment and pretty much all of them are tasked to ensure that the king's visit doesn't attract an enemy air attack from

Sicily. Meanwhile, the Royal Navy will be tying down the Grand Harbour even more tightly than normal. A lone sniper is harder to defend against, but I will ensure that the army is on full alert. I'll certainly ensure that every rooftop and vantage point overlooking the balcony on the front of this building is guarded, in case they are trying to double-bluff us.'

'I imagine that an itinerary for the king has only been worked out at very short notice,' said Bob. 'It seems to me that likely areas of attack might be those where a visit could be anticipated in advance. A balcony appearance here is an obvious example. Could you tell us what the king is due to do on his visit so we can work out the most easily predictable elements?'

The colonel fetched a piece of paper from a nearby desk, then came back and sat down.

'Please don't take any notes. For obvious reasons, this is classified as top secret. The king is due to land by boat in Valletta from the cruiser HMS *Aurora* at 9.30 a.m. He will then drive with the governor to this building in the back of a car. As we're talking about a possible sniper, it pains me to say that the rear part of the car will be open, in other words, the foldable hood will be down. As the idea is to allow the people of Malta to see their king, I doubt if that's negotiable.

'Once here the king will inspect the George Cross he awarded to Malta in April last year and attend a meeting. He will then make an appearance - as the SD has guessed - on the balcony. We're expecting a large crowd in Palace Square. He and the governor will then be driven, in the same open car, to Senglea to visit the naval dockyards. As they are still badly damaged he will be shown the underground workshops which are actually beneath Senglea itself.

'The king will then walk through part of Senglea with a senior local cleric to see the scale of the damage for himself. After that, he will travel to Verdala Palace, which is the governor's summer residence, south of Mdina and not far from the west coast. He will meet senior military officers and have lunch. After lunch, the king will visit Mosta and then tour some of the airfields on the island accompanied by Air Vice-Marshal Park. He is then due to return here for dinner with Lord Gort before returning to HMS *Aurora,* which will sail for Tripoli at 10 p.m.'

Bob leaned forwards. 'I take two things of particular significance from that beyond the balcony appearance we've already discussed. The first is that a visit to the dockyards is very predictable, so could have been planned for by the SD agents. The second is that they chose to base themselves in Senglea, which again flags up the dockyard visit as high risk and suggests that the planned walk through part of the area is also particularly risky even if it's not predictable. Will it be possible to step up security for both those elements of the visit?'

'It will,' said Colonel Miller. 'I'll make sure we put a ring of soldiers around the part of Victory Street that he'll be visiting that should deter anyone trying to assassinate the king there. We'll do the same at the dockyards.'

'Where exactly will he be going in the dockyards?' asked Bob. 'They're pretty extensive.'

'The car carrying the king will drive to what the navy calls Hamilton Dock, a dry dock off French Creek. The entrance to the underground areas that the king will visit is close by.'

'Thank you,' said Bob. 'Now you've heard what we've had to say, what do you intend to do?'

'I will wake the governor, which given how busy he's going to be later today will not be well received. I will recommend that he signals the king's private secretary on board HMS *Aurora* to alert him to the problem but say that we believe the visit should proceed. Let's hope that turns out to be sound advice.' Colonel Miller smiled grimly.

CHAPTER THIRTY-FOUR

'Why do you want to come here, Bob?' asked Monique. 'Of all the places where Dieter might be intending to try to kill the king today, why the dockyards?'

It was just after 8 a.m. Neither Bob nor Monique had much sleep after being dropped off at the Osborne Hotel by Wilfred Masterton. Bob knew that even after getting to bed he'd lain awake for a long time trying to grapple with the ideas fighting for position in his head.

'I think the entrance to the dockyards is near the landward end of the peninsula,' said Bob. 'Yes, this is it.'

Bob had hoped that security would be tight and it was. He and Monique had to show their security passes at three separate checkpoints before she was able to drive their Royal Navy staff car to Hamilton Dock.

When they stopped and got out of the car they were approached by two naval ratings carrying rifles, who asked to see their passes again.

Bob pointed at a tunnel entrance cut into the base of the sheer wall that rose high above this side of the dockyard. 'You wouldn't need all those people coming and going to know that was the entrance to the navy's underground workshops, would you, Monique?'

'No, you wouldn't. Now come on, humour me. I also spent half the night working out that we should come here, but I want to know if your reasoning is the same as mine.'

'I asked myself two questions,' said Bob. 'The first was about the areas of greatest risk and the second was about our capacity to add anything to the security that will already be in place. I think that the balcony of the Governor's Palace is the most dangerous place the king will be all day, but I can't see how you and I can do anything to add to the security the army will be providing now they are aware of the danger.

'The same argument applies to what seems to me to be the second most dangerous element of the king's itinerary, his walk around Victory Street in Senglea. There's nothing we can do that soldiers with rifles can't do better.

'Here, though, it's a bit more complicated. We've seen how tight security is in the dockyard itself, but is that enough? Let's think about how it's going to work later this morning. Presumably, the king's car will come in through the gate we used and drive here. We need to think about where it's likely to stop.'

'The driver will be a bit limited if they are driving something large, expensive and unwieldy,' said Monique. 'We've got the dry dock behind us here, but how much closer to the workshops will the car be able to get?'

'It will have to come to pretty much where we're standing and then turn down the access road which might get it 50 yards closer to the entrance to the workshops. But then the car will have to turn around.'

Bob looked up at the top of the wall rising above them. 'What interests me is the idea that someone with a rifle up there on this side of Senglea might take a shot at the king. This sheer wall cuts the angle down if the king were to get out of his car right by the entrance to the workshops. But we've been told that the rear of the car will be open to allow people to see King George. Let's assume that while the king is in the workshops, the driver turns the car around here and reverses back towards the entrance. When he drives away he will pass right in front of where we're standing and anyone in an open-topped car is going to be vulnerable to a shot from any of the ruined buildings we can see up there.'

'That's a long shot, especially at a man in a moving car,' said Monique. 'But then we have to assume that Dieter has been picked because he's good. We need to check, but won't that be within the area the army is sealing off because of the king's walk in Senglea?'

'As you say, we need to check,' said Bob.

*

Monique pulled the car off the cleared part of the road where Victory Street broadened in front of a ruined church. Men in army uniforms carrying rifles were jumping out of lorries and dispersing into the surrounding ruins.

An army major was directing operations and Monique walked over to him with Bob. The major saluted and Bob responded before introducing himself.

'How can I help, sir?'

'Colonel Miller in the governor's office said you'd be making sure that the area where the king is due to walk later is secure,' said Bob. 'How far to the south-west of here does your area cover? Does it go as far as the ruined buildings overlooking the dockyards?'

'No, it doesn't, sir. This map shows what we're covering.' The major held out a folded street map with an area ringed in pencil. 'I'm told that the king is likely to walk along this section of Victory Street and then back along a short length of the street to its north-east. On the south-west side, we're going one street back, which doesn't take us as far as you have in mind.'

'Is there any possibility of extending your area to include those buildings?' asked Bob, running his finger along the area of the map he was interested in.

'I'm sorry, sir, but that's a decision for someone paid more than me. If I extend my coverage on that side I'll weaken the rest of it. I'm ordered to let people into the area after checking them for bombs or weapons, so it's going to be a complex operation and I need every man I've got.'

'What time are you expecting the king to arrive?'

'11.45 a.m., sir.'

'Thank you major.' Bob turned away and walked with Monique back to the car.

'Surely you can get hold of someone with the authority to provide more troops,' said Monique.

'I'm not sure,' said Bob. 'We need to remember that the most likely places of danger are being covered, quite thoroughly as we've just seen.

'I'm also very conscious that for our theory to hold water, we have to assume that Dieter is capable of shooting a man in the back of a moving car from quite some distance away. That same man in that same car is going to be driving through the streets of Valletta very soon, and then around the Grand Harbour to here. I'm sure there must be any number of places on his route, some of them capable of being predicted in advance by the SD, where a good shot with a rifle might stand a much better chance of killing the king.'

'And yet they chose Senglea for their base for some reason,' said Monique, 'and I've not heard a convincing one yet. Wilfred Masterton went as far as saying that if they'd chosen Valletta or Sliema with more people still living around them, they'd probably have gone unnoticed.'

'I know, and I agree,' said Bob. 'But we're not going to be able to convince the army to provide more troops or redefine the area it's protecting in Senglea based solely on our joint instinct that it should.'

*

The day was shaping up to be another warm one and Monique moved the car so it would be in the shadow of the ruined church. She then donned her sunhat and sunglasses and walked with Bob along one of the shattered streets leading off Victory Road in the direction of French Creek, walking around piles of rubble from bombed buildings.

It only took a couple of minutes for them to emerge onto what in better times had been a road running along the south-west side of Senglea. The collapsed buildings now made it almost impassible on foot, never mind in a vehicle.

On the far side of the road was a stone wall of perhaps six or seven feet in height with a wall walk along the side facing them. In places, the wall had also been damaged. Bob walked a short distance to their right, where a set of stone steps at an angle in the wall gave access to the wall walk, then climbed them.

Monique followed and found that they were standing a considerable height above where they'd been a short time earlier and they were looking over the top of the sheer stone wall that they'd seen rising above the entrance to the navy's underground workshops. Hamilton Dock was below them and the rest of the dockyards around French Creek could be made out clearly.

Bob looked down, and then at the ruined buildings behind them on the other side of the street.

'You can see the upper floors of some of the buildings behind us from down there, so they have to be contenders for a roost for a sniper even though the ones that still have walls don't seem to have floors. Otherwise, the only place where you'd be able to get any sort of a rifle shot at the king's car would be from this wall walk itself.

'There are a couple of places where the wall has been damaged, said Monique. You could shelter in the rubble there and get a clear shot downwards to the dockyard from road level.'

'That might be Dieter's best bet,' said Bob.

Monique looked at her watch. We know the king is due in Senglea at 11.45 a.m., which means he'll be leaving the dockyard down there a few minutes earlier. Dieter won't know any timings but if this is where he intends to strike from, he's probably seen the increased security down below and knows he's guessed right about the king visiting the dockyards. We also need to guard against the possibility of Dieter taking his shot when the king arrives at the dockyard rather than when he leaves. I think we need to find somewhere to keep out of sight here, settle down early and simply wait it out.'

'I agree,' said Bob. 'But it's hot. Let's head back to Victory Street and get the army to loan us a couple of full water bottles.'

'If we're going to do that I'll borrow a rifle too,' said Monique. 'That will ensure we're not outgunned.'

*

Monique looked at her watch again. The time seemed to creep

by. She and Bob had found some shade and some shelter from view by sitting on stone blocks amongst the rubble on either side of the doorway inside a bombed-out building. That allowed them to keep watch in both directions along the street.

Monique wondered if she'd dozed when she felt Bob tap on her arm. He put his finger to his lips and touched his ear. She held her breath and then heard a stone move behind them in the building. Monique's pistol was already cocked and the Lee-Enfield rifle she'd borrowed was ready to fire as soon as she moved the safety catch to its forward position.

Another stone moved and then there was a grunt from somewhere above her. She realised that someone had entered the building from its rear and was climbing up the structure to a higher level. Monique looked at Bob and pointed upwards. He nodded.

They both slowly stood up. Monique left the rifle on the ground where it was, and took three careful paces away from the doorway, holding her pistol ready and looking up to see who was above them. She couldn't see anyone but it sounded like someone was moving very slowly and carefully almost immediately above her head.

She took another step to try to get a better view up through the remains of the floor above but kicked a stone that skittered across the floor and the noises from above ceased.

Monique found she was holding her breath. She could see Bob looking anxiously back at her and knew he'd have no view up to the floor above from his position. She motioned to him to stay where he was and he nodded. Then she looked down to ensure she made no more noise and shifted her weight to allow her to start to move again.

Suddenly there was a crash as a large section of stonework

fell from above. Monique ducked sideways into the remains of an adjacent room as the debris landed in a cloud of dust where she'd been standing only a moment before.

She heard Bob shout 'He's outside!' and then there were three gunshots in rapid succession, the first from a rifle and the second and third from a pistol. Monique scrambled over the debris and ran out into the street to find Bob standing with his Walther PPK in his hand. A few yards away was a man lying on his back with a sniper rifle on the ground beside him.

Bob looked at her. 'He jumped down into the street from the floor above and ran towards the wall. When I shouted he turned and fired. He missed. I didn't.'

Monique walked over to the man, who had two obvious gunshot wounds in his chest. She felt the side of his neck, then stood up.

'I'd introduce you to Dieter, Bob, but there's no point because he's dead.'

She turned at the sound of running feet. A soldier with his rifle held ready was quickly followed by two more men and the major.

'Hello major,' said Bob, putting his pistol back in his shoulder holster. 'I think you can stand your men down. This is the gentleman who was trying to kill the king.'

EPILOGUE

Bob and Monique waited at the top of the steps leading up to the ruined church close to where she'd left the car. Bob hadn't been sure what a royal visit would involve and found himself surprised when a long stream of cars drove into the broader part of Victory Street and came to a halt. It was easy to spot the king's car. It was flying a royal standard and closely followed by a pair of military police motorcyclists. The vehicle in front had a film camera mounted on a tripod in its rear, with a cameraman pointing it back towards the king's car.

As Colonel Miller had said, the king's car also had a hood that would otherwise have hidden the rear of the car but was folded back, allowing the king to be seen by the people of Malta. In his white naval uniform, he certainly stood out more than the man sitting next to him, who was wearing an army field marshal's uniform. Bob guessed he was the governor, Lord Gort.

Bob realised that it would have been very easy for Dieter to see his target from a distance, even if the actual shot might have been more difficult.

The crowds cheered as the king and his entourage got out of their cars and Bob's view began to be obscured as some of the onlookers realised the steps would be a good vantage point. The king was introduced to a man in clerical garb wearing a broad-brimmed hat who then led him off along Victory Street on foot, flanked by military policemen. To Bob's surprise, it looked like everyone else who had been in the convoy then followed. A couple of men in civilian suits stayed close to the king and the cleric. Behind them was Lord Gort, and then a stream of others.

'They aren't giving him much chance to get any real feeling for the place, are they?' asked Monique.

'I suppose that's the price you pay for fame and power,' said Bob.

The crowd continued to swell while the king and his entourage were out of sight, having turned along a side road. A little later cheering broke out anew as he reappeared and walked slowly back towards the cars, deep in conversation with the cleric and still followed by a gaggle of men wearing uniforms or suits.

There was a touch on Bob's left arm. 'Can you come with me, group captain? And you, Madame Dubois?'

Bob turned sharply to his blind side and saw Colonel Miller. 'Yes, of course.'

'This way, please.' Miller turned and led Bob and Monique down the steps and then over towards the line of stationary cars.

A civilian was standing by the side of the king's car.

'This is Alec Hardinge, the king's private secretary,' said Miller.

'Hello Group Captain. Hello Madame Dubois. The king has asked for a brief word with the two of you. If you hop in the back of the car and pull down the folding seats, the king will join you in a moment. Lord Gort will keep the others talking for a few minutes.' Hardinge opened the back door of the car.

Monique got in first and Bob followed. There were pull-down seats at the front of the rear compartment of the car, quite like those in London taxis, so they pulled them down and sat on them.

'This isn't quite what I expected,' said Bob.

Monique smiled nervously. 'Nor me. I got a lot of dust on

my clothes when Dieter tried to collapse the building onto me. I wish I could have got more of it off.'

The back door on the other side of the car opened and the king got in.

'P-p-please stay seated, both of you.' The king sat on the edge of the bench seat at the back of the car and leaned forwards. There was a lot of noise from the crowd and Bob assumed this was so he could make himself heard.

'I thought I recognised the names, though I don't believe you were with MI11 when the two of you rescued me from capture in Caithness last year. A-a-and congratulations on your promotion, Group Captain Sutherland.'

'Thank you, Your Majesty,' said Bob.

'I wanted a brief word simply to thank you for ensuring the last of the SD assassins is no longer a threat.'

'We're relieved we found him, sir,' said Bob. 'A lot of credit should go to MI5, who found the rest of them last night.'

'I'm sure, but it's the two of you who have made the rest of my visit to Malta more relaxing than it might have been.'

'Do you call this relaxing, Your Majesty?' asked Monique.

The king smiled. 'Everything's relative, Madame Dubois. I understand I'm now going for lunch at the governor's summer palace. I would be grateful if the two of you could join me.'

Bob saw Monique brush at her skirt.

'Don't worry if you're showing the signs of an active morning, Madame Dubois,' said the king. 'And that reminds me. I see you are wearing your medal ribbon as a Commander of the Royal Victorian Order, Group Captain.'

'Yes, sir. I'm very grateful.'

'A-a-after our last encounter, I gave instructions for that honour to be given to both of you and I was rather peeved to discover later that yours had not been awarded, Madame Dubois, because of some sort of bureaucratic wrangle about the name you were using when we met. I will ensure that omission is remedied after today.'

'Thank you, sir,' said Monique.

The king looked out of the car. 'Lord Gort did a splendid job holding back the Germans for long enough to allow most of our army to escape at Dunkirk, but I get the sense he might be fighting a losing battle here. Thank you both again.'

Bob got out of the car first and held the door open for Monique. As she got out of the car, Lord Gort was getting into the far side. Bob saluted and then took a few steps backwards, away from the car.

Monique walked over to join him. 'I wonder if Verdala Palace is shown on the map the navy left in the car?'

'There's no need,' said Bob. 'If we simply join the end of this convoy, it will take us there.'

Monique smiled. 'It's been an eventful honeymoon. We've drunk the Station Hotel dry of champagne, you've shot down your twenty-fifth enemy aircraft, I've been awarded my first medal, and we're going for lunch with the king. That really will be quite a story to tell our grandchildren.'

AUTHOR'S NOTE

This book is a work of fiction and should be read as such. Except as noted below, all characters are fictional and any resemblances to real people, either living or dead, are purely coincidental.

Likewise, many of the events that are described in this book are the products of the author's imagination. Others did take place.

Let's start with the characters. Some of the characters who appear between the pages of this book occupy posts that existed at the time, but except as noted below they are all fictional. These include the private secretary to the governor of Malta, the executive officer of the 10th Submarine Flotilla, and the station commander of RAF Ta Kali.

Some of the others who appear in this book were real people.

King George VI did visit Malta on the 20th of June 1943 and his itinerary was as I have described: though his brief meeting with Bob and Monique in the back of his car in Senglea is fictional, as is the plot to assassinate him. Lord Gort did serve as the governor of Malta and Air Vice-Marshal Sir Keith Park was the RAF commander in Malta at the time this book is set.

Other real people to feature or be discussed in the book are the Russian ballet dancer Vera Trefilova; the king's private secretary Alec Hardinge; and the actor Leslie Howard, whose tragic death happened on the 1st of June 1943 in the circumstances described.

Group Captain Robert Sutherland is an invented character, though he has a career in the Royal Air Force that will be recognised by anyone familiar with the life and achievements of Squadron Leader Archibald McKellar, DSO, DFC and Bar. Bob Sutherland's family background and pre-war employment were very different to Archibald McKellar's, but the two share an eminent list of achievements during the Battle of Britain. Squadron Leader McKellar was tragically killed when he was shot down on the 1st of November 1940, whereas the fictional Group Captain Sutherland was only wounded when he was shot down on the same day, allowing him to play a leading role in this book and its five predecessors.

And Madame Monique Dubois? She is a fictional alias for a real woman. The real Vera Eriksen, or Vera Schalburg, or take your pick from any number of other aliases, had a story that was both complex and very dark. She disappeared during the war after the two German spies she landed with at Port Gordon on the Moray Firth were tried and executed by the British for espionage.

A hint of Monique's story emerges from the pages of this book but to get a fuller picture you should read my first novel, *Eyes Turned Skywards.*

Military Intelligence, Section 11, or MI11, was a real organisation that had a role in maintaining military security. Its organisation and other aspects of its operations described in this book are entirely fictional.

The Security Service (MI5) and the Secret Intelligence Service (SIS or MI6) both existed, and both continue to exist at the time of writing. The role of Bletchley Park in intercepting German communications encrypted by Enigma machines was much as suggested here, as was the reference to the project as 'Ultra'.

Moving on to the events that take place in the book, they are a blend of the fictional and the real. Amongst the real events referred to are the Venlo Incident in 1939, the building of new airfields on the islands of Malta and Gozo, and the extension of the runway at Gibraltar. The front page of the Daily Mirror on Monday the 14th of June 1943 reported the stories that Monique reads out to Bob in their hotel suite. Fictional events in the book include the loss of HMS *Ursus,* a submarine that never actually existed.

Let's now turn to places that appear in this story.

The Isle of Skye and Kyle of Lochalsh were very much as they appear in this book in 1943, as was the operation of the Skye ferry and the bus service between Kyleakin and Portree. The remarkably high fare charged by the latter is taken from a 1937 timetable.

Gibraltar in 1943 was much as I describe it and the problems of infiltration by enemy agents and saboteurs were real.

In many ways, Malta is the central character in this book. The descriptions in the story of its heroic resistance during World War Two are as real as I have been able to make them. As background, I have drawn on many sources including books, films and personal visits. A book I would highly recommend to anyone wanting to know more would be James Holland's superb *Fortress Malta: an Island Under Siege.*

Having said that, when an author is 'playing away' there is inevitably a greater risk of misunderstandings or errors. This is particularly the case in Malta because of wider changes that have taken place since the war, especially its gaining independence from Britain in 1964 and becoming a republic ten years later.

Over the past eight decades, many place names and street names in Malta have changed. I have tried wherever possible to use the names that would have been used by my characters at the time the book is set.

Another complicating factor in representing Malta as it would have been in 1943 is the fact that it had been damaged so badly by over 3,000 air raids. Old photographs have helped me describe what it was like, but a layer of imagination has also proved necessary.

Real locations used in the book include the excellent Osborne Hotel, whose 1943 form and layout have been based on pictures and plans that remain on display in the hotel. Fort St Angelo, Hagar Qim, 3 Scots Street, Manoel Island and the Xara Palace (now a luxury hotel) are all real and in each case, I've used some artistic licence in reimagining them in 1943. The same is true of places like Mdina, Marsaxlokk, Marfa, Mosta and Victoria: as well as Valletta, Senglea and Vittoriosa. The last of these is now known as Birgu.

Cirkewwa is now the main ferry terminal for the crossing to Gozo. Its layout in 1943 as described in this book is largely imagined.

St John's Co-Cathedral in Valletta and the Rotunda of Mosta both exist and would have appeared to my characters very much as described in the book.

Captain Bianchi's is fictional, though Strait Street is real and was as disreputable as described in this book at the time. The King Edward Hotel and the Victoria and Albert Hotel are both fictional. St Dominic's House is fictional but has borrowed its location from a real Carmelite care home.

The Eye of Horus, also known as the Eye of Osiris, is a symbol that still appears on many traditional Maltese fishing boats. The story behind it is as told in this book.

To conclude, in my view a fiction writer should create a

world that feels right to his or her readers. When the world in question is as far removed in so many ways, some predictable and others not, as 1943 is from today, then it is inevitable that false assumptions will be made and facts will be misunderstood. If you find errors within this book I apologise and can only hope that they have not got in the way of your enjoyment of the story.